MW01676463

# The Infinitum Government

## Volume One

Megan Derr

The Infinitum Government, Volume One
By Megan Derr

Published by Less Than Three Press LLC

All rights reserved. No part of this book may be used or reproduced in any manner without written permission of the publisher, except for the purpose of reviews.

Edited by Caitlin Penny and Samantha M. Derr
Cover designed by Lainey Durand

This book is a work of fiction and as such all characters and situations are fictitious. Any resemblance to actual people, places, or events is coincidental.

Print Edition March 2012

Copyright © 2012 by Megan Derr

Printed in the United States of America
ISBN 9781936202935

# The Infinitum Government
## Volume One

Megan Derr

# Table of Contents

# Kidnapped

## Book One

# Prologue

**PLANET 5118208 (REHAB), REHABILITATION CENTER 2.2, SECTOR 9.9**

"Hey, Cyan. What the hell is a Draconis?"

Cyan quirked a brow as he strode into the break room and dropped down on the small, battered couch against the far wall. His boots rang on the metal floors that were everywhere in Rehab. "The dumb questions you ask, one would think you live in a closet."

"Damn fucking near. A closet full of violent assholes."

Cyan snorted. "You work on Rehab, Sean. You should know damn near every race in the IG. I know my training didn't fail; therefore, you're an idiot."

Sean rolled his eyes. "Fuck you. Unlike you, Cyan, some of us don't think it's fun to memorize all those dry texts you insist on reading. There is life outside Rehab."

"I prefer life in Rehab," Cyan said with a shrug. Sean started to taunt him more, but it turned into a soft curse when his in-lens fritzed, the information in the thin device shooting sparks of pain through his eye. "Problem, Sean?" Cyan asked, looking at him with concern and some amusement.

"In-lens has had it," Sean replied. That could turn into a really nasty problem. He struggled not to panic. He'd known it was getting on, but had pushed off getting a new one even though he knew the risks, because it was so hard to get a replacement. He'd have to pop over to Mars at end of shift and finally take care of the problem. "Guess that fucking Hellcat in 9.1.2 nailed me harder than I thought."

Cyan snickered. "Yeah, I prefer being nailed by Hellcats in an entirely different way."

"You and the rest of the stars," said a warm, amused female voice. They both turned to look at Tiffany, the systems analyst for the sector nine, wing two secluded network. In the dingy gray and black coloring of the break room, her Helior-red hair was a near blinding beacon. "At least you're inoculated, Sean."

"At least it was a Hellcat and not a fucking Sardoran," Cyan muttered. Sean snickered. "It's not funny," Cyan griped.

"That you seem to have some sort of 'come and get me' tattoo that only tentacle races can see? Yes, it is."

"Fuck you." Sean just snickered again. Cyan kicked him.

"Okay, okay," Sean said. He motioned to the file still in his lap, touching the screen to wake it back up. "So what's a Draconis?"

"Surprised you haven't heard of them, actually," Cyan said. "They're causing quite the controversy in the IG right now. Genetically engineered race designed by the Coni. It's a magics capable planet in the third quad. Their magics are diverse, ranging from basic elementals to defensive magics, but not very powerful. They created the Draconis to be legal supplements to increase their power. It's kinda cool what they did, actually."

Tiffany looked up from her own datapad, in-lens flashing as she kept constant watch on her systems. "Yeah, they *mate* and increase their partner's magics. So romantic!"

Cyan rolled his eyes. "Something like that."

"Mate?" Sean asked, looking back down at the file. The words *Mateless—Keep Isolated* were typed in green, rather than black like the rest. It meant 'fucking pay attention.'

"They bond and something in their make-up sort of attaches to whoever they bond with, causing some sort of reaction that increases the magics of both the Draconis and the person bonded. Most call that person a Draconis 'mate', though the term 'match' is also used since they can't bond with just anyone. No one knows why Draconis match the way they do, not even the Coni."

Tiffany looked up again. "Part of the controversy surrounding them is that they should have only ever matched with Coni, but these days they're matching with species all across the stars. It's causing loads of problems."

"Yeah," Cyan agreed. "It would suck to be suddenly stuck with someone you never met and unable to separate, because the further apart a Draconis and his match get, the weaker their magics get. Can you imagine? Being a magics capable who suddenly can't use his magics unless the Draconis he got stuck with was nearby?"

Sean frowned. "It can't be *that* hard to live without magics. Humans have been doing it forever."

"Spoken like a true human," Cyan said lightly. "That's what they'd tell you, Sean. Humans don't have magics, so we can't understand. I say lucky us, but that's probably my human bias speaking."

Tiffany shrugged. "It all evens out."

"Debatable," Cyan said. "Humans don't have magics, but that doesn't mean we should have all the ruling power."

Tiffany started to reply to that, but Sean cut them off before they could start arguing again. He didn't need to put up with yet another political debate. "This file says he's been arrested for murder. Patricide, specifically. Damn."

"Oh?" Cyan asked, leaning over to read the datapad for himself. "Huh. He's half-Draconis, half-human. That should be interesting. Father was the human."

"I wonder why he's being placed in 9.9. He only killed one guy. Fuck, the Klorin in 9.8.2 killed six people, and he's only got a life sentence."

Cyan tapped the bright green letters Sean had read before. "He's unmatched, which means he could possibly match with anyone magics capable in here. Lists his magics as being defensive, meaning he can probably heal, stuff like that. Still, if he has anything that could help him escape ... "

"They would have collared him," Sean said, grimacing at the thought of the magics-numbing collars, barely keeping from touching a hand to his throat.

"Yeah, but if he matches then his magics will increase in power."

"Ah," Sean said in comprehension. If that happened, his power would exceed the limits of the collar, which would then conceivably allow the prisoner to escape. Not that he'd ever get off Rehab, not unless he had some truly impressive magics.

"So we're on break after this shift," Cyan said in an abrupt conversation shift. "Wanna take a jaunt somewhere?"

Sean thought a moment. "Sure. Got anywhere in mind?"

"Was thinking Bangkok, or we could rent a private ship and just cruise."

"Or we could cruise leisurely to Bangkok and back," Sean said with a grin. "I've been wanting a ship of my own forever. Just go wherever the hell whenever the hell I want. Got enough points for it and a pilot license. Should get around to actually getting the ship."

Cyan's eyes began to gleam. "You should commission one. Get a sweet custom class with top grade materials. I bet you could even commission a Zero-caliber company to build it. Oh, man. Can you imagine? A gremlin built ship?"

"That would kick ass," Sean said, matching Cyan's eagerness. "Zero companies have serious waiting lists, though. I probably wouldn't get it for at least a term." He grinned. "Would be worth the wait, though. Want to help me start designing it? We could peruse the shipyards here instead of going to Bangkok. I know there's a few Zero-grade companies on Mars; there are always combat class ships docking for repairs and upgrades."

"Men," Tiffany sighed in tolerant amusement. "If you're not discussing your dicks, it's weapons or starships."

"Hey," Cyan said defensively. "We have to know weapons. I'm wearing two dozen at the moment. It would be rather detrimental to my health if I grabbed a stinger instead of a painter when trying to put down a Traxen."

Sean winced at the thought, lightly touching the long, sharp baton slung into its loop low on his left thigh, then the thicker baton set with a nozzle right beside it. Yeah, didn't want to mix up those two, especially when a Traxen was involved. "Come to my house when we get out of here and we can start on the prelim work."

"Cool," Cyan said with a grin right as their in-lens flared with an arrival alert. "Oh, hey. There's our Draconis."

"Should be interesting," Sean replied, tucking away the folder he'd been reading. "Hopefully getting him into solitaire goes without a hitch." Standing up, Cyan one step behind him, Sean moved to the break room door and swiftly punched in the codes to let them out. No matter what, not a single door in Rehab opened without proper codes. Even the locker room required them for entering and leaving.

As the door slid open and Sean passed through, additional sensors scanned his in-lens and his blood for the appropriate electronic and chemical keys. Behind him, Cyan was just as thoroughly checked.

Back in the main portion of Rehab, they swiftly made their way down long halls and through rooms, ignoring the jeers and calls from various prisoners when they passed different cellblocks. The floors and stairs were all grated metal to make cleanup easier when things went sour with a prisoner.

They worked in sector nine, the hardest sector on Rehab. It was the one reserved for the most dangerous adult male prisoners in the stars. That day they were assigned to wings eight and nine, and that meant all incoming prisoners for those areas would be theirs to personally escort to their cells.

In this sector, things often went wrong. Men who committed murder and much worse had no compunctions against resisting authority. It was only part of the reason Rehab guards went through some of the most rigorous training in the Infinitum Government.

Finally they made their way through the maze-like halls, coming to a halt at the edge of Dock 5, where Authority combat class ship was already going through the last of its landing procedures.

"It's about time you two showed up," a man with a bald head and massive mustache barked. "McCracken. Noor. Where the fuck have you been?"

"Break, Captain Waters." Cyan replied, unfazed. "We get those. We're here on time."

"Insubordination," Waters muttered, but subsided. "Fall in."

Cyan and Sean took their places at the edge of the dock as the ship opened and a ramp extended. The prisoner file hadn't included a picture, and they'd moved on to talking about ships before Sean had thought to ask what Draconis looked like. Whatever he'd been picturing, it wasn't anything like the handsome man that was led from the ship, hands bound and a thick magics-dampening collar around his neck. The gray uniforms worn by the IG soldiers escorting him only brought out the brilliance of his scales.

Sean realized he was staring, but could not help it. The Draconis was tall, with dark green hair about shoulder length, messy looking. He was bare-chested, as most high class criminals were, his skin human looking; it had a faint gold-brown to it, as though he had a tan, but covering most of it (leaving only much of his torso, the inside of his arms, and his hands bare) were rich green-gold scales. They were beautiful. More scales curved along his cheekbones and brushing just below his green ey—

Pain shot through Sean's head, and he dropped to his knees, clutching his head in agony. People started shouting all around him, and he briefly heard Cyan call his name, then hands grabbed him roughly and he was pressed up against something unbelievably hot.

Then just as suddenly, the noise died. He jerked away from what he realized was someone holding him—and realized it was the prisoner. Sean stared at the man in disbelief, noting from their surroundings that they were on the Auth ship. He reached for his stunner, thumbing it to the highest level.

"Sleep," the Draconis said.

Sean crumpled.

### COMBAT CLASS STARSHIP C-81261518, THE *RAZOR*

He woke with a groan and realized almost immediately that he was bound. Testing the restraints, Sean realized they were his own fucking cuffs. Rehab guards always carried four sets. One pair secured his arms to a pipe above his head, and another around his ankles secured to the footboard of the bed. He could feel the weight of the magics collar around his throat, and he bet that was the reason for the nausea as well.

So he was well and truly fucking trapped. Damn it.

What in the fucking hell had happened?

The door chimed, then opened, and Sean stared wide-eyed. He remembered. There'd been pain, and then the Draconis had taken him. "You!" he snarled. "What the fuck did you do? Why am I here?" He recoiled as best he could as the Draconis approached, realizing for the first time that he was dressed only in his black workpants and faded black undershirt. Gone were his jacket, all his weapons and keys, even his damned boots. "What the fuck is going on?"

"You're human, yet we matched," the Draconis said. "I have never met a magics capable human, though I've heard before such mutants occasionally appear. I also heard they never get to live long."

Sean went still and wondered if it was actually possible for a person to feel himself going pale. "Magics capable?" He tried to activate his in-lens and realized he couldn't. He struggled to fight off panic. No, no, no. "How—" The words cut off, Sean unable to say them.

"How did I know?" the Draconis asked. "Like I said, we've matched."

"Matched?" Sean repeated, feeling sick as he realized what that meant. All that he'd recently learned from Cyan about Draconis came flooding back. "How did we match? I can't match! I'm not supposed to have fucking magics!" His life was over. Done. They would kill him now. All his life he'd hidden his magics, done everything he could to be normal. He'd even tricked everyone and gotten into Rehab, where he thought he'd finally be safe. No one with magics capability worked Rehab, just like none of the ruling authorities in the IG could be magics capable.

"What are you going to do with me?" Sean asked dully. He wished Cyan were there. His oldest friend was calm about everything; the perfect Rehabber. He'd probably already be out of his cuffs and taking over the ship.

Wait; this was an IG military ship. Combat class at that. No civilian should have been able to pilot the damned thing. "How the fuck are you flying this ship?"

The Draconis smirked briefly, but did not answer the question. "What's your name?"

"None of your business," Sean snapped. What was he going to do? He couldn't call for help because the minute help arrived, they'd kill him. There was nowhere else for him to go. What was he supposed to do? "I want to know what the fuck you're going to do with me."

"I don't know," the Draconis admitted, misery flashing across his face. "I didn't know I'd match with anyone on Rehab, never mind a Rehabber. This completely screws up all my plans."

Sean glowered at him. "Which were what?" he demanded. "You were going to Rehab. Solitary confinement."

The Draconis ignored him. "I can't just dump you off somewhere, unfortunately. We're matched. I need my magics." He rubbed his forehead tiredly. "Damn it."

It was only adding insult to injury, Sean thought, that the prisoner was hardly a chore to look at. The more dangerous the prisoner, the less he wore upon arrival. That made for some hideous sights. The Draconis was a fine exception—or would have been, had he not cuffed Sean to a bed and were he not saying what sounded suspiciously like he would be kidnapping Sean for an indeterminate length of time.

"Are you going to leave me like this?"

"I should let you go?" the Draconis asked. "Not that stupid, thanks. I managed to put you to sleep once, but given we're matched, that's not going to keep working. I'm a total civilian; you'd kick my ass."

"So, what? You just cart me around the stars in order to keep using your magics?"

"Once my mission is accomplished, I'll be more than happy to let you go."

"You'd lose your magics."

The Draconis shrugged. "I'd learn to manage."

Sean was silent, not buying a word of it. The Draconis had started to speak again when his in-lens suddenly flashed blue. Incoming call, if it was on standard settings ... though that begged the question of how he was wired to the ship, but Sean realized tiredly that there were already a dozen mysteries pertaining to the Draconis. What was one more?

"This is Spring," said a sharp voice.

"This is Fall," the Draconis replied. "What's your location?"

"Close," the voice snapped. "What in the stars have you done now? This was supposed to be a simple matter, and you've bungled it quite nicely. I wish Winter would give an order to wring your neck."

"I'm sure he will at this point," the Draconis sighed. "It's not my fault I matched with a magics capable Rehab guard."

Spring groaned. "Only you. Rendezvous in fifteen minutes. Be ready. Spring out."

The Draconis gave an affirmative reply, but Spring had already cut the connection. He looked at Sean. "I'm truly sorry."

"Yeah," Sean said tiredly. It wasn't the Draconis' fault he was magics capable. If what Cyan had said was true, it wasn't his fault they'd matched either. "There's no way to ... unmatch?"

"No," the Draconis said. "I'm afraid we're stuck. It's part of the reason people hate us." His face twisted with anger and bitterness.

"So you turn around and kill them?" Sean asked.

Genuine hurt and agony filled the Draconis' face. Then his expression turned bitter. "Not that I expect a Rehabber to believe me, since no one else did, but I didn't mean to kill him. We were fighting; it got out of control."

"As mad as I got with my dad, I never fucking killed him," Sean said. It was stupid to argue about this, but he couldn't seem to help himself. If he stayed quiet too long, he'd give in to his panic.

That handsome face hardened, but Sean could see there was pain as well. "Your father wasn't trying to destroy your entire race," the Draconis said. "Look, neither of us wants you here. I promise, as soon as I can, I'll drop you off somewhere and be done. Until then, stop throwing insults at me. I'm well aware I'm a murderer and escaped convict. I don't need constant reminding." Sean nodded. It wasn't as though he could argue much, was it?

"I guess I'll have to put you to sleep again," the Draconis sighed. "Stars, I really didn't need this."

"I'm not going to put up a fight," Sean said with a sigh of his own, conceding reluctant defeat. Really, it was better for him to be kidnapped. "Where the hell am I supposed to go? If they caught us, they'd lock me up right beside you—if they didn't drag me into a dark corner and kill me. I have no fucking choice, really, but to go with you. So just fucking unlock me. You don't hurt me, I won't hurt you."

The Draconis frowned at him, then shrugged and moved to undo his cuffs. Sean slumped as soon as he was free, working the soreness out of his wrists and ankles. He froze as the Draconis deactivated and unlocked the collar around his neck. Calloused hands, surprisingly warm, circled his wrists. There was a brief, tingling heat and then Sean realized his wrists felt better. He jerked his head up. "You ... healed me?"

"Yes," the Draconis said. "You could heal yourself, you know. It's the magics you got from me. I got teleportation from you. Most impressive."

Teleportation? That was his magics? And healing from the Draconis? Those were two of the more powerful defensive magics. Sean swallowed. He'd never known his magics; his entire life had been about *hiding* his magics, not learning them. "Thanks," he said, and pulled his wrists free of the Draconis' touch. "Uh. My name is Sean. Sean Noor."

"Mendel Ekard. I truly am sorry about this."

"It doesn't matter," Sean said tiredly. "Let's just do whatever it is we're doing. I'll figure out the rest later." Nodding and looking as miserable as Sean felt, Mendel turned and led the way out of the room.

# Chapter One

*One term later*

PLANET NUMBER 2051225 (TELVE), IMPERIAL TOWER

"Einn!"

Looking up at the sound of his name, Einn shook off his brooding, and said, "Lark, I was starting to worry. Did you get it?"

"Yeah," Lark replied, looking as tired and strained as Einn felt. He impatiently shoved back an overlong strand of reddish-brown hair and set down the small case he was carrying. "Finally had to break the bastard's nose to get it, but it hardly upset me to do so."

Einn grunted and waited impatiently as Lark opened the case and pushed the lid up, then extracted the injector inside. Loading a capsule, he pressed it to Einn's arm and pulled the trigger. Einn grunted again from the brief burst of pain, the icy wash of serum that flooded his system. He closed his eyes, slumping in relief.

He listened to Lark inject himself, then slowly dragged his eyes open and tilted his head back to look up at the spire of the Telve Imperial Tower. It seemed almost endless, the way it vanished into the high, dark clouds above. Lights were slowly turning on, activated by the steady descent of night. A breeze sprung up, making him shiver.

His coat was nearby, but Einn left it. The climb was going to be long and arduous, even for him, and extraneous fabric would only impede him. Lark sat down next to him and handed him a sac of water. His skin was a dark, dusky red, lurid against Einn's gray-toned skin. Einn sucked the water down, then crumbled the empty sac and shoved it into the pocket of the jacket he was leaving behind. "Everything is ready?"

"Yeah," Lark said. "Ship is prepped; we can run faster than a Kreskan in a whorehouse."

Einn snorted, mouth quirking in an almost smile. "Just make sure you're here to catch him."

"Don't tell me how to do my job," Lark groused. "I've been breaking the law a lot longer than you." He restlessly pulled out the stunner from a holster strapped to his thigh and fussed with it for a minute, before shoving it back into the holster. "I really can't fucking wait to get off this planet. Who in the stars is so special he hides on goddamn *Telve*? No one comes here unless they want to die a slow and painful death."

Rolling his eyes, Einn replied, "We've been here two whole days, and no one has killed us."

"We have omnipasses," Lark replied. "I really don't get why this guy is so special."

Einn called up the file with a thought, his in-lens flashing and data moving across his right eye. "He's one of the most famous scientists in the IG, with a specialty in the evolution of magics. As to why he's here on Telve: he can kill with just one touch of his hands. Not even the Telve are immune, even though he's half-Telven. Worse, not even humans are immune, since the ability is some sort of environmental magics. What do they call it—micro-environmental or something like that?"

"I'm a pirate, how should I know what it's called? I prefer to know as little as possible, anyway," Lark said tightly. The in-lens in his left eye flashed. "City is closing up for the night and the tower is sealing. We are officially locked up tight. Only way in is you, rock spider. I'll be waiting on the ship. Don't screw up."

Einn nodded and stretched out his long legs, then stood and did the same with his arms. He flexed his longer fingers and again eyed the tower. Despite everything, he could not help the thrill of anticipation that raced up his spine, pumped through his blood, and sped his heartbeat. He hadn't been to his home planet of Fornar in five terms—a little *over* a decade, actually—and he had no desire to return, but the love of climbing had never left him. Even travelling the stars could not completely compare to climbing, defying gravity solely by skill and will.

Full dark fell, and Einn clasped Lark's hand briefly. "Cling to the rocks."

"Good luck to you, too," Lark replied, smiling briefly.

Einn nodded and strode off, creeping from the greenery where they'd been hiding and racing toward the tower. No guards impeded him; this close to the Imperial Tower, the Telven relied on magics and their reputation for protection.

His in-lens flashed as he called up necessary specs to avoid the traps that sought to impede him, slipping easily across the lawn, over a low wall, and finally into the courtyard. He darted quickly across the stones, boots nearly soundless on the dark stones.

Reaching the towers, he smiled in anticipation and examined his options, eyes seeing easily in the early evening dark. Examining the spire, he planned his hand and foot holds, then reached up, grabbed hold of the first one, and began to climb. He moved at an easy, steady pace, trusting only his skill because he had a long way to go and, by the end, would need his magics.

A light came on in a room as he passed it by, and Einn froze—but after a few minutes, the light went out again, and with a soft sigh of relief, he kept climbing. Up and up he went, until he reached the halfway point. He didn't look down, simply adjusted his balance and rested for a few minutes. Sweat coated his brow, made the nape his neck wet and itchy, but Einn ignored it.

When he was rested, he resumed his climb, this time using his magics as the air got thinner and colder, and the stones grew more poorly maintained than those on the bottom half of the tower. He climbed until he was another quarter of the way up, then slowly stepped halfway around the tower, before pulling himself onto a balcony that had the small, white marking he had been told would identify it.

Dropping neatly onto the balcony, Einn gingerly tested the door, lip curling in disgust when it simply slid open. Only a fool assumed that being high off the ground was sufficient protection. Slipping into the room, Einn stood a moment to get his bearings. His in-lens flashed again, calling up blue prints. Einn dismissed them, then turned left and strode down a short hallway to a room at the south end of the apartment.

A single bed and a bureau were the only pieces of furniture, and he could just see a door that led to a bathroom. Einn stifled a sigh, wishing he were anywhere else in the world, but his arm still throbbed where Lark had injected him, reminding him all too well why he wasn't anywhere else. He took a step closer to the bed—then froze as the man in it stirred. "Who is there?" demanded a sharp, clipped voice. "Lights!"

Einn narrowed his eyes as the lights came up, and smoothly drew his stunner. He stared at the man sleeping naked in the bed. The file hadn't contained a picture, but it had contained a description: dusky skin, violet eyes, black hair with streaks of white, broad build, average height. Einn smiled with exaggerated congeniality. "Dr. Bikendi?"

Bikendi glared at him but said nothing, though Einn saw his hand start to move. "I wouldn't try that if I were you," Einn said, motioning with his stunner. "I'm afraid your presence has been requested, and I am here to serve as your escort."

"Escort yourself right out of my room, and I hope you break your neck on the way down, you fucking Fornarian," Bikendi snarled.

"Being rude won't help anything," Einn said, and pulled the trigger on his stunner. Bikendi jerked as he was hit and cried out in pain before he slumped, unconscious, on his bed. Holstering his stunner, Einn went to the bureau to find some clothes. Throwing them on the bed, he first pulled out gloves and yanked them on, then took out another set and tugged them onto Bikendi's hands. The last thing he needed was to actually let Bikendi's hands touch him and wind up dead. He'd put up with too fucking much to die so stupidly.

Picking up the clothes, he got Bikendi into them with some effort, then lifted him up and settled him over one shoulder. Walking back down the hallway, he laid Bikendi down on the floor right in front of the balcony door. From the pouch strapped to his left thigh, he pulled out the descent device that he and Lark had picked up once they knew their latest assignment.

When the device was strapped to Bikendi and the poor bastard was as ready as he was going to be, Einn hefted him again and moved out onto the balcony. His in-lens flashed as he communicated with Lark, waiting patiently at the base of the tower. When Lark replied, he threw Bikendi off the balcony, closed the balcony door, and then began the long climb down.

Down was always easier than up. Einn relied on his magics ability to stick to any surface and descended as quickly as he possibly could, and as soon as the ground was close enough, he let go and went into a controlled fall, rolling as he hit the ground. He quickly regained his feet and bolted back across the courtyard, over the wall, across the lawn, and away into the night.

Einn reached the port in record time, dripping sweat and dizzy with exertion. He bolted up the gangway of the *Dragonfly*, in-lens flashing as he ordered the doors to close behind him. When he reached the bridge, he heard Lark speaking to the traffic towers, clearing them for departure.

### CUSTOM CLASS STARSHIP X-11944654, THE *DRAGONFLY*

Einn didn't start breathing properly until they were well away, cruising as fast as they dared until Telve was a blip in the distance. He collapsed in the communications chair. "Thank the skies."

Lark grunted in agreement. "Bikendi is in the holding cell, still out cold. Better call and say the job is done, get the drop off coordinates."

"Yeah, yeah," Einn grumbled, ignoring that for the moment and going to the medic station. He pulled out a towel to wipe the worst of the sweat from his face and neck. Throwing the towel aside, he finally went back to the comm station and punched in a long string of numbers. A moment later, a face appeared on the main screen.

The man was breathtakingly beautiful. He had a narrow, elegant face, eyes the soft gray of the Brelar cliffs of Einn's home, and golden brown hair woven into a braid that fell past his hips, brilliant against his dark green and black robes. His nails were long, gleaming with dark green polish as he set aside the data pad he had been reading. "Captain," he greeted coolly in the smooth, elegant tones of one who had spent his entire life on Zero.

"We have him," Einn said.

Smiling in a way that always made Einn want to shudder, the man replied, "Good. I'll relay the drop off coordinates." He ended the call before either of them could reply. Einn slumped over the console, burying his face in one hand.

Lark let out a sigh that expressed every thought in Einn's head. "I wonder how much longer we'll have to do this before he finally just fucking kills us."

"Too much longer," Einn said bitterly. He glared at the console as it chimed an incoming message, and mashed the necessary buttons to accept it and read the message that popped up on the screen. *2147151, 5.14.9586540 09.37 19:30 ZT*. "Ship 958650," Einn muttered and rotated his chair around to the master console. "Registered Merchant Class, *The Serpent*."

Lark glanced at the message, and then moved to the navigation and pilot console. "Bangkok. That's in Quad 3. We'll have to go to Helior and request a light jump, otherwise we'll never make the meet time." He pinched the bridge of his nose and stood up. "I'm going to make us some food and wake-ups; we're clearly going to need them."

"Don't we always?" Einn said. Lark did not reply, but Einn hadn't expected him to. Left alone on the bridge, he began to put together permits and light jump requests, pausing frequently to rub his eyes when his vision blurred. He looked up with a grateful smile when Lark reappeared and set a plate of food and a small glass filled with a thick, dark red substance in front of him. He made a face and drank it quickly. "I really can't wait for the day we no longer have to drink this shit. I would like to get a real bout of rest."

"I would like not to be poisoned," Lark said bitterly, and settled down at navigation again, quickly chugging his own wake-up. "This is what, the tenth scientist we've taken?"

Einn nodded, and then said tersely, "If we're going to Bangkok, we're probably picking up more ... "

"Victims," Lark finished, voice flat. "We really should have just let the bastard kill us."

"It wouldn't have done any good," Einn reminded him for the thousandth time. "We'd be dead and he'd just be using someone else." He didn't bother to add that someone else probably would not have been keeping careful track of everything they did in the hopes that they, or whoever found their bodies someday, might be able to make use of the information to save the people they were kidnapping.

Lark grunted, but said nothing further.

Einn wolfed down his food, then went back to work. "Permits are ready. Contacting the Helior Light Gate." He punched in the contact codes, and the main screen lit up to display a man with dark red skin and dark brown hair. He was dressed in the uniform of the Infinitum Government's army, the Authorities: a dark gray jacket that fastened with silver frogs at the right shoulder. "Sergeant, this is ship X-11944654. We're requesting a jump."

"Jump permits?" the sergeant asked.

"Sending now," Einn replied, and punched a couple of buttons on his console.

A moment later, the sergeant grunted, and said, "Permits verified, sending jump protocols and clearance codes. You'll be permitted to jump in three hours ZT and have a two-hour window. Fee is five hundred points."

"Transferring funds now," Einn said, in-lens flashing as he activated the ship accounts, and with a few more button presses, he transferred the money. "Thank you, sergeant." The sergeant grunted and the screen went dark. Einn yawned and slumped in his chair. "I really fucking hope we get a little bit of down time in Bangkok. If I have to survive on wake-up much longer, I won't have to worry about the next injection; I'll just die from exhaustion."

Lark did not reply, scowling at his screen while he fussed with the navigation and pilot controls. "You should go check on Bikendi," he said eventually. "He should be awake by now. I left food for him in the mess."

Einn nodded and stood. "I'll look in on him, then I'm going to clean up. Buzz if you need me."

"I will," Lark said, and went back to fussing with his controls. Einn sighed and walked down the hall to the mess at the back of their small ship, retrieving the tray of food on the small counter. Back in the hall, he went down a short set of winding stairs to the below deck area, which housed the guts of the ship, a couple of storage rooms, and the holding cell.

He flicked on the lights and peered through the bars at Bikendi, who glared right back with eyes that glowed lavender. "Doctor."

"Who are you, blood bag, and why in the hell are you kidnapping me?"

"I'm just following orders," Einn said. "I don't know what the fuck they intend to do with you, though I can guess, given your reputation."

Bikendi smiled coldly and flourished his hands, still in the gloves Einn had put on them. "Which reputation?"

"I'm sure both are useful," Einn said, and lifted a small flap at the bottom of the cage, sliding the tray through it. "Eat up." He stood up and turned away.

"Why are you doing this?" Bikendi asked, his tone that of a scientist: curious, thoughtful, emotionless. He might have been discussing his latest experiment. "Is it for points? For pleasure?"

Einn balled his hand into a fist, but did not reply, simply walked away. Upstairs, he went into the room across from the kitchen. One side of the room held two beds, one above the other. He hated ship beds; they did not accommodate for the exaggerated build of Fornarians—but given he could count on one hand the number of other Fornarians he had seen in space, he supposed it was fair enough.

The other side of the room held a washing area, blocked off by a half wall. He stripped out of his clothes and stepped into the tiled area, using a rough pad and dry soap to get himself as clean as was possible in the middle of nowhere on a junker custom ship only just small enough for two people to manage on their own.

*Why are you doing this?*

Every single one of them asked that question, as though they expected the answer to make a difference. Not a one of them could offer him the only thing they needed: a way out of the prettily painted clutches that held them fast. Einn scrubbed down viciously, wishing he could wash away the past term as easily.

But he couldn't. His crew was dead, save for Lark, and they would both die as soon as they ceased to be useful. Einn wasn't stupid—there was no way that they would ever be given the antidote to the ticking time bombs in their system. They knew too much, had done too much. Once there was no one else for them to kidnap, that was the end of it.

He'd left home to do something more than climb cliffs and crawl through caves. He had wanted to see the stars. He'd wanted an adventure. If he had known he would end up a pirate, and then the kidnapping expert of an IG bastard—

Well, it didn't matter. They could not go back and change anything; they could only cling to the futile hope that they would find a way out of the mess. Until then, best only to think about reaching Helior, then on to Bangkok. They would pass Bikendi off, get their next assignment, and carry on same as they had for the past term.

One way or another, the nightmare would eventually end. They'd find a way out, they'd get carted off to Rehab, or they'd die. Einn wasn't sure how much he cared about which of those outcomes came to pass—except, if that were true, he'd let the damned poison kill him.

Swearing softly, he wiped himself down and strode to the set of storage units built into the wall beside the bunks. He took out fresh clothes and pulled them on, then sat down on the lower bunk to lace up his boots. They were slightly impractical for space, but he wasn't comfortable if he wasn't in climbing shoes of some sort. Standard bunks were not built with Fornarians in mind, but neither was anything else in space, which gave him a decided edge. No one else would have been able to take Bikendi from his room in the Imperial Tower so easily.

Dressed, he returned to the bridge and took over the controls so Lark could get cleaned up as well. He prodded without interest, tweaking their course, seeing what other ships were out and about, and making note of a couple that could possibly be threats, even though they were far enough away they weren't likely to attack his small, unremarkable ship.

Settling back, he brought up news feeds, idly scrolling through stories. His mouth tightened as he caught the headline of one, an update on the raging debate about the fate of the Draconis. It listed off scientists likely to assist on each side of the debate, political figures, lawyers, IG thoughts—

Einn dismissed the story, then shut down the feed and looked over the star course again. Satisfied all was still well, he pushed his chair over to the ship console and called up the diagnostics, because if he had actual down time, it was best to spend it on the ship. The very last thing they needed was for it to break down; they already had enough problems.

Einn really hoped that they got a breather when they reached Bangkok. Skies above! Something good had to go their way, just once. What better place than the planet where 'all dreams come true'? They could not keep going the way they were—something had to give.

# Chapter Two

**PLANET 5118208 (REHAB), REHABILITATION CENTER 2.2, SECTOR NINE**

"Damn it," Cyan managed, but the word turned into a choked off squeak as the Sardoran managed to get a tentacle around his throat. His head knocked hard as the bastard slammed him into the wall. Cyan fumbled for his stinger even as more tentacles came for him. Stars a-fucking-bove, he hated Sardorans.

Gritting his teeth as he was slammed to the floor and the fucking creature got too close, Cyan thumbed the stinger to its lowest setting and drove it into the Sardoran, pressing the activation button. The Sardoran snarled at the shot of pain, and Cyan managed to break free, dropping to the hard metal grating with a grunt. Twisting, he got to his knees and lunged at the retreating Sardoran, grasping the stinger and thumbing the power all the way up, before zapping the fucker again. Then he threw himself back, hands flat on the grating, flipping over in a backward handspring and landing neatly in a crouch, standing as he watched the Sardoran twitch and writhe and scream in pain.

When it finally fell still, Cyan stalked over and gave it another jolt just to be certain. After he was absolutely certain the Sardoran was unconscious, he began to roughly kick it across the grating and down into the special pool that would be its cell for the next three terms. "Stupid. Fucking. Sardorans," he muttered, punctuating each word with a hard kick and stepping hard on stray tentacles whenever they happened to get in his way until, at last, the floor was clear, and he'd locked the Sardoran up.

He rounded on Captain Waters, who stood well out of the way up the stairs. "Where the fuck were you?" he snapped.

"Watching the show," Waters replied, smoothing his mustache, brown eyes full of mirth. "Honestly. Is there some Sardoran blood in you? Or do you just wear 'Sardorans, please fuck me senseless' cologne?"

"Go to fucking hell," Cyan said in disgust, rubbing his throat. Sardoran skin always left him with a goddamn rash; something in their skin didn't like his, even if he did seem to be the hottest thing Sardorans had ever seen. "Stop fucking assigning me to 9.2.4."

Waters grinned. "And lose the best free entertainment around? No way."

"Fuck you," Cyan muttered, slinging his stinger back in its loop on his pants. He systematically went about ensuring all his other weapons were in place. He was covering 9.2.4 and 9.2.5, which meant he carried fifteen weapons instead of the usual twelve—all three additions were meant for killing, not merely restraining.

Weapons accounted for, he moved on to his keys. As a First Class Guard, he was in possession of 150 keys, and they came in a wide variety of forms. First were the chem-keys, special chemicals that needed renewing every five hours. He kept the pills in a pocket low on the front of his jacket, left-hand side—ten of those. Next were the microchips attached at the start of each shift to the heavy black fabric of his jacket—fifty of those. Fifteen clearance codes were saved to his in-lens, updated every ten hours. Twenty-five key cards and five old-fashioned metal keys that were obsolete everywhere but Rehab. The green bands he wore on his upper arm held another ten codes, twenty-five were in the microchip in his brain, and his fingerprints served as a final ten.

When he'd verified he had all his keys, Cyan took the datapad Waters held out and quickly signed it, acknowledging the newest prisoner was caged and secured.

"Make the fucking newbies clean this place up. I'm hitting the showers."

"Then going on break," Waters added.

"Break?" Cyan asked, then grimaced. "Oh, yeah. Fine. Whatever. See you in a month." Heaving a sigh, he scrubbed a hand over his hair, cut so short that it was only barely possible to tell it was black, and began the long walk through the wings until he finally reached the locker room.

Going to his lockers, he quickly began to put away all his weapons, scanning each one in before hanging it up. Next went the keys, stripped off and locked up in a box that itself required six keys. He closed and locked both the box and his first locker, before throwing his keys in the security drop box and striding back to his lockers to open the second of the two. Stripping off his clothes, he tossed them toward the hamper, then grabbed a towel and walked to the shower area.

Turning on the water of the furthest shower, Cyan sighed as the pounding heat soothed his aching muscles. He stood like that for several minutes, just letting the hot water drive everything away. Several minutes later, hearing noise in the locker room, he began finally to move. Reaching for the soap, which smelled vaguely like lemons, he began to scrub away the day. Beneath the abrasive soap, traces of the Sardoran vanished, a light anesthetic healing the sting from a Hellcat cut and a bruise administered by a pissed off Telsken.

Cyan's body was all tight muscle with not a spare ounce of fat anywhere, rippling with every movement. From head to toe, he bore the scars of a life spent as a Rehab guard—one who had made it all the way to First Class: a burn along his right upper arm, Hellcat scratches down his side and one leg, and at least a dozen other marks that spelled out plainer than words the rough life led by Rehabbers. He ran his fingers over his stomach, where a livid set of five long, deep scratches were forever imprinted. Most of his scars had come from Rehab, but not all of them.

Cyan opened his eyes, pale dove gray, as he heard others spilling into the showers. Nodding to them, Cyan quickly scrubbed his hair clean, and then strode back into the locker room. Unlocking his second locker, he quickly pulled on soft denim pants and a white undershirt, then a dark green, long-sleeved shirt. Making certain one last time that all was accounted for, he sat down to tug on his socks and boots, then sealed his locker and walked out.

Out in the guard docks, he grabbed a bench and waited for a shuttle to Mars to arrive. It was, as always, almost completely silent. Only a faint hum of machinery buzzed and thrummed, a sound so familiar he barely heard it anymore. The air was thick with dark clouds that would never go away, one of many lingering results of the Last War, which had resulted in the planet being turned into a Rehabilitation Planet.

Everything was dull gray, concrete and metal, with more alarm systems than even most guards knew about scattered and cleverly hidden. No one and nothing escaped from Rehab—except one fucking Draconis after he'd matched with a stupid, fucking, magics capable human, who had never told his goddamn best friend he was magics capable. It sat heavy and bitter on Cyan, even a full term later, that Sean had never completely trusted him.

He'd told Sean his own deepest secret and Sean had not shared his. Why? Cyan knew he should let it go—Sean probably had a good reason—but it still hurt. They'd done everything together ever since they'd met, after Cyan had arrived on Mars at age eighteen. Sean had been the friend he'd never had back home, had been the reason he'd found a life on Mars he would never have had otherwise. Yet it seemed Sean had always held something back. And if he'd held one thing back ...

Miserably, Cyan cut the thought off. It didn't matter—none of it mattered. What mattered was being able to punch Sean for it someday. Every damned day he hoped to hear something, and every day he heard nothing. No clue had ever turned up, only the combat ship in which the Draconis had escaped with Sean. By the time authorities had reached it, the ship had been little more than space debris. The search was still open, but shunted to the very bottom of the IG to-do list.

Thankfully. On top of being angry at and worried about Sean, Cyan had feared the whole thing would reveal his own secrets and he would rather die than *ever* return to Zero. He wasn't doing it. When the IG had finally grown bored and wandered away to attend other matters, Cyan had nearly passed out from relief.

Stupid fucking Sean.

Cyan's thoughts broke off as a shuttle arrived, and he waited impatiently while the next shift disembarked, waving and greeting absently, nodding to the others on his shift who clambered onto the shuttle with him.

He picked a seat in the back and stared blankly out the window as the shuttle took off, wishing he were still working, because on Rehab, there was no way to think about anything other than the job. He had an entire month to kill and nothing to fill the time. There were things he could do, of course, but it wasn't the same. He wanted his best friend back, even if it seemed Sean had never entirely trusted him.

Maybe he'd take a trip like the one that had been waylaid by Sean's stupid fucking vanishing trick. Yeah, go to Bangkok, take his mind off everything.

The thought wasn't as cheering as it should have been.

### PLANET 1311819 (MARS), SETTLEMENT 2.1 (CANADIA)

Cyan stirred from his light doze as the ship touched down, quickly regaining his senses. Throwing himself into the line of those disembarking, he chatted easily about prisoners and protocol with his fellow Rehabbers. As they entered the terminal and began to disperse, there was a slight shift in the level and tone of chatter. Cyan ignored it, as did his comrades. It didn't matter how many times people saw them, they were intimidated. Rehabbers were crazy, after all: violent, loved to fight, and never lost one.

Cyan shot a glare at an old woman when her whispers got too loud, and she guiltily dropped her hand, which had been pointing at his notably short hair. Longer hair was more fashionable; only dock laborers and Rehabbers tended to go with the cropped hair that was just short of completely shaved, and laborers did not have the 'menacing' air of Rehabbers.

Rolling his eyes, Cyan left the terminal behind and strode through the streets. Mars was divided up into hundreds of settlements, and it was said they all paralleled countries and cities, all of which had existed on Earth before the Last War. He lived on Settlement 2.1, one of the larger; its traditional name was Canadia, but most just went by the number.

Moving quickly, knowing the streets as well as he knew the wards and wings of Rehab, Cyan finally came to the little section of houses at the edge of the northeast quadrant where he'd spent the last ten years of his life when he wasn't on Rehab. Stifling a yawn, he strode past his own house and keyed open Sean's.

As miserable as he still was by Sean's departure one term later, it was Sean's mother who'd been hit hardest. Sean's father had died two terms ago, only half a term after Sean had joined Cyan on Rehab. Losing her son, her only remaining family, had been nearly too much for the poor, sweet lady to bear.

Whistling, Cyan stepped inside—and immediately stopped. Something was wrong. This time of day, Alice was usually making tea and fussing with her plants. She had a Vrill rose that had cost most of her savings, something she'd waited her entire life to purchase.

A sick feeling in the pit of his stomach, Cyan cut through the house to the back where it spilled into a small greenhouse. He swore softly when he saw a small heap in the very back, lying far too still. Kneeling, he checked Alice for injuries, softly calling her name. Her eyes fluttered open after a moment, dim and weak, but the very same bright blue as Sean's. "Cyan."

"Alice, what's wrong? Why didn't you call to let me know you weren't feeling well?"

"Doesn't matter," Alice whispered. "Nothing to do except wait. I'm too old."

Cyan felt cold fear wash through him. "What are you saying, Alice?"

"Dying, silly boy. Wish I could see my son ... "

Biting back an angry retort, Cyan slowly got her back into the house and into bed. "Is there anything I can get you?" he asked. She pointed weakly at the door to her bathroom, and Cyan went to investigate. It didn't take him long to find the little bottles of prescribed drugs tucked behind lotions and tinctures. His mouth tightened as he examined the bottles and realized she'd been hiding her illness for a long damned time.

Returning to the bedroom, he said, "Alice, you should have said something. It's not right, keeping it to yourself. I would have helped you—I want to help you."

"Didn't want anyone worrying about me," she said with a tired smile. "I'm old; it's about time I moved on. Just wish I could see my boy."

Cyan held her hand tight, kissing the knuckles, then one wrinkled cheek. "I wish I could bring Sean to you, Alice."

Alice stared at her hands, rubbing one thumb over his. "Would you, Cyan? I would like to tell him goodbye, though I've put off asking because I know he's in danger ... " A tear slipped down one cheek.

"I don't know where to find him, Alice," Cyan said, vowing to punch Sean good and hard if he ever saw the bastard again. Letting go of his hand, Alice fumbled with a drawer of her nightstand. Gently, Cyan urged her to lie back down and opened the drawer himself. "What did you need?"

"Datapad," Alice whispered. "Diary." She whispered a long string of numbers and letters, and Cyan rapidly punched them in at the demand for a password. "Search—3765.419.28."

Cyan did as ordered and swore softly as the diary entry came up. It was simple, nothing more than a string of numbers, but he immediately understood. Once upon a time, he'd been made to memorize hundreds of planetary serial numbers—usually just called PSNs. He seldom forgot something once it was memorized, another element of his upbringing. Cyan stared at the numbers, mind already working.

**03-07-11181911-3554**

Quad Three, Sector Seven. The rest of the number identified the actual planet, which was Kreska. The last four numbers meant the location was actually the moon of Kreska, rather than the planet itself. Sean was on the moon of Kreska and Alice had known all along. Why hadn't Sean told him? Cyan tried not to feel hurt. Of course he should have been cautious in who he told—

With a rough sound, Cyan turned off the datapad. He kissed Alice's cheek. "I'll go get Sean for you, Alice. Stay here and rest, all right? You call Waters if anything happens."

"I will," Alice said. "Thank you, Cyan. You know I always counted you my boy, too."

"I know," Cyan said softly, a sharp pang in his chest. "Rest, now. Before you know it, I'll be back with Sean." Making certain Alice had everything she needed close to hand and shooting off a communication to Waters, he walked swiftly to his own house and began to pack.

Clothes. Datapad. In-lens. Stunner. Extra cartridge. Rifling through his closet, Cyan finally unearthed the holster for the stunner, fitting it over his shoulders. He double-checked the stunner and cartridge, and then slid them into place. Reaching back into the closet, he tugged on a plain black jacket, rolling his shoulders so everything settled properly. Next, he double-checked his permits and licenses to carry the concealed stunner, as well as his Rehab ID and clearances.

Better to travel incognito, but if he had to throw his weight around, he would. The only real problem he was going to have was that no one had ever really believed him when he'd claimed ignorance of Sean being magics capable. Cyan didn't blame them—he still couldn't forgive Sean for not telling him.

But it meant IG officials were still watching him, if covertly. They had said months ago he was no longer under suspicion, but Cyan wasn't stupid. He knew better than anyone realized how the IG worked. They were still watching him. That meant he'd have to be really fucking careful they didn't find his actions suspicious.

Bangkok was right at the border of the second and third quads, making it a nearly perfect halfway point between Mars and Kreska. If he got to Bangkok, the IG would likely lose any interest in him after a couple of days. Everyone went to Bangkok, all for the same reasons. The Star of Delights was called thus for extremely good reasons.

All Cyan would have to do was find a way to slip out of Bangkok and get to Kreska. Not easy to do, but not impossible. If a magics capable human could vanish from the stars, Cyan could slip undetected out of Bangkok.

Even after a term, it was hard to believe Sean was magics capable. He knew there were IG scientists who believed that it was only a matter of time before humans started evolving magics; mingling and mixing with so many magics capable races, it was to be expected. However, Cyan had never expected to encounter a reality that validated their theories. He definitely hadn't thought it would be his best friend.

The Infinitum Government was run by humans because they were the only species in existence that was not magics capable. Every official from the Grand Chancellor down through the Lower Chancellors, the High and Low Councilors, the Authorities, and Rehabilitation Guards were all human. No one employed in a government role was magics capable.

It was important that humans never gain magics capability because the greatest danger with those who *were* capable was the vulnerability to all magics—mind control, telepathy, telekinesis, and hundreds upon hundreds more. It was too dangerous to let magics capable beings run the government; there were too many chances for things to go horribly wrong. If humans suddenly became magics capable, the entire power structure would collapse and war would result.

Cyan didn't give a fuck, except that it meant his biggest problem wasn't going to be finding Sean—it would be getting Sean home to see his mother. Should the wrong people ever find Sean, they would kill him. That, however, was a problem for later. First, he had to get to Sean.

Swearing softly and refusing to admit he might be happy about getting to see Sean again, even if the circumstances fucking sucked, Cyan slung the strap of his duffle bag over his chest. He locked the door as he left, setting the codes for a long absence—meaning the house would shut down and run on the bare essentials until he returned. Waters would stop by to deal with shit like food and all. The bastard might stick him with the Sardorans, but Waters looked after his own.

Making his way back to the terminal, Cyan bypassed everything by flashing his RCCs—Rehab clearance codes—, since Rehabbers got special treatment, due to the vigorous and highly specialized training that even the Authorities did not experience. He stopped briefly at one security desk where all his stuff was quickly cleared. At the ticket desk, he booked the first flight out.

# Chapter Three

**PLANET 0315149 (CONT), PRIVATE ESTATE OF GRAE DRALL**

"No sign of a struggle," Sean said, picking through the various and sundry objects in Lady Jundel's room. "She must have been taken in her sleep, which is rather impressive, knowing what little I do of your mother."

Mendel said nothing; merely continued to examine the room, a grim expression on his face. Sean wished he knew what to say to at least get Mendel to calm down, but one term later and they still seemed to be strangers in too many ways. He watched Mendel surreptitiously, admiring him despite the futility of it all. He could admire Mendel until the day he died, and Mendel would neither notice nor care. Mendel's only interest in life was in saving the Draconis.

Sean could not blame him for that either, not when he knew what it was like for people to want him dead. The existence of a magics capable human was the death knell of human control of the IG. When they eventually got caught, no one would bother to arrest them—between him being a mutant and Mendel being a convicted felon, they would shoot on sight.

In Sean's mind, that meant they should enjoy what they could for as long as they could. He was more than willing to enjoy his kidnapper-turned-friend, but he could crawl naked into Mendel's bed, lubed up and ready to go, and Mendel wouldn't notice because he was too busy compiling a report or examining star charts.

Putting the thoughts aside, because there were definitely more important matters at present, Sean sat down at Jundel's desk and activated her work unit. It was a handsome piece, built into a dark wood desk, everything motion activated and state of the art. No Draconis really wanted to be matched, but Jundel had definitely made one of the best matches possible in Lord Drall. Sean activated the screens and half a dozen squares of light lit up around him.

Well, he knew where Mendel got his 'all work, no play' modus operandi. He fussed with the work unit for a few minutes, then pulled out his own data pad and synched them, calling up his cracks to hack into her system. Jundel was no idiot, however; it would take several minutes for him to get into it—and if it all held true to the rest of the kidnappings, there would be no clues.

Across the room, Mendel was rifling through a jewelry box, a too-familiar pensive frown on his face. Sean went over to him, lightly touching his shoulder. "We'll find her, Mendel. I'm sorry she was one of the victims."

"It was a logical choice," Mendel said, putting a necklace he had been holding back in the case. "She said herself it could happen and I told her to take the necessary precautions, but of course she did not listen."

Sean's mouth curved up in one corner in a fond half-smile. "No, I would imagine she didn't. Your family does not seem the listening sort."

Mendel shrugged. "Listening goes both ways."

"I know, I was teasing," Sean said, then shook his head. "Never mind. I'm running cracks now. Maybe her unit will turn up something. You say she was a good choice for the kidnappers, but it seems strange to me they would pick such high profile victims. Lord Drall and Lady Jundel are two of the most well-known supporters for the continued existence of the Draconis. Until now, the kidnappers were keeping everything low key, but this latest snatch will cause the problem to go straight to the media. What were they thinking?"

"That my mother and Lord Drall are a perfect example of what the Conis and Draconis were meant to be," Mendel said, moving to the unit and watching impatiently while Sean's cracks slowly whittled down its security. "Everyone else they've kidnapped has been a Draconis matched with a non-Coni. Whatever the hells they're doing, they would need a control. I'm surprised they have not addressed that sooner. But who knows, we know absolutely nothing about what's going on past what we can conjecture based on the persons kidnapped."

Sean nodded and rested his hand lightly on Mendel's back. "I'm sure they're already regretting it, and maybe we'll get a break now that it will finally come to media attention—"

"I don't want it coming to media attention!" Mendel snapped. "If it goes too far, whoever it is might panic and just kill all of them. While this was quiet, we stood a chance. But now ... "

"They won't murder that many people," Sean tried to reassure, but before he could say anything further, both their in-lens lit up and a voice spoke in their ears.

"Get what you can and get back on the ship. Just got word from Winter that another kidnapping has gone down. These fuckers are even better than we thought because they snatched Dr. Itzal Bikendi from the Imperial Tower of Telve."

Sean's brows shot up at that. Beside him, Mendel looked just as shocked. Who the hell was brazen enough to kidnap someone from Telve? From the stars damned *Imperial Tower*? "We're on our way," he replied, then looked at Mendel. "Do you want to wait to see what we'll learn from searching the unit?"

"No," Mendel said. "Winter can send someone else to look into it. Lock it down so only IA can mess with it."

"You got it," Sean replied, and immediately went to work, tapping his datapad and activating a full keyboard. It shimmered green and blue in the air in front of him, flaring orange as he hit the keys and uploaded a program to keep running cracks, simultaneously setting up his own securities and sealing up the protocols to transmit later to Winter, who could pass it on to whatever agent he assigned to finish the job they'd started.

When he was done, Sean put his datapad to rest and slid it into its holster on his thigh. "All set. Let's go see what Telve can tell us." He took Mendel's arm, tugged him close, and for a brief, stolen moment enjoyed his warmth and salty-sweet scent. Then he called up his magics, and they vanished from the room.

### CUSTOM CLASS STARSHIP Z-28922942, THE *BRILLIANT*

Mendel strode off as soon as they reappeared in the transport room, not looking back. Sean sighed and followed him, but veered off halfway to the bridge to go to the mess. He knew for a fact that Mendel had not eaten so much as a bite since hearing of his mother's kidnapping, and whatever the idiot thought, he would do no one any favors by starving himself.

A few minutes later, carefully carrying three trays of food, Sean joined the other two on the bridge. "So who is this guy you said was kidnapped, Karmikel?"

Karmikel looked up from where he was bent over the center console with Mendel, arguing over the best route to take. "Do you live under a rock?"

"If by rock, you mean 'vaguely illegal custom class starship as the magics capable human mate of a convicted felon', then yes, I live under a rock," Sean replied dryly.

"Fair enough," Karmikel said, impatiently shoving back strands of honey-gold hair. His scales and skin were the same shade, making him look like a Draconis crafted from the finest gold leaf. "Dr. Itzal Bikendi is the leading geneticist in the IG, and he has a long list of specialties, but he's best known for supporting the theory of lost magics."

When no one bothered to explain what that meant, Sean rolled his eyes, and asked, "What is the theory of lost magics?"

"Bikendi, along with a small handful of other scientists, believes that humans once possessed magics and that they were suppressed for reasons not yet known. That they were suppressed to the point that it now seems humans do not possess magics. Bikendi believes that, eventually, humans will possess magics again. Bikendi would count you proof of that theory," Mendel explained.

"I've never heard that theory." Of course, Sean conceded, he'd never given a damn about science. He hadn't dared, not when he was a lab rat waiting to happen.

Mendel shrugged. "It's not a popular theory within the IG, obviously. The only reason no one shuts Bikendi up is that he is both brilliant and deadly."

"What do you mean?"

Mendel answered, "He can kill with just a touch of his hand, drain a person's energy, and convert it to whatever energy he needs. It's an especially fascinating magics in that it's micro-environmental, meaning he can kill even humans. He studies magics and genetics in the hopes of overcoming his own magics, or so it's said. He lives on the primary moon of Telve; I can't think why in the stars he was down planet."

"Could be any number of reasons," Sean said, and shoved a tray at him, forcing Mendel to take it or let it drop. "It's not like you can keep up with the everyday lives of every scientist and Draconis in the IG. We have our hands full as it is. My main concern is Telve and whether they'll let us poke around."

Karmikel snorted. "What the hell is the point of Winter if he can't get us cleared for that?"

As if sensing he had been mentioned, the main comm screen lit up with an incoming communication. Karmikel accepted it via his in-lens and the screen flared to life, displaying a man who looked to be in his forties, with broad shoulders and the mien of a man long-used to authority. He was dressed in the black and silver formal uniform of the IG, a stark contrast to his white-blond hair, the whole adding an almost silvery touch to his pale blue eyes. "I have obtained passes for you to enter Telve, though it will obviously be covertly. Spring, they are not willing to risk your presence, so you will remain on the ship while the others investigate."

"But—"

"It's non-negotiable," Winter said firmly. "I have an agent in Telve working on something else. He will be your escort. I have transmitted all pertinent information, as well as clearance for the light gate. Contact me if you have any questions. Winter out."

Sean frowned when Mendel set his tray of food down, clearly dismissing it. "I'm not staying on the damned ship! I'm the scientist; I'm the only one who will understand whatever we look at." The words shouldn't have stung, but they did because Sean might not have been a scientist, but he wasn't a fucking idiot either. He knew enough to know what to bring back to Mendel. "I'm not just going to sit here being useless—"

"I'm not useless because I usually stay on the ship," Karmikel snapped. "If you didn't want to be stuck on the ship, then you shouldn't have committed murder! You're a felon; deal with the consequences." For a moment, Sean thought Mendel was going to launch himself at Karmikel and break his face. Sean had never seen Mendel resort to violence, but from what little he'd inferred from Karmikel, he could more than hold his own in a fight.

It made Sean all the more curious about what had happened the night Mendel had killed his father, but as with everything else about himself, Mendel didn't discuss it. He was the single most infuriating person Sean had ever met. Even getting *Cyan* to talk about himself was not as difficult as getting Mendel to talk about anything other than his cause.

The tension finally broke when Mendel turned sharply on his heel and left the bridge. Karmikel made a face and bent back over the three-dimensional star chart display, in-lens flashing as he mucked with courses, settling on the best one. "You have a death wish," Sean remarked.

"Che," Karmikel said dismissively. "I wish he would punch me. Holding back all that rage is exactly what caused that fight between them in the first place. He needs to learn to let it go, and while I don't really want to be his punching bag ... well, it's hardly the first time someone has come at me looking to cave my head in. I don't care."

"I think we all need a damned break," Sean said, and sighed at the abandoned food. He tried to ignore it, but in the end just couldn't. Picking it up, he headed off to find Mendel. "Vicky," he said, speaking to the AI that ran the *Brilliant*, "Where is Mendel?"

*"Laboratory,"* Vicky replied.

"Thanks," Sean said, and took the stairs up to the third level, which had mostly been converted into a research laboratory and office space. His own work area was in the south-most corner. Mendel stood in the middle of the room, poring over data that lit up the primary work table. Clearly impatient, he dismissed whatever he was reading and called up something new.

Sean drew a deep breath, steeling himself for an argument, then let it out slowly and walked forward. He froze the table with a touch and a command from his in-lens, and then set the tray of food over whatever Mendel was reading. "You really need to eat, Mendel."

"I don't need you telling me what to do," Mendel said coolly, shoving the tray aside and unfreezing his table, resuming work. "I am busy. I will eat when I feel like it."

"You haven't eaten in two days," Sean countered.

Mendel ignored him. Sean stifled a sigh and raked a hand through his overlong hair—then grabbed Mendel, spun him around, and swept his legs out from under him. He pinned Mendel to the floor, straddling him so his arms were pinned to his sides. "You're being an ass. You don't help anyone by overworking and starving yourself. How many fucking times do we have to have this argument?"

"Until you stop nagging me," Mendel said curtly. "I have taken care of myself this long; I will continue to do—"

"It's not just about you!" Sean snapped. "It's about everyone you're trying to help; it's about your mother working her ass off to help you. It's about—" He bit off the word 'me', because whatever he might wish, whatever he might want, it wasn't about him. Mendel was truly sorry that they had matched, Sean knew that, but he didn't want Mendel to be *sorry*. He wanted Mendel to give a damn, to want to make them more than just comrades in arms. He liked to say they were friends, but he knew it was just tarting up a working relationship. "Do you know why Rehabbers are unbeatable?"

Mendel snorted. "I know they think they're unbeatable."

Sean jabbed him, hard. "Fuck you. I'm being serious—would it kill you to cooperate with me for five fucking minutes? Rehabbers are unbeatable because we train and train and train. We have to be better than all the different kinds of criminals we deal with every day. Not only do we train, but we work on rigid schedules, and part of that schedule is regular, month-long breaks. Do you know why those are important?" Mendel remained stonily silent, but Sean pushed on, refusing to be daunted. "A Rehabber who can't let go and unwind is a danger to himself and others. Too much work and not enough downtime leaves you too tense to function properly. The best Rehabbers are the ones who walk away from the job for a bit and clear their heads. You need to clear your fucking head, and you need to eat."

"Fine," Mendel replied.

"You could *listen* to me, instead of just saying what you think I want to hear," Sean said. Mendel glared at him. Sean wondered what had happened to the man who had first kidnapped him a term ago, the one who had apologized and looked contrite, and had compelled Sean to give this whole crazy thing a chance instead of waiting for the first opportunity to escape.

"Oh, forget it." He climbed off Mendel and stepped away. "I wish you would at least eat so I could worry a little less about you. Would it really kill you to remember that people do worry about you?"

"I have been fine so far, and there is no reason for you to worry about me," Mendel replied. Sean balled his hands into fists, and then forced himself to relax. He watched in silence as Mendel picked at the food, but did not bother to actually eat any of it. Sean had fixed his favorites—well, the closest anyone could have to favorites when it came to travel food—but Mendel may as well have been picking at everything he hated for all the enthusiasm he showed.

Sean shouldn't have been hurt. "Of course I should worry about you," he said.

"There is absolutely no reason for you to worry about me," Mendel repeated flatly, and shoved his food away again. When Sean said nothing, he finally looked up—and Sean punched him. Before Mendel could recover, Sean punched him again, then tripped him up and planted a booted foot on Mendel's chest.

"No reason for me to worry?" he yelled. "Is that really how selfish you've become, that you think I have no fucking reason to worry about a man who holds my life in his hands? You work yourself to death, you worry yourself to death, you don't eat, you don't sleep, and every day you get angrier and more hostile. One day, you're going to get yourself killed, and I'll die right alongside you. If you feel so fucking bad that we matched? Try to show it by giving a damn that every time you risk your life, you risk mine. Eat your fucking food."

Not waiting for a reply, Sean stormed off, going back downstairs, past the main level and down to the bottom level. Storming down the walkway, metal grate floor ringing with the force of his steps, Sean kept going until he reached the engine room.

It was always oddly quiet, a testament to the quality of the engines and how well the entire ship had been built. Everything had a muffled quality to it, and it was one of the few places on the ship the other two never bothered to go.

Sean sat down at the engineer's workbench, restlessly picking up and putting down all the tools he had left there the last time he had worked on the engines. Karmikel was one hell of a pilot, but like most pilots that Sean knew, he seemed to have little to no patience for the nuts and bolts of a starship. How the hell he and Mendel had kept the *Brilliant* running for so long by themselves was a matter of probability or luck.

Sean had not been aboard for more than a couple of weeks before he had found himself playing the roles of engineer and technician. They were contributions that Mendel and Karmikel made full use of, but Sean couldn't remember either one saying anything to him about it. Normally, he took it in stride; they were both self-contained, quick to push people away. Given their personal histories, he could not blame them.

Right then, however, he was more than happy to blame Mendel for a great deal. What in the stars was Sean doing anyway, gallivanting about from planet to planet, untangling conspiracies and working with covert agents? He was a fucking Rehab guard.

Unfortunately, he was also matched to Mendel, and no matter how badly he thought it would be best if he just left, he did not want to leave. He liked the work he was doing, and he wanted more than anything to actually get along with Mendel. Instead, no matter what he did or said, there was always guilt and anger wedged between them.

He was tempted to go back and heal the bruises and bloody nose with which he'd left Mendel, but Mendel was capable of healing himself and Sean would probably just wind up punching him again. Instead, he flopped back down on the bench, pillowing his head on a cleaning rag, and stayed in the engine room until Karmikel called him to the bridge. As he left the engine room, Sean tried to convince himself that he wasn't disappointed Mendel had never bothered to seek him out.

# Chapter Four

**PLANET 2147151 (BANGKOK), RED DRAGON PAVILION**

Einn threw back a shot of Bangkok spiced rum then chased it with a swallow of dark Fornarian beer. He looked around the dive, restless, wanting *something*—a fight, a fuck, anything to expend energy. It made him antsy that they had been given downtime and their serum a full day ahead of time. They were being prepared for something particularly unpleasant, and he really did not want to know what—but he would still try to enjoy the break.

If only he knew what to do with himself. He couldn't remember the last time he'd *had* free time. Lark had vanished, skies alone knew where, but they'd had no company but each other for far too long. Whatever Lark was doing, Einn hoped he was enjoying it.

He scanned the bar again, fingers drumming restlessly. Nothing caught his eye, so he returned his attention to his beer and wondered where else he should try. He didn't really want to go further into Bangkok; he was happier at the fringes. Finishing his beer, he signaled a passing waitress for another and activated his in-lens to see what amusements might be had in the area.

A sudden lull in the barroom din made him look up, and Einn immediately saw the reason for the silence in the doorway. IG goons—they all had the same look about them. They weren't in uniform, but the arrogant way they moved, the close cropped hair, the way their eyes scanned the room in a way no civilian bothered marked them. Could be criminals, but criminals didn't draw that kind of attention—only someone with the law behind him bothered.

The man on the right was the taller, with dark bronze skin, pale blond hair, dark eyes, a broad build and stern, handsome face. Men hastened to get out of his way, and though he scarcely seemed to pay attention, Einn had the impression that he was very aware of everything going on around him. The man next to him was shorter, more compact, but no less muscled or impressive. They both moved with the fluid grace of fighters and were dressed in the sort of loose, but well-fitted clothing that suited hand to hand combat: it allowed them to move easily, but wouldn't get in their way.

Auths, he would bet; only military-type thugs had that particular look about them. He looked again at the shorter one, who wouldn't even reach Einn's shoulders. He was handsome, and if he ever let his hair grow out, eased the tense set to his features, he'd flirt at the edge of pretty. Too bad he was Auth, because Einn probably would have bought him a drink, and then invited him upstairs or out back for a fuck. Einn had always liked them small and feisty.

He watched the men as they settled at the bar and ordered drinks, knowing he should tear his eyes away, but not quite able. The waitress appeared with his new beer, and Einn was momentarily distracted. When he looked back toward the bar, he accidentally met the idle gaze of the shorter man—and froze, startled, when the man smirked at him, a message as old as time.

Einn quirked one brow and took a sip of his beer. Before he could act on the man's invitation, another waitress materialized with a fresh shot of Bangkok spiced rum. "With compliments," she said, and scurried off. Einn laughed and gestured with a jerk of his head for the man to join him.

Clapping his friend on the back, the man left the bar and strode toward him, the dingy bar lights falling across his face in a way that made it truly beautiful for a moment. It sent a shiver down Einn's spine, but not one of lust—of fear. But why? The man reminded him of someone, he realized. Who? Before he could figure it out, the man was at his table. "Thanks for the rum," Einn said.

"Sure," the man replied. "Don't see Fornarians very often."

"No, but I sure as stars hear *that* often," Einn replied.

The man laughed, and then looked him up and down slowly. His eyes were gray, pale as smoke, full of speculation and heat. Another shiver lanced down Einn's spine, but this time it was equal parts fear and lust. He ignored the former in favor of the latter. "I bet there's a lot you hear often."

"Maybe. Doesn't mean I agree with, or to, any of it."

"So you're saying you're *not* interested in fucking me?"

Einn stopped with his beer halfway to his mouth; he was used to blunt, but that was remarkably blunt even for his crowd. He rather liked it: no fuss, no muss. So many races could be so fussy about such things, even when they bragged they weren't. It was one of the few things he missed about home: the simplicity of sex. "I rather like the sound of that offer, actually. I was just thinking I was in the mood for a fight or a fuck."

"I can provide both, but fighting isn't nearly as much fun—too much like work."

Finishing his beer, Einn stood up and dropped a few tokens on the table. "Where?"

"I've got a room across the street, a couple of hours left on it. I'm leaving Bangkok in a few hours, nothing to do until then."

Einn nodded and followed him out, admiring the man's ass the whole way. There was nothing better than spending a couple of hours with someone just as eager as him to fuck and move on. He didn't like clingy types; Lark was the only friend and attachment he needed.

The man led him up a couple flights of stairs to a room even dingier than the rundown bar, but the bed looked clean, and the man's bag was already packed and ready to go. Hardly unusual to spend the last few hours in port getting laid. Veteran star hoppers seldom got the chance for such things and took them where they could. "Got a name?"

"Cyan. You?"

"Einn. Get naked," Einn ordered, stripping off his own shirt. He started to undo his belt, but got distracted by the sight before him as Cyan shucked his clothes to reveal a tight, honed body that bore more scars and marks than Einn could count. His eyes went to one in particular, a long, jagged tear that could have only been made by a very particular kind of weapon—a weapon that was found in only one place in all the IG. "You're not an Auth—you're fucking Rehab."

"Is that a problem?" Cyan asked, pausing with his shirt still in his hands.

Einn contemplated all the reasons it was stupid for a criminal to be anywhere near a fucking Rehab guard—then eyed that exceptional Rehab's chest and decided that 'fucking Rehab' really was the only thing he wanted to do. "No," he said.

"Good." Cyan threw his shirt aside and shoved his pants down, then stepped out of them and toward Einn at the same time—and shoved. Einn stumbled back, hit the bed, and fell down on it, swearing softly. Any complaints, however, were immediately forgotten in favor of focusing on the man suddenly on top of him.

He grunted as Cyan kissed him, a bit surprised, but recovering from it quickly and returning the kiss with pleasure. It wasn't something most of his crowd bothered with, and it was always nice to find someone who did bother. Einn liked kissing as much as liked all the rest of it.

Speaking of the rest of it ... he slid his long fingers along Cyan's skin, loving the softness of it, the ripple of hard muscle beneath. Reaching his prize, he grabbed Cyan's ass tightly and pulled him so they were flush together, rubbing their hard cocks together and causing Cyan to moan. Einn tore his mouth away and lapped at whatever skin he could reach. "That's right, Rehab, moan for me." He got a hand between them and wrapped it around Cyan's cock. "You handle criminals all day, every day, don't you? Is this what you do on your off time, make yourself the bitch?"

Cyan let out a huff of laughter—then made Einn jump by leaning down and biting his shoulder, *hard.* "I'm no one's bitch, rock spider."

Einn just snorted in amusement and let go of Cyan's cock to get a better grip on him, then abruptly turned them over, pinning Cyan to the bed. He settled between Cyan's legs and bent down to kiss him again, biting down on his bottom lip, making Cyan grunt. Drawing back a bit, he asked, "Got anything?"

"Be prepared for anything," Cyan retorted, the motto of the Rehab guards. He shoved a hand beneath his pillow, and then tossed something at Einn. Uncapping the small tube, Einn slicked his fingers and shifted to slide one inside Cyan. "I'm not fragile," Cyan said.

Laughing, Einn added a second, stretching Cyan quickly. He grinned when Cyan tugged at him impatiently. "Do I look delicate to you, rock spider?"

"You look like you could leave me for dead if you felt like it," Einn replied, grinning as he removed his fingers and lined up his cock. He hovered there, waited until Cyan started to yell at him again—then thrust inside in one sudden move, all the way to the hilt, making Cyan arch up into him, swearing. "Better?"

Cyan just held fast to his shoulders, digging in with his short nails, gray eyes flashing as he said, "It'll be better if you *move.*"

"Bossy, I like that," Einn said, and kissed him hard to stop whatever threat was about to come next. Pulling back, he lifted Cyan's legs to his shoulders, held tightly, and began to fuck him in earnest, pulling out and slamming back in, moving faster, harder, and Cyan ordered it, giving all that was demanded, all that Cyan seemed to want to take.

It had been a while since he'd done anyone who could so easily take it all and just beg for more. Einn dragged it out as long as he could, savoring it, wanting a good memory to jerk himself off to on solitary nights, but at last it all became too much, and he finally sank into Cyan's tight body one last time and came with a muffled cry.

He took one last kiss, loving the way Cyan returned it, then finally drew back and slipped from Cyan's body. Einn flopped down on the bed, shoving strands of his light blond hair from his face and staring up at the cracked, dirty ceiling. "I feel there should be a saying about Rehabbers and fucking them, but none comes to mind."

Cyan laughed and slowly rolled out of bed. "Better to fuck us than fuck *with* us?" Einn snorted in amusement, idly admiring the ass he'd just ridden before Cyan vanished into the washroom. He reappeared shortly and gathered up his clothes. When he was dressed, he slung his sole bag over his shoulder, and then glanced at Einn. "Room is good for another hour. Thanks for the ride, rock spider. Good luck in your travels." He waved and was gone.

Einn smiled faintly, then dragged himself up and went into the washroom to clean up. Pulling his clothes back on, he activated his in-lens to check the time and saw he had a message from Lark telling him to get back to the ship.

Stifling a sigh, pleasant buzz from the last hour dying as he was dragged kicking and screaming back to reality, Einn double-checked he had everything and left the cheap room. Weaving his way through the crowded streets, he left the Red Dragon Pavilion, left behind the glamour of the towers and their surrounding glitter altogether, heading down to the more familiar grit and grime of the port.

Weaving his way through the seeming maze of ships, warehouses, yards, and guard outposts, he finally reached the section where the *Dragonfly* was docked. Walking up the gangway, he met Lark at the top. "What's up?"

"I just got back, there's a message waiting for us. Figured I should call you before I listened to it. You look rested."

"Slept all of yesterday, and ... expended some energy today," Einn smirked. "You?"

Lark shrugged, his way of saying he'd done essentially the same. If he hadn't gotten laid, he would have been a hell of a lot more grouchy. "Come on, then, time to get back to kidnapping."

Einn made a face, but obediently followed him into the ship and to the bridge.

CUSTOM CLASS STARSHIP X-11944654, THE *DRAGONFLY*

Lark moved to the comm and punched a couple of buttons, calling up the message. Einn read the numbers that flashed up on the screen, and then punched another button, downloading the two files that had come with the message to his in-lens. He grunted. "Another Draconis and his match."

Einn felt sick, knowing they were responsible for the missing Draconis that the news feeds kept mentioning. The story had not caught major interest yet. Missing people were an all too common occurrence, but Einn wasn't stupid. They were kidnapping matched Draconis and scientists—some of them very famous, like Bikendi. The public might not have been aware of everything that was going on, but the IG would have noticed a correlation by now.

It was only a matter of time before IG officials showed up to arrest him; he was damned lucky that Cyan really had been just a fuck. Einn wondered if he'd been hoping for arrest. Not that it would have done any good—the poison would kill them long before anyone could get a real antidote to them, given they had been assured the poison was unique. Einn always wondered just how many people had died because of it and how many others would die after them.

He *hated* being helpless. If he ever got the chance to kill the bastard—

Einn cut the thought off, knowing rage would accomplish nothing. The best thing to do was cooperate until they found an opening. Sitting down at the comm, he began to prepare for departure. Several minutes later, they were away from Bangkok, and he was reading through the files on their latest targets. "Looks like they just left Bangkok as well. They're on a ship called the *Huntress*, X-82142089. Why didn't he tell us sooner? We could have grabbed them on Bangkok."

"Hardly," Lark said. "It would have been a mess, and you know it. We'll have an easier time of it taking them in space." His eye flashed while he reviewed the data himself. "It's a harmless custom class, looks like a converted leisure class to judge by these specs. It won't have real weapons; they wouldn't dare risk not registering firepower. It'll be tricky, but we've handled worse."

Einn nodded. "Locate it, then. Let's get this over with."

In reply, Lark simply took the pilot and navigation seat, and set to work. An hour later, he said, "Got it. Punching coordinates now."

"Bringing up anti-tracking shields," Einn ordered, rapidly punching buttons, eye flashing as he transmitted codes and protocols to activate the weapons and defense systems that were not strictly legal on their civilian ship. Beautiful as she was, though, the *Dragonfly* was nothing like the ship he had lost when his crew had been slaughtered, leaving him and Lark enslaved.

"Approaching now," Lark said. "Ready on my mark."

Einn nodded, hands poised to strike. When Lark said, "Now!" he fired, sending stunner pulses at the ship in front of them, three bursts of fire that completely disabled it, leaving the ship little more than a floating casket in the middle of space.

Standing, he followed Lark from the bridge and to the transport room, moving to the platform while Lark keyed in the necessary information at the control panel. Minutes later, they vanished from their ship—and Einn barely ducked in time as someone swung a punch at him when they reappeared on the *Huntress.*

Einn drew his stunner and fired, but the man dodged out of the way just in time. Firing again, Einn said, "Freeze or you'll be killed instead of maimed!"

"Well, well, if it's not the rock spider." The voice registered a moment before the man himself did, and Einn stared in shock at Cyan, who coolly faced him down. "I told you, rock spider, it's better to fuck a Rehabber than fuck with one—did you want to test that theory?" Before Einn could speak, Lark fired his own stunner, forcing Cyan to jump back and divide his attention between the two of them. "What in the fuck is going on here? Two man pirate team?"

"Something like that," Einn said, and started firing again, because business was business. Cyan bolted, realizing he could not stand up against two stunners in such confined quarters.

"Damn it," Lark swore. "Is he really Rehab?"

Einn grunted and led the way from the transport room, stunner at the ready as they began to carefully explore each room. They finally found the two they were after huddled in the main leisure room, fumbling with communication devices that weren't going to work no matter what they did. He frowned, realizing Cyan was missing. "Where is the Rehabber?"

"Here!"

Einn whipped around, but too late, as a booted foot connected with the side of his face and sent him crashing to the ground. He regained his footing, but only to be knocked down again. He heard Lark cry out, saw him run toward them, and snarled, "Do the job! He can't get both of us at the same time!"

Cyan grunted and made to go for Lark, who was bearing down on the other two people on the ship. Einn stood up, wiped blood from his mouth—then leapt up and touched the ceiling, then brought his legs up. Sticking to the ceiling, he crawled along it toward Cyan.

The Draconis and his pale-faced match pointed, and Cyan whipped around—and looked up too late as Einn let go and dropped down on top of him, pinning Cyan to the floor and knocking him out cold. "Damn it!" he swore, while Lark took care of the other two, stunning them into unconsciousness. "This ship only had the two passengers listed. What in the stars is a vacationing Rehab guard doing with them?"

Lark made a face. "Fuck if I know. What do we do with him?"

"He's going to have to come with us," Einn said. "Otherwise, we have to kill him. If we just leave him, he's got more than enough information on us to cause a lot of problems."

"So we're fucked like a Vrill prostitute going for half price," Lark said. "Wonderful. Secure him, then, and let's get the fuck out of here. I say we blow the ship; that'll slow down any investigation."

Einn nodded and dug out a pair of cuffs from the pouch on his thigh, binding Cyan's wrists. "Of all the people to run into, I swear by the cliffs!"

"You know the guy?" Lark asked, hefting the small Draconis over one shoulder.

"I just fucked him three hours ago," Einn replied.

Lark's brows shot up, but then he shook his head. "You should gamble, given the odds that play to your favor. Come on, the longer we linger, the likelier the danger."

Nodding, Einn stood and hefted Cyan up and over his shoulder, following Lark back through the ship to the transport room. When they were laid out on the transport, he went back for the Draconis' match, a delicate-looking Vrill as green and lovely as they were known to be. Lifting the woman up in his arms, he carried her to the transport.

Half an hour later, all three captives were in holding. Lark scowled at them. "What in the fuck are we going to do with a Rehabber? He'll be missed a lot sooner than the other two and not in a good way. We'll be killed for this."

"I don't know," Einn snapped. "We'll figure something out. Right now, we have a ship to blow up. Let's do that, get out of here, and then we'll deal with the Rehabber."

"Fine," Lark bit out, and stomped off to the storage locker where they kept the explosives. Einn sighed, and went to ready the ship for a quick departure.

# Chapter Five

CUSTOM CLASS STARSHIP X-11944654, THE *DRAGONFLY*

Cyan was handcuffed to a wall and more than a little pissed about it. They were heavy cuffs, thick, wide, and stiff. They were also the kind that required a code to unlock, too tight to maneuver out of easily, and prone to cause permanent damage if worn too long. Even Rehab didn't use them very often. The minute he managed to get free, he was going to *murder* someone, starting with that stars damned Fornarian. He jerked at his cuffs, annoyed when they stayed in place, then forced himself to subside. He'd get nowhere if he damaged his own wrists.

On the far side of the holding cell, near the door, a slight-statured Draconis and his Vrill lover—and match, Cyan suspected, though they'd never said as much—huddled together. Cyan frowned at them, pensive, wondering what in the hell was going on.

He was still fairly certain no one was after him; it was too much coincidence that the Fornarian he'd fucked had been sent after him. One, he wasn't IG. Two, he was definitely a criminal, probably a pirate or mercenary. Three, if he had been sent after Cyan and was under orders to take him back home no matter what, he would have taken him *before* they fucked.

Well, possibly after; things like morals and ethics were not always preferred in IG goons, especially magics capable that were not officially on the payroll. What a pity the Fornarian—Einn, that was his name—was turning out to be such an annoyance, because he'd definitely been an excellent fuck. Cyan huffed irritably and wondered when someone would come along to talk to them.

He looked at the couple again, and asked, "Any idea why they've kidnapped you?"

"N-no," the Draconis said.

Cyan narrowed his eyes. "You're lying. I don't have time for bullshit. Tell me what you know, or I can't figure out a way to help you."

"There are rumors," the Vrill woman said, ignoring the scowl the Draconis shot her.

"Rumors?" Cyan pressed gently, as though he were talking to the scared prisoners in Rehab that had committed petty crimes and were really only locked up to serve some politician's agenda.

"That Draconis are vanishing—being kidnapped," the woman said. "Always matched Draconis. No one knows how many people are actually missing. We thought it was just a paranoid rumor, a scare tactic, since the trial for the Draconis is going before the Star Assembly next term."

Cyan grunted, turning that over in his mind. It would not surprise him to learn there was something that fishy going on. He could name half a dozen politicians on Zero who would not hesitate to use the Draconis and the raging debate about them for personal agendas.

Memories, a too-familiar face, flooded his mind, and Cyan hastily turned away from things he had sworn never to think about again. He had left that life behind. He was Cyan McCracken, Rehabber—and currently, prisoner.

He was going to fracture that Fornarian's face in ten places. "So you think you're the latest victims. Anything else you can tell me about these rumors?"

"No," the Vrill said. "So far as I know, no one knows anything, just that Draconis and their matches keep vanishing. What's going to happen to us?" She started crying quietly, milky white tears trailing down her pale green skin. The Draconis, who had dark skin and blue-black scales, cuddled her close and whispered words that Cyan could not quite catch.

Not that he really needed to catch them. He left them alone and looked more carefully around the holding cell, but it remained a fruitless endeavor. Einn and his Helior buddy knew their work and had obviously known it would be suicide to give Cyan even the slightest bit of leverage.

He could not believe he was handcuffed to the wall of a holding cell on a pirate ship because Einn had *dropped on him from the ceiling*. Cyan wanted to beat his head into the wall for being taken so fucking easily. He was a First Class Rehabber—he didn't lose because someone dropped on him! Fucking rock spiders. "Have they come by and said anything?"

"They brought food a little while ago; you were still asleep," the woman said.

Cyan frowned. "That doesn't make sense. Were they keeping me unconscious?"

"Yes," the Draconis said. "The Helioran came in shortly after we flew off—and I think they blew up our ship—and cuffed you, then injected you with something."

Mentally adding 'break Helioran's face after Fornarian's' to his to-do list, Cyan asked, "Can you tell me anything about them? Is it just two of them?"

"Just two, sweetheart, and it's rude to gossip." Einn beamed when Cyan glared at him. "I see you're finally awake. Don't start causing trouble, or we'll put you back to sleep."

Cyan beamed back. "Come on in and try it."

Einn chuckled, winding his long fingers around the bars of the holding cell. "I'm not quite that stupid, but nice try. Stop causing trouble in the ranks, Rehab. I knocked you out once, I can do it again."

"We'll just see," Cyan retorted.

Not replying, Einn pulled a canister from his pouch and shook it, then shoved it threw the bars and pressed down on the nozzle trigger. A fine mist filled the small cell. Cyan sucked in his breath and held it. The others saw him do it too late and succumbed to the sleeper spray. Einn pressed a button out of view on the wall, and a fan kicked up. A few minutes later, the room was clear, and Einn pushed more buttons, turning off the fan and opening the door. "Let's get going," he said, and Cyan heard a grumbled reply before the red-skinned man from earlier appeared and helped Einn haul the two unconscious figures from the cell.

Definitely mercenaries, he thought. Pirates did not travel on such small ships, or with just a two man crew. But mercenaries hired to kidnap people—that was the sort of job perfect for two men and a small, custom class ship. Interesting that they went custom class; mercs usually went with merchant or fleet class ships. Custom class ships stood out more readily and had to be registered in more places due to the non-standard parts that put them in custom class.

Cyan watched in silence as they dragged the captives away and closed the door. "You can't leave me in here forever!" No reply came, and Cyan kicked angrily at the ground with the heel of his boot. Unfortunately, they *could* keep him there as long as they liked. He frowned at that. Why were they keeping him locked up? It would have been smarter for the mercenaries just to kill him.

Stars, had they somehow figured out who he was? No, he had taken care of that—anyone who looked him up would find information only on Cyan McCracken. There was absolutely nothing that connected him to Zero or his godforsaken brother. Cyan's mouth tightened as things he'd not thought of for five and a half terms tried to surface. Had it really been that long?

Cyan sighed softly. He hoped to the stars that the bastards let him go before anyone realized that he was missing. He did not want to know what would happen if anyone found out Jade Alexander's twin brother had been kidnapped. He had done his damnedest to walk away from that life; he did not want to be dragged back into it and definitely not this way. "Sean," he muttered, "I'm going to fucking kill you."

He waited through several minutes of doing nothing but avoiding the thoughts in his head, then grew bored with holding still. His shoulders were getting sore from being held up high and out, and his arms liked the arrangement even less. At least the bastards had left his legs free.

Pulling his legs in close, Cyan tested whether or not he would be able to get to his feet. No, he determined after a moment, he was definitely not going to be standing. He really wished they had not been smart enough to go through his clothes and empty all his pockets. They had also, to judge by the lack of weight in his boots, checked those, too. Bastards.

What were they going to do with him? Stars, he still wanted to know why they hadn't killed him.

He also wanted to know why it was always the good fucks who turned out to be so much trouble once they had their clothes back on. Cyan let his head fall back to thunk against the wall. He would not have been nearly so pissed about his predicament if he hadn't actually sort of liked the bastard he had spent all of an hour with. He'd been shameless and fun, and Cyan had been smiling in memory of their hour together when the ship had gone dead in the water.

It was always the good lays, that was certifiable fact. He sighed and tried to think of how the fuck he was supposed to get out of his predicament. If they didn't know who he was, he could possibly play to that. Stars knew nobody wanted to piss off Jade. If he told them the truth, they might let him go. On the other hand, they might just keep him for ransom, at which point things would *really* get ugly. He would never turn Jade's wrath on another, even a couple of good-for-nothing mercs.

Figuring it all out was giving him a fucking headache. He was going to—

Cyan's thoughts froze as he heard footsteps on the metal grating walkway outside, and he looked up with a glare when Einn filled the cell doorway. "So what are you going to do with me now that you've disposed of your captives? Are they alive?"

"They're alive and should stay that way," Einn said, but Cyan had the impression he wasn't entirely certain of that. "As to you, I have no idea. You've become a problem of the highest order."

Cyan sneered, "I think the only problems on this ship are the two mercenary scumbags kidnapping innocent people. I refuse to be sorry about fucking up your plans. Kill me if you're going to kill me, and if you're not, then do something else and do it fast." Before someone figured out they'd kidnapped Cyan Alexander.

"In that much of a hurry to die?" Einn asked, looking startled by his vehemence.

"I have somewhere I need to be, and I need to be there soon," Cyan replied.

Einn cocked his head. "That's why you were on that ship. I'm going to hazard wherever you were bound, you didn't want people knowing where you were going, which is why you weren't listed on the passenger manifest." Cyan didn't bother to confirm the obvious. "Where are you headed?"

"What the fuck does it matter?"

Einn crouched down, and Cyan tried not to notice, but it was hard *not* to notice the lithe way Fornarians moved. They were so rare that he'd never encountered one in Rehab, and Rehab usually had at least three of everything. Every part of them was just a little bit longer than was normal on a human—longer legs, longer arms, longer fingers. They were so skinny—on any other race they'd look malnourished or ill—but Fornarians were a study in minimalism. The gray-toned skin that blended into the cliffs of their planet, the spindly limbs, the sharp eyes that could see well in daylight and darkness, the way they moved and could stick to any surface ... it all combined to give them the nickname 'rock spider'.

Cyan had only ever met one before, when he'd spent a whole week of leave on Bangkok, and she'd been a fabulous time the whole week. When he'd gone to the bar with

Sigma after chancing upon him, he'd only meant to go for a couple of beers and catch up with an old friend, but he'd seen Einn and his ability to think had dropped straight to his cock. It so *figured* he was a fucking mercenary and completely screwing Cyan over in the worst way.

"Where are you headed?"

"It's none of your fucking business, merc," Cyan snapped. "I'm not playing games with you, so kill me or drop me off or whatever, but stop trying to hold a conversation. Rehabbers don't associate with the prisoners; we just lock them up."

Einn just replied, "Pirate, actually."

Cyan started to reply with something hostile, but stopped short. "What?"

"We're pirates."

"What's the fucking difference?"

Mouth twisting in a cynical smile, Einn said, "Pirates just steal. Mercs will do anything."

"Stealing *people* really seems more a merc thing to me," Cyan snapped.

Einn sighed, but said nothing, simply stood back up and stretched out his long limbs. Cyan really hated that he could not tear his eyes away. "We could take you somewhere in return for your silence."

"Fuck—" Cyan stopped. They were mercenaries—pirates—whatever, criminals. He did not bargain with criminals ... but time was short and he had literally no other way to get to Kreska, and if he didn't do something, he was going to die and his death would cause way more trouble than it was worth. "Fine," he bit out, hating it, hating himself, hating the whole fucking universe, but fuck if he had a choice. "I need to get to Kreska. Take me there, we're even. You let me go, I keep my mouth shut."

"Really?"

"I'm not going to waste my time lying. Do we have a deal or not?"

Einn regarded him warily, even as he punched a button to open the door. "What are you going to do if I let you go?"

"Punch you in the face," Cyan said. Einn laughed and crouched in front of him, in-lens flashing while he probably communicated with the Helioran elsewhere in the ship.

"Guess there's no escaping that," Einn said lightly, and stood up to input the code on the cuff on his right wrist, and then his left. Cyan immediately kicked his legs out from under him, straddled him, and punched Einn in the jaw, exactly as promised. He shook out his hand and flexed the fingers, always forgetting just how fucking dense and *hard* Fornarians were under their thick skin.

"Bastard," he said, and stood up, leaving Einn lying on the floor. "Where's my stuff?"

Einn snorted as he stood up, testing his jaw and looking amused. "I actually expected you to hit harder. I'm not dumb enough to give your weapons back, Rehab. You'll get them when we dump you on Kreska. Come on, I'll show you the ship. She ain't much to look at, but she's a good ship."

Cyan nodded, agreeing with that statement; from what he could see, she was a good ship, for all she was a bit rundown and clearly survived on used parts and limited repair. "Who's the Helioran?"

"Lark—he's the one who does most of the piloting and navigation," Einn replied. "I'm more the comm."

"And you share the kidnapping duties?"

Einn ignored him and bowed mockingly when they reached the bridge. "Welcome to the *Dragonfly*, Rehab. Your home away from home until we get rid of you on Kreska."

"The sooner the better," Cyan said.

"It amuses me that you had no trouble fucking me, but it gets your panties in a twist to have to deal with me otherwise. How typically Rehab and high society of you to keep to such a double standard."

Cyan rounded on him, barely resisting an urge to punch first and ask questions later. "You didn't have problems risking your partner by fucking a Rehab, so don't preach to me, rock spider. Don't call me high society, either. I'm not."

Einn snorted. "Who are you fooling? You might try to speak like a commoner, but when you're pissed, your words start getting that clipped tone only Zero-types have. You might be Rehab now, but I'll bet you grew up on Zero."

Well, fuck the stars and everything in them. Cyan thought he'd kicked his accent. Shit, shit, and shit. "Fuck you," he said, and whirled around—and nearly crashed into the missing partner. Lark, he recalled. "I hope you're not as annoying as him."

"Less annoying, more violent," Lark replied, folding his arms across his chest. "Though so far as that goes, I don't think either of us is as bad as you."

Cyan smiled his Rehab smile. "Matter of perspective, I guess. Rehabbers and criminals get along like Sardorans and Avarri."

"At least you didn't say Fornarians and Kreskans," Einn commented dryly.

Despite himself, Cyan snorted in amusement. "I think we both know I'm no locked-down, virginal Kreskan. I don't suppose I could get something to eat and possibly be pointed to the head?"

"That way," Lark said, gesturing. "Second to last door on the left. Mess is last on the right. Don't go anywhere else."

"Got it," Cyan said, lifting a hand as he strode off.

Get to Kreska. Kill Sean for putting him through all this bullshit. Go home.

Hopefully he would be able to do all of that before anyone noticed he was missing and that the ship he'd been on had been blown up by pirates. He *really* did not need to be the reason the IG flipped out and started tearing down the stars to find him.

Despite his best efforts, thoughts of the life he'd left behind crept to the forefront of Cyan's mind. He couldn't even remember the last time he'd seen Jade other than on news reports, and those were few and far between. Jade was a beauty, knew he was a beauty, but he detested being fawned over. Beauty was a weapon to him, and attention on a large scale diluted its power. Cyan's hand curled into a fist, but he forced it to relax as he slipped into the head, and finally was able to relieve himself.

Washing his hands with dry soap, he went into the mess and grimaced at the limited offerings. Stars, he had not missed starship travel. Stifling another sigh, he went about fixing food, going ahead and making enough for three from habit. He had not travelled so roughly in years, but he had not forgotten how to do it.

Carrying all the food back to the bridge, he hovered at the edge. "Want food?"

They looked up, surprised and cautiously pleased. "Yes?" Einn said, and shut down the comm where he was working. "Uh, thanks."

Shrugging, Cyan handed over their trays, and then stole the only spare seat over by the engineer's seat. In larger ships, the engineer usually remained in the engine rooms. On smaller ships everything was consolidated on the bridge to maximize on resources and make the power last as long as possible. He ate in silence, not really certain what he was supposed to say; even his extensive etiquette lessons did not cover 'polite conversations with one's kidnappers'.

Cyan glanced up through his lashes, looking over Lark and Einn. His gaze lingered on Einn, unable to resist. No matter how much he hated to admit it, Einn was attractive. Everything about him just *did* it for Cyan, and he completely hated that another bedroom romp or six was out of the question. Not that fucking on starships was ever as easy as net shows and bad porn made it out to be.

Rolling his eyes at himself, Cyan poked at his food and slowly made himself eat, wishing he was back on Rehab getting attacked by a Sardoran—even *that* was better than the mess in which he was currently stuck.

# Chapter Six

**PLANET NUMBER 2051225 (TELVE), IMPERIAL TOWER**

"I don't understand how the hell they got in." Sean glanced at their escort, a rough-looking Danubian Hellcat with brown-red feline ears and hair, dusty brown skin, and sharp yellow-green eyes. "We've checked the security systems a hundred times looking for even the smallest bug. No strangers, no unusual guests of any sort. Nothing. Whoever they are, they're fucking ghosts."

"No such thing as a ghost, Lius," Sean said.

Lius shrugged irritably, ears twitching. He kicked the floor with one booted foot and flexed his claws. "May as well be, and it amounts to the same thing. No one just hacks security without leaving some sort of trace. The fucking *gremlins* leave signs, even if they're the only ones who can see those signs later." His ears twitched again.

Sean shrugged and moved to the balcony, looking down. They were shockingly high up; the kidnapping had definitely been no easy feat. No one just walked into the Imperial Tower of Telve without being noticed in some way. Most of the galaxy was terrified of the blood-drinking, xenophobic Telve. They would not tread—

Xenophobic. Sean leaned further over the balcony, reaching out to run his hands along the surface of the tower. It was completely unmarred, exempting the normal wear and tear any building suffered after centuries of existence. Because no damage had been done to the tower, everyone had determined the kidnappers had hacked security to gain access to the tower and worked their way up from the inside.

He paused when he saw something. Kneeling, he reached his hands through the railings of the balcony and rubbed the white mark he had spied that would have been easily missed if he hadn't already been thinking that someone had done the impossible after all. His fingers came away covered in chalk.

Smirking, Sean stood and returned to the room where Karmikel and Lius were still poking around. "How well do the two of you know your IG races?" They both gave him withering looks, clearly offended he had to ask two top tier Internal Affairs operatives how well they knew anything. "All right, then, smartasses," he said, "name me the race that wouldn't need to break into the tower because he can literally climb any surface, has no fear of heights, and would leave no trace because he would not need special equipment for even this difficult a climb."

"A fucking Fornarian!" Lius swore, and Karmikel looked just as irritated with himself. "How the stars did we miss that?"

"In your defense—in everyone's defense—Fornarians are even more xenophobic than Telvens. I doubt there are even twenty registered as space travelers."

"Seventeen," Lius said. "The last time I had to look up that sort of thing there were seventeen Fornarians who had registered to leave their planet and travel the stars. The number goes up to twenty-one if you include those on the Star Assembly, but they never leave Zero. I don't know what the seventeen are doing, mostly geo work, I think. Stars take it! A fucking Fornarian."

Karmikel, as usual, had already overcome his anger and moved on with his ruthless efficiency. "The Telven will be relieved to know their security has not been breached, though I'm sure now they will endeavor to create a surface that even rock spiders can't stick to."

"Good luck with that," Lius said, rubbing one ear. "Why do you think they do geo work? No one has found a place they can't climb up or down. Well, if we're looking for a Fornarian, that just made the job stupid easy. But call if you girls need help, anyway."

Sean gestured crudely, and waited while Karmikel let the Telve know they were leaving. When Karmikel had finished, he took Karmikel's arm and said to Lius, "Thanks for the help."

"Yeah, yeah," Lius said. "Just find the kidnappers before I have to do it for you."

Karmikel rolled his eyes as Sean lead the way to the balcony and, once outside, teleported them back to the ship.

### CUSTOM CLASS STARSHIP Z-28922942, THE *BRILLIANT*

"We have problems," Mendel said, as they appeared on the bridge. "There's been another kidnapping."

Sean nodded, but did not reply. He was too startled by Winter, who was on the main screen and looked the grimmest that Sean had ever seen him—and given that grim was Winter's default, that was bad.

Their codenames were largely superfluous, meant only as a precaution should they be overheard, though the chances of that were extremely slim. Zero-grade security and technology was nothing to sneer at; even gremlins were impressed with it, and they literally had electricity in their blood. Winter, however, remained largely a mystery to him.

If Mendel and Karmikel knew who he really was, they had never said or even hinted at it. He was the shadowy head of the IG's Internal Affairs, a network of agents who did a shocking number of things behind the scenes. Nearly all of them were magics capable, which meant they definitely did not work officially for the IG. No government position of any sort could be held by a magics capable being.

Still, Sean had his suspicions as to who the man was, though he doubted he would ever know for certain. "What's wrong, Winter?" he asked. "You don't usually look *this* upset over the kidnappings."

Winter's mouth only tightened. "Yesterday, at 17:05 ZT, a leisure class starship, the *Huntress*, X-82142089, was destroyed. It was registered with two travelers. However, we have reason to believe that they were transporting an unregistered guest who is now also missing. It's possible he's dead, though we are hoping he was taken hostage. Unfortunately, they were expert about blowing up the *Huntress* and not enough of it remains to tell if there was a body onboard when it was destroyed."

Karmikel gestured impatiently. "Who is this 'guest' that obviously has the IG panicking?"

"No one knows yet, outside of a very small group of people. The man they were transporting, and who is missing, presumed dead, is Cyan McCracken, also known as Lord Cyan Alexander."

Sean paled. On either side of him, Karmikel and Mendel swore. "Why in the hell were they stupid enough to kill or kidnap the twin brother of Lower Chancellor Alexander?" Mendel demanded. "Who is that stupid?"

"I doubt they know," Winter replied. "After Lord Alexander surrendered his title, he changed his name and worked hard to live a completely different life. He has not been Lord Alexander for more than five terms. He never put himself in the spotlight as his brother has, and they look almost nothing alike for all they are twins. You know more about the kidnappers than all my other agents. You will find them, determine if Lord Alexander is alive, and if he is, you will retrieve him."

"If he's dead?" Karmikel asked.

"Let us hope he is not."

Sean swallowed, and then asked, "What was he doing so far from home? He lives on Mars, and it's possible he was on leave, but it seems strange he was so far from home."

"He was taken just outside of Bangkok, less than an hour after departure," Winter replied. "We believe he was simply on vacation, though that does not entirely explain why he was not on the passenger manifest for the *Huntress.*"

"He was my best friend. Ever since I was kidnapped, I bet the IG has been keeping an eye on him. He was probably just trying to be left alone," Sean said, biting his lip, then added, "But Cyan isn't that stupid or reckless. He knows what would happen if he went missing; he dreaded going back to Zero. He wouldn't cause himself or anyone else trouble by sneaking around like that. There must be another reason."

Winter shook his head. "We don't know yet; I've dispatched agents to look into the matter. As I get more information, I will send it your way. Did you learn anything useful at Telve?"

"We're ninety-eight percent certain that a Fornarian did the kidnapping," Sean said, forcing himself to focus on business, even if the back of his mind was flailing with worry and panic. Cyan *had* to be alive; nobody got the drop on a Rehab, especially Cyan. "No one could have snuck up from the inside; Bikendi's room was over a hundred stories high. That left only the outside, but there were no visible signs of climbing, only a chalked mark on the outside ledge of the balcony."

"To indicate which balcony," Winter said, smiling in a way that made his codename so apropos. "You're right, only a Fornarian could have made that climb without leaving a single trace. Well done. I'll send you all the information I have on Fornarians registered to travel. That should narrow things down considerably. Keep me apprised." The screen went dark, leaving the bridge in a sudden silence.

Sean turned around and left, heading for his room and sitting down on his bunk. He buried his face in his hands. Cyan wasn't dead. He couldn't be dead. What in the stars had he been up to? Sean scrubbed at his face and tried to focus, but all he could think about was the last time he'd seen Cyan. They'd been screwing off in the break room.

They'd been planning to build a ship because Cyan had more money than god.

Cyan was supposed to be alive and well on Mars or Rehab, planning all the ways he was going to kill Sean when they met up again. Not that Sean had ever thought they would meet again; his life had been over the moment his secret was revealed. Thinking about that did not help matters, so he tried not to dwell on it. Cyan ... stars have mercy, he hoped Cyan was alive.

A knock on the door startled him from his thoughts, and Sean reluctantly punched the release button by his bunk to open it. "What?" he asked tersely when Mendel stepped into the room. They had barely spoken since their fight, and every word they did exchange pertained to business. Sean was certain Karmikel would kill them sometime soon just to gain some peace, but Sean refused to bend. He'd done nothing but bend for an entire term.

"For whatever little my opinion is worth," Mendel said, "I do not believe your friend is dead. It does not fit the MO of the kidnappers. I surmise they took him and do not yet know who it is they have taken. If they *do* know, they are even less likely to kill him."

Some of the tension in Sean's shoulders eased as he recognized the awkward attempt at comforting for what it was. Mendel was an ass, but sometimes the man he had probably been before his life shattered slipped through, and he was only an awkward scientist who was more comfortable with his lab than people. "Thank you," Sean said gruffly. "I had hoped that was the case, but it's good to hear it from someone else."

"We were going to start re-analyzing data factoring in a Fornarian. I thought you would want to help."

Sean nodded, then drew a deep breath and let it out slowly, before standing up and heading for the door. Mendel stepped aside, but not quite far enough for Sean to avoid brushing against him. Whatever the bond between them, touching seemed to jolt it slightly, leaving something akin to an electric charge brushing along his skin.

He moved hastily on, pretending not to be painfully aware of every part of Mendel, who had proven time and again that he wanted no real part of Sean. Mendel called his name, but Sean pretended not to hear him, simply heading for the bridge where Karmikel had already pulled up all their files on the kidnappings. "Seven scientists and eleven couples so far, twenty-nine people total," Karmikel said when he saw Sean. "This is all assuming they haven't kidnapped individual, unmatched Draconis, and we've simply never noticed."

"I'm sure we would have noticed by now," Sean said. "Missing persons reports on single Draconis have never matched up. I'm more interested in what we know of the kidnappers, now that we have a real clue as to their identities."

Karmikel nodded and shifted files around, bringing up their notes on the kidnappers. The amount of information they had was pathetically small; no matter how hard they tried, they were working against pros. "Probably not a large group of men, but it's hard to say for certain. They use a small, light ship. They're experienced space travelers, good at getting in and out of ports quickly. We're probably looking for free mercenaries or pirates, rather than corporate goons. One is a Fornarian—" He stopped as his in-lens flashed, then shifted the information on the screen again. "Here's all the info on Fornarians from Winter. Seventeen, all right. Hmm ... interesting collection, all told. More than a few possible candidates, at a glance."

"Go through them one by one, in more detail," Mendel said from right behind Sean, making him jump. How had he not heard the bastard arrive? "One of them must be it; unregistered travelers do not go unnoticed long."

Sean moved away and sat down at the chair by the star chart table. "Well, almost half that list can go away—three are underage, two only have permits for public travel, and two are retired."

"Three more can go," Mendel said, folding his arms across his chest and standing in front of the screen, Karmikel to his right at the comm station. "They're scientists aboard research vessels. We'd know if they were missing or going on kidnapping jaunts."

Karmikel dismissed the indicated files. "That leaves seven. One is fresh out of a Rehab in quad four ... sector six, I think."

"Yeah, six," Sean said. "That's Rehab 4.3, third Rehab built by the IG in that quad, one of only three that is the sole occupant of an entire planet. The entire thing was wiped by the Sentas Plague fifty terms ago. It's the only Rehab licensed to perform executions, though only on the order of the Grand Chancellor and a majority vote of the Star Assembly."

Mendel shook his head. "I was nearly sent there, but they thought your Rehab would be a better fit, since I stood less chance of being 'accidentally' killed there."

Sean grunted. "Very true. So what does the file say on this guy?"

"Says he was arrested for disorderly behavior, repeat offender. They let him off the first couple of times, but the third time they locked him up for the night, and the fourth they had to arrest him. He appears to have been no better in Rehab, at least at first, but he was only released a half term ago. Not our guy."

"Five left," Sean said, and it did not take them long to discard two more, leaving only three. "Hakon, Adalsteinn, and Pall. Why don't any of them have surnames?"

Mendel shifted to half-face Sean behind him, and replied, "Fornarians don't have surnames. Their native language doesn't even have a word for differentiating 'given name' and 'surname'. They don't really even have words for family, sister, mother, etcetera. The closest they come to surnames is tacking on what section of caves and cliffs they come from, and as they seldom travel even on their own planet, it's largely irrelevant."

Sean nodded and looked again at the three men on the screen. "Hakon is a geo explorer, but he hasn't been with any planet exploration team in well over a term. Adalsteinn is listed as a free traveler, and no further information is given. Pall was arrested for suspicion of piracy a term ago, but let go when no evidence could be found to make it stick."

"I'll send them back to Winter, see what else he can dig up on them," Karmikel said. "My points are on Adalsteinn or Pall, though. They're both perfect for it. Adalsteinn has a permit to travel wherever, whenever, and then has nothing further attached to his name? Not even a job history. That is a pirate if ever I've caught one."

Laughing, because Karmikel had excelled at pirate capture before he'd been seduced away by Internal Affairs, Sean said, "I guess if Winter can pin him down, we'll go for him first. Anything else we need to do? Where are we headed?"

"Bangkok," Karmikel replied. "We should be there in a few hours. So you know this guy? Is he really *the* Cyan Alexander?"

Sean nodded. "Yeah, he is. I couldn't believe it the day he told me. We were a little drunk, sitting in our room in Bangkok. I made a joke about the points he had; Rehabbers earn high wages, but even so, Cyan has a lot. He got bitter, then quiet."

"You can't tell they're related," Karmikel said. "They're night and day." He punched a couple of buttons and brought up the two Alexander brothers. Sean stared in wonder, to actually see the brothers side by side. Other than their pale gray eyes, and a bit of something in the shape of their faces, it was impossible to tell they were related.

Cyan had black hair and gray eyes, and was handsome in a rough and tumble sort of way, short and built. Any sign of the noble he had once been was long gone. Well, mostly. Sean had wondered for years what was so weird about Cyan's accent—something about it just seemed off. It wasn't until Cyan told him his real identity that Sean figured it out:  when Cyan got pissed off, his clipped Zero accent came out. But Cyan had always been so proud of mastering 'common speech' that Sean had never had the heart to tell him.

Beside him, Lower Chancellor Jade Alexander was a cool, breathtaking beauty, the very definition of what it meant to be Zero elite. He was tall and willowy, with dark gold hair that fell to his thighs and was woven into a braid. He was dressed in an ornate violet and lavender robe, the fastenings holding it shut shaped like the infinity symbol of the IG. His nails were long, sharp looking, and painted the same violet as his robe.

Stories of the Lower Chancellor were legend, and Cyan had never confirmed which of the tales were fact, fiction, or exaggeration. Sean had never asked, not when speaking of his twin brother put that look of pain and anger on Cyan's face. Though there was no love lost between the brothers, Sean knew enough to know that the Lower Chancellor would rip apart the stars to locate Cyan. In Cyan's words, only Jade was allowed to make Cyan's life a living nightmare. No one and nothing would take that pleasure from him.

Sean turned away from the screen. "I'll be in the engine room; there's a couple of things worth picking up if we're going to be in Bangkok, and I want to be sure I get the right serial numbers." He walked off, once more ignoring the way Mendel tried to catch his attention.

If Mendel wanted to repair things, he was just going to have to try harder. Sean wasn't in the mood to make it easy.

# Chapter Seven

**CUSTOM CLASS STARSHIP X-11944654, THE *DRAGONFLY***

Einn was going stir crazy. He did not like that Jade had not contacted them for *days*. They were going to need their next dose of the serum soon; he could already feel the fever creeping up. It was the first of many symptoms, and they would get progressively worse.

He rubbed his forehead with one hand, restlessly pacing the bridge. Lark was off sleeping, and he had last seen Cyan reorganizing the mess because apparently he was *that* bored. Einn kept trying to sit still and do something constructive, but it just was not working. He wanted to know why Jade was ignoring them; at the very least, he should have sent them a new job.

What if the silence meant he was done with them, and he was just waiting for the poison to do its work? Fear made Einn's blood run cold, and he spun anxiously back around, stalking back toward the u-shaped arrangement of consoles. Sitting down, he pushed his chair over to the comm station and called up news feeds, desperate for any distraction.

For half an hour, Einn clicked through various feeds, nothing in particular catching his attention. He was always afraid the kidnappings would reach the media, but so far, they had escaped detection. He did not want to know what Jade would do to them if they ever slipped up enough they alerted the media to their activities.

Clearly there was nothing capable of distracting him—

Einn froze over the off button as Cyan's image flashed across the comm screen. He activated the sound with a thought to his in-lens. *–missing since yesterday, when the ship he was on exploded just outside of Bangkok. Foul play is suspected, especially with his brother, Lower Chancellor Alexander, deep in policy revisions. This will be the second* *great tragedy to befall the Alexander family, the last being—*

"Cyan!" Einn bellowed, storming from the bridge. Cyan appeared from the mess, looking startled—but not surprised, Einn noted. He flew down the hall, grabbing Cyan and slamming him against the wall. "You're all over the stars-damned news! Lord Cyan Alexander, brother of a fucking Lower Chancellor!"

"Damn it," Cyan said, letting his head thunk against the wall behind him and staring up at the ceiling. "I was hoping they would manage to keep it out of the fucking media."

Einn shook him hard. "Why in the stars did you not tell me who you are? Do know what could happen now?!"

Cyan sneered at him. "Forgive me if I don't feel sorry for a couple of pirates-turned-professional kidnappers."

"You don't understand anything!" Einn snarled, letting him go to haul back and punch him—

—only to somehow wind up on his back on the floor and staring up at Cyan, the hall lights right behind his head, forcing Einn to squint. "Fucking Rehab."

Cyan only grunted in reply. "A criminal is a criminal, and I'm trained to deal with all of you. Don't forget it." He stood up, letting Einn go.

"I don't care what you are," Einn said, slowly standing. "A deal is a deal, and you don't strike me as the sort to go back on your word. We give you transport to Kreska, you don't turn us in. Not fucking telling me you're really the Lower Chancellor's brother counts as turning us in. If they find us, they won't arrest us, they'll just kill us! I've worked too fucking hard and lost too fucking much to lose now because of a brat prince!" He pushed past Cyan to wake up Lark, because they needed to figure something out *fast* before Jade really did finally let them die a very slow, very painful death.

Einn swallowed, all his old fears returning. Stars in the sky, cliffs that reached toward them, he was *tired* of being afraid all the time. It was one thing to live a life of piracy, stealing back from the bottom dwellers too powerful for the law to control; it was quite another to kidnap people because he was poisoned with something only Jade knew how to fix.

A hand caught his wrist, stopping him. He jerked free and whipped around. "What?" he demanded—then stopped, because Cyan's expression gave nothing away, but Einn saw the fear in his eyes. He had begun to think Cyan didn't know how to fear. Even locked up and with his life in danger, he'd just been pissed.

"You're right, I'm sorry. I kept silent because I was hoping like hell they would keep it from coming to light. I haven't been Cyan Alexander for eleven years. Get me to Kreska; I'll do what I can to help, and once I'm there, I'll assure everyone I'm fine and just could not contact anyone 'til then."

"Fine," Einn conceded, because what else was he supposed to say? Admit that he was working for Jade? Cyan wouldn't believe him, and even if he did, what good would it do? It wasn't as if Cyan would help them or something. Einn didn't really get the whole family thing, for all that he'd seen it more than most Fornarians, but he knew one thing: family stuck together. Cyan would choose his brother over a couple of pieces of space junk without hesitation. "Wait, what do you mean you haven't been Alexander for eleven years?"

Cyan looked at him in surprise. "Have I actually managed to meet the only person in the IG who doesn't know all that old gossip?"

Einn made a face and strode past him back to the bridge. "My apologies for having better things to do with my life than keep up with space gossip. Zero and its precious cave stars are of no interest to me."

"Cave stars?" Cyan repeated, staring at him blankly.

"Sorry, I don't think that translates well," Einn said with a sigh, in-lens flashing as he called up a manual translator. He sighed again after a moment and gave up. "It's a type of lizard, I think. That's the closest I can find. But it glows in the dark, that's why they're called cave stars. They're rare, easily spooked, and anyone who accidentally hurts one gets in trouble."

Cyan laughed. "Sounds like Zero to me."

"No wonder you have the fancy accent when you're pissed off," Einn groused. "I'm honestly surprised you didn't have it when we were fucking, too, as bossy as you get." Only after he said the words did he realize he probably should not have brought that up. One, he really did not need to be reminded of just how much he enjoyed fucking Cyan.

Two, he really did not need to be reminded just how easily Cyan could kill him. Cyan looked as though he wanted to do exactly that for a moment, then he just turned on his heel and strode off. Einn followed and saw him slumped at the comm station, watching the news on the main screen, arms folded across his chest. He winced when he saw an old picture of himself dressed in Zero finery, standing alongside his brother.

Einn could not believe they were related. "You don't look anything like him," he said, then wondered when he had started speaking without thinking.

"I'm aware of that," Cyan said tightly. "He's five minutes older and fifty times—" He cut himself off, but Einn heard the unspoken *better-looking* anyway. Cyan certainly did not seem to doubt his looks, but Einn imagined anyone would feel at least a little inferior standing next to Jade. "He looks like our mother."

"Too pretty for my taste," Einn said. "I like my men to look like men." Cyan seemed to ignore him, but his fingers eased where they'd been digging into the fabric of his shirt. Einn forced himself to look away because otherwise he'd try something stupid. Despite the galaxy-wide problems between them, it was hard not to remember their one-off, or avoid thinking about how much he wouldn't mind a second round. He was not generally into repeats, but something about Cyan would not leave his head.

Or maybe he was tense and afraid and stuck on a starship. Einn sighed, and for a moment, wished he could have been like every other Fornarian back home, content to spend his life climbing and living in dark, quiet caves away from all but the most essential of technology. Of course, thoughts of home quickly reminded him of all the reasons he had wanted to leave—

But honestly, cliffs and caves did not come with the great big mess his life had become, and *stars,* he wanted a drink. Or to hit something. Or both.

Cyan sighed, breaking Einn from his light-jumping thoughts, and turned off the main screen. He tilted his head back over the chair, staring up at the ceiling and looking so *lost* that Einn wished he knew what to say. "So, tell me this gossip I'm supposed to know. Unless you don't want to talk about it, I mean. But I think you'd give a better accounting than the media feeds."

Behind him came the sound of boots on metal grating, and Lark spoke before anyone else could. "Six and a half terms ago, High Chancellor Carmine Alexander and Lady Isabelline Alexander were assassinated via sniper fire at the Eternity Ball. The assassin was never caught, and those responsible for it were never discovered. That particular Eternity Ball was celebrating the execution of the last Temperast. The extermination of the Temperast was a lifelong goal of the Alexander family, despite the controversy they stirred up by supporting it. No one knows why they were killed, but everyone believes it was largely due to the Temperast."

"The Temperast were pure evil," Cyan said, his voice the flattest—the coldest—Einn had ever heard it. "My parents did the right thing by wiping them out; that's the whole fucking *point* of Heartstone's Law." Einn said nothing, though he at least knew that law and that race. Heartstone's Law was the most notorious code in the IG:

*Any race deemed beyond all shadow of a reasonable doubt to be a threat to all other races, with no discernible purpose for their existence, or if said race is found to have been artificially created with no vital purpose and no place in the natural order is discovered, is to be annihilated.*

The Temperast were a genetically engineered race based on the Kemperast, but contorted to horrific proportions. If he recalled correctly, the Temperast had been able to 'eat' the magics energy of all magics capable races, a traumatic assault that usually left the victims dead.

He hadn't thought anyone was particularly upset that the Temperast were gone, but as he had told Cyan, he didn't pay attention to such things. The only rumors that had concerned him were those involving the sorts of people who could stand to be pirated and Auths.

"No race deserves to be exterminated," Lark said.

Cyan looked at him, expression fierce enough that Einn and Lark both took a step back before they caught themselves. "You never met a Temperast, and for that you should be grateful to my parents."

"I still don't get why you're here, wishing you weren't Lord Alexander."

"I'm not Lord Alexander," Cyan snapped. "My name is Cyan McCracken. I walked away from that life one term after my parents died, when I could no longer take it and I was old enough to make my own decisions. I switched my citizenship to Mars the day I turned eighteen, which made me legal in all quadrants, and I joined the Rehab Guard program the next day. I am *not* Cyan Alexander anymore."

Einn fell silent, not at all sure what he should say in the face of such vehemence. Beside him, however, Lark just snorted with impatience. "Poor little prince, unable to live without mummy and daddy?" Einn reared back as Cyan *moved.* How in the stars did he keep forgetting the bastard was Rehab?

Lark struggled to breath, pinned to the wall in a way that gave him no chance of escaping despite the fact Cyan was at least half a head shorter and not quite as broad. Einn moved to help, but then stopped, because he sensed that would only make matters worse. "I can and will kill you if you persist in shooting your mouth off about things you do not understand. My parents' deaths are not the reason I left." He threw Lark to the ground and walked back to his seat, ignoring the sounds Lark made as he struggled to breathe properly again and pull himself to his feet.

"Are you all right?" Einn asked, helping him up. "Cyan, knock it the fuck off, or we'll put you back in the hold."

Cyan smiled at him. "Try it, rock spider. Just try it."

"That's enough," Lark said, voice hoarse. "You're out of control, Rehab. There's no call for threats and violence. Stars, I thought the criminals were supposed to be the danger in Rehab."

"Not if you're a criminal," Cyan said, and Einn shivered—partly from fear, but also, he acknowledged in annoyance, partly from lust. He did not enjoy seeing Cyan rough up Lark, but he didn't mind Cyan a little on the hostile side.

Lark grimaced. "Stars. Your parents saw to the annihilation of an entire race, you have anger issues ... is your entire family unstable?" Einn almost rolled his eyes because they both knew the answer to that fucking question.

"My parents were good people," Cyan said quietly, going from furious to depressed in the blink of an eye. "You'll never know just how much they cared about everyone, to take on an issue they knew would probably get them killed. What's left of the family has issues, yes. Be grateful I'm not the sadistic, crazy one." He stood up and stormed out, leaving them in another ringing silence.

Sighing and taking the seat Cyan vacated, Lark fumbled through drawers until he came up with a med kit. "What in the name of the Wings are we supposed to do?" he asked. "If you haven't noticed, we're fucked harder than a Kreskan virgin going half price at a Bangkok flesh market."

"Succinctly put," Einn muttered, and collapsed in the nav seat. "I don't know. Tell him?"

Lark shook his head. "No way. I say we dump him on Kreska and pretend he never existed. That means you really need to stop giving him all those 'fuck me' looks you think you're hiding."

Einn made a face, but did not protest the accusation because it was true. If Cyan made him an offer, he'd accept it in a moment, even knowing all the reasons he should not. "But if he doesn't like his brother—"

"It's a bad idea," Lark snapped. "Zero sticks with Zero, no matter what they say. There is absolutely no telling what will happen if we find ourselves stuck in the middle of some sibling feud. We drop him on Kreska, then we run like hell and hope to the stars that Jade does not kill us for kidnapping his brother."

Nodding, letting the matter drop, Einn said, "Speaking of our boss, he hasn't contacted us in far too long. We don't have long left before—"

"I know," Lark bit out.

Einn thought again of Cyan, the way he had looked watching his brother. "Are you sure—"

"What do you think will happen if we tell him? That he'll magically fix all of our problems? Forget it. Either he'll turn on us or he'll be dragged down into the mess with us," Lark said. "Ignorant people are happier for being so."

"Those who never fall, also never climb," Einn countered.

Lark made a sharp, impatient motion with his hand. "He ran away from his damn brother; I don't see it playing out well for anyone—"

"But Jade must already know, or will soon, given he's the one who sent us after the *Huntress*," Einn said.

"Which is probably why he hasn't contacted us," Lark said. "He must be mired in the matter of his missing brother, never mind all the ghosts they're pulling from graves. There's nothing people like more than reliving the old tragedies of others."

Einn shook his head, not quite following that one for a moment. Graves, burial, right. Not something he saw on Fornar or in space. On Fornar, bodies were thrown to the ground well below the shrouding mists, and in space, bodies were incinerated or thrown into the nearest sun. "Dealing with people talking about his dead parents won't keep Jade busy forever. I don't like keeping quiet, not now when I know he might not side—"

"But you don't know for sure!" Lark snapped. "Zero sticks with Zero when it comes down to it, and blood sticks to blood. That never changes."

The bitterness in his tone drew Einn up short the way it always did when it slipped into Lark's tone. He knew some of Lark's history, but not much. He'd been orphaned, grown up in the slums, eventually got work in the docks. The docks were a brutal place for anyone, but apparently much worse for those with no ties to anyone or anything. Lark had never elaborated on what he'd endured, but it wasn't really necessary.

Einn was grateful he didn't really understand the whole family thing people seemed obsessed with; all it seemed to cause was problems. "So you really think that's what we should do? Say nothing, dump him off, and run?"

"Yes," Lark said, and gave up fussing with the med kit. Picking it up, he left the bridge, leaving Einn with only the silence for company again.

With nothing better to do and curiosity still clawing at him—and not so secretly desperate for a reason to tell Cyan everything—Einn went to the comm station and searched the IG network for every scrap of information pertaining to the Alexander family.

"Having fun?"

Einn jumped and tried to turn at the same time, succeeding only in nearly falling flat on his face and giving himself new bruises. "Not really. I want a better idea of just who the hell is on my ship and how much trouble it's going to cause me."

"A lot," Cyan said flatly. "I left home because Jade is crazy. I don't care how smooth he behaves in public, and I can never prove it, but my brother went insane that day."

"That day? The day your parents ... "

"The day my parents were shot, leaving very little of their heads intact," Cyan said flatly, eyes dark as he met Einn's. "Whoever contracted that hit wanted it messy, wanted it flashy, and they got their points' worth. Jade was standing with them and had the closest possible view when their heads were all but popped—"

Einn didn't think, just reacted, tugging Cyan close and holding him, hating that hard, jagged edge to his voice, the one that said it took a lot of practice to sound that brutally indifferent. Cyan stiffened in his arms, but didn't pull away. "Where were you?"

"Across the room behind a pillar, making out with the son of a Lower Chancellor," Cyan said. "I didn't know what was going on at first, didn't know 'til I heard Jade screaming that whatever was wrong, it was my family suffering. Their bodies—" He broke off and fell silent, then finally shoved Einn away. "Anyway, Jade was never the same after that, and he never forgave me for not wanting revenge."

He abruptly pulled up his shirt, displaying a long line of scratches across his stomach. Being Rehab, the wounds could have been from something gained through work—but Lark had an exact duplicate of those scratches on his chest. They had only met Jade in person once, but once was more than enough. "I'm sorry," Einn said. "Siblings aren't supposed to do that sort of thing, I know."

Cyan looked at him, and then laughed softly, some of his tension bleeding away. "I always forget Fornarians have no real concept of family."

Einn shrugged, feeling uncomfortable. "I get it a little bit. Hard not to pick it up when you have to learn IG Common and when you leave home to travel the stars. But no, I don't really get it."

"Must be nice," Cyan said. "Sorry to interrupt your research." He turned away, and Einn reached out to grab his arm, not thinking. "What?"

"I—I don't know," Einn admitted. "There's a saying we have on Fornar; I don't really know your equivalent, but it goes 'it's never an easy climb to the top, but it's always worth it.'"

Cyan smiled faintly and gently pulled his arm free. "I guess that makes sense because you carry nothing when you climb. The journey is a lot different when you have more than your life to lose, but thanks. Dinner will be ready shortly."

Einn frowned at his retreating back and continued to stand there and frown long after Cyan was gone. Stupid. He didn't even know what he wanted to say, so why say anything at all? Sighing and raking a hand through his overlong hair, Einn went to find something to take his frustration out on.

# Chapter Eight

CUSTOM CLASS STARSHIP X-11944654, THE *DRAGONFLY*

Cyan wanted to punch something. He wanted to punch *Jade*. Always his problems circled back to goddamn Jade.

He drew a deep breath and let it out slowly—then punched the wall anyway, grimacing briefly at the pain that resulted. He was not jealous of Jade; he'd overcome that a long time ago. Jade was crazy—sadistic—and Cyan hated him.

Unconsciously, he ran his hand over the scars he'd shown Einn, remembering the night Jade had put them there. It had been just days after the funeral. Cyan had barely stopped crying and Jade had been cold as ice once he'd woken up. His eyes had been different, and while Cyan had never gotten along with his brother, that was the first time he'd been scared of him.

Nothing had happened until he'd tried to tell Jade to let it go, to leave it, to move on. *That* had been the true beginning of the end. Every slap, every hit, every mark of nails; all the cruel words and taunts had started that day. Jade would never forgive him for not being there, for not wanting revenge.

Cyan swallowed as he remembered the cold air on his skin, the ropes biting into his wrists and ankles, the sun as it slowly set and the sky filled with stars. When Jade had finally freed him, Cyan had run and never looked back. One year later, he'd arrived on Mars with a new identity.

Jade continued on, because of course Cyan could ever *prove* anything. He punched the wall again, the throbbing in his hand almost a relief. Anything was better than dredging up memories of his past. He tried to focus on the mess, on putting dinner together. Food was not something anyone typically tasked to him, but after enduring the efforts of his shipmates, Cyan was willing to improve his own skills. He hadn't thought it was possible to make travel food worse, but he hadn't thought his brother would turn into a sadistic bastard, either.

He went through the motions, pulling out packets, containers, trays to put it all on, activating the water heater, and frowning that the water levels were getting low. Well, they should be landing somewhere soon, they could restock—

Oh, what the stars was wrong with him? He was a temporary passenger, and barely one step above full hostage at that. Cyan rubbed his temples and sorely wished there was some way to release all his pent up nervous energy. His traitorous mind immediately went to Einn, and Cyan wondered what the hell was wrong with him that he was thinking of fucking his jailer.

It almost made him laugh as he belatedly appreciated the irony of being the captive for once. Then he was reminded of the lower level prisoners who tried to seduce some of the guards. When it worked, those Rehabbers were fired immediately and banned from ever again working a Rehab. Cyan had seen it happen once; he had no idea what had happened to the man after he'd been removed from his duties.

He closed his eyes and tried to put his mind on a path that would not drive him insane—well, more insane. For all that he called Jade the crazy one, Cyan wasn't certain he was much better. Shaking his head, he opened his eyes and focused again on the food. When it was ready, he found Lark in the engine room, before slowly making his way to the bridge.

Einn was still at the comm station, though it looked as though he was clicking through entertainment vids. He turned it off when he heard Cyan and swiveled around in his chair. "Thanks," he said, then hesitated before dropping his eyes to his food.

Cyan was tempted to smile, because Einn was all confidence getting picked up in a bar, but when it was clear he was trying to comfort—well, he obviously felt about as confident as a Kreskan in a brothel. Damn it, Einn was his captor; Cyan should not be growing to like him. He licked his lips, not quite certain what to say, just as Einn looked up. Their eyes locked.

"There's something—Lark doesn't want us saying—"

"What are talking about?" Cyan asked, but before either of them could say anything further, the bridge consoles blew up with lights and alarms.

Einn swore and whirled around, dashing to the navigation console. "Bottom dwellers!" he snarled, and at Cyan's blank look, clarified, "Pirates." His in-lens flashed as he worked, doing what, Cyan didn't know. "Lark, get to the bridge! Pirates!" He looked at Cyan. "You should—"

"Please don't tell me I should take cover or something," Cyan said, amused and annoyed all at once. "Why would pirates attack this bucket?"

"Parts," Lark said, as he appeared. "They only attack ships like this in search of parts."

Einn grunted. "Brace yourself. We can't counter the firepower I'm reading." Cyan didn't ask or comment; simply took a chair and strapped himself in, holding tightly as only a moment later, the ship rocked with the force of impact. He unbuckled himself once all seemed clear.

"They're hacking our teleport system," Einn said, and unlocked a cabinet, throwing them stunners. Cyan whistled when he saw they'd been illegally modified for fatal shots. Deactivating the safety, he tucked it into his waistband and bolted from the bridge.

He met them as they came out of the transport room, taking two completely by surprise. The third had enough time and wits to attack him, but a space thug was no match for Rehab. Cyan broke his nose with a well-placed fist, then swept his feet out from under him, grabbed his head and slammed it into the metal grating of the floor.

The whirring sound of a stunner drew Cyan's attention, but before he could pin down the exact source and dodge, the stunner fired. He realized the shooter wasn't aiming at him when two more pirates dropped to the ground from shots fired almost directly behind Cyan. He turned and looked at Einn, who shook his head. "Rehabbers. It's true what they say about you guys being crazy."

"Rehabber, you're almost as bloodthirsty as a Telven, I swear," Lark said, holstering his stunner. "Think they'll send another wave? How—fuck." He stopped as four more men spilled into the hallway, spread-stunners at the ready.

"Get up," said the man tucked back behind the other three—clearly their leader. He spoke with a Mars accent, a hint of the Britania colony to it. "Well, well, Hood's protégé. We heard you were dead, Einn. I see you have your little red bird at your side still."

Einn said nothing, but Cyan did not miss his tension, the tight set of his mouth. "Still alive, Smoke. Why the hell are you bothering me?"

"Happy coincidence, eh?" Smoke drawled. "Looking at the state of my men, I should just kill you and have done. I think you deserve something slower, though, don't you?"

"Fall to the bottom and stay there," Einn snarled and raised his stunner—

—but Cyan lifted his own and shot out the fire extinguishing systems on the ceiling, causing a burst of fine white powder to fall over them, turning the hall into mist-shrouded chaos. Closing his eyes, he drew back and waited until someone finally blundered into him. It took only a moment to determine it was not Lark or Einn.

Snapping the man's neck, Cyan cast the body aside and waited—but then head the tell-tale sound of the transporter firing up. A moment later, there was only silence. It was finally broken by the sound of Lark swearing loudly and colorfully, and a banging sound, which was followed by more swearing before the fans finally kicked on.

A few minutes later, the hallway was clear, and Cyan made a face at the bodies lying in the hallway. He looked as Einn strode off, cursing, and vanished into the bridge. Following, Cyan watched while he worked at the comm station, punching in numbers so quickly that Cyan couldn't follow. "What are you doing?"

"Making certain they're gone, for one." He paused, and after a couple of minutes said, "Looks like they are, and we're lucky Smoke didn't decide just to blow us up. Then again, I'm sure he wants to kill me in a much more personal way, the same way I'd prefer to kill him." He slammed one last button. "There, that should buy us time for a bit. Lark, get us out of here."

"Working on it," Lark replied.

Cyan shook his head and fell silent, letting them work. He watched in admiration, realizing after a few minutes that Einn was hacking the starship networks, though he couldn't quite piece out what Einn was doing. He startled when Einn suddenly looked up. "Is it a Rehab thing, the way I can feel you staring?"

"Not that I'm aware," Cyan replied, smirking. "Though, they do teach us to be intimidating and I was one of the best guards on the payroll." He caught Lark rolling his eyes and snickered. Turning back to Einn, he said, "So what exactly are you doing besides breaking laws?"

Einn looked at him in surprise. "No derisive tone?"

"I have no issue with pirates fucking over other pirates," Cyan said.

"I'm changing the flight plans they registered with the IG Star Command. They hacked us to get to our teleport, kind of like what we did with the *Huntress.* It's risky because it provides a chance to back hack, which is exactly what I did. Now, I'm tweaking their registered flight plans to line up with when we attacked the *Huntress*, along with a couple of other things. It won't work forever, but it will throw the IG off our trail long enough to hopefully find a cave to hide in."

Cyan smiled. "I can't tell if you mean that literally or figuratively."

"Either works."

Lark snorted, drawing their attention. "If you two are done flirting, we have ship damage to repair. They didn't breach anything, thankfully, but we're not safe to fly for long until we can get real fixes in place."

"Got it covered," Cyan said. "I would kill for an in-lens right now. Just give me a datapad with the specs, and I'll get started on repairs." He started to turn away, but suddenly remembered. "What were you going to tell me, Einn, before all this happened?"

Einn froze, and then tried to hide it, but not before Lark caught it—and only then did Cyan remember that Einn had said something about Lark not wanting him to know whatever it was. Stars, what he wouldn't give to be back in the uncomplicated world of Rehab. "Einn," Lark hissed.

"I just think—" They both stopped as the comm station began to light up with an incoming call. Cyan's brows shot up at the stricken look on their faces. He moved before they could, slamming the receive button right before Einn grabbed him and yanked him away.

The main screen flickered to life—and Cyan felt his heart drop into his stomach as he looked into his twin brother's face. Jade smiled his cold, sadistic smile; the very one everyone else called beautiful. Cyan trembled with fear against Einn, barely noticing that the hands holding his arms tightened. "What—"

"Brother," Jade purred, flicking the nails of one hand, the deep red paint on them glistening. "All the stars are aflutter with news of your disappearance. I've had idiots stopping by all day long to comfort me. I think they're all afraid I'll fall into hysterics."

Cyan snarled, vibrating with tension, wanting badly to lunge at Jade and break his stupid, fucking, oh so perfect face. "They're stupid for thinking you ever *stopped* having hysterics. Why in the stars—" His eyes widened as the obvious belatedly struck him. "You're working for Jade! You sons of bitches!" He threw all of his weight back, sending Einn off balance, then twisted free, whipped around, and punched him square in the face.

When Lark came at him, Cyan nailed him in the gut, then the jaw, and Lark tumbled unconscious to the floor.

"Prisoners," Einn gasped out around his bloody nose.

Cyan barely heard the word, chose to ignore it, and turned back around to face his smirking brother. "What in the *stars* is going on?"

Jade laughed and settled back in his seat, gold hair braided as always and vibrant against his dark crimson robe. "They're mine, and they do my bidding because otherwise they will end up dead. How fortuitous that you have joined their crew, because their next assignment is going to be difficult."

"I don't do your bidding," Cyan snapped. "If you think I'm just going to stand by—"

"All those muscles and skills you acquired in that hovel cannot change the fact that you are a worthless coward, darling brother. If you attempt to circumvent me, I am more than willing to let your friends die. If you do anything other than my bidding, I will be more than willing to see to it the scientists and their experiments begin to die. I can always have my men fetch more, after all."

Cyan felt sick. "I don't understand—"

"No, you never do," Jade said with cold condescension. "I will put it to you plainly, sweet brother. On my orders, those two men you just beat up kidnap various persons across the IG. You will join them and continue to take who I tell you, when I tell you, until I see fit to tell you to stop."

"Fuck you."

Jade sighed and tsked softly, shaking his head. "You continue to disregard what I am telling you—that you have no choice, because if you do not obey me, the poison that infects my little pirates will kill them when I withhold the serum that keeps them alive. Should that not work, I will begin to kill off those they have already stolen, and you can fetch the replacements yourself. There are plenty of people to kill, brother dear, and their lives are in your hand."

"I hate you," Cyan replied.

"A pity," Jade said with a laugh. "You know how much I love you, brother."

Cyan said nothing, merely killed the connection, bringing a merciful silence to the bridge. "What is going on?" he asked. Einn grunted, making him turn around, and he almost smiled to see that Einn had already healed most of the damage Cyan had done to his nose. He spoke before could catch himself. "You guys really do have harder bones and stuff, don't you?"

"Fall off enough cliffs, and the Cave Carver takes pity and makes you harder to break," Einn said. "Did you have to knock Lark out? We're not as evil as you clearly think—and I'm not saying I blame you, but you could listen before you turn violent."

Sighing, Cyan knelt and hefted Lark over his shoulder. "Sorry. Let me put him in his bunk." He left the bridge, and with some effort, managed to get Lark into the lower bunk and comfortably settled. Sighing again, he headed back to the bridge.

Einn handed him a bottle. "Zero brandy."

"Thanks," Cyan replied, and took a generous swallow, relishing the way it burned and made his eyes water. He collapsed in the nearest chair, and then asked again, "What is going on?"

"When I left Fornar, it was with nothing," Einn said quietly. "I fell in with a bad group and couldn't find my way out. They were attacked one day, and this guy ... He called himself 'Hood', and if he had another name, I never knew it. He—he was a pirate, but not the usual sort. He took me in, taught me the ropes, and it wasn't long before I actually became his second in command. We stole from all sorts of space junk, the sorts of men who make known criminals look like saints. We took everything we could and sold it off, gave the money to others."

He fell silent, and Cyan could only stare. "So—you're vigilantes?"

"A pirate is a pirate," Einn replied. "Anyway, one day, we got wind of this job, and it seemed too good to be true, and I tried to say that, but Hood wouldn't listen. It went wrong in the worst way, and four of the crew died before we could get away."

"Including Hood."

Einn nodded. "After that, I became captain. One term after that ... " His fingers tightened on the bottle of brandy, and he drank down two swallows before he finally continued speaking. "We were led into a trap, and everyone was killed except me and Lark. Jade had sprung the whole thing; I still don't know why he chose *us.* He infected us with some sort of poison that needs regular doses of a special serum to keep it from becoming fatal. I don't think there's a permanent cure."

"There is," Cyan said grimly. "I know that poison; my mother's family was renowned in the field of toxins. Jade had been studying to follow in those footsteps when our parents were killed, and he switched to politics. There is a cure, but Jade is the only one who knows how to make it. So you have to kidnap people for him or die?"

"Yes. We thought about defying him, but he'd just find someone else if we were dead, and ... well, we know all the people we've stolen and take notes of every drop off, every target. We make note of every last detail that we think of in the hopes someday it'll be useful—to us or someone else." Einn set the bottle aside and covered his face with his hands. "I'm sorry we dragged you into it. I wanted to tell you; Lark said 'no'. I was going to do it, anyway—"

Cyan just laughed bitterly. "Of all the ships, in all the stars."

"You could just run," Einn said quietly. "Lay me out cold, run for your fucking life. Jade can't do shit if you run away."

"Clearly you do not yet know my brother well," Cyan replied, stealing the bottle of brandy and downing a generous portion of it. "He has me right where he has always wanted: in his hold, unable to wriggle free. If I leave now, he will leave a pile of bodies before me wherever I hide. I'm stuck, and he knows it. He loves it."

"I'm sorry," Einn said softly. "We'd hoped to get you to Kreska before everything went wrong."

Cyan shook his head. "Forget it, just forget it." He drank more brandy, before letting Einn take the bottle back to drink himself, and they both ignored the comm station when it notified them of a waiting message.

# Chapter Nine

CUSTOM CLASS STARSHIP Z-28922942, THE *BRILLIANT*

"Adalsteinn, known pirate. Beyond that, there isn't much actually known. He is twenty-nine years of age, Zero Standard Reckoning, about thirty-one by Fornar reckoning. He comes from the Broken Green caves, which is the southeastern portion of the planet. He was a top-ranked climber when he left Fornar at age seventeen, ZSR, and was logged on various planets before falling off the IG's grid one term later." Winter's in-lens flashed as he rifled through data. "However, he is well known in other circles, and I have men in the right places. He fell in with a pirate called Vermin roughly a term after he left Fornar. Intel says Vermin was slaughtered by the Hood gang, and Adalsteinn joined up with them."

Karmikel grunted. "Vermin—he was bad news. I wasn't at all upset to hear someone had killed him. Hood—that's one of the vigilante gangs. He was killed a couple terms ago, I heard."

"Correct," Winter replied. "Just over two terms ago, Hood was killed in an ugly clash with another pirate gang. Rumor has it that Adalsteinn took the Captain's reins. A term ago, his ship was found as nothing more than bits of space debris. Bodies of the crew could not be located, so no one knows if they are alive or dead. Adalsteinn has not been seen or heard of since, not by anyone who is talking, anyway."

Sean sighed. "So Adalsteinn is the guy we're looking for, I would say. It all lines up too neatly."

"He's a vigilante-type, though," Karmikel said, scowling at the data on the screen beside Winter. "It just doesn't make sense one of that ilk would resort to this."

"What's a vigilante-type?"

Karmikel flapped a hand impatiently. "I don't know what you would call them on Mars. They like to attack powerful, corrupt type persons, then they give the stolen goods away to the less fortunate."

Sean burst out laughing. "He's a Robin Hood: steals from the rich to give to the poor."

"I hadn't realized the job was in the name," Karmikel said, shaking his head. "Yeah, that's basically it. There's a handful of them. They think they're heroes of some sort."

On the screen, Winter smiled faintly with amusement. "Indeed, I have more than a few operatives who began as such. I wonder what would drive a vigilante to become a more standard sort of criminal. Kidnapping is dangerous work; either the kidnappers or the victims always die."

"Do we have any information on the rest of the crew?" Karmikel asked. "They're probably dead, but the more information we have, the better."

Winter nodded. "One moment." His in-lens flashed, and after a moment, the new information began to fill the right side of the screen. "Hood captained a merchant class vessel called *The Nottingham*. It was an M line, which means it could sustain a maximum crew of fifteen. His was rumored to be smaller than that, though no one could ever confirm it. We have information on only four: Hood, Adalsteinn, a Hellcat name unknown, and a Helioran believed to be named Lark Vallant—"

"I know him," Karmikel said, staring at the images that flashed on the screen. They weren't very good images: a standard dock worker employee photo, several years out of date and a security scan image that only caught a partial profile. He was handsome, with the dusky red skin common to most of the planet Helior. "I've seen him before the couple of times I crossed paths with Hood. Never spoke to him, obviously, but I definitely remember seeing him."

Nodding, Winter resumed, "He was a dock worker in the city of Skyrun, the IG capital of Helior. Excellent work records, but a long criminal history. Petty stuff, mostly:

theft, prostitution, disturbing the peace. The usual assortment for that group."

Sean snorted in amusement. "There's a place that still outlaws prostitution?"

"Many, actually," Winter replied with equal amusement. "Vallant dropped off the grid several terms ago when he was sixteen, ZSR, about nineteen by Helior reckoning. He never reappeared anywhere except in sightings and rumors connecting him to Hood's crew. *The Nottingham* was completely obliterated when it was discovered. If anyone survived, it would be a certified miracle."

Mendel stirred from the back of the bridge where he had been sitting quietly the entire time. "How was the ship destroyed, exactly? It does not seem to me, reading all that you have sent to us, that Hood and his crew should have been so easily massacred. If even half these rumored attacks can be definitively attributed to them, they are no one to trifle with."

"Hood was hardcore," Karmikel said, before Winter could reply. "I never chased him, though I was offered good money to do so a few times. He really was what he claimed—he found the blackest bastards in the stars and left them naked. I'm sure one of his victims found a crew willing to take him on; there's always somebody willing to take money."

"Well, they never got to enjoy it because *The Nottingham* wasn't the only ship found in pieces. The other ship, we could find no registry."

Sean's brow shot up at that. "No registry? A ghost ship? That's not possible. Any ship caught without registration is halted, if not simply obliterated if found in the wrong place. They can't leave the shipyards where they're built without being registered."

Karmikel laughed and looked at him with amusement. "Rehabbers. You're so cute in what you don't know about being a criminal."

"Fuck you," Sean said.

"Unregistered ships usually come from decommissioned ships. They use artificial protocols and IDs to get from port to port; the best way to nail a ship for having an artificial registry is to check its light jump history. Ports almost never care about how legal a ship is. I can't tell you how many ports a term receive violations for negligence in record keeping. We've had accounts of one ship docking six times in one day, because the port workers just log the numbers and never bother to cross check and validate. They're too short on manpower and too long on apathy. Of those six times, only one was the legally registered ship. The others are all ghost ships."

"So why do they get hung up on light jumps?"

"Because the light gates are IG maintained, and they *do* cross check and validate all IDs and protocols," Winter said. "Without the right numbers, no one is given permission to light jump. Faking those would take IG intervention or cracks of a very high caliber."

Sean nodded. "Fascinating, but I think we've wandered off point. If this Adalsteinn is the guy we're looking for, and he's supposed to be dead, then how in the stars are we supposed to find him? We can hop around all the planets where the kidnappings took place, or the planets closest when the kidnappings happened in space, but without knowing what ship to track, we're looking for 'a Fornarian', which is useful, but not useful enough."

"Well, only eleven ships left Bangkok at the relevant times, and only three went in the correct direction: the *Huntress,* the *Argov,* and *the Dragonfly*. So I would wager the *Argov* and the *Dragonfly* are the best places to start." Winter put up the data for both ships. "The *Dragonfly* is a custom class starship registered to an in-lens merchant on Mars. Registries and merchant logs all check out; they use light gates extensively." He pulled up more information, but did not bother listing it all out. "The *Argov,* on the other hand, was docked twice in the same hour on Krawl."

"Unregistered ship," Sean said. "So that's the one we want. How do we track it now?"

Karmikel laughed and started typing furiously, in-lens flashing as he transmitted passwords, codes, and orders while he worked. "We track that registry and see where else it shows up. Ships like to use one for a few stints, since it makes it look more credible. If they were good, they could hack the system and alter any duplicates, but if they were that good, they would find other ways around the registry problem. So, it looks like it appeared right *here* two days ago. I say we start there; I know all the haunts in that area and who is best to ask."

"Do it, then," Winter said. "You have all you need to get there. Keep me apprised."

"Copy that," Karmikel said, and ended the call. Silence fell while he worked, plotting their course and looking the happiest Sean had seen him for days.

He shook his head, amused. "You never look happier than when you are doing this sort of thing. How did IA coax you away?"

Karmikel paused and looked at him in surprise, his usual terse demeanor absent. "I got tired of being a bad guy and being used. I worked for Three Moon Industries as a 'security consultant', which is just business speak for corporate mercenary. It became less and less about hunting pirates, and more about shady dealings and getting rid of the competition. I stumbled across IA agents looking to nail my boss. I helped them. I'm good at what I do, and IA had an opening." He turned back to his console and resumed typing.

Sean chuckled and left him to it. "I'll be in the engine room; call me when we get wherever we're going."

"Copy that," Karmikel said absently.

Leaving the bridge, Sean paused in the mess to fix something to drink, and then carried his steaming mug down to the engine room. They had something to work with, he thought with cautious relief. They would find Cyan, damn it. Sean would kill every last one of the damned pirates involved in the kidnapping.

He took a sip of his tea, grimacing at the staleness of it, but grateful that there was tea at all. Stars, he could not wait to spend time on land again. Of course, thinking that reminded him that his chances on land were going to be infinitesimal.

It was something he preferred not to think about. Eventually, the matter of the Draconis would be decided. No matter what the outcome, though, he and Mendel would not live. He winced, thinking about it. Mendel never should have matched on Rehab. He should have been serving his life sentence. It was no kind of life, but it wasn't dead.

Now, because Mendel was matched to him, the IG had every reason in the world to execute them. Sean's hands tightened around the warm metallic mug. As much as he hated the way Mendel treated him, could he really blame him? It was not as though matching to Sean had ever done Mendel any real favors.

He frowned at his tea, wishing it would provide answers, even if he didn't quite know the questions. The sound of familiar footsteps drew his attention, and he looked up slowly. "Mendel. Did you need something?" Mendel opened his mouth, but closed it again and hovered in the doorway. Sean sighed and looked at his tea again. "What?" he asked more curtly.

"I feel like, no matter what I say, it is going to be the wrong thing," Mendel said. "You've said more to me now than you have in days."

Sean felt that was a slight exaggeration, but he was pleased in a stupid, petty, lonely way that Mendel was so acutely aware of how little Sean spoke to him. It was more attention than Mendel had ever seemed to pay before. "I never had a problem with what you said; my issue was that you never said much of anything. We've been together for over a term, yet I feel like we barely know each other."

Mendel didn't say anything, but Sean heard him move further into the room and looked up to see Mendel standing right in front of him. "I just want this to work," Mendel said. "If we don't make a big enough difference, the IG will kill us."

"We're going to die, anyway," Sean said, and set his tea aside, tangling his fingers together and letting them dangle between his knees. "It doesn't matter what we do, who we save, or what difference we make. I'm too much of a risk to be allowed to live, and you are a runaway murderer. That will make getting an execution approved easy."

"It was self-defense," Mendel said quietly. "We were fighting and it got out of hand, but he was the one who tried to kill me first. You've never asked. In all this time, you've never even brought it up."

Sean looked up in surprise. "Why would I?"

"You're chained to a killer. I would think you'd want a few points of the matter clarified."

"I don't give a damn," Sean said, annoyed. He stood up so hastily that Mendel was forced to take a couple of steps back. He looked up at Mendel, always stupidly pleased that Mendel was taller. Sean had never cared to be the one who towered. He was intimidating enough being Rehab; he didn't want to loom, too. "You're my partner—my match." Mendel could be his lover, too, but Sean was not going to beat his head against that wall at the moment. "It doesn't matter to me if you are or aren't a killer. We're a team, whether you like it or not."

Mendel frowned. "You should not be stuck—"

"I'm not stuck with you!" Sean bellowed, startling them both. He did not stop though, simply plunging on. "The moment you freed me, I could have killed you or knocked you out. I could have fixed my in-lens, said it was a mistake, and that you'd done something else to escape. I could have fled at every last fucking port we've stopped in and gone to ground. Stars, Mendel, I could teleport away whenever I fucking feel like it. But I haven't—I've stayed right here.

With you. I am not in danger because I'm with you, Mendel, but they will use you as an excuse to kill me, because if I live, I'm a liability to the entire infrastructure of the IG."

Silence fell, and they just stared at each other. Finally, Mendel said, "Perhaps we are arguing semantics about who is actually stuck with whom."

Sean laughed. "You're such a fucking scientist."

"I'm sor—"

"If you say you're sorry, I will break your nose."

Mendel lifted his eyes to the ceiling, and Sean laughed at such an honest look of exasperation from someone whose perpetual expression was 'stone-faced'. "Then what do you want me to say?"

"I'm not telling you what to say," Sean snapped, levity gone.

"That's not what I meant," Mendel sighed. "Forget it. I am sorry to disturb you. I wish people would just leave me to my lab work." He spun on his heel and strode out. Sean winced because that time was definitely his fault. He bolted after Mendel and snagged his wrist, jerking him about-face. "What?" Mendel asked.

Sean suddenly had a better idea exactly how Mendel must have felt walking into the engine room. "I'm sorry."

"Are we ever going to say anything else?"

"You are the one who is all work, all the time. I realize our work is important, but I meant what I said—breaks are necessary to maintain peak performance, even if that break is just goofing off for ten minutes. One term and we barely know each other, and sooner rather than later we will be dead. It's depressing to me that the one person who should most understand how I feel is a virtual stranger rather than a real friend."

Mendel stared at him in silence, and Sean could see that he'd never really thought about it that way before. "Even before I— I've always been too focused on work."

Sean shoved at him gently. "You're an idiot, but there is hope for you, I suppose. Try working on doing other things."

"Like—"

"If you ask me 'like what'—"

"Stop finishing my sentences!"

Sean laughed and shoved him gently again, then stepped closer, right up into Mendel's personal space, leaning up so they almost nose to nose. "If you honestly cannot think of a single thing to do with free time, your own bedroom, and a willing match, there's really no hope for you, Mendel."

He drew back and strode past Mendel before he could reply, leaving him to mull over that for a bit. Maybe, just maybe, Mendel would eventually act on it.

# Chapter Ten

**PLANET 6182854 (PARTHON), TIPTE PORT CITY**

"I hate silk spiders," Einn groused.

Lark grunted in agreement, and Cyan rolled his eyes at both of them. "Parthon isn't that bad."

"It's not that bad the way a long fall isn't that bad," Einn retorted. "I feel like I'm violating protocol every time I draw a breath. This planet is more irritating than Zero."

Cyan laughed. "Zero is nowhere near as bad as everyone likes to say."

Lark sneered at that. "Spoken like a true lord who never had to live as a denizen of Zero beyond the Palace of Eternity and the sprawling city surrounding it."

"I made it as Rehab," Cyan replied. "Zero isn't as soft and whimsical as you seem to think. I didn't learn how to kick your ass by sipping tea all day."

"You haven't kicked my ass," Lark said. Cyan only smirked.

"Whatever," Einn said, cutting them off before they decided to spar. He pointedly ignored the way it annoyed him that Cyan was practically making Lark an offer. Lark and Cyan had no interest in each other, so there was nothing to be annoyed about. What was wrong with him? "I still hate Parthon."

"I always thought Vrill was far more pretentious," Cyan said. "Where exactly are we supposed to meet this guy who has your temp antidote?"

Einn's in-lens flashed, and he pointed, "Not far now; just at the end of this street, turn right, couple buildings down. I think I know the bar, though I've never been in it. I really hope this goes without a hitch." He sighed.

Cyan's brows rose. "Why wouldn't it go without a hitch? We're just picking up medicine."

"Half these fucking deliverymen seem to realize we're picking up something important," Lark said sourly. "They think they can extort more money by withholding it, at which point Einn and I have to get violent."

"I see," Cyan said. His hands flexed, clearly in anticipation of a fight.

Einn shook his head in amusement. "Are you ever not spoiling for a fight?"

Cyan laughed. "Fighting or fucking: only way I ever handled anything. My parents despaired of making a proper politician of me—a proper anything of me."

"Somehow, I'm not surprised," Einn replied, struggling to ignore the memories that were increasingly difficult to push away. Cyan approaching him so boldly in the bar, riding him with no inhibitions or hesitations. Einn swallowed and stopped trying to hold a conversation, focusing on the task ahead of them.

The bar reeked of the flowery cigarettes popular on Parthon, but there was an underlying sticky-sweet scent that made Einn tense. In all the stars, only one thing had that particular scent: Soul, one of the few substances completely outlawed by the IG. There were absolutely no exceptions, and being caught in possession of Soul was a ticket straight to Rehab. The potent drug had a long list of side-effects, all of them nasty, but the notorious high it gave made the damned drug impossible to eradicate. The points it raked in didn't hurt, either.

"Let's get in and out," Lark said grimly.

"Agreed," Einn said, and beside him, Cyan nodded. Einn squinted through the haze of acrid smoke, searching—ah, there he was. Parthon pretty, all rigid and still and smug. Einn couldn't stand silk spiders. Parthon was one of the wealthiest planets in the IG simply because of the trade they did in textiles. No planet in the IG could match the quality of Parthon silk and all the other fabrics they churned out. The silk and the inherently poisonous nature of Parthon had earned them the nickname 'silk spiders'.

It irritated Einn beyond all words that Fornarians were often called 'rock spiders'. He wanted nothing in common with Parthon. He scowled at the delivery man who only smirked back, pale blue skin sickly looking in the weak light. All Parthons had that faint blue tinge to their skin, the side-effect of a natural immunity to a chemical in the air that was toxic to off planet visitors.

Einn loathed the inoculation necessary for visiting Parthon because it made everything taste like metal for days after. Just one more reason he hated Parthon. Or maybe he was just in a bad mood, since being half a day from dying a slow and painful death tended to make him cranky.

Einn led the way through the crowded bar and sat directly across from the deliveryman. Why Jade couldn't make it easy, he did not know, except perhaps that it was Jade. Cyan and Lark took the two remaining seats, the four of them forming a loose circle around the rickety table in the back of the bar. "Got it?" Einn asked.

The man ignored him in favor of finishing his drink, one of the syrupy concoctions that Parthons loved. Einn forced himself to display a patience he did not feel. When he finally finished his drink, the man asked, "Got my money?"

"We don't owe you money," Lark said flatly.

Smirking, the man replied, "You do if you want your precious little box." Einn started to reply to that, but almost faster than he could follow, Cyan lunged from his seat and swung a punch that made Einn wince when he heard the man's nose break. He knew exactly how much Cyan's fist hurt and had never been more grateful that his bones were harder to damage.

The man went down, out cold, blood gushing everywhere from his shattered nose. Around them, the bar went silent for a moment, then business resumed like normal. In a Soul-dealing bar, no one asked questions or called the Auths. Reaching under the man's chair, Cyan grabbed the small metal case that held their antidote, stood up, and strode out of the bar without looking back.

Einn shared a look with Lark, who rolled his eyes, then hastened after Cyan. They walked quickly through the crowded streets and back to the rooms they'd rented closer to the docks. Once inside, Cyan set the case on one of the beds and opened it. He picked up the injector and loaded it, then cocked an eyebrow at them. "Well? Which of you girls is going first?"

"Who suddenly voted you mom?" Lark asked sourly, but shoved up his sleeve. Cyan injected him, and Einn stepped up. "There," Cyan said when he was done. "That will set you to rights for a few days, correct?"

"Yeah," Einn replied gruffly, meeting Cyan's gaze and suddenly noticing for the first time that his gray eyes had the barest flecks of blue in them. Pretty, Einn thought, before he could stop himself from thinking something so idiotic. "I'm sorry for dragging you into this."

"You can make it up to me later," Cyan replied, putting the injector gun away. Einn wondered if he was allowed to construe innuendo in those words, or if Cyan was just being matter of fact.

Lark made a disgusted noise. "The ship won't be ready until tomorrow morning. I am going to go find something to do, because if I have to watch the two of you make 'fuck me' eyes at each other for five more seconds, I'm going to shriek like a Vrill left on Krawl." He didn't wait for their replies, simply stomping out and not quite slamming the door behind him.

"Fuck me eyes?" Cyan repeated, sounding amused.

Einn laughed. "Should I bother trying to deny it?"

"Not much point," Cyan said. "Even when I thought you were a kidnapping bastard, I still wanted you. But wanting to do something and doing it are two different things."

True enough, and there was no point in arguing the point—yet Einn wanted to argue. He didn't get it, but he wasn't going to lie about it either. Whatever the reason,

Cyan was in his blood. Einn wanted to get him out. "I think that, no matter all the reasons we shouldn't, thinking about it and constantly telling ourselves not to is far more distracting."

Cyan looked at him, clearly startled. Then he went back to being amused. "Convenient logic?"

"Doesn't make it less true," Einn said, and reached out with one long arm to wrap his fingers around Cyan's wrist, feeling the way Cyan shivered. He pulled Cyan close and bent his head down. "So what's it going to be—" His words were cut off by a kiss, and Einn had not realized the degree to which he had missed those kisses, and just how poorly he remembered them. Memory was just no substitute for the real thing. He grunted and kissed back, letting go of Cyan's wrist to wrap around his body and haul him closer, up.

Reacting to the movement, Cyan wrapped his own arms around Einn's neck, his legs around Einn's waist. Einn murmured in soft approval, and then lowered Cyan to the bed, climbing on top of him. Cyan wasted no time in loosening his arms to begin pulling and shoving at Einn's clothes, all while never quite able to stop kissing him. Einn chuckled and drew back, pulling off his shirt and getting Cyan's off next. "You really are something, Rehab." He bent to put his mouth to Cyan's skin, lapping at the myriad scars marring it. No part of Cyan seemed unmarred; every bit of it held the history of some prisoner or fight. He nuzzled against the tell-tale marks that had been left by Jade's claws. "These must have hurt."

"Jade mixes poison into his nail paints," Cyan said. "It burned for days; I thought I was going to die. Couldn't do anything, but pull against my bonds."

Einn stilled at that, looked up with surprise—that Cyan said anything at all and at the words themselves. "Bonds?"

Cyan's mouth twisted. "When I started to really defy him, Jade took to tying me down. First, just in my bed, but he got more creative later."

"Mercy of the fallen," Einn said, and kissed him hard. No wonder Cyan was such a fighter. Something like that, men either fell or learned to fight. Cyan kissed him back hard, splitting his own lip. Einn lapped the blood away, then nipped his jaw, down his throat, working his way slowly back down Cyan's torso until he encountered his pants.

Smirking, Einn opened Cyan's pants and pulled out his cock, laughing at the way Cyan swore and thrust into his touch. Einn stroked him once, twice, ran his thumb over the head, chuckling at the look Cyan gave him. Hovering, doing nothing for a few more seconds, he gave in only when Cyan's body rippled in that sinuous way that was a warning sign of impending violence. Einn licked his cock and sucked it down, working with lips and tongue, and chuckling at the hands that fisted in his hair. He took Cyan deep, nearly to the point he couldn't breathe, but loving every moment of having Cyan so thoroughly under his control.

Cyan made a sharp, keening sort of noise the moment before he came, thrusting one last time into Einn's mouth. Einn swallowed it all, slowly pulling off Cyan's cock once he stilled, nuzzling against his surprisingly soft skin, before slowly crawling back up his body to take a kiss. "Nice, rock spider," Cyan said, licking at his lips. "Going to fuck me now?"

"Rehab: so impatient," Einn replied with a laugh. "Get naked."

"Get off me."

"I thought you were supposed to be getting me off."

Cyan rolled his eyes and shoved, and Einn obediently moved, lying down beside him on the narrow bed and watching with pleasure while Cyan stripped off the rest of his clothes. He was small, short, all tight compact muscle and lithe movement as he climbed back onto the bed. The perfect build for space travel, unlike Einn's too tall, too long form. So different from everything Einn had known on Fornar, and one of the best parts of leaving home. Einn grabbed him and rolled them over, once more pinning Cyan to the bed, loving that Cyan let him.

It made him want to find out what else Cyan would let him do. He ran his hands over Cyan's body, mapping it, memorizing it, confounded as to why he was so obsessed, but not interested in exploring why. In space, the point was to savor, not to wonder. He took another kiss, and then nipped hard at Cyan's throat, loving the flavor of him, smoky and musky with a faint hint of sweet beneath it all.

Reaching back to one of the many pockets on his pants, Einn pulled out the tube of lube he'd stashed there earlier in the hopes of finding a way to take his mind off Cyan if they had enough downtime. So far, his day was looking to be far better than he had dared hope. Slicking his fingers, he pressed one inside Cyan's body, pushing his legs further apart to get better access. Cyan obliged, move into the touch, hands grasping at the bed for leverage.

"I should kidnap Rehabbers more often," Einn murmured, as he added a second finger.

"Go to hell," Cyan replied. "Stop playing around and fuck me."

Einn chuckled. "Your patience is your finest quality." He withdrew his fingers and opened his pants, pulling Cyan's legs up and lining up his cock. He pressed in slowly, and then at the look Cyan gave him, thrust all the way in hard. "Better?"

Cyan gave him a murderous look. "If you don't know what you're doing, pirate, I'll be happy—damn it!" He swore as Einn pulled out and slammed back in. "Better."

Laughing again, Einn began to move the way they both wanted, thrusting hard and fast and deep until he could do nothing but gasp for every breath, watch the emotions that played across Cyan's face, feel sweat slid along his skin, dampen his hair. Cyan in passion was a thing to behold, and Einn stored it away in his mind with the countless other memories he wanted to hold fast.

Best of all was the way Cyan looked when he came, Einn's name on his lips, those gray eyes looking blue for a single moment. Einn followed almost immediately after, burying himself to the hilt in Cyan's tight body and collapsing on top of him as exhaustion took him in the wake of the release of long-pent up sexual tension. He grunted when Cyan shoved him off, purposely leaving one arm and leg draped over him. "So bossy, even when you're being fucked," Einn teased. "Must be that fancy Zero blood of yours."

"Go to hell," Cyan said again, the words almost cheerful, too lazy to even open his eyes when he spoke. "I don't think the man who couldn't even be bothered to take his pants and boots off has any right to bitch about my impatience."

Einn smirked. "I was far too eager to fuck you to bother with undressing."

"I rest my case," Cyan said around a yawn. "Rock spiders."

Not replying, Einn just rolled away to actually undress, then lay back down. It was weird, staying in bed with another person. He'd done it before, but not for a long time, and usually only because it was more convenient to stay a few minutes than clean up and go elsewhere.

He yawned himself and realized he felt better than he had in a long time. Perhaps it was finally getting Cyan out of his blood—except that as he fell asleep, all he could think about was doing it all over again.

Einn gasped as he woke, hit by too many sensations to sort them all out. He groaned when he saw Cyan between his legs, sucking him off as if he were under a life or death order to do so. "Sky above," Einn said on another groan. "That's almost as fine as your ass."

Cyan laughed around his cock, eliciting a rough noise from Einn. Flopping back down on the bed, Einn simply enjoyed the ride, admiring Cyan and the way he looked sucking cock, head bowed, dark hair grown out slightly from the severe Rehab cut—

Those eyes, looking up at him through long, dark lashes. It was the last little bit Einn needed to come hard in Cyan's mouth. Cyan took most of it, but a thin line of come trailed from the corner of his mouth. Sitting up, Einn pulled Cyan up and licked it away, then kissed him deeply. He fisted Cyan's cock, began to stroke him off—

And they both jumped as his in-lens flashed, alerting them that the ship was ready and there was a message waiting. Einn ignored it and finished stroking Cyan off, kissing him hard as Cyan came with a soft cry.

Panting, Einn dismissed the annoying alerts. "So much for round three."

Cyan rolled his eyes, but Einn could see he was just as disappointed. "Let's get cleaned up," he said, climbing out of bed and going to the wall to punch in commands for the bath.

Einn sighed and focused on getting clean, on the problem awaiting them when they returned to the ship. Even that was preferable to wondering why in the stars Cyan seemed even more deeply embedded than he had before. The fucking was supposed to fix the problem, not make it worse.

It wasn't a problem he knew how to fix, and he had enough problems.

Einn shook his head, banishing the thoughts, and climbed out of bed to get clean.

# Chapter Eleven

CUSTOM CLASS STARSHIP X-11944654, THE *DRAGONFLY*

"Hello, darling brother."

"Go to hell, Jade."

Jade laughed. He was, Cyan thought irritably, even more beautiful than usual. Jade always looked his best in black. The severity of it brought out his pale skin and the gold of his hair. The long nails that were Jade's pride and joy gleamed with gold paint, matching the pale gold on his lips and the ribbon that secured his braid.

Jade was breathtaking, and Cyan always felt ugly next to him, a last little insult that Jade thrived on the same way he thrived on *all* of Cyan's pain and insecurity. Cyan was sore from Einn's very thorough fucking, but even that solid proof that someone wanted him could not compete against his feeling like a failed clone of his stunning twin brother.

It was a stupid thing to focus on, but it was also the easiest. If he thought about anything else where Jade was concerned, he would start to lose it.

The hardest part of it all was that Jade was the one who had first understood him, the one who knew that Cyan hated the political life. It was Jade who had coaxed him into taking martial arts lessons, pointed him to those things that had stilled Cyan's restlessness. Once upon a time, they had behaved like normal brothers. It had never been an easy, comfortable relationship, but they'd had their own strange bond. Sometimes he thought it all a dream. It might as well have been.

"I have your new assignment," Jade finally said, smile razor sharp and dipped in poison. "He is both scientist and experiment, and the most difficult to obtain. We nearly had him once, but he slipped away due to circumstances no one could have anticipated. You will find him and his match, and capture them."

Images flashed on the screen, and Cyan felt like he was going to throw up. Sean's face filled the screen next to an image of a Draconis. It was the damned Draconis who had ruined everything by bonding with Sean. Cyan's hands balled into fists, and he made himself relax only because he would not lose his temper in front of his brother.

"Mendel Ekard, geneticist and convicted murderer," Jade said. "Patricide, as it happens. His father was a Councilor of the third quad and spoke vehemently for the extermination of the Draconis." He laughed, and Cyan fought a shudder. "His match is Sean Noor, former Rehab guard, mutant magics capable human. Be on guard, because it is suspected that Mendel also travels with this man." Another Draconis flashed on the screen. He was remarkably beautiful, Cyan noted, all cream and gold, features narrow and delicate.

"That's Karmikel Aurum," Lark said, sounding surprised. Cyan looked at him—and drew up short at the look of longing that flitted across Lark's face before it was hidden under his stony mask. "I don't believe it; he dropped out of the stars ages ago. Why would he be with those two?"

Jade shrugged. "Lieutenant Aurum worked as a security consultant for Three Moon Industries; he quit that position two terms ago for reasons unknown. It's believed he was bought out by another corporation. I've no idea which, and I do not care. He's dangerous, as are the other two. You will have to find them first, but I cannot imagine finding an old friend will be a problem for you, will it, brother?"

Cyan said nothing, merely glared at him. Laughing, Jade cut the connection. Heavy silence fell over the bridge, and Cyan sat down before he gave in to the urge to start hitting things. Jade had not even bothered to reiterate all his threats; he knew it wasn't necessary. Cyan would help Einn and Lark kidnap his best friend, or people would die.

He slammed his fist down on the nav console, only barely avoiding the controls themselves. "Stars damn him."

"Agreed," Einn said, glaring as he brought up all the information that Jade had left them.

Cyan could not stand to look at Sean's face, the way he was smiling faintly, unable not to even in an official image. He focused on the two Draconis and his curiosity instead. "How do you know that one—Karmikel, wasn't it?" he asked Lark.

It was Einn who replied, "We crossed paths a couple of times. He's one of the best damn pirate hunters in the stars—or was, anyway. He just up and vanished one day, and no one knew where he went. We half-figured someone had finally managed to kill him, but if that were true, the bastard would have bragged about it long and loud. At which point Lark would have murdered him, because he's always had a bit of a thing—" He broke off with a pained grunt and gave Lark a look that was equal part scowl and pout. "Was that called for?"

"Yes," Lark said with a grunt.

Cyan almost laughed. "So what more do we know about Mendel and Karmikel? How ironic that I have to go after Sean when that was the whole fucking point of my being in space."

"Oh?" Einn said, when Lark shot him one last warning look and stepped away. "Why are you trying to find him?"

Sighing, Cyan replied, "Because his mother is dying and her final wish is to see her son." Silence fell at his words, only the whir of the machinery to keep it from being absolute.

"Cliffs," Einn sighed. "How are we going to get out of this mess? I feel like we're trying to untangle ourselves from Vrill thorn-ivy." Cyan grimaced with agreement. Einn struck the comm station with his fist. "I wish we could just turn the bottom dweller in—he's the Lower Chancellor! He shouldn't be doing this! I don't understand *why* he's doing it."

Cyan stirred at that, because it was a question he should have asked himself already, and being distracted by how much he wanted Einn and how much he hated his brother were not good excuses. "Jade only gets his hands dirty when he wants to hurt someone. He isn't Lower Chancellor at age twenty-nine because he asked please. He threw all three of his predecessors out of office by dragging them into the mud, but getting none on himself."

Lark quirked a brow at him. "How do you know that? People love him; he won the vote for the position by a record-breaking margin. The Star Assembly could find no fault with him, and of course he has the lineage."

"You seem to know an awful lot about it," Cyan said, surprised. "You don't seem the type for politics."

"Politics, no," Lark said, mouth twisting in a cynical smile. "Politicians, yes. They paid well, always pay well, for services rendered. They like to talk, and they'll do it all night with very little encouragement. I learned a lot listening to them mostly because they thought I was too stupid to understand what they were saying." His smile turned into a smirk.

Cyan laughed. "The best politicians are the ones who say nothing at all outside of an official capacity. My father was notorious for being silent, and Jade has that skill. The only person I ever saw match Jade full measure was a man nearly twenty years his senior ... " His mouth twisted with bitter memories and a few sweet.

"They say it's only a matter of time before he becomes High Chancellor."

"That won't happen," Cyan said. "High Chancellor is too restrictive. You only become High Chancellor when you're destined for Grand Chancellor or the Grand Chancellor wants to keep an eye on you. Jade can get away with more as a Lower Chancellor. All he'll do is ensure that someone useful to him is put in the High Chancellor's seat." He turned to look at the nav station, staring at the star course they were on without really seeing it, mind occupied with thoughts of his brother. What was Jade up to? Looking up again, he asked, "You said you kept records on everyone you've kidnapped?"

Einn nodded and moved to the data station, calling up all sorts of files, his in-lens flashing as it transmitted his personal access codes. He put it up on the main screen. "Eleven Draconis and their matches, and seven scientists from all over the IG. If there's a correlation past the obvious, we haven't seen it; the scientists don't even all do the same kind of research."

Cyan looked pensively over the images and data that flashed up on the screen. "They all spoke at the Temperast hearings, one way or another. The scientists, I mean. Three of them actually spoke at the hearings, three contributed research, but were excused from presenting, and one was permitted to give sealed testimony that was read only by the Grand Chancellor, the High Chancellor, and the panel of judges."

"Sealed testimony?" Einn echoed.

"Because giving it publically would have endangered her life," Cyan replied, and indicated the woman in question. "Sarah Cohen is the sister of the High Chancellor, though he was only a Lower Chancellor back then. Their ancestors were the ones who helped develop the Temperast. No one except those I just listed was allowed to read what she contributed to the argument, but it's largely believed she spoke for the prosecution and supported the termination. I haven't spoken to any of the Cohen family for years, but I know the case fractured them badly. But her brother *is* High Chancellor now, and doing well at it. He won't be able to stand against Jade whenever Jade decides to put someone else in that spot, but he's done well enough while he's had it."

Cyan pointed out two more images. "These two were excused due to old age; the journey to Zero would have been far too arduous for them, never mind the rigors of a trial that lasted for two terms. The last, Dr. Bikendi Itzal, was excused because of his magics."

"The way he can kill with a touch, you mean," Einn said. "I had to put gloves on his hands before I could take him."

Cyan nodded. "That's right. It's a strange combination of being half-Telven, half-Kemperast. He's been a subject as often as he's been a scientist. His research was crucial to the entire matter; they say without his contribution, the case may not have been won. I believe they are trying to coax him into the Draconis trial to do the same thing."

Dismissing the scientists, Cyan pulled up the Draconis and their matches. "It's interesting that of the eleven pairs, only two are Coni/Draconis matches. The rest ... it's quite the mix, isn't it? A Vrill, a Hellcat, a Krawl ... It's wild how broadly the Draconis have matched, since they were created just a few generations back. They were never meant to match with anyone except the Coni, and their scale colors have gone beyond the original scope. Then you have Mendel who matched with Sean—nowhere in the Draconis gene structure should it have been possible to create a Draconis who could match with a race that's not even supposed to have magics."

Lark grunted. "It's no mystery to me that genetic research has been outlawed in three of the four quads. I wish they'd outlaw it altogether, before someone develops something worse."

"What could be worse than the Temperast?" Einn asked. "No one has annihilated a race since those things on Kreska were destroyed centuries ago."

Cyan swore as an idea came to him, looking at the array of people who had been taken. "I don't want to know what could be worse. Hopefully we never find out. What we do need to find out is why someone is kidnapping these people. It obviously has to do with the pending trial to decide the fate of the Draconis. But are the kidnappings to impede the trial? To push for their destruction, or for their survival?"

"Does it matter, really?" Einn asked. "Your brother is going to let us die, eventually. Soon, I think. I'm just getting that feeling that there won't be many more serum injections in my future."

"You're not dying!" Cyan snapped. "Once we find Sean, everything will change. I'm not letting Jade kill any of you."

Lark sneered at him and kicked idly at the cabinet below the nav station. "I'd like to know how you're going to obtain this miracle cure. You said yourself it's of Jade's design, and he's the only one who can fix us."

"I don't know yet," Cyan said, "but I'll figure it out. Jade isn't getting away with this. I slipped through his fingers once, I can do it again."

Einn glanced at him, expression unreadable. "I guess if anyone could, it would be his brother."

Cyan smiled tightly. "It doesn't come without cost, slipping free of Jade's hold, but as you said: if anyone could, it'll be me. He won't kill me, just make me wish I was dead."

"He's on Zero, more than likely, and if not, then some planet far from here," Einn said. "He's nowhere close to us, I'm pretty sure. That would be stupid given the way he's blackmailing us. You make it sound like he's going to snatch you out of thin air."

"Jade couldn't touch me before, not when I was out of his quad and a Rehab guard. Now, however, I'm missing, presumed dead, but actually consorting with criminals. Jade can do whatever he wants to do me; the only question is when he'll do it." He abruptly turned and left the bridge, wishing the *Dragonfly* were not such a small ship. He felt as though there was nowhere to go, as if he was trapped all over again. Tied to his bed. Tied out in the yard. Left to starve and dehydrate, bake under the sun and freeze under the moon.

Beaten, humiliated, imprisoned ... and Jade's cold laughter, his pretty poison smiles, the way he charmed everyone else while breaking his twin brother. Cyan hated most that Jade's abuse had worked: he would always wonder how different things might have been if he had been standing with his family as he should have been instead of sneaking off to steal kisses. His mother had begged him not to wander off, and his father had given him one of those looks, but Cyan hadn't been interested in anything but the pretty mouth of a young man whose name he could no longer remember.

If he had been there, like he'd been told, as he should have been, would he have wound up as broken as Jade? Or could he have saved his brother?

Cyan finally found himself in the holding cell he hadn't visited since Einn had freed him. What was he doing here? Footsteps made him whip around and bring his hands up for a fight—but on seeing Einn in the doorway, he tried to relax. "Sorry," he said, feeling stupid.

"You're fine," Einn replied, cocking his head. "Well, you're not fine, not really, but I won't take it personally if you want to hit me again. You've got a mean punch; you may yet crack my bones."

The words were almost enough to make Cyan smile. "Sorry to storm off."

Einn shrugged and strode into the cell, crowding into Cyan's space and forcing him up against the wall. He towered over him in a way that should have been threatening, or at least annoying—but Cyan only found it oddly comforting and fought an urge to lean into him. Einn was a good time, even if Cyan shouldn't indulge, but that was all he was. Cyan wasn't cut out for serious shit, and Einn was literally incapable, even pretending for two seconds that Cyan wanted serious.

Which he didn't. They barely knew each other. Cyan was a former Lord of Zero turned Rehab, and Einn was a pirate. When their fucked up adventure finally ended, they'd go their separate ways and never look back. Serious wasn't even an option.

That didn't stop him from leaning into the touch when Einn touched his face, cautiously at first, then more firmly when Cyan didn't recoil. His fingers were long, and Cyan should have been used to that by now, but it always startled him how much further Einn could reach, how much further his touch could go. He dragged his eyes up and met Einn's gold gaze, so vivid against his light gray skin, the paler gold of his hair. "You don't have to concern yourself with me, pirate."

"I know, and I keep trying not to, but then I keep doing it anyway," Einn replied, looking as lost as Cyan felt. "I wish I knew why."

Cyan nodded, knowing how he felt and probably hating it just as much. He'd thought that bout in the room they'd rented would scratch an itch, finally get Einn out of his system. Instead, he'd woken up wanting Einn even more. As hard as he tried to dislike him, to keep a distance, it seemed every new thing he learned just made him like Einn more.

Cyan wished he knew why, too, so he could fix the problem and regain his equilibrium. He was going to need every last bit of himself when he finally confronted Jade. He didn't need to be distracted by Einn, no matter how fascinating and sexy and ... and Cyan didn't know what, he just wished it wasn't.

But it was hard to think about anything else when those long, thin fingers were stroking his skin in an attempt at comfort, something Cyan just wasn't used to. Hard to focus his thoughts when he could smell Einn, could feel his body heat, when Einn was blocking out the rest of the world exactly the way Cyan wanted. Sighing softly, he finally gave in to the urge to move closer, to reach up and wrap his arms around Einn, greedily attacking his mouth and wrapping his legs around Einn's waist as Einn hefted him up and braced him against the wall. Sex wasn't the smart thing, but it was distracting and about the only thing Cyan felt he understood at the moment.

# Chapter Twelve

**UNREGISTERED MERCHANT CLASS STARSHIP**

Sean frowned as he examined the bridge of *The Argus,* the captured captain, and other crew. "We've been duped."

"Yes," Mendel agreed lightly. "There's no way this is the ship behind the kidnappings."

"It was a dead match," Sean muttered. Absently using his magics to heal a cut on his arm, he moved to the ship's master console at the captain's seat and pulled out his datapad, quickly synching and cracking the security codes with only a few minutes' work. "Subpar computer work," he commented, and began to work his way through the information that practically fell into his lap. "Someone hacked them, rewrote their logs and registries. I don't get why, though."

Karmikel snorted and kicked the seated captain in the thigh. "Who hacked your ship?" When the captain remained silent, Karmikel kicked him again, harder. "We can play this game all night, Smoke, or you can tell me what's what. Who'd you tussle with that gave you that head wound, and then hacked your system?"

"Hood's rock spider and that Helioran slut he ran with," Smoke said sullenly. "Should have killed them when I had the chance."

Karmikel nodded. "No doubt, but you were always too cocky to last forever."

"You never caught me."

"I don't waste my time on the small jobs, Smoke. People paid me to go after pros, not amateurs. If you're what they consider pro these days, I'm glad I got out of the business." Karmikel drew his stunner and knocked Smoke out before he could reply. Holstering the stunner, he knelt and double-checked Smoke's pulse, then turned to Sean, and asked, "Got any new information for us?"

Sean pursed his lips, eyes on his data screen, in-lens flashing as he worked. "Whoever did this knew what he was doing and knew not to waste time hiding his work overmuch. He knew it would be found, and just made it good enough to buy time. The information he planted lines up too neatly with exactly what we're looking for. I think Adalsteinn and Lark were behind this hack."

"To buy time to get away since by now they must know who Cyan is?" Mendel asked, and when Sean nodded, continued, "Now we've got proof that they did it, and we also know now that they were on the *Dragonfly*. Was the risk of revealing that worth buying time?"

"Guess that depends on whether or not we can find them," Sean said. He disconnected his datapad and stowed it in its holster on his thigh. "We should get back to our ship and figure out the next step; there's nothing more this ship can tell us."

Karmikel nodded in agreement, checking over the cuffs holding the crew captive one last time. "Winter said he was sending a ship into the area to arrest them. We should be gone before it gets here." As if on cue, their in-lens lit up with a communication from *the Brilliant*. "Ship approaching," Karmikel grunted. "Auths, all right—the *Scythe.* Winter wasn't lying; we need to be gone. If the *Scythe* spots us, they'll Heartstone us."

Sean rolled his eyes as Karmikel and Mendel walked over to him, but didn't comment; only took hold of both of them as they reached him and teleported them all back to their ship. On the *Brilliant,* he settled into his seat on the bridge to upload and begin analyzing the collected data.

"We're clear," Karmikel said some time later, and Sean looked up, glancing at the console and seeing an hour had passed. "Winter says they were taken into custody, and the *Scythe* was instructed not to look a gift horse in the mouth. What have you learned, Sean?"

"Nothing good," Sean said, frowning as he looked over his data again. "These guys have connections—serious connections. I'm only looking at the data that the unregistered ship logged while it was hacking the *Dragonfly*, and I can tell you they have the sorts of things they shouldn't."

Mendel asked, "Like what?"

"Like I don't know exactly, but I recognize enough of it to know some of these number strings are high level IG-issue. These guys have serious government clearance, unless I'm sorely mistaken. They're fractured, because the hack didn't finish—" Sean broke off and transmitted it all to the main screen. "Here and here," he said, pointing to two lines of numbers. "These are IG pass codes for something. They're similar to what we get on Rehab, the only reason I recognized them at all."

"They're merchant licenses," Karmikel said. "Zero class licenses at that, meaning they have permission to trade everywhere without needing to get special permits for certain planets. Not entirely unusual for merchants, especially in-lens merchants who might sell military-grade in-lens. Still ... " Karmikel frowned. "Can you pick out anything else?"

"Something that looks like a light gate protocol, maybe?" Sean pulled it up. "I've only ever light-jumped on public ships; I don't really know what they look like, but this seemed to be like what you've talked about before."

Karmikel grunted. "Yeah, that's a light jump protocol. Stars damn them." He scrubbed at his face, then punched buttons on the main comm. A couple of minutes later, Winter appeared on the main screen. "They have inside help," Karmikel said without preamble. "Deep inside help. We were also tricked—Adalsteinn isn't with the pirates; he's on the *Dragonfly*."

"Show me what you've got."

At Karmikel's gesture, Sean obediently transmitted all the information they had managed to get. Winter was silent for several long minutes as he read through it all. His expression steadily moved from somber to angry. "Yes, it would seem they do have inside help," he said at last. "This is all the information you have?"

Sean nodded. "Yes. I'm sorry there's not more—"

"Do not be," Winter interrupted, smiling tiredly. "There is more here than you might think. Information embedded in the information; it only takes the right expert to extract it. I happen to have such an expert on staff and should have the identity of the leak in a few days. What are your plans now?"

"Can you trace the *Dragonfly?*" Karmikel asked.

"I will try, but if these codes originate where I suspect, then no, we will not be able to trace it. Your best chance for following the *Dragonfly* is to follow where it makes port. You learned nothing from the pirates?"

"They attacked the *Dragonfly* for parts, got their asses kicked," Karmikel said.

Mendel added, "They knew Adalsteinn and Vallant, so there is no doubt now that they are definitely who we are hunting. They made no mention of Cyan, but if he's a prisoner, they wouldn't."

Winter nodded. "I will let you know what I learn as soon as I learn it. Find the *Dragonfly,* keep me apprised." The screen went dark.

"This just keeps getting more and more complicated," Sean sighed, and swiveled his chair around to activate his work station again, pulling back the information he'd transferred to the main screen. "Let's see if the *Dragonfly* has hit any other ports recently, and if there's a pattern to all their other stops."

"We should head back to base for a time," Mendel said abruptly. "We could stand to be off ship for more than a couple of hours, and there are more resources there."

"The ship could use real work, too," Karmikel conceded. "We're close to Kreska from here; it can't hurt to rest on real land for a few days." He bent over his console and began typing furiously.

Mendel nodded, and said, "I will be in my lab. I am still hoping to figure out what exactly they are hoping to achieve with all these kidnappings. But if Winter can now figure out who 'they' are, perhaps my efforts are superfluous. All the same. Call if you need me."

Sean watched him go, disappointed that Mendel did not even look his way. Stifling a sigh, he went back to work, slowly pulling up every scrap of information he could find on the *Dragonfly*, using codes Winter had given him to pull up its registry history.

For several minutes, the only sounds on the bridge were the hum and whir of machinery and the occasional rustle of clothes. Sean jumped when Karmikel abruptly said, "You *do* know he's in love with you, right?"

Scowling at all the data he had just accidentally deleted, Sean recalled it, then turned around and shifted his glare to Karmikel. "What?"

Karmikel just met the glare with that half-amused, half-sneering look of his. "I don't know that I can put it any plainer. He does love you, that's probably why he's making such a mess of it all." Sean frowned, then turned back around and resumed typing. He'd barely gotten two words down before Karmikel continued, "You should ask about his family. It would explain why he's so aggravating."

Sean slammed his hands down on his workstation. "Why do *you* know so much, and since when do you care?"

"Mendel was my partner well before you appeared," Karmikel replied. "I was the one who set up an escape plan after he was convicted—the escape plan *you* ruined, and we nearly didn't get away because of it. I don't like working with strangers, that's why I know so much. It's a policy you should try taking up. There'd be a lot less sighing and arguing between the two of you. I always cared. Who the fuck else is going to when nearly every star in the IG wants us exterminated?" He threw his hands up and went back to work.

Sean sighed and stood up, leaving the bridge and heading upstairs to Mendel's lab. When he stepped inside, Mendel was sitting at his work station in the corner, clearly sifting through articles and journals, and other such research documents. He looked up at the sound of footsteps and stared at Sean in surprise. "Is something wrong?"

"I think you and I have been doing *everything* wrong."

Mendel went still, then made a face. "What did I do this time?"

"I said we—more or less. I do mean *we*." Mendel just stared blankly. Sean almost smiled, because Mendel really did just look lost. Stepping in closer, so he was just barely brushing against Mendel's arm, Sean tilted Mendel's face up, then bent and kissed him. Mendel jerked in surprise, but Sean held his head fast in both hands and kissed him again. Mendel made a rough noise, and then one hand rested lightly on Sean's hip as Mendel turned in his seat to get a better angle.

After a moment, the hand on his hip slid around his waist. Sean shifted to accommodate their odd positioning, only to wind up hitting his foot against the chair and upsetting his balance, tumbling to land in Mendel's lap. He broke the kiss with a laugh, then dove right back in to another. Mendel tasted sweet, like the Helior cherries he liked so much. For someone who seemed so uncertain much of the time, he certainly kissed like a pro. Sean finally drew back, licking his lips. "Stars, why haven't we done that sooner?"

"I believe the main reason was that I work too much and am not very pleasant about it," Mendel said, looking somewhat stunned by the kisses and the way Sean was settled on his lap.

Sean smiled. "I bite my tongue too much and overreact when I finally do speak, and then ignore you. As methods go, there are a few flaws."

Mendel returned the smile with a faint one of his own. "Flaws all around?"

In reply, Sean kissed him again, wanting to feel that cute half-smile he'd never seen before. "We're communicating now, at least."

"I do not know that this is communicating, per se, but I do prefer it to you punching me."

Sean winced. "I'm sorry—"

"Don't. I deserved it."

"I made you an offer the other day. You never took me up on it, but you're certainly kissing me back right now, so I can't think you were disinterested."

Mendel shook his head. "I was afraid of screwing up. I'm good at that. Really good at it, if you take into account that the last time I argued with someone, I killed him."

Sean kissed him again, soft and reassuring, hating the anguish in Mendel's voice and face. "I don't get it—clearly it was self-defense, if your father attacked you first. That should have factored into the trial and gotten you a much lighter sentence."

"You really don't know anything about it, do you?" Mendel said.

Making a face, feeling like an idiot, Sean said, "No. I never watch the news. Hell, I didn't even know what a Draconis was until we got your arrival report. I deal with crime nearly every day; when I'm not working, I don't go watching the news for more. After I wound up matched to you, it felt like snooping to hear it from someone else. If I was going to learn about it, I was going to hear it from you."

Mendel smiled at him, shy and pleased, and nothing like the cold, aggressive workaholic that had stressed Sean to no end. "You said that before; I'd forgotten 'til now."

"So tell me what happened," Sean said quietly, carding a hand through Mendel's long hair. He slid off Mendel's lap and leaned against his work station, feet stretched out between Mendel's. It wouldn't be hard at all to move forward, straddle Mendel properly, and better explore his mouth.

Maybe in a bit. Serious first, then fun.

Drawing a deep breath, Mendel let it out slowly, and then said, "Ekard is my mother's name. My father's name was Martin Cohen."

The name jolted through Sean, and he stared at Mendel dumbfounded. "You—you can't mean Cohen as in *High Chancellor* Cohen."

"My uncle," Mendel said.

Sean could only stare for a moment. "Now I'm astonished you only got a life sentence. They could have gotten execution approved easily for murdering the High Chancellor's brother."

Mendel hesitated, then replied, "I think Winter had a hand in that, though he's never brought it up. I wasn't—still am not—really part of IA. I was just consulting for them on some illegal experiments, helping them catch all parties. Karmikel was my contact and my partner when we were afield. We had been working on it for a term and a half when everything went wrong.

"I was home visiting my mother and found out that my father—part of the ambassador assembly on Coni—was supporting the annihilation of the Draconis. He should not have been involved at all, but there was a leak and word got out. I lost it. I barely remember that entire day." His face shut down, eyes dark and hard as he stared at the floor. Sean reached out and cupped his cheek, and Mendel turned into the touch, eyes sliding shut. "I took it when he wouldn't acknowledge me, when he shunned my mother. But to declare that we would be better off dead ... It was a mess. I was rushed through a mockery of a trial, the entire scandal kept as quiet as possible. Then you. Then we were assigned to figure out the kidnappings."

"Stars," Sean said. "They really *will* execute us when this is all over—they don't have a choice."

Mendel made a face. "I just want to know why he wanted the Draconis wiped out. It's especially strange when the High Chancellor vehemently opposes Heartstone's Law. He's always supported the continued existence of the Draconis. He'd never allow his brother to tarnish his political image by opposing him that way, or perhaps I just don't understand politics."

"No, you've hit that mark precisely. It's strange they would be on opposite sides."

"There is also the fact that the Cohen family is famous in the arena of genetic research," Mendel continued. "My father's ancestors were heavily involved in the creation of the Temperast. That's why—" He cut himself off, but it wasn't hard for Sean to silently finish the sentence. Mendel had gone into genetics in hopes of drawing his father's attention, of binding himself to a family that did not want him.

"It does seem strange your father would be for something your uncle is against. Did they not get along?"

Mendel shrugged. "They seemed to get on well the two occasions I saw them together."

"So the Cohens helped create the Temperast?" Sean asked, grimacing.

"Yes," Mendel said. "Everyone knows only terrible things about the Temperast, but they were a marvel of genetic artistry. It took decades to get as far as they did, and it is a tragedy that something meant to be good took such a horrible turn. It was a blow to the Cohen reputation when they were exterminated. They have mostly recovered now, but they will probably never enjoy the levels of prestige they once did."

Sean pursed his lips. "Maybe they think by supporting the Draconis, they'll regain more of that lost ground? Not to mention the permits they'd recover to help with further experiments that may be required as a condition of the Draconis' continued survival."

Mendel nodded, frowning in that way of his that said he was lost in thought. He went abruptly still. "How did I miss that?" he asked. "Stars take it!"

"Miss what?" Sean asked, hastily getting out of Mendel's way as he all but threw himself at his work station. He began typing furiously, lost in his work as quickly as that. Sean smiled faintly, brushed a strand of hair from Mendel's face, and left him to it.

Returning to the bridge, he sat down and resumed his own work. "So are you two done moping, now?" Karmikel asked.

"Yeah. I think Mendel may have cracked the motive for the kidnappings. I'm sure he'll let us know in a few hours when he's checked, double-checked, and quadruple-checked."

Karmikel rolled his eyes. "So all it took to solve the damned mystery was Mendel getting fucked?"

"No fucking took place, not that it's any of your business," Sean replied, amused.

Smirking, Karmikel said, "Well, then, I guess you'll know what your duty is when he hits a snag in the research. We'll reach Kreska in twenty-seven hours."

"Copy that," Sean replied, and settled into his work.

# Chapter Thirteen

**PLANET 11181911 (KRESKA), HEARTSTONE TAVERN & INN**

"Thanks," Cyan said, taking the beer Einn pushed across the table toward him. Instead of drinking it, however, he only traced the rim of the glass with his finger. Einn frowned, but said nothing. He never knew what to say, no matter how hard he tried to figure it out. Comfort wasn't something he did. Distraction he could do, but even sex only went so far.

Einn hated it—hated that he wanted to comfort, hated that he didn't know how, hated that the problem existed. With each passing day, the fierce Cyan he'd known in the bar, cuffed to a wall, was sinking below the surface of a tense, anxious, quiet man he scarcely knew at all. Einn wanted to fix it, wanted to make Cyan smile again. He had no idea *why*, though; he'd never felt such a compulsion before, not even with Hood or Lark.

Dealing with Cyan felt a lot like going on his first solo climb, except he couldn't see his handholds, couldn't feel them, and had no idea what would happen if he lost his grip and fell. "Where's Lark?" he finally asked, scowling moodily at his beer. Kreskans made shitty beer; he might as well have been drinking water.

"Still working on getting us moon access," Cyan replied, and finally took a sip of beer, grimacing. "This tastes like shit."

Einn smiled. "All they had." That they could sell legally, anyway, and he wasn't in the mood to get the good stuff, even if the legal stuff tasted like they'd scraped dirt off the floor and mixed it with water.

Cyan made a face. "Lark seemed pretty confident he could get us access. Didn't say much more than that, but you know Lark." Einn nodded, amused that Cyan seemed to know Lark, too, after only a matter of days. It was far too easy to forget the way they had begun, and for brief moments, to forget their motivations.

"So what shall we do in the mean time? Were you able to learn anything about what your brother is up to?"

Shaking his head, Cyan said, "Science isn't Jade's thing. Politics are Jade's game. If he is involving himself in this, there is a political agenda beneath it all, but I can't deduce it by victims. I've tried everything I can think of, but nothing political pans out. I can't even tell which side he's on, though I know publically he supports the continued survival of the Draconis. If I know Jade, which unfortunately I do, no one will know what he's doing until it's done. Like I've said before, only one man is Jade's equal, and he is two decades older."

"Who is that?" Einn asked, genuinely curious.

Cyan hesitated, then said, "Pyotr Kavalerov."

Einn blinked. "Kavalerov—that's the name of the Grand Chancellor. He's a lot more than twenty years older than Jade."

"Not the Grand Chancellor, that's Arkadii Kavalerov. Pyotr is his nephew, the son of his late brother."

"I didn't know the Grand Chancellor had a nephew," Einn replied, and took another swallow of beer. "Then again, I couldn't tell you anything about the guy, not even if he's married, though I think he is?"

Cyan laughed. "He is. Lady Veronika is very sweet. Not many outside of Zero know of Pyotr, and if they do know of him, they don't know much. He's very low key, despite being as powerful and ... well, he and Jade are a lot alike in strange ways: intense, too smart, too *clever*, and while I wouldn't call Pyotr insane, there are plenty on Zero who would. He is Commander of the Authority Special Forces."

"Stars! I can't imagine it's easy to become leader of the toughest bastards in space."

"Toughest?" Cyan sneered. "I can kick the ass of any Auth, even those prissy special forces."

"Second toughest," Einn corrected. "Sorry. So Jade's equal is the Special Forces Commander—that makes sense."

Cyan's mouth tilted in a smile that made Einn feel unsettled. That was a Zero smile, if ever he'd seen one; the smile of a man who knew a cave complex by heart, knew all the ways to go, what routes to take, and how to make people go through them the way he wanted. Cyan might claim to want nothing to do with Zero and that he would do poorly there, but Einn suspected he would be damned good at it. "Not just that, though that would almost be enough. Only a very select group of people know that he is also head of Internal Affairs."

Einn choked on his beer. "There's no such thing as Internal Affairs! Everyone knows that's just a conspiracy theory; the IG doesn't need a special, secret group of people to supervise it."

"Don't they?" Cyan said with a return of that cynical smile. "My brother certainly is not being watched closely enough. Wouldn't it be useful for a group of secret operatives to be working on this kidnapping, tracing it back to its source?"

"I don't believe it," Einn said. "Next you'll tell me they're all magics capable." Cyan laughed and drank his beer. Einn stared at him. "You're serious. Magics capable beings aren't allowed in *any* government position."

"Which would be why they're not officially anything, but they're there," Cyan replied.

Finishing his own beer, Einn shoved their glasses away and just continued to stare at Cyan for several minutes. "You shouldn't be telling me all this."

"I trust you," Cyan said quietly, speaking to the table. "I don't know why, but I do." Einn couldn't think of a reason he should either. Nor could he seem to come up with a reply; breathing properly had abruptly consumed all of his attention. Cyan looked up, eyes dark. "Einn—if something happens to me—"

"Huh? Like what? Nothing is going to happen to anyone, except maybe me getting arrested, and I'm not letting the Auths get me *now.*"

Mouth twisting into that Zero smile again, Cyan said, "It's Jade—something will always happen. If it does—I have no right to ask, I know, we barely know each other, but I *do* trust you. If something happens, would you get Sean back to his mother? I—"

"I'll do it," Einn said, meeting his gaze. He had never given a damn about anyone's eyes before. Stars, he couldn't even say with any certainty the color of Lark's eyes. But he thought he would always remember Cyan's, pale gray and blue-flecked. "I won't need to, because nothing is going to happen, but I will."

The smile Cyan gave him then ruined Einn's ability to think right alongside his ability to breathe. What in the stars was wrong with him? He shook himself, called for more shitty beer, and changed the subject. "So I guess you go back to Rehab when this is all over?"

"I don't know," Cyan said. "I suspect I'll be on Zero for at least a little while."

Einn fought disappointment. It would have been one thing to stop over on Mars, but was quite another to go anywhere near Zero. Assuming, of course, that Cyan would want to see him again after it was all over. "Well, if you ever want to give up a life of law-abiding and take up piracy—"

He was interrupted when Lark abruptly appeared at the table, sat down, and stole Einn's fresh beer. Lark downed half of it in one go, ignoring the way Einn glared at him. Couldn't he have waited ten more minutes to show back up? "What's your problem?" Lark finally asked.

"Nothing."

Lark rolled his eyes, finished the beer, then said, "Good news is, I've got us passage to the moon. Bad news is that we can't go until day after tomorrow."

Cyan made a face. "Why so long? Why is it so damned difficult to get to the moon here?"

"Smugglers," Einn and Lark said together, then Lark continued, "Kreska is supremely uptight, everyone knows that. Even the Vrill have nothing on a locked-down Kreskan. But the Kreskans are also kinda two-faced. Their import laws are the strictest in the IG to preserve the 'sanctity and identity of the planet' or whatever."

"But they probably want all the perks they say they don't," Cyan said.

"Exactly," Lark confirmed. "Kreska has two things in abundance: prudes and smugglers."

"I don't see what all this has to do with the moon."

Einn explained, "Kreska's moon used to be a research and military facility, back when Kreska actually had a military. Only a small portion of the planet is inhabited, and it's one of the few planets that developed a planetary identity long before they joined the IG."

"I remember that," Cyan said. "I studied it in school. Mars had a huge problem with planetary identity. It took a good twenty-five terms for the colonies to really settle into the idea of planetary leaders and send reps to the Star Assembly. Some planets, like Trax and Salath, still have problems."

"Right," Lark replied. "Kreska never had those problems. They're also out of the way enough that no one cares about the fact they walk around with sticks shoved proudly up their neither regions. Traffic around here is too slow for pirates to bother, and honestly, even if there was more traffic, picking on a Kreskan is like kicking a callio."

"I get what you're saying, but what in the stars is a callio?"

Lark frowned in annoyance. "Translators skip over the stupidest things." His in-lens flashed, and then he pulled out his datapad and brought up an image before flipping it to Cyan. He stared at it thoughtfully, then brought up an image of his own and flipped it back. "Looks like a dog."

"Sort of," Lark agreed, studying Cyan's image. He tucked the datapad away again, and said, "Anyway—Kreska is a pass through spot for smugglers. Mostly alcohol, I think, but they'll smuggle almost anything. I think flesh and Soul are the only two things you'll never see pass through here. The moon is a popular place for them to hide their shit between moves, though you won't hear any natives admit to knowing anything about it."

Cyan made a face. "So there's lot of bootleg around here, and I still get shitty beer."

Einn smiled. "I can get good stuff, but it would have drawn attention."

"Yeah, I know," Cyan said, waving the words aside. "So we have to wait until these smugglers are going up to the moon?"

Lark nodded. "Right. If they make too many runs, the few token Auths around here who actually give a damn would notice, so we're waiting for their next scheduled run. Once we land, we'll have three hours to find Sean and the others, otherwise we're stuck there until the smugglers return or we can no longer breathe. I'll let you figure out which is likely to happen first." He snagged Cyan's beer and drank it down.

"So what are we supposed to do for nearly two days?" Cyan asked. "Admire the scenery?"

Rolling his eyes, Lark replied, "You two don't seem to have a problem keeping yourselves occupied. Don't whine to the man *not* getting laid, 'cause he won't feel sorry for you. This beer tastes like shit. I'm going to go find a decent place for food and drink. I'll see you ringers later."

Cyan scowled at his retreating form. "I know that time he purposely used a word that wouldn't translate. What in the stars is a ringer?"

"No idea," Einn said. "What do you think Jade is going to do? I should probably be braced for it if I'm going to be of any help."

"He'll take me and try to kill the rest of you. I won't let that happen, but the price of your lives will be me."

"No."

"You don't know Jade—"

"The man has been blackmailing me for a term! He poisoned me! After he slaughtered my crew—" Einn pushed the memories away. The fire, the smoke, the way he'd barely gotten into gear in time to avoid being killed by space itself. The bodies.

Jade, beautiful, cold, smelling like something sweet and sharp. His hard smile with that edge to it that made Einn's blood run cold. Those who spent too much time in the deepest, darkest caves had that kind of smile. Too much of that sort of deep dark always broke a man.

"He tied me down," Cyan said quietly. "Left me in the private garden too far away for anyone to hear my screams for help. He left me there, naked and alone, for days. All day the sun burned, and at night it turned cold, and every day he came and tried to make me see his reason, to make me join him. When he finally let me go, as soon as I could move properly again, I ran."

"Why is he still free?" Einn demanded. "He should be locked up!"

"No way to prove it, and at that time, Zero was mired in enough tragedy and controversy. It would not have helped anything. Jade is a good Chancellor, which is the irony in all of this."

Einn glared. "He's not a good anything! Look at what he's done to us!"

"Jade would be even worse if I had tried to get him locked up, trust me."

"If you say so."

Cyan sighed and raked a hand through his hair, then abruptly stood up. "I'm going for a walk." He walked off without waiting for a reply, leaving Einn alone at the table.

"The least I could get for all this is a decent fucking beer," Einn groused, transmitting points to the table scanner. He left the bar, and then lingered outside, not certain where Cyan had gone.

"You're Fornarian, right?"

Einn grimaced at the way she mispronounced it, saying the 'nar' syllable like 'bar' instead of 'bare', but said, "Yes, I am." She looked innocuous enough, but Einn knew a hooker when he saw one, even on Kreska where they pretended they were all pure as cave crystal. She looked him up and down appraisingly, and he supposed he passed muster because her demeanor shifted slightly.

"Hear you guys are a good time."

"Yes," Einn said, "but not me, I'm taken. He just left ahead of me, did you see him?"

She cocked her head. "Weird. Not that military type that just stomped out?"

Einn nodded, "Yes, that's him. Where did he go?"

She smirked at him, saying nothing, but finally relented just as Einn had decided to go for his stunner. "Oh, don't panic. He went towards the woods, that way."

Einn took off in the direction she pointed, not sure what he was doing or why—

He'd told her he was taken. Einn tripped as his own words registered, nearly falling face first on the ground. He grimaced. 'I'm taken' was a phrase he'd picked up after leaving home, and he'd heard it any number of times. Not the sort of phrase he'd ever used himself, though, and he shouldn't have been using it then.

Frowning, Einn continued toward the woods at a slower pace, fingers twitching again for his stunner. He had no love of wild land, even on a boring planet like Kreska. He forced himself to relax because it *was* Kreska—a trio of pirates was probably the most excitement they'd seen for terms.

It wasn't hard to pick up Cyan's trail once he entered the woods; city types were so easy to follow once they left their cities. Einn finally spotted him well into the trees, sitting alongside a creek and idly tossing in stones and bits of stick.

Cyan snapped to his feet when he heard Einn approach, braced for attack. As always, Einn was impressed by how quickly Cyan could move. It wasn't something he had ever really seen before. Plenty of people who could move quickly, but no one like Cyan. Then again, the stories of Rehab guards were nigh on legendary in the stars. It wasn't the cells that kept the prisoners in—it was the Rehabbers.

Cyan relaxed when he saw it was Einn. "Did you need something?"

"I didn't mean to upset you," Einn said. "You're right. I don't know Jade like you do. If—if you say that it's better he's still free, I believe you."

"Forget it. Jade should be locked up. He should be put in solitary confinement at the very least. But if someone actually tried to do it ... " He trailed off and just shook his head, sitting back down. "You didn't have to come out here; I wasn't upset with you, not really. I'm upset about Jade."

Einn snorted and sat down beside him, then stretched out in the grass, boots not quite reaching the water. "Yeah, I'd much rather be in that dingy bar drinking shitty beer than out here with you."

Cyan went still, and Einn inwardly cringed at his own words. Stars, he really was losing his mind. Cyan looked at him. "You shouldn't want anything to do with me."

"I know. I keep trying to remind myself of that."

"I'm a runaway noble with a crazy, sadistic brother who will do anything to make me miserable. When this is over, I'll be on Rehab or back on Zero. That's just the start of reasons to avoid me."

Einn countered, "I'm Fornarian, and that's enough for anyone. I'm a pirate, a kidnapper, and if I'm really lucky, I'll come out of all this a fugitive, but more than likely I'll wind up dead or arrested. I'm no prize myself."

Cyan sighed, and Einn agreed wholeheartedly. He reached out and tugged, bringing Cyan down to sprawl on top of him. He splayed a hand across Cyan's back, the feel of Cyan against him already so familiar and somehow reassuring. "So are there any good reasons for this?"

"No," Cyan said softly, even as he rested his head on Einn's chest. "Just can't seem to help myself."

"Yeah," Einn agreed, and stared up at the trees, the bits of yellow-green sky peeking through. He listened to the sound of Cyan's breathing.

He jerked slightly when Cyan broke the silence. "So why did you leave Fornar?"

"I thought the stars were beautiful," Einn said before he thought. But it was the honest answer. "Fornar is ... I love my home, but it was never enough."

"Never enough," Cyan echoed. "That sounds right."

They lapsed into silence again. It should have been uncomfortable, and it was a little, but not nearly as much as Einn would have expected. He liked the quiet, the feel of Cyan against him, able to feel it every time he drew breath. It felt like they were the only two around for miles.

Cyan lifted his head, and Einn didn't even hesitate, just drew him in for a kiss, slow and sweet. He was, he suspected, a fool. He also did not care. "Cyan—"

Before he could try again to ask about seeing each other when it all over, his in-lens flashed with an urgent alert from Lark. Activating his earpiece, Einn barked, "What? I will throw you to the bottom—"

"Spare me your weird, rock spider threats," Lark cut in. "Get your asses back to the tavern because they're here."

Einn frowned. "Who? The smugglers"

"Sean and Mendel! Get here now!"

Lark cut out, and Einn scrambled to his feet, pulling Cyan up with him. "Your friend is here, apparently."

Cyan's mouth tightened into a thin line. "Let's get this over with and hope we all come out of it alive."

# Chapter Fourteen

PLANET 11181911 (KRESKA), HEARTSTONE TAVERN & INN

Adrenaline pumped through Cyan's blood, every part of him on high alert. It was happening—whatever *it* was. The moment was upon them and there'd be no going back. Cyan could *feel* it, that nausea in his gut, the cold shiver down his spine, a dryness in the back of his throat. He could feel Jade's presence like a perversion of a lover's touch.

He walked with Einn back into town, fighting an urge to grab him in a desperate bid for comfort. He had survived the past eleven years on his own; he would not undo five and a half terms of work by acting weak now. It was time to think about what was to come and not the way Einn had kicked his heart to a furious pace long before Lark had contacted them.

What was he doing with Einn? Whatever it was, he shouldn't be doing it, because there was no future in it. "Around back," Einn said, snapping Cyan back to where his thoughts should have been. They looped around the tavern, Einn taking the lead, and slipped in a back entrance. At the end of the hallway, Lark leaned against a wall, waiting for them. When they reached him, he pushed off the wall and led the way up two flights of stairs, then down another set of hallways to a room all the way at the back of the building.

He drew his stunner and gestured to Cyan and Einn. When they were all ready, he blew the lock, and Cyan slipped inside, leading the way into the room. Sean, Mendel, and the other Draconis—Karmikel—stared at him in shock. "Cyan!" Sean cried out and bolted toward him—and bellowed when Mendel grabbed him.

"What's with the pirates?" Mendel asked, as Karmikel lifted a stunner—

And screamed in pain. Behind Cyan, Einn did the same. Cyan whipped around, saw Einn on his knees, holding his head. He knew that scream, that agony—but there was no way—

"You son of a bitch!" Karmikel snarled, raising his stunner again and thumbing it to a more dangerous level of power. One hand was still pressed to his head as he glared murder at Einn. "I will *kill* you."

"You can't," barked Mendel, letting go of Sean to grab Karmikel and take his stunner. Instead, he stumbled back onto the bed, reeling from a punch to his jaw. "If you kill him, Karmikel, you'll die too!"

Karmikel snarled, "I don't care! I did not manage to go unmatched for thirty-two years only to match *now* to a fucking pirate!" He screamed in rage and aimed the stunner—

—and dropped like a rock when Lark knocked him out from behind. Catching Karmikel up before he hit the ground, Lark laid him out on one of the beds. Cyan's brows rose at the uncharacteristic gesture, but he said nothing. "What in the stars just happened?" Einn demanded. "My head is killing me, and the rest of me feels like I took a hard fall a couple of days ago."

"You and Karmikel just matched," Sean said. "Cyan—what is going on?"

"A lot," Cyan sighed.

Lark added, "It just got more complicated. I cannot believe you *matched*, Einn! With him, of all people! Can't you stop causing us more trouble? Don't we have enough?"

"How was I supposed to know that would happen?" Einn snapped.

Mendel broke into the fight, asking, "So you are Adalsteinn?"

"Call me Adalsteinn again and I will break your face," Einn snapped. "The name is Einn."

Despite everything, Cyan laughed. "Adalsteinn?"

"Shut up."

A banging on the door made them all jump, and Sean swore softly as he went to deal with the inn staff. He left the rest of them standing around, awkwardly staring at one another. "You couldn't just knock?" Mendel finally asked.

Cyan made a face. "No time to talk. We needed to grab and *go*." They still needed to grab and go, because that feeling in his gut was getting stronger.

"I do not understand—you were taken hostage. Why are you cooperating with pirates?"

"It's complicated," Cyan repeated. "We'll explain everything later. I don't even know where to start."

"How about the reason ... " Mendel trailed off just as a shiver of fear lanced up Cyan's spine. Turning slowly around, Cyan watched as Sean was thrown onto the bed, and the familiar form of Jade's favorite henchman filled the archway.

"Hello, love," Rall said in a congenial tone, and though he had always tried hard to affect a Zero accent, still his Britania colony roots slipped through. "There's someone who'd like a word with you."

Cyan grabbed Einn's hands as he tried to stand, stilling him. "Sean," he said. "You promised." He kissed Einn quickly, knowing the display of a weakness would get back to his brother, but unable to resist. He wished he could have taken a longer lasting kiss, but it would have to suffice. Standing up, he strode over to Rall. "Just take me. Leave them alone."

"My only order is to take you," Rall said, and grabbed him, yanked him close—too close. Rall had always loved violating personal space. "Long time no see, love."

Cyan said nothing. Rall chuckled and let him go to wrap a too-familiar collar around Cyan's throat. Cyan did not react, but cringed inwardly, hating that Einn and Sean had to see him like this—captured, dragged away, once more under Jade's control.

He fought an urge to look back at Einn for comfort. He'd never had anyone to turn to for that—not even Sean, the only person he considered a real friend. It was stupid to want to seek Einn out now, and he could not afford to be stupid. There was no guarantee Einn would still want him, anyway. One thing for a pirate to want a tough Rehabber, but a collared weakling?

Cyan swallowed and kept his gaze straight ahead as Rall dragged him from the room. Out in the hallway, two still figures caught his eye—and he stumbled, realizing what he was looking at, choked with disbelief and terror. "Those—they can't be!"

The two figures were roughly male in appearance, though Cyan knew from reports that reproduction had never been in their design. Their eyes were solid pools of glistening black, skin such a deep purple it may as well be black, with an iridescent shine that gleamed wetly in the dim hallway light.

Cyan tried to twist free, get away, go back to Einn, Sean, the others. He had to save them! "No! You can't do this! They were exterminated! Einn!" He broke free, heard Einn call his name, then screamed in agony as Rall triggered the collar.

He collapsed, clawing futilely at the collar, begging desperately as he watched the two Temperast slip into the inn room, heard Rall's orders to take Sean and Mendel, and kill the rest. He whimpered when the collar jolted him again, then passed out.

LEISURE CLASS STARSHIP 31899205, *THE MONTE CRISTO*

Cyan woke up in bed—tethered to it, in fact. He shivered, not surprised to realize the only thing he was wearing was the collar. It was much harder for a prisoner to escape when he was naked. He had not seen *The Monte Cristo* for years, but she was as familiar as ever. Beautiful, elegant, and one of the only things in the stars of which Jade was truly fond.

It was on the large side for a leisure class vessel, with five bedrooms and six leisure rooms. His parents had paid a fortune for the ship, but they had hated to travel in the more perfunctory IG-appointed ships. His own bedroom had changed little, still decorated in blue and green, all his old training weapons on the walls. The room was just cool enough to be uncomfortable, and Cyan shivered at the memory as much as the temperature. Eleven years, and he might as well have run away yesterday.

Abruptly, everything from Kreska came back to him—Rall, the Temperast. Stars, how could there be any Temperast left alive? Why was Jade tangled up with them? Jade had sided with their parents on the matter. People had admired how staunchly so young a man had supported his parents on such a complicated matter. He would never betray their memory by siding with the Temperast.

Einn, Lark. Dead, along with Karmikel. Sean and Mendel ... stars knew where they were, if they had been taken as he vaguely recalled. Because of him. Because of Jade. *Einn.* Cyan swallowed, flooded with memories of every little thing he had ever noted about Einn. How still and quiet he'd been in that bar on Bangkok when everyone else was so rowdy and noisy. His hot little smirk, his laugh, those sweet, awkward smiles when he was trying to do something he didn't think he knew how to do. The sure, confident way he had attacked the *Huntress*. The way he could be so serious, but clearly preferred not to be. The sinuous way he moved, his pale gold hair against his pale gray skin, and his eyes the color of real gold. The awkward way he tried to comfort and the confident way he fucked.

Dead. Whatever was between him and Einn, Cyan would never get to explore it, because Einn was dead, because Cyan was too much of a guilt-ridden coward to turn Jade in when he should have. Cyan buried his face in his hands, bitterly aware he had just enough give to do so, hating the feel of the chain on his right wrist, the weight of the collar around his neck. They served as reminders, though. He had to keep it together, had to get through this and escape again. He was all that Sean and Mendel had left, and they were all he had left. He wouldn't fail them, too.

The sound of the door sliding open made him tense, and he knew before looking up that Jade had arrived.

Jade was dressed in IG formal wear: black robes with silver clasps in the shape of the IG's infinity crest. His hair was in its usual braid, bound with black ribbon, and his nails gleamed black dusted with silver shimmer. He was the epitome of beauty in the eyes of most, and he knew it. "What a lovely surprise," Jade said. "Hours and hours of tedious arguing with my councilors, but I return to my ship to find my beloved brother waiting for me. Delightful."

"Go to hell."

Laughing, Jade locked the door, then moved to the foot of the bed and looked at him. "Rehab has been good for you, brother, though all those muscles won't overcome your cowardice."

"Better a coward than you."

Silence was Jade's only reply as he left the bed to move to the table beside it. A tray had been set on it with a pot of tea and a delicate looking tea cup made of Krawl glass. Jade poured the tea, and the smell made Cyan want to throw up. Expensive, delicate, a balance of bitter and sweet: Vrill esora tea, their mother's favorite. Cyan hated it.

Jade took a sip, and the silence stretched on. Cyan lay down and stared up at the ceiling, waiting for Jade to finally make his move.

"So what did you think of the Temperast?"

The words made Cyan gasp with pain, then bite down so hard on his lip that he drew blood. Jade had brought it up on purpose, and Cyan should have been better braced for it. "You hate the Temperast, just like Mom and Dad. There was no reason for you to murder Einn, Lark, and Karmikel."

"Reason enough," Jade said. "No one will miss a couple of pirates and a glorified bounty hunter."

Cyan barely bit back the words, *I will.*

Jade laughed and set his tea down with a soft clink. "Never say that my heartless, work-obsessed *little* brother developed a weak spot for pirates. You know, it's not actually healthy to fall in love with your kidnapper, right? The studies on the matter are countless."

"Like you would know anything about mental health," Cyan retorted, and grunted when Jade slapped him, nails slicing his cheek and searing the skin with whatever was in Jade's nail paint. "I'm not in love with anyone," he said, even as he knew it was a waste of time. He wasn't in love and never would be, because Einn was *dead*. Slowly turning his head, he asked, "Why are you doing all of this, Jade? The Temperast, the Draconis—you have no interest in such things. Your only scientific interest is in your poisons and toxins. Why genetics?"

Jade trailed his nails lightly across Cyan's skin. "Dear little brother, I have only ever wanted one thing, you know that."

Cyan frowned. "You can't get revenge, because no one knows who was behind the hits, Jade. After so many years, I doubt ... " He trailed off at the look on Jade's face, then whispered, "You figured it out."

Jade's smile was cold, but his eyes burned hot. "I found him."

"Who?"

"Why should I tell you?" Jade said with a laugh. "You said to let it go. You said it didn't matter. You ran away. You can remain ignorant!" He turned sharply away, still laughing as he left the room.

Cyan screamed and struggled to get free, succumbing to all the rage and fear and pain, just screaming until he could not scream anymore. He tore the bedding from the mattress and threw it, struggled against his bonds, beat and threw and broke whatever he could reach until he collapsed from sheer exhaustion.

*~*~*

When he woke again, the room had been set to rights, and he'd been completely chained down to the bed on his back with arms spread and attached to the headboard, his ankles bound together and secured to the footboard. Damn it. He turned his head and saw Jade once more at the table, sipping tea and reading from his datapad.

Slowly, Jade looked up and clucked disapprovingly. "It's not healthy to succumb to these fits of yours, brother. You know that."

Cyan said nothing; just shifted to look at the ceiling again, braced for what he knew was coming. He felt Jade's nails lightly rest on his stomach, right over the old scars. He drew a breath and bit back a scream of agony as Jade tore the old wounds open. It hurt—burned, even worse than his cheek had earlier. He felt the blood pool, run over his body, down his sides to soak into the bedding. The cuts weren't deep, but they were enough. "That should keep you from succumbing to further fits. Can't have you hurting yourself," Jade said, and patted his cheek.

"No, that's for you to do," Cyan said dully. Jade returned to his seat and picked up his tea again. "What are you going to do to me?"

"Take you home where you belong," Jade replied. "You were gone eleven years. I've had enough of your nonsense. Look at all the harm done by cowardice. You belong on Zero, and that is where I'm taking you. Perhaps this time, you'll realize that it's a stupid idea to run away from me. I admit, I am impressed you managed it. For years, I thought Pyotr must have helped you."

Cyan laughed. "Pyotr was too busy fawning over you like all the others to give a damn about me. He didn't help me, and if he had, it would only be because with me gone, your attention would have been that much more on him."

Jade made a derisive noise. "It's true," Cyan whispered, but he knew Jade would never concede it. The relationship between Jade and Pyotr was beyond his ability to understand, but he knew there was one. If there wasn't something there, Jade would have already killed the only person who could be deemed his equal. "So what does revenge have to do with the Draconis and Temperast?"

"The Temperast started this, so they will end it," Jade said, and Cyan gave up. He would get no explanation, only more cryptic replies. He settled for saving his strength. Eventually, Jade would have to release him. Best to be ready when that opportunity came. He'd given in to one useless fit; he wouldn't be that stupid again.

"I hate you," he whispered.

"You hate yourself more, though," Jade replied, "and that is all I want, if you will not stand with me."

Closing his eyes, Cyan tried to block out Jade's presence and focus only on escape and finding Sean. He opened them again at the sound of movement, however, tensed for another attack. Jade stared down at him, and Cyan stared back. Almost thirty and he still did not understand how they were related. "I should have turned you in when I had the chance."

"That would have been the action of a brave man, and you are a coward," Jade replied. "Even now, you cower." He started to say more, but his in-lens flashed, and instead he smirked. "How neatly the pieces come together and fall into my hand. I'll be back in a bit, dear brother. Do stay out of trouble while I'm gone."

He left, and Cyan pulled at his bonds, testing them. He would not be able to get out of them on his own, which meant he definitely had to wait until they had to move him. So he would not get a chance until he was on Zero. Some Rehabber he was  proving to be.

Resigned, Cyan tried to make himself get some sleep.

# Chapter Fifteen

PLANET 11181911 (KRESKA), HEARTSTONE TAVERN & INN

Sean snapped awake, flooded with fear and healing magics. He glanced at Mendel, but the fear on Mendel's face had him glancing toward the source of it—and realized why he was afraid. He'd glimpsed them in the hall, but hadn't been able to believe that he was seeing what he thought: Temperast.

He drew the stunner at his thigh and fired, hitting the nearer of the two Temperast dead center in the chest. The damned thing barely noticed. Sean rolled off the bed, landing in a crouch as he thumbed his stunner to a fatal level of power and fired three more times in rapid succession.

"Stunners won't kill them," Mendel said. "Temperast were designed with a resistance."

"If they get their hands on us, we're dead," Sean said, abandoning his stunner for the dagger in his boot.

Lark drew his own knife, and said, "Only you," before jumping onto the bed and throwing himself at the Temperast, knocking them both down, landing atop one fully and attacking it with his knife. Sean licked his lips as the other one smiled at them and stood up again to resume walking toward them. He wondered if being human would give him any chance of surviving when it touched him. He tensed, feeling Mendel behind him, knowing there was nothing they could do because they could not risk getting close—

"Light!" Karmikel screamed, startling Sean, and he only just remembered to close his eyes in time as Karmikel flooded the room with blinding, white-gold light. Sean waited until the light faded, then threw his dagger, catching the blinded Temperast in the throat. It made a wet, gurgling noise, but even as it tried futilely to save its own life, Lark appeared behind it, smeared with purple-black blood, and grabbed the dagger. He yanked it out, then slit the Temperast's throat properly, throwing it back to join the corpse of the other.

Wiping blood from his face, Lark glanced at Karmikel. "I've heard of that little trick of yours. Handy." Karmikel grunted.

"Those were Temperast," Sean said. "They were all exterminated."

Mendel made a face. "I am not at all surprised to learn that someone kept the means to recreate them. These two were killed far too easily, according to what I have read on the Temperast. I think they have not been alive long. We should be glad that they were new, and we had Lark. Thank you." Lark shrugged the words aside.

Sean's attention shifted as Adalsteinn—Einn—finally stood up. He had been quiet and still the entire time, and Sean wondered suddenly if he'd had a plan of his own. "Where have they taken Cyan?" When no one replied, Einn's voice took on an edge that was a blend of anger and desperation. "Where is Cyan?"

"I don't know," Sean said. "He seemed to know the man who took him and what was going on. Well, other than the Temperast. No one could predict that. Cyan can handle himself; I'm sure he's got a plan. You don't need to worry; he'll contact us soon, I have no doubt."

Einn's face twisted. "Jade, he was taken back to Jade—but where? I have to save him." He strode to the door and scowled when Lark stopped him with a hand to his chest. "Get out of my way."

"So you can die of the poison in your system? So Auths can arrest you? So you can bungle your way around the stars trying to stop a Lower Chancellor?"

Einn punched him, sending Lark reeling into the wall, then sat down on the nearest bed and buried his fingers in his hair. Sean stared at him, taken aback. What in the stars was going on? "I don't understand why Cyan was *cooperating* with you."

Einn laughed bitterly. "Jade didn't give him a choice."

"There's a lot to explain," Lark added, when Sean and Mendel only looked more confused.

Karmikel nodded. "We should get to the moon—Winter will meet us there. He's already sending someone to handle this mess and we need to get out of here. Come on." They followed Karmikel out of the room, sneaking out the back way of the inn, then used back streets and alleyways until they reached port. "Come on, we're taking my ship. Yours will be dealt with."

Einn grumbled something Sean didn't catch, but followed them onto the ship. Once they were on the bridge, he whipped around. Sean recoiled, bumping into Mendel behind him. "Don't you care at all? Cyan only left Mars because of you, and you don't even care that Jade has him now!"

"I care!" Sean snapped. "But like I said before, Cyan can handle himself. He's never needed anyone to help him with anything. He's the best guard on Rehab, and I've never seen him get in trouble he couldn't get out of. He always said it was best just to stay out of his way. If you knew him at all, you wouldn't be overreacting."

To his surprise, Einn sneered at him. "You know him so well, do you? Then you know about his brother?"

"Cyan never talks about it," Sean replied. "He only says that his brother is crazy and hates him."

"Well, he told me exactly what his brother used to do him, and if you honestly think Cyan doesn't need us, you don't deserve to call yourself his friend!"

Sean stared at him, startled and stung. "I *am* his friend—he *told* you? He told *you?*"

"Yes," Einn said. "He also made me promise to get you home, if something happened to him."

"Why?" Sean demanded.

Einn hesitated, anger falling away, then said in a tone clearly meant to be gentle, "Your mother is sick. She wanted to see you one last time. Cyan was trying to find you and take you home to see her."

"What—" Cold disbelief shot through Sean, making everything go numb for a moment. He couldn't breathe. His mother. "My mom—my mom—" He went easily when Mendel pulled him close, held him. Sean wanted to go home. He was tangled up in the problems of the stars, and all the while the one person who had loved him unconditionally his entire life was *dying*.

"We'll figure out a way," Mendel said softly. "I promise." Sean didn't reply; just let the words comfort him, even as he knew the promise was futile. There were bigger concerns afoot than a boy and his mother.

He pushed away from Mendel and went numbly through the motions of helping Karmikel get the ship out of port. Karmikel did not really need his help, but Sean often did it anyway, and they worked together in their usual easy silence. A short time later, he helped dock the ship just outside their base on the moon, a large building that had once been a research facility. "Home sweet home," Sean muttered bitterly.

### PLANET 11181911-3554 (MOON OF KRESKA), ABANDONED RESEARCH FACILITY

Sean woke the building systems, and the lights flickered on. "When will Winter be here?"

"Five hours ZT," Karmikel replied. He led the way inside and down a narrow hall that led to a large room, then collapsed on a beat up sofa. "So let's start talking."

Two hours later, Sean said, "What a mess. So what in the stars do we do now?"

"I don't care what the rest of you bottom dwellers do," Einn snapped. "I am going to save Cyan."

Mendel replied, "You can't go off on your own. Distance will weaken the bond, and you will no longer have your magics."

"Then I'll do it without them," Einn snarled. "I am not doing anything else until I get Cyan back. I climbed the Tresso Cliff in half a day without my magics. I don't need them. I'm not just leaving him." Silence fell in the wake of his words, and Sean could practically see the way he was trembling with anger and tension.

"Ringers," Lark said dryly. "Everyone goes crazy when they become ringers. Sit down before you pass out, Einn. We'll rescue your crazy Rehab princess, but we need a better plan than 'stomp around like an angry Krawl'."

"Bottom dweller," Einn said sourly, but Sean saw him smile faintly as he sat down.

Lark snorted. "It's not an insult if I don't get why it should be, Einn. I keep telling you that."

"None of the Helioran insults I've used in the past worked either."

"I'm immune to insult," Lark said. "Now, are you done looming and snarling?" Einn grimaced, but said nothing.

Sean went to get drinks, too restless to keep still any longer. Cyan, his mother. It was all a fucking mess, and it was all his fault. He turned at the sound of footsteps and stared at Mendel hovering in the doorway, not really certain what to say or do. Mendel crossed the room and pulled Sean close, then kissed him. Sean clung tightly and kissed back feverishly, needing the warmth and reassurance—the distraction, however brief. When they finally pulled apart, he said, "Do you know how much easier everyone's life would be if I hadn't been born a fucking mutant?"

"Easier, maybe, but not better," Mendel replied quietly. "Don't get so focused on the negatives that you dismiss the positives. I did that once and nearly had my jaw broken for it." He smiled faintly, and Sean could not help but smile back. "We'll figure something out, Sean. Don't we always?"

Sean nodded. "I hope Winter can help, because we're going to need his resources."

"He'll help; he always does." Mendel helped Sean finish pouring the drinks and preparing food, then carried it all back to the main room, arranging it all on the low table in the middle of the circle of sofas and chairs.

"The *Melee* contacted us," Karmikel said. "Lius said he should have some promising information for us in a little while. There was a suspicious ship in port and men trying to nose around the *Dragonfly*. He'll let us know more once he's certain of the information."

Sean nodded. "Good. I hope whatever they learn gives us a solid lead. We still don't know where they take the victims."

"Maybe our combined knowledge will give us some idea," Einn said, clearly still annoyed at the lack of inaction, but resigned to it—for the moment. Sean sensed he would not remain complacent for long. "There's got to be *something*. Cyan said he was certain the motive was political, but he could not find anything that connected all the pieces. Jade is Lower Chancellor of the fourth quad; if he wanted to arrange for genetic experiments, he is literally the only chancellor who did not need special permission. All he had to do was hire the scientists and victims he instead kidnapped, and clear it all with the IG, who would grant him any favor he wanted. Cyan didn't think it had to do with the policy revisions going on, either."

"It has something to do with the Temperast," Mendel said. "I've been examining everything from that angle for the past few days, and the two that attacked us down planet only confirm my suspicions. It all fits too perfectly: every one of the scientists taken has the right background, professional and/or personal, for Temperast studies. Stars, Dr. Bikendi himself could be both scientist and subject. He's almost exactly what the scientists who created the Temperast were aiming for: can absorb energy, kill with a touch, hard to kill in turn. He's damn near a natural-born

Temperast. The rest of the victims, the Draconis and their matches, either have magics wanted for the Temperast or magics that would serve as bases to develop something else. I don't know about political motives, but even Jade would not be able to get permission if he wanted to experiment with Temperast."

"They don't need Draconis specifically if they're just researching magics," Karmikel said. "So why Draconis?"

"I have not yet gathered sufficient proof for my hypothesis, but I suspect the main point is control. It's the bond they are studying. Temperast were not on the same sentient level as the rest of us; they were merely living weapons. That was the biggest problem with their existence: they were weapons with no safety and always set to fatal. I suspect they want to take the bonding element of the Draconis and use a variation of it for the Temperast."

"It's a good idea," Sean said. "The bond would exert control, and the Temperast can't go too far because distance would weaken their powers. They'd be forced to stay close, obey, and keep their matches alive."

"No one needs living weapons," Lark said scathingly.

"Which means they probably need living batteries even less," Karmikel said bitterly. "They'll exterminate us right alongside whatever other Temperast happen still to be alive, like that nasty bunch from before."

"The Temperast were dangerous, uncontrollable, and ultimately pointless," Lark said. "You're dangerous and kind of bitchy, but not useless."

"Bitchy?" Karmikel repeated in a soft tone that made Sean wince reflexively. He'd seen what had happened to the last person to provoke that particular tone.

Either Lark was oblivious to the danger or simply did not care. "Definitely bitchy, like some shrieking woman on market day who paid too much for a cut of kesto."

"Woman!" Karmikel snarled and reached for his stunner. "I'm not a woman."

Lark smirked. "Certainly pretty enough, and like I said, bitchy enough." He started to say more, but caught the look Einn was giving him. "What?" he snapped.

"Nothing," Einn said, motioning lazily with one hand. "I've just never seen you flirt before; it's kind of strange."

Lark folded his arms across his chest. "I'm not flirting. I just hadn't realized the notorious Lieutenant Aurum was such a princess when he was out of his corporate thug uniform."

"You wish you could see me out of uniform," Karmikel retorted, and let his stunner slide back into the holster from which he'd half-pulled it. Lark sneered at him and Karmikel sneered back. Sean rolled his eyes.

"So what does all this matching mean?" Einn asked, drawing Karmikel's hostility. "I don't want to be matched to anyone. I'm a pirate. You're clearly government now. That's the exact opposite of a good idea."

Karmikel made a face. "You don't need to tell me that." He hesitated a beat, then added, "I'm Internal Affairs. I'm liaison to Mendel, who is an unofficial consultant on this case."

"Great," Einn replied. "I'm stuck with you—what, forever?—because the Coni have a seriously bottom dweller view about how batteries should operate?"

"At least you aren't the battery," Mendel said coldly.

"At least you knew it would happen!" Einn snapped. "I'm not Coni. I'm not even from the same damned quad! Why would I match with one of you? I'm a *pirate*, I can't be matched to an IG secret goon!"

"You're telling me," Karmikel muttered. His in-lens flashed. "Winter is here."

Sean stood up and went to the dock, guiding in a beautiful combat-class starship that he could not tear his eyes from. The words *Shangri La* were written in black on the prow. Several minutes after the ship settled, the main hatch opened and a gangway slid down. A man appeared in the doorway, skinny and gangly, and tall in a unique way. But, Sean noticed, he was not quite as exaggerated as Einn. As he drew closer, Sean saw that he was only half-Fornarian. He had the dusky skin common to humans on Bangkok and the Nippon settlement on Mars, with a close-cropped goatee and dark brown hair. He wore the IG formal uniform, black with silver trim and fastenings, but there were no marks of rank anywhere on it. He carried three visible stunners, which in Sean's experience meant there was at least two more that weren't visible.

The man smiled as he reached the bottom of the gangway and gave a casual salute. "Hello, hello. So you're the mutant causing all the fuss, then. Nice to meet you. My name is Raoul, personal bodyguard to the Commander."

Sean said nothing; merely looked at him, not glancing away as the others filed in behind him. Raoul chuckled. "I came to ascertain that the perimeter is secure. May I safely assume all is well, Rehab?"

"Bangkok," Lark muttered, and Sean realized he was right—the man had a faint, but noticeable Bangkok accent, eliminating the possibility he was from Mars. Not that of the upper class, but the lower, what everyone called the Bangkok cattle that kept the dragons fed.

Raoul smiled in a way that seemed friendly at first, but definitely had ice to it. But in reply to the carelessly muttered word, he only laughed. "Bangkok spider, that's me. I'll ask you one more time: are the premises secure?"

"Secure," Sean replied. "Unless you're worried about the drunk smugglers wandering around the rest of the moon."

"They are of no concern," Raoul said. He turned and whistled, and a moment later, a familiar man with broad shoulders, pale blond hair, and sharp blue eyes appeared and walked down the gangway. "I told you the dramatics were unnecessary, Raoul."

"I'm paid to ignore you, not listen to you. Let's get to your shadowy stuff, then. What's that odd phrase you're always using?"

"Cloak and dagger."

"That's the one," Raoul said. "Let's get to it. You're due to meet you-know-who in a few hours and can't be late."

"I have assistants to heckle me about that, Raoul," Winter replied lightly, then turned to face the group properly. "Greetings. I am sorry we must meet under such circumstances. I do not understand, though, why Cohen kidnapped Cyan."

"Cohen?" Sean repeated, staring at him blankly. "But—it was Jade who took him; it was Jade doing everything."

Winter's eyes went glacier, and Sean recoiled. "Jade," he repeated softly. "Are you certain?"

"Yes," Lark said, holding a hand against Einn's chest to steady him when it was clear he wanted to launch himself at Winter and throttle the man for daring to ask if they were sure.

Beside Winter, Raoul shifted minutely. Sean grimaced. "It was definitely Jade behind it, and if you would please all avoid killing one another, we can talk and figure it all out."

"Jade," Winter repeated again, mouth tight and eyes flashing with something that Sean didn't understand. Not bothering to reply, he turned on his heel and led the way back to their living quarters.

# Chapter Sixteen

**PLANET 11181911-3554 (MOON OF KRESKA), ABANDONED FACILITY**

"So you didn't know it was Jade? Who the stars is Cohen?" Einn demanded. "Jade has always been the one behind this mess." He glared at the blue-eyed man, refusing to back down from his gaze no matter how intense it was.

They were beautiful eyes, the clearest, sharpest blue he had ever seen. But they also held shadows, that *something* that made him want to stay far away, even as he forced himself to maintain eye contact. It was like looking into Jade's eyes. Realization struck him. "You're Pyotr Kavalerov."

"Guilty as charged," Pyotr said with a weary smile. "Those codes given to me, taken from the ship that hacked yours—they originated from High Chancellor Cohen's office. No one but he could have issued those codes. They come from his datapad or his main work station, in the office only he uses. Those are the only two places from which such codes can be generated."

Sean shrugged. "He got hacked or infiltrated."

"Improbable."

"But not impossible," Einn said. "It doesn't take a high-caliber hacker to do that, not if it was an inside job. At that point, all it would really take is someone who knows the man and the system, like a certain Lower Chancellor."

Pyotr nodded. "Jade could do it, I do not deny that. Hmm ... "

"What?" Einn demanded, not liking the look that slid across his face. "You know something. He has Cyan; I'm not sitting around here forever. What do you know?"

"Revenge," Pyotr said, after a moment. "I believe Jade's machinations are all about revenge."

Lark went for his stunner, as did Karmikel. Lark snapped, "Stop being cryptic. Our friend has been kidnapped by that psychopath, and Einn and I will die in a matter of days from the poison Jade put in our system, not to mention all the people still missing. I will kill you and your bodyguard if you do not say something useful."

Pyotr laughed, lightly placing a hand on Raoul's chest. "No need for threats. I am here to help, despite your beliefs to the contrary."

"I don't trust anyone with eyes like yours," Einn said.

"Eyes like mine?" Pyotr asked, but Einn could see he understood perfectly. "Indeed. Let us start with the most crucial part of your statement:  Jade has poisoned you?" He half-turned, looking at Raoul, who nodded and stepped away to communicate with someone else on the ship. A couple of minutes later, a man came out and joined them.

"Constantine here is an expert on poisons; he will work out a cure, and in the meantime, can give you something to hold you over."

Einn frowned, but held out his arm when Constantine indicated he should, grunting as he drew blood. Constantine smiled absently at him, then moved on to Lark. When he was done drawing blood, he glanced at Pyotr and gestured, then left as abruptly as he had arrived. Pyotr smiled faintly. "He says he will get to work, but he would not be surprised if he has seen the poison before. Those who use them in this manner tend to have favorites, and a victim always crops up."

"So why is he doing this?" Lark demanded.

"Jade has always wanted vengeance for the death of his parents," Pyotr replied. "We found the shooter many years ago, though that is not public knowledge. Unfortunately, he was dead when we found him. We have never been able to figure out who contracted the hit. Jade never mentions it, but he has never given up his quest for vengeance."

Sean shook his head. "I don't see what this has to do with High Chancellor Cohen."

"Cohen's family was most responsible for the Temperast back when they were first created. Again, it is not common knowledge, but they broke several rules in the making of them and paid many fines. They were very upset about the loss, and it strained the friendship between the Cohen and Alexander families. When Lord and Lady Alexander were killed, they were, of course, investigated as primary suspects. The investigation quickly cleared them, however, and Cohen became High Chancellor two terms later. He helped raise Jade and Cyan after their parents' death, repairing the friendship between their families."

Einn's brows shot up. "You're saying the investigators who cleared him were wrong."

Pyotr nodded. "So it would seem, if Jade is seeking revenge as I now suspect. I can't believe I missed it all this time ... " He shook his head. "All evidence points to Cohen. The codes used by the *Dragonfly* were all generated by him. Lius' team just finished going over the *Dragonfly* and found more evidence that they say was recently placed by the men they apprehended, engineered to implicate Cohen. The other ship they captured also bears signatures of Cohen. Nowhere at all is there evidence of Jade." He looked at Einn and Lark. "I believe the two of you and Cyan are the only ones who can testify to Jade's involvement."

Yeah, him testify. Einn sneered at the idea of anyone believing a couple of pirates over a popular Lower Chancellor. "So you're telling me that the last term, the nightmare we've been living, all those people we kidnapped—everything was for someone's *revenge*? Tell me again why the stars Jade isn't in Rehab?"

"Not just revenge," Pyotr said. "Revenge is not the only thing afoot. It is Cohen, after all, and something to do with genetic research. That's too much coincidence. I do not think Jade did all this for revenge—I think he is *using* it for revenge."

Mendel spoke up from where he and Sean had been sitting on a couch, listening quietly to the exchange. "We were attacked by Temperast."

"Yes, Karmikel told me," Pyotr said. "I am looking into that. In the meantime, you have a rescue mission to launch."

Einn slumped with relief. Finally, *finally* they were going to save Cyan—

"The *Melee* was able to capture the men who I think were meant to take Sean and Mendel to wherever the other victims are being kept." Pyotr smiled, and Einn could see perfectly how and why he was head of Special Forces and Internal Affairs. "If Lius is correct, and he generally is in these matters, then the men he captured are taking you to a way station. From there, another group will transport you to the actual facility."

Sean swore. "You want us to go—to be 'captured' and figure out where they're being held, lead everyone else there."

"Yes," Pyotr replied. "You will infiltrate the facility, gather whatever intel you can, and relay it back to the *Brilliant*, which will be standing by for your signal to attack the facility, rescue the captives, and arrest everyone else." He pulled a case from inside his jacket and tossed it to Mendel. "Track chems. They taste a bit metallic and might make you nauseous for a brief time, but otherwise are fine. The chems will last one hundred Zero hours. Still, delay taking them as long as you can. Karmikel, as ever, is your point man."

"I'm not doing this!" Einn snarled, surging to his feet. Didn't any of them *care*? All he could see was Cyan's face, those scars on his stomach, the deeper scars in his eyes. That awful look of *goodbye*, the taste of it in his last kiss. No one wanted to save him. "I'm going after Cyan; the rest of you can fall to the bottom for all I care."

Pyotr shook his head. "I will handle Cyan—"

Einn rounded on him. "I've seen what Jade did to him, I've heard Cyan's stories. It's no wonder that Cyan calls you Jade's match—you really are just like him! I'm not doing *anything* else until I save Cyan, and if I have to do it alone, fine." He turned sharply and stormed from the room, before he added 'murdered Commander of Special Forces' to his list of crimes.

He raked a hand through his hair, wishing he could get around to cutting it. Then he shoved the stupid thought aside and focused only on Cyan. He would have to get the *Dragonfly* back somehow, or figure out how to steal another ship. But even the smallest ships needed a minimum of two people to crew it. Well, he would scale that cliff when he reached it.

The first cliff he had to scale was finding a space suit that would fit him, since his only way to get back down planet was the smugglers. Space suits fitted to Fornarian sizes, however, were in short supply. Several minutes of searching through a surprising number of them only resulted in two that were so close it was infuriating. Einn sucked in air and let it out on an irritated sigh.

Footsteps made him whip around. He scowled at Lark. "I hope you're not going to try and talk sense into me or something."

"I'm a prostitute, a thief, a pirate, a kidnapper, and best friends with a Fornarian," Lark drawled. "No one will ever accuse me of having sense. I came to tell you how to stow away on the *Shangri La*."

Einn grinned. "I can do that?"

Lark nodded. "I worked on a few of them when I was actually gainfully employed. The shipyard I worked at did a lot of government issue ships. They have some ... allowances ... if you know what you're doing."

"No man knows what he's doing better than you."

Smiling faintly, Lark crossed the room to Einn and flourished an injection gun. "Here, Constantine already worked up his version of Jade's serum. Apparently, they *have* seen it before, and with our fresh samples of it, Constantine says he should be able to get a cure in a few days." Einn pulled up his sleeve and Lark injected him.

Setting the spent gun on a nearby shelf, Lark moved to the table in the middle of the room and cleared it off. Pulling out his datapad, he called up information and projected it to the table surface. Einn looked over the schematics. "You shouldn't have these."

"Pirate," Lark said wryly, looking at him.

Einn laughed. "Good point. So tell me what to do."

"Climb on top of the ship here," Lark said, and went on to explain in great detail how Einn could get inside the ship and to the engine room, where he'd be able to hide.

Einn listened carefully, memorizing everything and more than a little impressed, as ever, by Lark's knowledge. Whatever flippant things Lark said about himself and his colorful past, he deserved to be more than a criminal waiting for the inevitable day the law caught up to him. "What are you going to do?"

"Tag along with the Hero Brigade and keep them from realizing you're long gone until too late," Lark said. "We're caught, anyway. Maybe cooperating now will reduce my sentence later."

"And Karmikel is very pretty."

Lark shoved him, and then put away his datapad. "Just remember to stay in the engine room, because otherwise all their fancy scanners will pick you up. I don't know where they're headed after this, but eventually they'll return to Zero. You'll be able to tell when you've arrived there; the landing procedures take a good hour and the ship is heavily searched before anyone is allowed off. They won't find you, however, not if you stay where I told you."

Einn nodded. "I know when to do as I'm told."

Grunting, Lark continued, "After the ship is empty, but before they lock it down completely, go out the way you came in. From the docks, you shouldn't have trouble getting to the public areas of Zero. No one there watches the docks nearly as well as they should. The codes Jade gave us should still work for a bit, so you'll be able to get to the private estate areas, I think. If not, I'm sure you'll improvise. I don't know where the Alexander Estate is, however—"

"I can figure it out from there," Einn said. "Cyan will hopefully be able to get us off Zero again. Thanks, Lark."

Lark shrugged the words aside. "Just don't die or get arrested."

"I won't," Einn replied. "Be careful not to do either yourself. Watch that group; I trust them less than a Bangkok sharp."

"Smart man," Lark laughed. "Get going, I'll ensure they don't mark your absence until too damn late."

Einn nodded, and neither of them bothered to mention the poison still in their systems. What was the point? As Lark ventured off, he took a different door out of the storage room, going down a hall that bypassed the main living room, slowly finding his way back to the hangar. He paused as he passed an office and slipped inside to snatch up a few things that looked as though they might be useful: an old datapad, an extra stunner charge, and a knife that looked to be Rehab issue. That would make Cyan laugh.

Tucking it all away, he ventured on to the hangar. He finally reached it by way of a door that was at the opposite end of the one he'd used before when Pyotr had arrived. Closing it quietly, he immediately turned and began to climb up the wall, hands sticking easily to the smooth, metal surface. When he reached the top of the ship, he gingerly leapt from the wall, landing smoothly. Crawling across the ship, he reached the innocuous-looking hatch Lark had described.

Prying it open was as stupidly easy as Lark had promised, if one knew what to do. Lowering himself inside the ship, Einn pulled the panel back in place, secured it, then slowly climbed down deeper into the ship.

From there, it was roughly an hour of nerve-wracking crawling, climbing, hiding, and nearly panicking when he barely avoided being caught by three guards. He wondered if Lark knew how much tension was involved and scowled when he decided Lark was probably laughing himself silly. Finally, *finally*, he reached the engine room. Bypassing the main power coils, he entered the room just beyond it. Lark had said it would hold the back-up coils, but unless Einn was mistaken, those were warp coils.

The door to the engine room should have been locked. It was standard procedure even on civilian ships to keep certain parts of the ship restricted, a safety feature that the crew of the Commander's ship should have been following. But the arrogance and laziness of such men had always been a pirate's greatest weapon, and Einn was more than happy to take advantage of it.

In the warp coils room, he once more climbed a wall, and then across the ceiling to the panel directly over the almost too-warm coils. Einn wanted badly to poke around, because he'd *heard* of ships that did not need gates to light jump, but the cost was preventative, and the IG made a lot of its money on the light gates. The engineering that must have been involved with designing such a thing—

Shaking his head at himself, he pried open the panel directly over the coils. Tucking the screws he'd removed into a pocket of his shirt, he swung the panel aside on its remaining screw, then crawled up inside. He could barely fit; how in the world did anyone else? As promised by Lark, there was a crawl space for someone to lay in, a leftover from when the ship was being constructed.

According to Lark, such spaces were supposed to be eliminated when the work was finished, but lazy, underpaid shipyard workers seldom bothered, the general inspectors were only moderately less lazy, and the IG inspectors had better things to do with their time than look for work holes they probably didn't even know about.

Reaching down, Einn pulled the panel back into place and restored the screws. Assured it was as it should be, he withdrew into the crawl space and settled in for several hours of not moving. No one knew the crawl space was there since it dead-ended almost immediately behind him, and the heat and power emanations of the coils would keep anyone from registering his presence. All he had to do was not give himself away.

The passage was only just large enough to accommodate an average human, and Einn wondered how they dealt with it, given that in his experience, precious few people could endure such confinement. It wasn't really all that bad; it reminded him of home. Everyone remarked on the notorious cliffs of Fornar, but few people ever seemed to recall—or even know—that Fornar revolved as much around exploring the caves that riddled the cliffs as the cliffs themselves. The caves were endless complexes of twisting channels, dark holes, endless falls, pools of clear water, ice, wide caverns, and spaces too small for even a babe.

Twice in his life he had gotten stuck in places where he dared not move, and could only hope that someone would come along and find him sooner rather than later. They always had, because that was how the systems worked—but there were still too many tragedies, and Einn had feared more than once that he might become the next.

Lying low in a ship was much easier than exploring a cave he could barely see inside of, even with his improved dark vision. The hard part was not going cave crazy with worry. His gut twisted all over again as he replayed that awful moment when Cyan had kissed him goodbye. The paleness of his skin, the look of resignation and fear on his face—the way that stars-cursed bastard had collared him.

Einn fisted his hands, aching to wrap them around the throat of that smug-looking bastard. Cyan shouldn't be collared like that, shouldn't be mistreated at all. Collars were for bottom dwelling scum like Jade and his henchman.

The screams had been the worst. He hadn't seen Cyan, but he'd heard those screams. He'd heard Cyan angry, happy, amused, hurt, and even scared. He knew every last whimper and plea and moan that Cyan made in passion. He would recognize Cyan's voice in a crowded room. He *never* again wanted to hear those screams of agony and pain. He closed his eyes, but that couldn't block the memory of those horrible screams.

Was Cyan okay? What was Jade doing to him? Stars, why hadn't he *done* something? Instead of acting, Einn had just sat there and let Cyan walk away. He'd let Cyan go back to that nightmare.

Would Cyan forgive him? Einn didn't know what Cyan had done to him, or how he'd done it, but Einn knew he was ... well, taken, he supposed, really was the only word for it. Was that what everyone said Fornarians couldn't comprehend? He wasn't sure he wanted it: the fear, the anxiety, the *addiction*.

He sensed it would be much easier to be matched to Karmikel, despite the annoyance of being magically bound to an IA operative he did not know. He could understand the matching. There was science in that, rules and limits, reasons.

Einn's obsession with Cyan made no sense at all, and it made even less sense that he would gladly die for a chance to figure it out.

Voices drew his attention, scattered his thoughts, and he looked down through the grating to just barely see a couple of engineers discussing something about the coils. One of them shifted, and Einn saw the markings of a master engineer on his left arm.

So he was probably right about the *Shangri La*'s ability to light jump without a gate. He could not think of any other reason the crew would include a master engineer. The only thing more expensive in regards to ships was hiring a gremlin to design the damn thing.

Einn heaved a sigh of relief when they finally left and settled himself a bit more comfortably. They likely would not return again for a while; best to try and doze while he had the chance. Thoughts still on Cyan, Einn slowly fell asleep.

# Chapter Seventeen

**PLANET 0000000 (ZERO), THE PALACE OF ETERNITY**

Cyan hadn't realized he'd missed Zero. Not all of it—he certainly had not missed the way every word was carefully measure and calculated, the backstabbing, the politics and the games. 'Zero chess' was what they called it, the art of surviving the cutthroat environment at the heart of the IG.

But he had missed the beauty of Zero, the wonder of it. If Zero had possessed another name before the IG claimed it, no one ever knew it. Until Zero, the IG had not had stationary headquarters, but had travelled the stars on a ship of legendary size. As the IG continued to grow in strength and numbers, however, that had become inadequate, and so the IG had begun to look for a real home.

They had found it on a planet that had clearly borne life at one point, but had been left barren when a plague had wiped out everything. The IG had the barren planet thoroughly scouted, and a full decade later, had claimed it as home. It had not been long before Zero was the epicenter of the IG; the dividing lines for the Quads began at Zero, and it was where anything of star-changing importance took place. Because of the Star Assembly, which required two representatives of every race to be present at all times, only on Zero was one guaranteed to see every single race in the IG. They were the only legal exception to the rule that magics capable were not allowed to hold government positions.

In Cyan's eyes, though, the true marvel was how the IG had worked to restore Zero to a place of beauty. The images in the archives showed a place of rock and dust, but Zero in the present day was lush with greenery, with pieces of hundreds of other planets brought in to create a planet of unparalleled beauty and luxury. The private areas were on one section of the planet, the public areas another, and crowning everything was the famous Palace of Eternity.

The Palace was enormous, made of gleaming white stone and towering higher than every other building on the planet. The twisting towers were capped with colorful globes and spires. Fountains, parks, the star mazes, the outbuildings, the Hall of the Star Assembly, the Great Archives—the Palace itself was a maze to newcomers and veterans alike.

The most famous part of the Palace was the floor of the great hall, where all visitors entered. All new arrivals, no matter how well-prepared, were *not* prepared for walking across the glass floor so well made it really did seem as they though walked on the water below. The Eternal Pool beneath the glass floor was so deep it was difficult to see clear down to the bottom, and it was populated with more creatures than anyone could count.

Cyan was given very little chance to appreciate all that he had missed of his homeland as he was quickly dragged along through the Palace to Jade's office. He endured greetings, expressions of relief that he was safe and that it was good to have him home again, all the while biting his tongue against trying to get someone to help him.

As much as he hated it, hated pretending that all was well, being stuck in the Palace was better than the moment he was dreading: when Jade finished his work and they went home. Cyan didn't want to see home again, no matter how much part of him missed all the good things about it. His mother had loved flowers, had spent so much of her personal funds filling the yard with Vrill and Mars roses. The house itself was several generations old, built by the first Alexander to move to Zero after taking a position in the Star Assembly with ambitions for Grand Chancellor—ambitions he had achieved. Since that long ago ancestor, no

Alexander had managed higher than Lower Chancellor, but his father had been poised to change that.

Once, Lower Chancellors had not been allowed to become High Chancellor, on the grounds that a Lower Chancellor would be too biased toward the quad that had once been under his command. That law had eased over the years, but it was still mostly preferred that High Chancellors not be pulled from Lower Chancellors.

Cyan knew everyone expected Jade to be High Chancellor someday. It just proved that no one really knew Jade; he had far more freedom, power, and control as Lower Chancellor. Climbing any higher up the ranks of the IG would only impede him.

He sat quietly on the couch in Jade's office, biting back an urge to scream, run, *anything*, but sit there quietly and endure. He could feel Rall's eyes on him from where he lurked on the opposite side of the room. Cyan's skin crawled, but he ignored it. No one liked Jade's First Assistant, and both Jade and Rall thrived on that knowledge.

When finally they were ready to leave, Cyan walked along quietly, not saying a word as they boarded a shuttle that took them to the private sectors, not looking at anyone as a second shuttle took them to the Alexander Estate.

Rall took his arm once they were inside and led him upstairs to his bedroom, Jade following right behind them. Cyan stilled as they entered the room he had not seen in more than a decade. It was like looking at the room of a stranger, even if it all looked familiar: his old clothes, expensive, ornate, and carelessly thrown about; his old training equipment and weapons; books and datapads, childhood toys he'd never been able to part with until forced to leave his whole life behind. He bent and picked up one of the books, turned it on, and saw it was a collection of manuals for Auth training.

He had nearly forgotten that, immersed in Rehab. He'd wanted to be an Authority, the only respectable job that he thought his parents might let him take and would make him happy. Except his parents had not been even remotely pleased. He'd been arguing with them the night they'd died. Defiant, he had fled their side the moment they had arrived at the Palace, sneaking off to make out with a boy his own age.

Stars, they had just been children, but so stubbornly sure they were adults. He'd been mad at his parents, jealous of his twin, angry at the whole world for being so unfair. Shaking his head, Cyan turned to Jade, and said, "So here we are again. Do you think you'll manage to keep me this time? Because you won't. Eventually I'll be gone ag—"

He screamed and dropped to his knees as Jade triggered the collar around his throat. Cyan tried to claw at it, but Rall had cuffed his hands the moment they were out of the public eye, and he could only scrabbled futilely until the pain finally abated. "Where will you go?" Jade asked. "To yet another faraway planet to start another new life? You could, I suppose, but will you? Thanks to you, all your friends are dead, or will be shortly. All I need now is for Sean and Mendel to lead Auths to the research facility to catch Cohen in the act."

Cyan felt as though he'd been slapped. "Cohen?" But—but Cohen had been exonerated. Cohen was their *friend.* Cyan wanted to scream, wanted to hit something. "Cohen killed our parents," he said dully instead.

Jade's cold smile was all the answer he needed.

"All of this was to get to Cohen," Cyan said. "Sean and Mendel are part of your plan. How will the Auths know where to find them?"

Jade only smirked and settled in the window seat on the far side of Cyan's room. "Your friends aren't stupid; they'll ensure there's a way they can be traced. If not, distress calls are useful things."

"I do not see how this is getting revenge for murder," Cyan said flatly. "Will he even realize you've set him up?"

Jade threw his head back and laughed. He stood up and moved closer to Cyan, laid his orange nails gently against Cyan's cheek. Cyan tensed for pain and did not relax when the nails slowly slid away without scratching him. "My, my, dear brother. You have been out of the loop. Don't you listen to the gossip at all?"

"I'm too busy working to listen to gossip, and I'm not interested in gossip about *you* anyway," Cyan retorted.

Ignoring the taunt, Jade replied, "I guess you never heard that *dear* Gary and I have been *good* friends for quite some time. Of course, I want to help him in his quest to bring back the Temperast and restore his family's honor." He smirked again, and added, "Though I think the loss of income interests him more than honor."

Cyan knew he would pay for it, but could not resist taunting, "You're fucking Cohen? He's nearly as old as our parents—but I suppose you did always have a thing for older men. Why Cohen? Did Pyotr turn you down?"

He screamed when Jade triggered the collar again, but managed to stay on his feet. Jade smiled his poisonous smile, and said, "I would be more careful of what you say, dear brother."

Panting, trembling with pain, Cyan just said, "You'll hurt me no matter what, so I may as well say whatever I please. Our family hates the Temperast, Jade. Cohen would never believe you'd betray our parents by helping to bring them back."

Jade smiled and tilted his head, the very image of seduction. Cyan wondered how many men and women had fallen for him over the years—and how few of them had come out unscathed. "Men will believe whatever I want them to believe because they like believing I want them."

Cyan made a face, not bothering to argue that. People had always fallen at Jade's feet, had brushed past Cyan to fawn over his more perfect twin. He'd hated it. He could work hard all day for crumbs of praise, screw up his courage to speak to someone, and Jade would still get praise and gifts and attention just because he was beautiful and possessed of a too-clever tongue.

"So you've been fucking Cohen so he'll never notice you've betrayed him until too late," Cyan said. "What happens after the Auths catch him?"

"He will see his work destroyed a second time and his family ruined forever."

Cyan did not bother to add 'like ours', but they both were thinking it. Jade would never see past the murders, or that Cyan had not supported him. "Must you do this? Why can't you let it go? Be happy that you have me, that we're alive."

"I *don't* have you," Jade said coldly. "You chose to ignore your family, to not care that our parents were *murdered*, to walk away—"

"They're dead!" Cyan shouted. "Getting revenge won't bring them back. They're gone. Instead of seeing *me*, instead of trying to be a family with what was left, you put all your attention on revenge. It's always about *you;* it always was. I was right there the whole time, and you never saw me. No one did. I'm your brother, your stars-damned twin, and even you never saw me except as something to mock and hurt."

Jade did not respond to the tirade at first, simply stared at him, until Cyan looked away with a rough sound. Finally, Jade said, "You're a fool and a coward. You never would accept who you are, you defied Mother and Father at every turn—"

"You helped me!" Cyan snarled. "You helped me learn to fight, pointed me to the Auths—"

Jade tossed his hair and smirked. "It kept you out of my way, made it easier to get what I wanted. If you had just accepted your life and made the most of it, I would have been forced to work a lot harder at getting what I wanted. Precious Cyan, so earnest and good and stubborn." He sneered.

Cyan said nothing.

"You ran from duty, from your family—you are very good at running, dear brother, I will concede that."

"I don't run all the time," Cyan whispered, even as the words cut. He *didn't* always run. He'd never run from a fight, except when it came to fighting Jade. Einn and the way he made Cyan feel terrified him, but he hadn't run away. Even now, as the agony of Einn being dead cut through him once more, he was glad for what he'd had, that he had not run as he probably should have.

Cyan's vision blurred. He'd been trying not to think about Einn because it just hurt too fucking much. "I will *never* forgive you for killing my friends, Jade. You can keep me prisoner all you like, it'll never make me give a damn about you. Not now."

Jade just laughed. "Your friends? Or is it that you're mad I killed your little Fornarian fuck toy?"

Cyan snarled and lunged blindly at Jade, screaming in agony when the collar activated, but keeping his hands around Jade's throat, squeezing with all the strength he had left. Nails raked his face, searing his skin and adding to the agony already tearing through him. He couldn't breathe, but he would be damned if he let go—

Rall tore him away and threw him on the bed, and Cyan finally gave up. The sound of the door closing made him glance up cautiously, and he glared when he saw Jade was still in the room, looming from the foot of the bed. "Rehab hasn't been good for you, brother."

"It's been great," Cyan replied, smugly enjoying the bruises already forming on Jade's throat, the way his voice was not quite as smooth as it had been only moments ago. "You still haven't explained why setting Cohen up to fall is revenge for murdering our parents."

"They'll find the evidence for that after they arrest him for everything else. When they do, he'll know he was played for a fool the entire time, exactly as he played Mother and Father, exactly as he thinks he has been playing me."

Cyan shook his head. "Mom and Dad would be appalled by your behavior. They'd be ashamed of you."

Jade tsked softly and moved around the bed to the side, reaching out to pat Cyan's head as he would a child's. "Cyan, our parents were ruthless politicians. They pushed hard to murder an entire race. No matter how they prettied it up, you of all people know that murder is murder. Our parents were not nice people. You would have finally gotten a taste of that if you really had gone ahead with your plans to defy them and joined the Auths."

"They would not have done as you did."

"You're a fool."

Cyan said nothing more, refusing to be further baited. No matter what Jade said, their parents had been good people. Jade was the only twisted one. "You can't keep me locked up forever, not when people know I'm here."

"You're shaken from your ordeal and only going to be further broken by the revelation that Cohen really was the killer. By the time people expect you to rejoin society, I'll have broken you." He dragged his nails lightly down Cyan's cheek, leaving livid red marks, but not quite breaking skin.

The door opened, and Rall entered carrying chains. Cyan tensed. He could take Rall, he knew that. Once upon a time, it was beyond his abilities, but he was the best of the best on Rehab now. He was better than any Auth. He could take Rall, and even Jade—maybe.

He needed to save Sean and Mendel, but he had absolutely no idea where they were or when Jade's scheming would all come to a head. If he left now, he'd be flying blind and likely in completely the wrong direction. He could run to Pyotr, but he had no faith in that quarter, and so late in the game, what could Pyotr really do?

Easier to wait until Sean and Mendel were arrested and hauled to Zero. They'd be arraigned or taken off quietly somewhere to be dealt with. Jade would be sure to tell him, just to torture him, and Cyan would figure out what to do then.

A sharp slap jerked him from his thoughts. "Pay attention."

Cyan glared at Jade, but said nothing, simply allowed Rall to chain him to the bed. He had no idea how he would get out of the chains, but that was a problem he would deal with later. "I hate you," he told Jade. Jade only smiled and patted his cheek, then turned and strode from the room, Rall on his heels, leaving Cyan alone.

He tugged experimentally at the chains, amused and annoyed that Jade had always preferred such old-fashioned, but regretfully effective means of keeping Cyan where he wanted. The locks, unfortunately, were *not* old-fashioned—they would require a passcode from Jade or Rall, but it was possible Cyan could fry it. His only real problem was the collar, but that would have to be endured until he could break it off. Hopefully, he'd last long enough *to* break it off.

Cyan stood up to see how far his chains would let him walk, unsurprised that he could only go a few steps from the bed—too far away from anything useful. Returning to the bed, he looked around his room, taking in the life he had left behind. The life to which he would probably be returning, one way or another. Either Jade would trap him here, or circumstances after Jade was arrested would. Not that he really cared. His only motivation was to save Sean and Mendel.

After that ... he just didn't know. His desire to build a life, a *real* life, had died with Einn.

# Chapter Eighteen

**PLANET 1529208 (KOLSTAR), RESEARCH FACILITY**

Sean's temper finally snapped. He turned on his heel and slammed his cuffed hands into the face of the guard who had grabbed his ass one time too many. The bastard dropped to the ground like a rock, blood pouring from his broken nose. Bending, Sean grabbed his stunner and clubbed him with the butt of it, then stood and aimed the stunner at the other two guards.

It happened quickly, too quickly for anyone to react properly. Sean didn't give them a chance to make up for lost time and didn't waste his own by telling them to drop their weapons and surrender. Instead, he fired, knocking them both out. "I am sick and tired of this stars-damned shit," he said, and dropped the stunner as more guards came pouring out of the facility. "One more of you Bangkok whores touches me, and I'll show you why no one fucks with Rehab. Collared and cuffed doesn't make me helpless."

Mendel chuckled as they were roughly hauled away. "I think you made your point." They were dragged into the building that loomed before them. It was made of rough, dark stone and marked only with numbers. Inside, the lights were dull, gleaming on slick blue tile and a dingy gray floor.

Sean glanced at the various rooms they passed, seeing what he could through the glass panels in each door. They all looked to be along the same lines of Mendel's laboratory on the *Brilliant.* So they were definitely in the right place, not that he'd ever had any doubt.

Eventually, they passed from the laboratories into what was clearly a wing of holding cells. If there was one thing Sean recognized on a moment, it was a prison. They were led to the very end of the hall and shoved roughly inside;

the door locked behind them with two different kinds of locks. Sean sneered at such slack security.

"I am astonished you were not beaten for taking out three of their guards in a temper tantrum."

"They're lucky it was only a temper tantrum," Sean muttered, then said more clearly, "They know I'm not one to fuck with, and that aside, they don't dare damage the goods. I would wager that you are of extreme importance, and they can't hurt me without risking you."

Mendel nodded, sitting down on one of the two small beds that were attached to the wall and meant to be folded up out of the way when not in use. In addition to the beds, there was a sink, a toilet, and a shelf meant to hold soap, washcloths, and other toiletries.

Sean rolled his eyes at that, but if the obviously amateur guards wanted to give him potential weapons, that was fine by him. "I wonder how long we'll stew here before something finally happens. Did you see anyone else? I didn't. This place could be empty, except they don't employ that many guards for an empty building."

"No, but I marked some of the equipment in the labs," Mendel replied. "Definitely a genetics facility, and not just for studying—at least three of the rooms I saw contained life pods. They are definitely trying to create something, not that we really needed confirmation at this point."

"To what end, though?" Sean asked. "It's all illegal; whatever they create will just be destroyed."

"Not if they successfully create a sentient being," Mendel replied. "That was the initial problem with the Draconis. We were meant to be sub-sentient, but wound up being fully sentient, and the IG code says that termination of a sentient being is murder."

Sean's mouth curved in a half-smile. "Nothing but trouble, Draconis."

Mendel tried to smile back, but it faltered and fell. "I may be trouble, but that doesn't mean I had to drag you—"

"Shut up," Sean said, cutting him off. "Whatever happens when this ends, I'm not sorry I met you. I've gotten to be *me* the past term, in a way I never have before. Even if we're fugitives, I haven't had to hide my magics or pretend I didn't have them. I think my only complaint in this whole mess is that I still haven't gotten to fuck you."

"Your priorities could use a recalibration," Mendel said, but he smiled, and that was all Sean cared about.

Sitting down beside him, Sean leaned in to take a kiss, annoyed that their still-bound hands kept him from touching. "Are they ever going to take these stupid cuffs off of us? I'd rather not cause trouble early by removing them myself."

"Not after your temper tantrum," Mendel replied with a laugh. "I'm more upset about the collars, but there is no way they'll give us a chance to use our magics."

"Not when we can teleport," Sean agreed. "But if they want me to behave, they should tell the guards to stop grabbing my ass. There's only one person with permission to do that."

Mendel laughed again. "I fully intend to make up for all the times I could have, but didn't, once we're out of here."

Sean smiled and kissed him again, trying to believe it would happen, but all he could see was that after this, they would just be moved to a different holding cell.

His thoughts were scattered by another kiss, and he decided thinking was definitely overrated. If he and Mendel had both done less thinking earlier on, they would have had more time together, instead of being on the same ship, but galaxies apart. Mendel's lips were soft and firm, his mouth warm, and he knew exactly how to kiss Sean to distraction.

He was so distracting, in fact, that Sean jumped when the door opened and someone cleared his throat. "Come on," the guard snapped when they jerked apart. He hauled Sean to his feet, and another grabbed Mendel, leading them back the way they'd come, then down another hallway and a third before stopping in front of a glass-front door.

They spoke to the two guards manning the door, one of whom then opened the door by typing in a long passcode and transmitting a second code via his in-lens. The door slid open, and Sean and Mendel were dragged inside and thrown to the floor. The guards departed, and Sean managed to get himself to his knees, then looked up.

As he'd expected, they were in a laboratory—and there were the life pods Mendel had mentioned seeing in other labs they'd passed. They were empty of specimens, but contained the pale, pink-ish nutrient fluid necessary for such experiments, so they were going to be used soon.

"Dr. Bikendi?" Mendel said, and Sean's gaze snapped to where Mendel was looking at a man who had, until then, gone unnoticed in one corner of the room. The man was of average height, with dusky skin and white hair streaked with black and glowing violet eyes—marks of the Telven. Sean shivered, thinking of the black-skinned Telve back on Rehab and their razor sharp fangs meant for drinking blood. This man's skin was more brown, though, since he was half Telven, half Kemperast.

So this was Dr. Itzal Bikendi, who was as feared for his heritage as he was respected for his brilliance. "What's going on?" Sean asked, slowly standing up.

"I would have thought that Mendel would have figured it out by now," Bikendi said, scowling at them and making no move to approach. He looked tired, haggard.

"We think we have the general idea," Mendel replied. "We're working on the theory that they want to recreate the Temperast, possibly with a Draconis-style bond."

Bikendi nodded. "Yes, but with some modifications. They want the Temperast to be powerless until matched, and for the Temperast to be the only ones affected by the bond while the soldiers bound to them are largely unaffected. They also want the bond to be tighter. Right now, for every bound couple, there is a twenty-one percent chance that when one person in the bond dies, the other will live. That is a seventy-nine percent chance that both parties will die. They—whoever they are, though I have my suspicions—want that percentage brought as close to one hundred percent as possible."

"Sub-sentient creatures that are forced to rely entirely upon their matches for life and power," Mendel said, "while simultaneously increasing the power and ability of their matches." He balled his trembling hands into fists. "They want to make the Temperast into weaponized Draconis."

"More or less," Bikendi agreed, looking more tired than ever. "I have been running the experiments as ordered, if only because I've nothing better to do with my time, and I do not have to hurt anyone to do my work. I will say I am damned tired of my own blood being drawn, but this is hardly the first group of morons to be overzealous on that point." He pushed up his sleeve to display the bruises and needle marks. "I do not much care for being the scientist and the experiment. You will not enjoy it either."

Mendel made a face in agreement. "Where is everyone else?"

"I have no idea. I have not left this room since I was dragged into it. Samples are brought to me; I never draw the blood myself. It would be a waste of time and resources to kill anyone, but that's all I can tell you."

"Most are probably in those other holding cells we passed," Sean said. "Or the labs, in the case of the other scientists. This place seems to have an abundance of space, so there's no easy way to pinpoint them exactly, unfortunately. So what do you need from me? I'm no scientist and I'm no Draconis."

"But you are a magics capable human," Bikendi pointed out. "You are also matched to Mendel, who is most qualified to help further my studies. They probably put you in here to make him more likely to cooperate—or so they can yank you away if he fails to cooperate. I will need blood samples from both of you."

Sean nodded and began to remove his jacket—then realized he was still cuffed. Bikendi muttered something

Sean didn't understand, then went to the door and rapped on it. A moment later, the door opened and a guard stepped inside. "What?"

"I cannot get work accomplished if they're cuffed," Bikendi said. "Remove their bindings."

"Boss' orders," the guard replied. "One's a killer, the other is ex-Rehab. They stay in the cuffs."

Bikendi sneered. "It is clear to me that I am surrounded by meatbags." Sean snorted at the uniquely Telven epithet, but one popular amongst criminals. He'd been called one so many times, he scarcely noticed any more. "Mendel is useless to me—to this whole endeavor—unless he can use his hands. What is he suppose do in chains, chitchat over tea? Make him useful or get him out of my sight."

The guard backhanded Bikendi, making the second guard laugh—it was all the distraction Sean needed. He swung his hands into the gut of the nearest guard, and when he doubled over, brought them down on the back of the guard's head. He dropped to the ground and Sean went for the next guy, catching him in the shoulder and knocking him into the counter, then nailing him in the groin. While he was distracted, Sean stole his stunner and fired, knocking him out. He rounded at the last guards, who was trying to retreat to call for help, and fired twice.

Dropping the stunner on the counter, he retrieved the cuff keys and freed Mendel, who immediately freed Sean. Flexing his wrists, Sean dragged the guards back out into the hall, stole another stunner and a knife, then returned to the lab. "Mendel, got that datapad?"

Mendel snorted in amusement and reached into his boot, pulling out a datapad about the length and width of two fingers. "I'm still surprised they did not find it."

Sean laughed. "Underpaid guards do underpaid work." Taking the datapad, he turned it on and pulled wires from his own boot, then used his newly acquired knife to pry off the cover of the door control panel. Syncing the datapad to the panel, he reached into his other boot and pulled out a small, thin case. He opened the case and quickly put the in-lens in place over his right eye.

Ready, he set to work, first jamming the door, then looking for cameras. "Do they not have eyes on this place?"

"No," Bikendi said. "Some of the equipment would interfere anyway, and the guards would have no idea what we're doing. The cells and halls are watched, but not the labs. We just get live attendants and periodic inspections."

Sean nodded and went back to work. It took surprisingly little effort to find what he needed and only a few minutes work to download it all to the datapad.

"We don't have much time," Mendel said.

"Don't need it," Sean said. "They didn't put up much security—guess he saw no point, given the whole operation was so secret. Also, if it's Cohen, he's too cocky for his own good."

Bikendi made a derisive noise. "He would have to be, to launch a scheme like this."

Sean smirked. "Well, he'll pay for it. The others will be here soon."

"It's good to know there is a scheme afoot," Bikendi grunted. "I am damned tired of being here. Took the IG long enough."

"Cohen is cocky, but he's had help that is far too smart for anyone's good," Sean replied and disconnected from the system. "There, I've grabbed damn near everything. If Cohen tries to have it all wiped when the Auths show up, it'll be too little, too late." He tossed the datapad back to Mendel, then restored the in-lens and wires to his own boots.

He returned the faceplate to the panel just before more guards showed up—five of them, all pissed off. Sean grabbed the stunner on the table and shot two of them before the third got to him. The Hellcat launched at him, poison-tipped claws slicing through Sean's' shirt and the skin beneath.

Sean grabbed him, slammed both their heads together, then sank a fist into the Hellcat's gut and threw him aside, shooting him to put him out entirely. By the time he was done with the Hellcat, Mendel had taken out the remaining two guards. Mendel glanced at him.

"As distracting as you are in Rehab mode, I cannot think it prudent to pick all these fights."

"If they're busy quelling trouble inside, they're less likely to notice trouble coming from the outside," Sean replied.

Mendel grunted and helped him cast the latest set of unconscious guards out into the hall. "You're playing a dangerous game."

"Yes," Bikendi snapped in agreement. "I think by now you have made your point. Get back in here." When the door closed, he punched in a sequence of numbers that set off warning lights and locked down the laboratory. "There. It will take them some time to sort that out, since it requires top-level clearance to cancel a hazard state from the outside, and I am fairly certain no such person is currently on the premises."

"You're brilliant," Sean said.

Bikendi just sneered at him. "Yes, I am. It is amazing what the mind can do when it is not severely damaged by pointless combat."

Sean laughed. "So what do we do now?"

"Work," Bikendi replied. "I am not going to waste all my time here; I may as well get some use out of being kidnapped. The information I've gathered will be useful to my own work. Now, blood samples. Mendel, my notes are over there if you want to read through them while I deal with your partner."

Laughing again, Sean stole a quick, firm kiss from Mendel, then sat where he was told so Bikendi could draw his blood.

# Chapter Nineteen

**PLANET 0000000 (ZERO), PORT PRIMUS**

Einn groaned in relief as he finally crawled free of the *Shangri La*. He never wanted to board another starship—ever. Slowly working out the stiffness in his limbs, he looked around to get his bearings.

It was hard not to gawk. He had always thought the tales of Zero must have at least been somewhat exaggerated, but near as he could tell at a glance, the tales were all true—Zero was beautiful. Einn could not tear his eyes away from the towering, shining building in the distance: the Palace of Eternity, the heart of the IG.

Someone bumped into him, recalling Einn to the task at hand. He was not there to stare like a babe fresh from his foundling cave; he was there for Cyan, and he would tear down the Palace itself to get him back.

Quickly moving away from the *Shangri La*, Einn wended his way through the maze-like port to the exit, heart kicking up a notch with trepidation. On most planets, the ports were public access. Securing ports was expensive and laborious, and most port workers had their hands full already. It was easier and cheaper to leave the ports accessible, and take the odd hit of criminal mischief—and there were plenty of ports that benefited from criminal activity.

Zero, of course, could afford to secure its ports. Importing or exporting anything on Zero was expensive and difficult: licenses, tariffs, and all the extras of both that went along with certain goods. Zero had never lacked for funds, and it poured a generous portion of those funds into security.

Reaching the access point, Einn handed over his stunner to the guards manning the security station. He then walked to the exit, drew a deep breath, and let it out slowly, then activated his in-lens, calling up the appropriate key codes given to him by Jade. To his immense relief, they worked, and Einn wasted no time in fleeing the port. Out in the public areas, he stopped a guide, and asked, "Alexander Estate?"

The guide smiled at him, though Einn supposed it was not programmed to do anything *but* smile, and replied in smooth tones, "Private Sector 3, Division 5, Estate 35-12548. Does that help you?"

"Yes, thank you," Einn said, and walked on, slowly finding his way to the transport platforms and getting in line for the one that would take him to Private Sector 3. When it was finally his turn, he stepped onto the platform and called up the necessary codes, though it took him a moment to locate them—and he was somewhat surprise that Jade had been so thorough. But he supposed that thoroughness was one of the things that made Jade so dangerous.

Einn wondered how long he had until someone finally deactivated all his access codes; hopefully not until he had saved Cyan. He *really* wondered how Cyan was going to get them off Zero, but there was no sense in worrying about that until he had Cyan. One cliff at a time, he reminded himself.

After arriving in the necessary sector, he checked a display map, then went to another transport platform, breathing another sigh of relief when his codes continued to work. Stepping out of the transport station when he arrived, he again found himself unable to do anything, but gawk. Shaking his head at the ridiculous amount of wealth towering around him, Einn checked a street board, used his in-lens to double check directions, and walked off toward the Alexander Estate.

When he reached it, he went back to gawking. *This* was the home Cyan had surrendered? Had walked away from without even a backward glance? This was what he had given up to settle for Rehab? It was beautiful, made of dark red stone with glass windows. Green grass covered the yard, though it was barely visible beneath the profusion of rosebushes. Einn shook his head at them: at least fifty bushes of Mars and Vrill roses. Such an extravagance made him dizzy. A walkway of bright white stone wended its way through and around the bushes, leading up to a door of dark green that matched the shutters framing the windows. Einn had never seen such a pretty, frivolous house.

He also saw no way in. Activating his datapad with his in-lens, he opened a security scan program, in-lens flashing as it analyzed the house and grounds. His datapad chirped faintly where it was still in its holster on his thigh, then sent back a confirmation that there were no security systems in place.

That was an out and out lie if ever he'd heard one, which meant it was an even nastier system than he'd been hoping to deal with—but he couldn't say he was surprised. Anyone who could afford roses like that, in that quantity, could afford the best security in the stars.

So how was he going to get in?

Einn kept walking, not wanting to draw attention to himself. He would make an attempt to break in once dark fell and hope for the best. He didn't have time for research or even much preparation. He really wished he had his magics right then, but he could still feel that awful muffled feeling in the back of his mind that told him he didn't. Whatever his bravado, being able to stick to things and heal himself were two things he greatly appreciated being able to do, and they would have been useful for climbing blind.

Worrying his bottom lip, Einn wandered around until he found a small, tidy-looking pub. Ordering a beer at the bar, he settled into a corner and contemplated his dilemma. There had to be a way in; he refused to be so close only to be flummoxed. He sipped at his beer and pulled out his datapad, running through what was available—legally and otherwise—on the types of security systems that could be guarding the Alexander Estate.

He looked up at the sound of someone approaching his table, reaching reflexively for his stunner before he remembered he'd had to leave it behind. He looked up—and froze in surprise when Raoul sat down across from him. Einn frowned.

Raoul smiled and drank his own beer. "You look remarkably healthy for someone crammed into that crawlspace for nearly two days."

"I've been in worse places for longer," Einn said. "We're adapted for it, you know that. What do you want?"

Raoul didn't reply as a waitress came up with a basket of fried Tehari. The sharp, salty smell made Einn's stomach growl. Raoul ate one, then nudged the basket toward Einn. "Eat. You'll need your strength."

Einn wasn't going to argue; it was possible the food was poisoned, but that was a sloppy way to get someone. If Raoul wanted him dead or captured, he'd already be out. "Take this, too," Raoul said, and tossed a small bottle filled with a dark green liquid into the basket. "Death by poison is not nearly flashy enough for a pirate."

Fishing out the bottle, Einn looked at it warily. "He found a cure for the poison that fast?"

"Constantine is very good at what he does," Raoul said. "He also worked nonstop to figure that out, but don't feel too sorry for him; he'll make a tidy sum from selling the formula. Drink it."

Einn obeyed, grimacing at the bitter taste, but not complaining otherwise—it was, after all, a cure. He chased the nasty taste with a few bites of food and a swallow of beer. "So what else do you want? You're not here just to be altruistic."

"My job is to protect Pyotr. I know everything that happens on his ship and in his office. No one boards the *Shangri La* without my being aware of it. Pyotr does not approve of your actions, but he doesn't condemn them either." Raoul tossed something else into the basket.

Einn ate another bite of tehari, and then picked up the little box. It was the length of half his finger and not quite half again as wide, made of black metal, and stamped with the infinity symbol of the IG on one side. The other side was stamped with a maker's mark he only recognized as one of the best in-lens makers in the IG. Why was Raoul giving him an in-lens case?

Flipping it open, Einn stared in bemusement at the two in-lenses inside, nestled in violet silk. The fine electronics around the edges glinted in the dim pub light, and the in-lens glass was so fine, he couldn't even really see it. "One for you, one for Cyan," Raoul said. "Don't let them fall into the wrong hands, though even if they did, they'd be useless. Those things are gremlin built, and it would take another gremlin to crack them. Never stops people from trying—and occasionally succeeding—though."

"Why?" Einn asked.

"Pyotr doesn't believe in wasting resources. Rescue Cyan. A ship will be waiting for you in Port Tertius, dock 3, section 21-B."

"Copy that," Einn said, deciding that questions would just have to wait until Cyan was safe. "Thanks."

"Oh, don't thank me," Raoul said with a grin, and set something else beside the basket, out of sight of the rest of the bar—a stunner, Einn noted. "Welcome to Internal Affairs. Don't screw up." He finished his beer, then stood and left as abruptly as he'd arrived, leaving Einn alone once more.

Einn picked up the stunner and smoothly tucked it away in his jacket. He carefully removed the in-lens he was already wearing, then picked up the one marked with a small 'E' in the silk in front of it. Fitting it over his right eye, he blinked to settle it into place. He froze while it activated, initializing information flashing across his eye, feeling the thrum as it verified his identity and searched out whatever it might need to connect to. Einn verified his datapad with a thought, then put the in-lens into rest.

How in the stars was it going to get him into the Alexander Estate? But even as he thought the question, the in-lens flashed back into life, bringing up codes, schematics, and a dozen other things that had Einn scrambling to put it to rest again.

Right. Expensive, sensitive equipment. Stars, he preferred working with old-model, black-market mod equipment. Putting aside thoughts of his late night activities for the moment, he enjoyed his beer and snack, then called the waitress over and ordered a full meal and a fresh beer.

As dark fell, Einn paid for his meal and made his way leisurely back to the Alexander Estate; by the time he reached it, full dark had fallen. He kept walking, then slipped in behind the house, heading down a smaller, less ornate walkway to a massive back porch and up to a set of glass-paned double doors. His in-lens flashed as it transmitted access codes when he passed through invisible gates, and flashed again when he reached the doors. They opened with the faintest click. Einn slipped inside and closed the door again behind him.

Inside, he called up the house blueprints, keeping them up as he moved carefully through the house. He froze on the stairs when he realized, too late, that someone else was on the stairs—

The bottom dweller who had collared Cyan. Einn reacted, but the other man reacted first, shoving him into the wall. Einn barely noticed, far more interested in the way his hand had reflexively *stuck* to the wall. He had his magics. So a ship was waiting for him, huh? Einn laughed.

"What's so funny?" the man demanded, slamming Einn's head into the wall. He then closed his hand around Einn's throat and squeezed. Einn didn't bother to tell him both were futile efforts, that he'd have to try a lot harder to injure or suffocate a Fornarian.

"Your face," Einn replied, and pulled the stunner Raoul had given him, firing almost before he'd fully aimed it.

The man dropped like a rock on the stairs, and Einn blasted him again for good measure. Holstering his stunner, huffing in annoyance, Einn dragged him down the stairs and into an empty room. Using the man's own clothes, Einn tied him and gagged him, then removed all his weapons and comms. Those he dumped in another room, then he locked both of them before finally returning to the stairs.

As he walked, stunner drawn this time, he made a mental note never to anger Pyotr Kavalerov. It was creepy—even frightening—how much power he had, and all the ways he was willing to use it. Einn did not like the idea of the IG having so much access to his private home.

At the top of the stairs, he called up the blueprints again and got his bearings. It really disturbed him that the map marked where Cyan would be. How had Pyotr—or whoever set up his in-lens—known where Cyan would be? Shaking the thought off as distracting, Einn moved quickly down the hallway to the appropriate door.

His in-lens flashed, displaying the necessary codes for the door scanner to read. After a moment, there was a muted click and chime. Einn pushed the door open and slipped inside, then pushed it closed again.

It took only a moment for him to spot Cyan on the bed. Relief flooded through him so hard and sudden, he trembled with it—but it turned to white hot rage as he drew closer and saw the scratches and bruises, the chains and that stars-damned collar. Reaching the bed, he lightly touched Cyan's cheek—and jumped when Cyan reared up, eyes wide with fright. "No—" Cyan froze, stared at him. He opened his mouth, but no words came out.

Einn cautiously moved close again, reaching out to him. "Cyan?"

"You're dead," Cyan whispered.

"What?"

"Well, well," said an all too familiar voice. Einn whipped around, raised his stunner—and reeled back when the bastard from before punched him in the face. He dropped, swearing and kicking out blindly as his eyes watered with pain. Looked like he knew how to hit a Fornarian after all.

"Rall, stop!" Cyan snarled.

Rall started to reply, but Einn used the distraction to land a more solid kick, and Rall went down with a cry, landing half on top of Einn. He struggled to get Rall off him, wishing irritably he had that handy little light trick of Karmikel's.

Einn screamed in surprise when the room filled with a burst of brilliant white-gold light, wondering why the hell it didn't hurt his eyes—

Questions for later, he thought, and with a snarl, shoved a temporarily blinded Rall off. He dove for his lost stunner—only to be kicked just as the light faded away. He saw Jade from the corner of his eye and wondered where the stars he'd come from. A wet, startled noise made them both turn and look to see that Cyan had gotten hold of a dagger and slit Rall's throat. Dropping the knife, Cyan fumbled with what looked like a control mechanism of some sort, and Einn saw Jade with an exact copy.

Einn knocked Jade to the floor and pinned him there, sticking himself to the floor even as he screamed in pain when Jade's nails sank into his skin.

He heard the burst of a stunner firing, then another, and Jade went limp beneath him. Einn slowly clambered to his feet, wincing at the bloody marks on both his sides, swearing as his healing magics made them sting all the more during the process of repair. He turned to look at Cyan, still tethered to the bed, but free of that awful collar. "Are you okay?"

Cyan laughed, a ragged, broken sound. "You're really—they said—I thought you were *dead.*"

Einn closed the short distance between them and caught Cyan up, kissing him so hard Cyan's lip split. He groaned, the feel and flavor of Cyan a balm. "I'm not dead."

"The Temperast?"

"*They* are dead. Are you okay?"

Cyan gave another of those shaky laughs. "I will be. I can't believe you're alive. They said you were all dead except for Sean and Mendel. You're alive, and you came for me—"

"I'll always come for you," Einn said fiercely, and kissed him again. Eventually, he drew back, and said, "As much as I love to see you naked, you need clothes if we're going to get out of here. Can you move? You look pretty banged up."

Making a face, Cyan said, "I've been beat worse by Traxens, if not quite so methodically. I'll be fine for a bit, and can rest on the ship. I'll have to raid Jade's room; I don't have any clothes here that will fit."

Einn tried to picture Cyan in Jade's ornate robes, and simply couldn't. Instead, he stole one last kiss, and then turned away to search Rall and Jade until he found keys to the chains. "I'll be back," Cyan said when he was finally free. "See to it Jade can't escape; he's going to Rehab this time."

"You got it," Einn said, and after Cyan had left, grabbed Jade and hauled him to the bed. Stripping Jade's clothes off, he put him in the collar, then attached the chains, making them too short for Jade to even get off the bed. Let him piss himself; Einn hoped when they found Jade, he was a filthy, furious mess.

Turning back to Rall, Einn stripped him of the weapons he'd regained and a few other items that could prove useful. He tucked it all away in the pockets of his pants and jackets. Out in the hallway, he locked the bedroom and checked his stunner.

"Einn!"

He holstered his stunner and turned around just as Cyan reached him, grunting when Cyan kissed him, awkward at first, but quickly smoothing out. "Hey," Einn said softly, lightly touching the scratches on Cyan's face, angry at Jade all over again.

"I still can't believe you're alive," Cyan said. "I'd given up. I was going to save Sean and Mendel, but after that ... all I could think about was you being dead."

Einn rubbed Cyan's bottom lip with his thumb. "It takes more than a couple of creepy goons to kill me. We should get moving. Karmikel is waiting for us. He must be, if I have my magics back."

"Speaking of Karmikel, that light trick must be his, 'cause that's not Fornarian magics. I thought you'd be slower to adjust to that, stubborn as you are—and reticent as Karmikel was."

"Accident," Einn said, and he told Cyan all that had transpired since he'd been taken as they left the house and headed for the ports.

Cyan laughed when he finished. "You've been busy. I'm sorry you were stuck in that crawl space for so long."

Einn shrugged the words aside. "I'm just happy to have you back. Now we need to go rescue the others, before Sean and Mendel get captured when it all goes south. Nice outfit, by the way."

"Go to hell," Cyan replied, tugging irritably at the ornate silk shirt and loose white silk trousers he wore. "I'm just grateful he at least had slacks; I wasn't wearing one of his damned robes."

Laughing, Einn got them through the various transports and back to the ports, then stopped. "I forgot! Here, this is for you. I even told you Raoul gave me two, and then completely forgot to give it to you." He pulled out the in-lens box and tossed it to Cyan. "From Pyotr, which makes me nervous, but they're damned useful."

Cyan frowned, but took out the in-lens and fit it into place over his right eye. "For better or worse, I guess."

Einn grunted in agreement. "So how do we get to where we need to be? This place is confusing, and I didn't think anything could be worse than Bangkok." Cyan laughed—a real laugh, which made Einn more relieved than he'd ever admit—and led the way through the carefully ordered chaos until at last the *Brilliant* came into view.

The door slid open and the gangway slid down as they approached, and Karmikel's acerbic voice came over the speaker. "In. Now."

Striding obediently up the gangway, Cyan on his heels, Einn led the way to the bridge where Karmikel was already busy getting them out of port. When they were well away, Karmikel rounded on them. "You're an idiot! This is exactly why I didn't want to match, and I'll be damned if I spend the rest of my life chasing after you and your stupid decisions."

"Saving Cyan wasn't stupid," Einn said. "Say that again and I'll knock you flat. That being said, I'm sorry. I don't want to be matched either, but you don't always get to pick your crew. You learn to build a team from the crew you get."

Karmikel scowled at him a moment longer, then gave a terse nod before turning back to his console. "Your light trick came in handy, by the way," Einn added. "So, thanks. You'll have to help me use it properly and tell me what stars else I can do now."

"You can tell me how not to stick to things," Karmikel groused, not bothering to turn around. "It's annoying."

Einn snickered. "Sure. Where's Lark?"

Karmikel made a face. "With Pyotr, though he wouldn't say why he insisted on taking Lark."

"Insurance?" Einn hazarded, not liking it. Karmikel did not reply, which was all the confirmation that Einn needed. So Lark was hostage until they did what Pyotr wanted. What was it Raoul had said? Pyotr wasn't pleased, but didn't condemn? So he'd been made Internal Affairs, but Lark was hostage until ... when? "If I have to assault the Commander of Special Forces to get Lark back, I will."

"I doubt that will be necessary, and that stars-cursed pirate could use the lesson in humility, anyway."

Cyan laughed. "I don't think Lark would appreciate being told he lacks humility. We'll get him back, but one thing at a time. Where are we headed?"

"If the chem trackers are to be trusted, we are headed for Kolstar. We should arrive in five hours, set to rendezvous in four with an Auth ship, the *Scythe.*"

"Good," Cyan replied. "I'm going to find better clothes." He strode out of the room and Einn followed him into one of the sleep cabins, watching as Cyan stripped, angry all over again at the bruises and scratches that covered him from head to toe.

"You need to rest," Einn said.

Cyan shrugged. "There's not really time."

"There's four hours," Einn said, and pushed away from the doorframe he'd been leaning against. He strode over to Cyan and grabbed him up, then carried him to the nearest bunk and set him down on it. "Sleep."

Cyan didn't reply, and cut off whatever he was about to ask. Einn didn't push, just sat down beside him, and bent to give Cyan a kiss. "Go to sleep, Rehab." Cyan nodded and turned away to lay on his side. Einn lay down next to him, pulling Cyan close, and didn't move until Cyan's slight trembling ceased and he finally fell asleep.

# Chapter Twenty

**CUSTOM CLASS STARSHIP Z-28922942, THE *BRILLIANT***

Cyan kept wanting to reach out and touch, reassure himself for the thousandth time that Einn was alive—that he was real and not some figment of Cyan's imagination while he lay, still trapped in his old room, waiting for the next round of misery.

He should have been convinced after waking up to see Einn had stayed with him while he slept. But the weight of the memory of the collar around his throat pressed more heavily upon him than even Einn's warm presence. He could not yet shake the awful feeling that had fallen over him when he'd thought Einn was dead.

Einn looked up from the comm he was monitoring and smiled. Cyan smiled back, though from the look Einn then gave him, the smile didn't quite succeed. "I'm fine," he said, before Einn could ask. "Shaken, not broken." Not now that he realized nobody had died. He still didn't like that they'd come close because of him, but damn it, they were alive. Rall was dead. Jade was going to Rehab. He'd learned his lesson there; he wouldn't fuck up a second time. "Are we almost there?"

"Yes," Karmikel replied, looking away from the main screen where he was monitoring space, the planet they were approaching, and the ship travelling with them. He had switched earlier from his in-lens to full on in-specs, communicating with the *Scythe* and contacts down planet. "Approaching Kolstar, cleared to travel planet-wide at will. Should reach base in minus twenty-five. Stand by to teleport in, be prepared for immediate action. *Don't* get yourselves killed." He shot Einn a glare for good measure, though some of the thunder was lost as half his face was covered by the flashing in-specs.

"Copy that," Einn drawled, unfolding from his seat and stretching as he stood up. Cyan watched him, unable to tear his eyes away at first. Finally, he shook himself and stood, then checked both of the stunners he carried, along with three knives and half a dozen bombsticks he'd found in a neglected arms trunk in a closet off the engine room.

He followed Einn from the bridge and down to the transport room, flexing his hands in anticipation of a good fight. *This* kind of violence he could handle—all too well. It was only Jade who made him weak. Shoving the thought aside, he reached out and touched Einn, resting a hand against his chest and smiling at the way he could just barely feel the bones of Einn's chest. "Any other race, I'd call you starved nearly to death, rock spider."

Einn snagged his arm and pulled him in close, then bent to kiss him. "I'm fine. Alive. You're not getting rid of me that easily."

Cyan smiled and started to say he was surprised he got Einn at all, but the lights flashed, warning them of imminent transport. They stepped onto the platform and, seconds later, vanished.

### PLANET 1529208 (KOLSTAR), RESEARCH FACILITY

They reappeared at the edge of a large group of Auths in their sharp gray uniforms. Cyan recognized the man in charge, but there was no chance to speak as everything abruptly turned into chaos. Guards streamed out of the facility they'd transported to, clearly not interested in surrendering peacefully—or surrendering at all. Cyan left the Auths to it and put his focus on getting through the melee and into the facility to find Sean and Mendel.

A guard came at him, blood streaming down his face, and Cyan put him out with a single stunner blast. Another rushed him from the right, and Cyan swung around, punched him, then stunned him. He pushed on, Einn close behind.

Inside the facility, the chaos only got worse. By the time they'd fought their way through, Cyan was sweaty, bloody, and ready for a nap. Why were there so many stars-damned guards? The entire operation had more of a cut-and-run feel that didn't mesh with the reckless attack by the excess of guards.

Finally, he reached the spot indicated by the chem tracers in Sean and Mendel's blood. He used his stunner to break the lock, and when the door still refused to budge, he pulled out a bombstick and affixed it to the door. "Clear!" he bellowed, and pounded on the door to warn anyone on the other side. Pressing the activation button, he shoved Einn down the hall, diving down a side hall just seconds before the door blew.

He didn't wait for the debris to settle; just burst from the side hall and back down the main hallway, barreling through the shattered door, stunner in his left hand, right hand free to—

To find Sean, Mendel, and two more figures lying unconscious on the floor of what appeared to be a lavish—overly lavish—office. He also saw an open door at the very back, behind the massive, ornate desk that took up a large portion of the room.

"I'll take care of things here," Einn said from behind him.

Cyan grunted an acknowledgment and took off, vaulting over the desk and sprinting down the narrow hallway beyond at full tilt. At the end, he nearly crashed into a small scout ship, the sort meant to regroup with a larger ship elsewhere, probably a combat or merchant class, the only two classes that employed such scout ships.

The ship's engines began to pulse and whir, and Cyan didn't hesitated—simply lit another bombstick and flung it, throwing himself out of the way as it blew out most of the bottom part of the tiny ship. He swore loudly as shrapnel sliced his right calf, but only paused long enough to make certain it wasn't a dangerous wound. Clambering to his feet, he limped as quickly as he could manage to the ship and aimed his stunner at the still-closed door. "Exit the ship. You are under arrest. If you resist arrest, you will be treated as armed and dangerous. Exit the ship!"

When nothing happened, he moved in closer, wishing there was some way to deactivate—then his in-lens flashed, syncing with the door control panel, and the door slid open. Cyan adjusted his grip on his stunner and limped inside.

He sneered when he found High Chancellor Cohen in the cockpit. "Do you want to go with dignity, Cohen, or should I just knock you out and drag you?"

Cohen glared at him. "You have no authority to—"

"I'm a First Class Rehabilitation Guard; I have all the authority I need," Cyan said curtly. "I've also been temporarily instated as a liaison to Internal Affairs, which gives me more authority. Stand up, get off the fucking ship, and don't try anything."

Cohen went from defensive to gentle and smooth. "Cyan, my boy, we're old friends. Surely—"

"You had my parents murdered," Cyan hissed, and shot him. Cohen slumped over in his seat, and Cyan holstered his stunner before he gave in to the urge to kill Cohen and be done with the bastard. He hefted Cohen up over his shoulder, awkward in the tight space, and he was not remotely sorry that Cohen was the one most jarred and knocked around by the endeavor. Panting, Cyan slowly limped out of the ship, then even more slowly made his way back down the hallway to the office where he'd left Einn.

When he finally reached it, he dropped Cohen to the floor, then collapsed himself. He groaned—and startled when someone grabbed him, then immediately relaxed when he realized it was Einn. "Thanks," Cyan said, as Einn carefully hauled him to his feet, and then continued to support him.

"Do you require medical attention?" asked a level, precise voice.

Cyan looked up and smiled at the man he'd recognized earlier, but had not been able to speak with: he had dark dusky skin and pale hair, and the sort of sharp eyes that seemed as though they missed nothing. He was dressed in the steel gray uniform of the Authorities and wore the marks of a Lieutenant. "Sigma," he greeted. "I'm not surprised in the least to see you here."

"Or I you," Sigma replied. "Do you need medical assistance?"

"No, I'm good."

Sigma nodded and glanced at the desk, surprise flooding his features. "That is the High Chancellor. Commander Kavalerov said this assignment would require discretion, but ... "

"High Chancellor Cohen is behind this entire operation. We have the evidence."

"Here!" Sean said suddenly, from where he was sitting against a wall, looking tired and pained. He tossed Cyan a mini datapad .

Cyan caught it neatly, then flipped it to Sigma, and added, "I also have it on good authority that he is guilty of the murders of Lord and Lady Alexander."

Sigma's brows rose, but he said only, "I will see the investigation is given renewed attention. I am under orders to get the four of you out of here quickly and quietly."

"We're going," Cyan said.

"You might work harder on the quickly part," Sigma said. "I will finish up here and contact Kavalerov should I need anything further from you. He will forward me your reports."

Cyan nodded and clasped his shoulder briefly in gratitude, then let Einn help him from the room. They paused at the door, waiting while Sean said farewell to the other two figures in the room. Belatedly, Cyan realized one of them was Dr. Bikendi.

"Remember what I said," Bikendi said to Sean.

"I can scarcely forget," Sean replied, smiling faintly. "Thank you."

Bikendi grunted and said nothing more, merely moved to go speak with Sigma. Cyan turned to Mendel and realized the woman he was embracing was a relation—mother, he guessed, by age and the way she was hugging him. Only mothers hugged like that; he felt a pang, recalling his own, then. He'd been too angry, those days he hadn't known were their last, to hug anyone.

Einn's arm tightened around him, and a soft kiss brushed Cyan's brow. "We need to go," Einn said, drawing Mendel's attention.

Mendel nodded, said something quietly to his mother, and with a last embrace, finally joined them, following them out into the main hallway and out of the research facility. A few minutes later, they reached the outer yard and Karmikel transported them back onto the ship, and the *Brilliant* sped rapidly away.

"Cyan!" Sean burst out once they appeared on the ship. He hugged Cyan tightly, and Cyan held him just as fiercely. "You're safe! We knew Einn would get you. I'm sorry you were dragged—"

"Forget it," Cyan interrupted, smiling. "Good things came out of it. So what do we do now, you think?"

"Now, we rendezvous with the *Shangri La*," Karmikel said from behind them. "One hour, be ready."

### COMBAT CLASS STARSHIP A-98147121, THE *SHANGRI LA*

Cyan bowed low to the tall, imperious, older look-a-like of Pyotr who stood before him. "Grand Chancellor. It's been a long time."

"Not so long you need be so formal," Grand Chancellor Arkadii Kavalerov replied, and beckoned Cyan closer. Cyan smiled and obediently hugged him.

"You're the same as ever."

Looking him over critically, Arkadii said, "You've grown into yourself—mostly, anyway." Cyan raised his brows. "We'll fix what's still missing," Arkadii said briskly, with a look that said it was pointless to ask, he would say nothing further. Cyan had gotten that look a lot, growing up.

Arkadii moved to his desk on the far side of the office he had clearly commandeered from Pyotr. "Sit, all of you. The Commander has just finished briefing me on this entire debacle." He slid a look toward Pyotr, and Cyan winced inwardly in sympathy. Six terms later, he still knew what it felt like to be given *that* look. "I have quite a mess on my hands," Arkadii said, sitting down and folding his hands on the desk. "My High Chancellor has been arrested for a list of crimes I shudder to look at. There is a warrant out for one of my Lower Chancellors, who has apparently gone missing—"

"Missing!" Einn burst out, rising from his chair. "He was chained to that damned bed! How the stars did he go missing?" he snarled, but sat again when Cyan tugged at him. Arkadii regarded him with amusement, and Einn tacked on a belated, "Your Lordship."

Snorting in further amusement, Arkadii answered, "He managed to escape, though the Auths I sent to retrieve him could not tell me how."

"Jade," Cyan said bitterly. "He always finds a way."

Arkadii replied in calm tones, "He cannot hide forever. For the present, I must sort out the lot of you. With the exception of Agent Aurum, every person in this room is either a criminal or dangerously close to being one. However, the circumstances are, to say the least, extenuating." He looked at Karmikel and actually smiled. "Thank you, Agent Aurum, for actually abiding by the laws you are sworn to uphold as closely as you are able, given your duties."

"I am proud to serve, Your Lordship."

"Kiss ass," Lark said, and Cyan wondered when he had entered the room. He nodded at Cyan and Einn, pointedly ignoring the nasty look Karmikel shot him.

Arkadii sighed, drawing their attention back to him. He leaned forward, hands still folded together, elbows on the desk. "In light of recent events, the reports submitted to me by various persons, and the recommendation submitted by Commander Kavalerov, I am officially instating Cyan Alexander, Adalsteinn, and Lark Vallant as Internal Affairs Agents. Given your colorful history, sadly a history that is common in the IA, you are on probation for a full term. At the end of that term, if you have performed admirably, you will be instated as full agents. Agent Aurum will be your handler during your trial term. If you do not work out as agents, other arrangements will be made. This is not a job offer; it is an order."

Karmikel sighed, but otherwise said nothing. Cyan winced to hear himself called 'Alexander' after so many years of being free of the name, but he had known that was how it would all end. Whatever he'd hoped, he'd known that in the end, he couldn't avoid it forever. "I liked being Rehab," he said anyway.

"Too bad," Arkadii snapped, then rounded on Pyotr. "You are being removed from your position."

Surprise flashed across Pyotr's normally guarded face, but in the next moment, he regained control of his expressions. "No—"

"It is not debatable," Arkadii said coldly, and Cyan could not remember ever seeing him so angry, least of all with the nephew on whom he had always doted. "Do you want to delve into why right now? You overstepped your bounds and you know it. I can go into detail." Pyotr said nothing. "You have one term to select and train a replacement," Arkadii said. "In the meantime, you are going to be appointed High Chancellor."

"I don't—"

Arkadii cut him off with a look. "I'm not interested in what you want or think, Pyotr. The IG is going to be in fits over the arrest of Cohen and the warrant out for Alexander. The Star Assembly will want reassurance that we are righting what has clearly gone very wrong. Appointing you will appease most and terrify the rest into keeping their mouths shut, and the rest of the Lower Chancellors will not dare cross me by voting against it. We will speak further in your quarters."

"Yes, Your Lordship," Pyotr said stiffly, then turned and left the room.

Turning back to the rest of the room, Arkadii said, "Gentlemen, I am sorry we must meet—and reunite—this way. I am sorry, too, that I must be so brief. Thank you for all that you have done, especially as I know most of you wanted no part of this debacle. I certainly did not. Suffice to say that while serving in the IA is your punishment, you will also be amply rewarded. Good day to you."

He left, and Cyan finally stood up, stretching out his sore muscles.

"So ... what about us?" Sean asked into the silence. "He never said anything about Mendel and me. What are we supposed to do?"

Cyan laughed. "Slip away. He is giving you a chance to escape. We've seen no one else on this ship. The only other person who really knows you're here is Sigma, and he'll never tell."

Karmikel removed a small box from his pouch and tossed it to Mendel. Staring at it in shock, Mendel slowly looked up at Karmikel. "This is the master key for the *Brilliant*."

"Take it and go away," Karmikel said sourly. "You've been a pain long enough.'

"But—I can't take your ship—"

"Shut up and go away," Karmikel snapped. "You can bet for all this hassle, I'll be demanding a better ship."

Mendel opened his mouth, then closed it again, and finally nodded. "Thank you. I hope we see you all again."

Cyan embraced Sean tightly, then shook Mendel's hand. "Take care of each other. Maybe we can visit sometime?"

Sean smiled. "We've been invited to be assistants and experiments by a certain scientist of notorious origins." His smile faded. "Of course, first we need to slip to Mars ... "

Hugging him again, Cyan said, "Give my love to your mother. I'm glad you're all right. I really thought I'd punch you when I saw you again, but I never got the chance, and now the moment's gone."

"I'm sure you'll think of another reason," Sean said with a crooked grin. "See you around, Lord Alexander."

"Fuck you," Cyan replied, and gave him a shove. "Go."

They went, and Cyan sighed as the door closed behind them. "So what do we do now?"

"The *Scythe* has agreed to return us to Zero," Karmikel said. "We'll have to go there to get you three officially set up as IA Agents."

Lark and Einn made faces. Cyan laughed. "At least you're not going to Rehab." The looks they gave him then were even more tragic, and Cyan laughed harder. "It can't be that bad!"

Karmikel looked at him as if he were an idiot. "If, after all that we've been through, you believe that, you're dumber than a Kreskan trying to stay pure in the Red Dragon district of Bangkok. You're Internal Affairs—it's always that bad."

Cyan shook his head, then looked at Einn and smiled. "There are perks." To his amusement, Lark and Karmikel rolled their eyes together, looking equally disgusted.

"I'm going to go beat my head against a wall," Karmikel groused. "I also need to start work on acquiring a new ship."

Lark's gaze followed him out, then slowly returned to the other two. "I'm glad you guys are safe."

"We're glad you're alright," Cyan said. "I'm sorry you were taken hostage."

"I've suffered worse than good food and a comfortable bed on a classy ship," Lark said. "Right now, I'm going back to that comfortable bed. Try to stay out of trouble for a few hours." He clapped them both on the shoulder, then departed, leaving Einn and Cyan alone.

Einn tugged him close, wrapping his long arms around Cyan. "As pirates, we accept that at some point, we're going to do time in Rehab. It's just a fact of life that pirates either die or get arrested. I have to admit, never thought my Rehab time would look this good."

Cyan laughed. "That's an awful line."

"Yours are never any better," Einn replied, just before Cyan kissed him.

# Chapter Twenty-One

CUSTOM CLASS STARSHIP Z-28922942, THE *BRILLIANT*

Sean helped Mendel get the *Brilliant* away from the *Shangri La*, the work familiar and distracting. He did not breathe properly until they were well out of sight, and no one tried to come after them.

It was stupid: he had technically been a fugitive for the past term. He should not feel like *more* of a fugitive just because they were running away. But he supposed he was more of one, really. Whatever his flaws, Pyotr had helped them, protected them, supported them. Now Pyotr was no longer there, and Mendel was no longer tied to the IA.

They were on their own, and the *Brilliant* their only protection until they could reach Bikendi, and even Bikendi was not the same as having the Auth Commander at their backs. "I can't believe the Grand Chancellor just let us go," Mendel said, breaking into Sean's thoughts. "We should be dead, or at the very least on our way to Rehab. He just ... let us go."

Sean smiled faintly. "I think you don't get to be Grand Chancellor of the Infinitum Government by being stupid. If he let us go, he has reasons, and I'm going to believe he knows it's despicable to want us dead just because I'm a mutant."

"You have a remarkably positive outlook," Mendel said, returning the smile.

"I'm still breathing, despite that whole mutant thing and our crazy adventures of the past term. We're as free as we could ever hope to be, on our way to Mars to retrieve my mother, and I have you. I've got all the reason in the world to have a positive outlook. There is also the fact that we have nothing to do between here and Mars."

"Nothing to do, hmm?" Mendel said, and wrapped his fingers around Sean's wrist, tugging him close. Sean splayed his hands across Mendel's chest. "I'm sure we could think of something."

Sean snickered. "No doubt you've got experiments to run." He leaned up and dragged his tongue across Mendel's lips, then took a proper kiss, slow and deep, leaving Sean breathless when they finally drew apart.

"Indeed," Mendel replied. He dragged Sean's arms up around his neck, then slid his hands back down Sean's arms, along his back, to finally twine around his waist. "The first experiment on my list is to determine just how loud and long you scream when you come."

The words made Sean jerk in surprise, then he laughed. "Now I have to ask what kind of lab equipment is required for that sort of experimentation."

"I'm not dignifying that awful line with an answer," Mendel said, rolling his eyes, and he kept Sean from providing his own answer by kissing him hard and grabbing his ass, grinding their bodies together. Sean moaned in approval and clung tightly, fingers twisted in Mendel's hair and a shiver running down his spine as Mendel nipped at his lips. He wasn't actually much for screaming; a lifelong habit of not attracting attention bled into all aspects of his life, but he half-thought Mendel might be able to make him do it.

Finally tearing away, he said, "We really shouldn't fuck on the bridge. Karmikel will sense it and cause the ship to self-destruct."

Mendel snorted in amusement, nibbling at his jaw. "Stop talking about other men." He pushed Sean playfully away, and ordered, "Lead the way."

Sean was tempted to just step close again, disregard his own words and push Mendel to the floor. But the floor was hardly comfortable, and there was a perfectly good bed a short distance away, so he made himself turn around and lead the way from the bridge and to the Captain's quarters.

In all the time they'd spent on the ship, he had never once seen Karmikel use the Captain's Quarters. Actually, Sean wasn't entirely certain he'd ever seen Karmikel leave the bridge, unless they had to go down planet. They really would have to repay Karmikel for parting with the ship he loved so dearly. Sean felt a momentary pang, reminded that being fugitives meant he would seldom, if ever, see his friends again.

He was distracted from the serious thoughts when Mendel grabbed him from behind and pushed him down onto the bed. Sean rolled over, staring up at Mendel, and the expression on Mendel's face went straight to his cock. "I should have known you'd be this take charge in bed," he said, sitting up to remove his boots.

"Focused," Mendel replied. "I believe you once punched me for being too focused."

Sean grinned, throwing his boots aside and starting on his jacket. "I am more than happy to have that focus on me."

"So am I," Mendel murmured, tossing aside the last of his own clothes and helping Sean with the rest of his, although helping turned into hindering when he insisted on caressing or kissing every part of Sean's body as it was revealed.

Mendel's green scales gleamed in the light that had turned on automatically when they entered the room, a stunning contrast to his smooth, tan skin. Naked at last, Sean pulled Mendel down on top of him, sucking up a mark on his throat and whimpering as Mendel's hands moved along his skin. He took a hungry kiss, jerking as their cocks rubbed together, leaving damp marks on his stomach.

Breaking the kiss, Mendel mouthed his way down Sean's body, biting his shoulder, licking his nipples, teasing with his fingers before following them with sharp little nips as he steadily worked his way lower. He hovered a moment, teasing, waiting until Sean yanked at his hair, before finally flicking his tongue over the head of Sean's cock. When Sean yanked at his hear again and swore at him, Mendel sucked him down properly, working tongue and throat. Sean fisted his hand in Mendel's hair more tightly than ever, thrusting into his hot mouth, panting and swearing and begging—

—and bellowing in outrage when Mendel abruptly pulled off his cock and reared up, then off the bed. "You son of a bitch!"

Mendel snickered at him and picked up his pants, rifling through them a moment before he came up with a small tube that made Sean forgive him a teensy bit. "I didn't know you were carrying lube around."

"Focused," Mendel repeated. "Also patient, upon occasion. I figured my chance would come." He pushed Sean's legs apart and settled between them, wasting no time in gently pushing in one slick finger. Sean moved into it, groaning his approval. Mendel kissed him, adding a second finger, and sucking up a mark on Sean's chest when he added a third a short time later.

Sean groaned again as the fingers withdrew, and Mendel's cock pushed inside him, slowly at first, and then all the way with a last, hard thrust. He gripped Mendel's back, nails biting, and said, "A little more focus, please."

Mendel laughed and, grabbing Sean's hips, obediently began to focus, thrusting hard and deep. Sean gasped and pleaded, holding so tightly to Mendel his nails left marks that would turn into bruises. He shouted as Mendel grabbed his cock and jerked Sean off in time with his thrusts.

He thought he may have very well shouted as he came, but wasn't entirely certain, more interested in committing to memory the way Mendel sounded when he came. Mendel collapsed on top of him, and Sean grunted at the weight, but did not shove him off quite yet.

After a few minutes, Mendel said, "While promising, I feel the first experiment was inconclusive. Many repeats may be required."

"Now who's coming up with stupid lines?" Sean replied, rolling his eyes. He shoved Mendel, then draped himself across Mendel's chest, leaning down to kiss him. "I think I need a nap, but then I'm all for it."

### PLANET 1311819 (MARS), SETTLEMENT 2.1 (CANADIA)

Sean breathed a sigh of relief as the main console chimed to warn him that someone was approaching the ship. His in-lens flashed as he transmitted an order to trigger the out-cameras, and he beamed when he saw an old Rehab buddy standing with his mother just outside the ship. "Open main," he ordered, and left the bridge.

As the main door slid open, he pressed the button to extend the gangway, then strode down it and embraced his mother tightly. "Mama, I'm so sorry."

She cried into his shoulder, thinner and frailer than when he'd last seen her, but still able to hold him tightly. "Oh, Sean, Sean, Sean ... " He kissed her cheek and hugged her again, then drew away and extended a hand to the man who had brought her.

"Thanks, Helm. I owe you big time for risking this for me."

"Fuck it," Helm said staunchly. "No one gets between a man and his mom. You take care, Sean. Tell Cyan we all said hey, too." He gave Sean a brief embrace and clapped him on the back. "Go." Then he turned and walked away, and Sean helped his mother slowly onto the *Brilliant*.

Onboard, he gave silent orders via in-lens for the ship to prepare for take-off, leaving Mendel to handle the details on the bridge. He led his mother to the mess and set her up at the table with a cup of fragrant tea. "Mama, I'm glad—" He swallowed roughly, taking in her pale skin, the way she looked so *small.* "It's good to see you," he said, unable to say that he was glad he hadn't been too late. "I love you, Mama."

She patted his hand and smiled at him, clearly happy despite the tears in her eyes. "I'm glad you're safe, Sean." Her eyes popped wide when she looked at something past him, and Sean smiled up at Mendel as he sat down on the bench beside him. "My, oh my. So this is why you're in hiding?"

"Yeah," Sean said softly. "Mendel, my mother. Mom, Mendel."

She extended her hand in greeting, and said, "My name is Alice. It's very nice to meet you after all this time. You don't look anything like those awful pictures they show on the feeds. Thank you for taking care of my son."

"You do remember the bit where he *kidnapped* me, right, Mom?"

"I also know what kind of fool trouble you can get yourself into," she said primly. "Anyway, I think we've all moved on from that kidnapping business. Where are we going, Sean?"

Sean rolled his eyes, but refilled her teacup, and said, "A friend of ours—well, mostly a friend of Mendel's—has invited us to stay with him. His name is Itzal Bikendi. He's a scientist like Mendel. He lives on the Moon of Telve."

Alice drew a sharp breath, eyes popping wide. "The bloodsucking planet? But they do not permit anyone to go there."

Mendel laughed. "They do whatever Bikendi wants because he improves their image. I promise, the Telve are not as bad as everyone says."

She nodded slowly, still looking nervous, and said, "So what happened, Sean? I thought I would never see you again, and now the feeds will talk about nothing else but the arrest of the High Chancellor and a warrant for Lower Chancellor Alexander, and how it's all tied up with experiments on Draconis. They say Draconis and their matches were kidnapped and tortured in labs! I thought—but you're safe."

"Yes, Mama, we're safe," Sean assured her, squeezing her hands. "We helped stop the kidnappings," he said, and told her all that he could about what had transpired over the past term. By the time he was finished, she looked exhausted. "Come on, Mama. I've got a bed made up for you." He led her to the Captain's Quarters, thoroughly cleaned and prepared for her, and got her settled in. She hugged him tightly again.

"I'm glad I got to see you again, baby," she whispered, holding him even more tightly.

He held her back just as fiercely, eyes stinging. "Me too, Mama. We'll take care of you, I promise." She lay down, and he kissed her cheek, then turned out the light and left her to sleep.

Back on the bridge, Mendel swept him up and kissed him. Sean knew from the look on his face that Mendel hadn't liked what he'd seen of his mother's condition, but he didn't say anything, and Sean was grateful. "Your mom is sweet. I'm glad she didn't try to kill me."

Sean laughed. "My mother always wanted me to settle down. How that happens is completely irrelevant. Thank you. How far are we from Telve?"

Mendel kissed him again. "A few hours now. Bikendi already sent us the landing protocols and permission codes from the Telve council, unofficially of course. He's excited, though he'll never say it."

"Excited to have captives who can contribute to his experiments as both subjects and assistants?" Sean responded dryly. "What exactly are we going to be helping him with, anyway? I never really followed what you guys were discussing back in the lab." He grimaced, recalling the facility. Their time there had been measured in hours only, but it had been too many hours as far as he was concerned.

Sighing, Mendel settled in the captain's seat and stretched his legs out in front of him, staring at the feeds and data readings scrawling across the main screen, machinery humming and chirping all around them, and seeming to enhance how quiet it was otherwise. "The Draconis have been getting more and more attention, but it's mostly been confined to the upper reaches of the IG. Until this debacle with the Chancellors, it was not a mainstream problem. Many scientists have been researching the Draconis, some toward the goal of exterminating, some toward the goal of supporting. Bikendi has been privately commissioned, by whom he will not say, to research the Draconis bond and how it is evolving. That evolution is one of the strongest arguments the pro-Draconis could hope for. You and I are a prime example of it, though Bikendi says that while we might be the most impossible, we're not the most fascinating."

"I see," Sean said, heartbeat kicking up. "So someday the Draconis may be able to argue for their survival in front of the Star Assembly."

Mendel nodded, and replied, "Not just someday—someday soon. Bikendi sent me word this morning that the IG has announced that there is to be a formal trial in one term, date still to be determined. We have one term to prove that the Draconis deserve to live. Apparently whoever is paying Bikendi has several other people on his payroll, and we are on course to put up quite a fight. He is going to tell us more about it when we arrive, as he dares not let information leak."

Shaking his head in amusement, Sean said, "I've been distracted, missing all these conversations with Bikendi you've had behind my back."

"You've been worried about your mom, and otherwise, yes, I have been trying very hard to keep you distracted," Mendel said, voice taking on a husky note.

"Alas, more distractions will have to wait." He shuddered at the idea of having sex while his mother was on board. To judge by Mendel's grimace, he agreed wholeheartedly. "Guess you'd better tell me more about what we're going to be doing for the next term. I hope—I hope we can do this."

Mendel seemed to understand what he meant and shrugged. "I don't see why we can't, and let us face it—we have no choice. But we've done well enough this far, and now we're not both working against the best thing to ever happen to us." He smiled and grasped Sean's wrist, tugging him until Sean fell into his lap. He wrapped his arms around Sean's waist and kissed him softly. "We'll be fine, and knowing Bikendi, we'll be too busy to attract trouble."

Sean nodded and took another kiss, as the *Brilliant* steadily headed toward their new home.

# Meant to Be

## Book Two

# Prologue

**PLANET 2154014 (TREDAD), CHELSAN HOMESTEAD**

Arkadii shuddered as he stepped out of his ship, futilely tugging at the collar of his heavy coat. He *hated* Tredad and he resented wholly that the reason he had returned after so many years was the reason he had left in the first place.

"High Chancellor," a lieutenant—he thought a lieutenant, anyway, damned snow—greeted, voice barely audible in the freezing wind.

Grunting in reply, Arkadii motioned for him to lead the way, trekking down an icy path toward the top-hatch of a house typical of the outer lying regions of Tredad—a circular building set deep into the earth, with a rounded roof built and treated to slough the never-ending snow. In the cities, there were no exterior doors; the only way to the frozen areas beyond the safe zones were the city gates. In the outer regions, however, there was no interconnecting underground world. It was every man for himself in the wild.

Stars, he hated Tredad; it was as feral as it was civilized. Unfortunately for him, he was the only civil member of his family. Fortunately, he'd gotten out before they'd broken him. Arkadii sighed as they finally reached the hatch, then grabbed the handle on one side and swung down to the first step with an ease he had apparently not forgotten in ten terms.

At the bottom, he neatly jumped the last two steps, landing smoothly. The smells of death hit him first, and Arkadii made a face. He had hoped that, after his Auth days, he would never again encounter the smell of a dead body or blood. He *hated* the smell of blood; it stuck in his mouth and ruined his appetite.

"What happened?" he asked curtly.

The lieutenant snapped a salute, but gratefully relaxed when Arkadii motioned that he should. He grimaced briefly, before recovering himself, and said in a voice that tried very hard to be coolly professional, "Murder-suicide, High Chancellor. Doc—that is, the doctor reports that there was a brutal struggle first and likely the man would have died of internal bleeding if he hadn't—"

Arkadii cut him off with another hand motion, unable to bear such a blunt, clumsy recitation of his brother's death. "Where is Captain September?"

"Here, my lord," September said, and with a jerk of his head, sent the lieutenant fleeing. "I apologize, my lord."

"Never mind," Arkadii dismissed, and looked around at the disaster—furniture broken, turned over. Damn near every object in the room appeared to have been thrown to the floor, and every bit of glass he saw was shattered. He looked away from the bloody hand he could see from behind the sofa. "What happened, Captain?"

September bowed his head and shoulders. "I am sorry for your loss, High Chancellor. It appears that Lord and Lady Chelsan fought, and in the scuffle, she was killed. He killed himself shortly thereafter."

"How?" Arkadii asked, not even sure why he bothered.

"Knife," September replied in the quiet voice of one who had given too many such reports, a tone the young lieutenant would not gain simply through practice. "We've tagged all the evidence, and I doubt the case will take long to process. It would already be well on its way, but the earnest lieutenant knew the family name."

Arkadii grunted, reluctantly impressed—not even people who had known him all ten of the terms he had worked for the IG really knew his surname had once been Chelsan. He sighed and shunted away those memories, focusing on the grimmer memories of his family.

"It's only the boy left to care for," September continued.

"The *what*?" Arkadii repeated, dread in his stomach.

September looked at him in surprise. "The boy—their son."

"They didn't have a son the last time I heard from them," Arkadii snapped, feeling about as sick as September suddenly looked. His brother *wouldn't* be that stupid—yes, he would, Arkadii conceded. He did not bother stifling his sigh. "Please tell me the boy did not witness all of this."

The tight set to September's mouth was all the answer Arkadii needed and didn't want. "Where is he now?"

"His bedroom. He won't leave it," September replied, and led the way in quick, even, military strides. Against the disaster of the living quarters, his sharp, steel-gray uniform and even gait were a glaring slice of order. Arkadii felt like an intruder, dressed in ornate robes of Parthon silk, with Treska diamonds in his ears and on his fingers.

In the small bedroom just off the main living area, a little boy huddled on a bed. The room was far too chilly, Arkadii thought reflexively, then felt stupid. In a matter of hours, the house would be empty. In a month, at most, someone else would be living in it. Tredad did not waste time on trivial things like sentiment and superstition; they were no substitute for a warm house.

The little boy, Arkadii noticed with a wrench to his chest, was the very image of himself at that age. If the boy was a day over six years—three in Tredad time—then he would be astonished. The boy was small for his age, with the white-blonde hair and sharp blue eyes so characteristic of Arkadii's family. He wasn't crying, or reacting at all, and that was something else Arkadii knew far too well. "What's your name?"

In reply, the boy just looked at the man standing nearby, a sergeant with a nasty, still-healing set of scars across one cheek. Hellcat scratches, Arkadii noted absently. "Pyotr Chelsan."

Pyotr. That had been their grandfather's name: the illustrious, oh, so perfect grandfather his brother had loathed, even after he had died in his sleep. Arkadii felt tired and at least twice his age. Arkadii knelt before Pyotr, and then frowned faintly. "Why does he look as though he has been showered and re-dressed?"

September hesitated a beat, and then said, "He was covered in blood, High Chancellor. I do mean covered. We thought it would reduce his trauma if we cleaned him up ... " Arkadii looked over his shoulder, at September's too-blank face, and felt a sick feeling his gut. He turned back to Pyotr and squeezed his shoulder gently. "My name is Arkadii. You may call—"

"Uncle," Pyotr said abruptly, though there was no inflection in the word.

"Yes," Arkadii said, startled, but before he could inquire further, Pyotr turned around neatly on one heel, with all the precision of a well-trained solder four times his age, and strode to the little blue chest at the foot of his bed. He opened it and pulled out a small wooden box, scuffed and shiny with age, and carried it back to Arkadii.

It made Arkadii's throat tight, to see that little box. What was it still doing around? He had been certain his family would throw out all his belongings when he ran away. He opened it, saw it was filled with picture folders—datapads meant to hold only one type of file, usually picture or documents, easily passed along from person to person without the risk of misplacing or sharing other data. They were also cheaper than standard datapads.

The ones in the box were years out of date; they looked so clunky compared to newer models. Arkadii picked one out and turned it on, surprised, and yet not, to see his own ten-year-old face flicker to life in front of him. He shut it off again, not needing the memories to flare any more to life than they already had. "So you know me."

"Papa talked," Pyotr said. "Mean things. Wrong things."

Arkadii raised his brows, wondering sadly what had happened to cause a little boy to understand far too much of the world. "Well, I doubt they were all wrong. The

Chelsan family has never been accused of being nice. Some say it's our fate. Do you know what that means?"

Pyotr shook his head.

"It means there's nothing we can do about it, any more than you can change the color of your hair or the blue of your eyes. You can alter them, disguise them, but not *truly* make them be a different color. Do you understand?"

Pyotr nodded solemnly, and Arkadii suspected he did, in fact, understand. "That's what everyone else says," he added. "Me, I didn't stay here to succumb to fate. I *did* change."

"Me, too?" Pyotr asked quietly.

Arkadii nodded and squeezed his shoulder again. "Yes. My name is Arkadii Kavalerov now; we'll change your name, too. Pack up everything you want to take you; the sergeant will assist you." He rose and jerked his head at Captain September to follow him into the hall. "What really happened?" Arkadii asked.

September sighed, sounding as old as Arkadii felt. "The man definitely killed the wife ... but he did not kill himself. My report will say suicide to my dying day, but that's not what happened here."

"Yes, it is," Arkadii said grimly. "Even after we die, that report will never say differently. Let us hope ... " Pyotr stepped out into the hallway and let the words remain unsaid, but September nodded. "See the bodies are destroyed, along with all personal effects. Send the report directly to me when it is completed. No one is to speak of what happened here, ever. See it is sealed with my mark."

"As you will, High Chancellor," September said softly, and touched his arm lightly before sliding away to see the orders carried out.

Arkadii held the same hand out to Pyotr, and said, "Come along, Petya. I will take you to my ship, and then to my home, and we will never have to see this awful place again."

Pyotr nodded and took his hand, and Arkadii put Tredad behind them both forever.

# Chapter One

COMBAT CLASS STARSHIP A-98147121, THE *SHANGRI LA*

Valendel stepped out of his shower, grabbing a towel as the water automatically shut off. He still could not believe he had his own shower—his own bedroom, his own *everything*. The few other times he had traveled by starship, everything had been communal and as unpleasant as that typically implied. He'd always thought combat class ships were even worse than civilian, but the *Shangri La* was the epitome of luxury.

He stepped into his cabin proper and finished toweling off, then threw the towel on the bed and picked up the sandcloth on the little set of shelves set into the wall over his bed. Starting with his arms, he began to slowly and meticulously polish his scales, wishing he had someone to help with his back, but making do. When the scales that covered the majority of his body gleamed, he polished the ones on his face, and then tucked the cloth back on the shelf.

Scales attended, Valendel combed his shoulder-length hair, before braiding it back and tying it off with a plain purple band. From the storage shelves set into the wall at the foot of the bed, he pulled out black pants and a dark purple t-shirt, and then sat down to lace on his heavy space boots. He hated the clunky things, but it was stupid to travel in anything else. Standing up, he shrugged into a light-weight, but durable black jacket, and slid his datapad into the holster strapped to his thigh.

Ready as he would ever be, Valendel drew a deep breath and let it out slowly. He lingered a moment more, wishing his nerves would settle. But they never did, so he gave up and abandoned the safety and quiet of his bedroom, and headed for the common room where everyone was gathering for dinner and a last update on everything before they landed on Telve.

Bikendi, he thought, heart kicking up several notches. After all the years of studying, reading, watching from afar ... he was *finally* going to meet the man he most admired in all the stars. There was *no one* more brilliant than Dr. Bikendi, no one more accomplished in genetics research—or anything else for that matter!

Valendel wasn't even certain why the defense team needed other scientists, when they already had Bikendi. He was just happy Bikendi was on *their* side, but if he weren't, then he wouldn't be the kind of man worth Valendel's support and admiration. He couldn't imagine a man as complicated as Bikendi picking to exterminate the Draconis, though.

"Val!" He jumped, half-turned, as a man who looked more like a pirate than an Auth strode toward him, clapped him on the back in greeting, then slung an arm over Val's shoulders and half-dragged him along down the hallway. "Enjoying yourself at all, Val? Ever been this far from Coni?"

"N-no," Val replied. "I mean—I am enjoying myself. I've never been so far from home. The Coni ... " He trailed off, because he didn't really need to say it: of all the Draconis-born, he was the strangest and most frustrating yet. Draconis had been made by crossing the Coni with a special native lizard. Those lizards came in only four colors: green, brown, yellow, black, with the occasional albino.

There was no explanation at all for the profusion of blue, red, orange, white, silver, gold, and myriad other Draconis spanning the stars. But they were not impossible. Valendel, and his pale violet scales, were a complete anomaly. He also possessed no magics; or at best, whatever magics he had were completely dormant. He was nineteen-years-old by Zero Standard Time, twenty-one by Coni time, so if he had magics at all, they should have long manifested in some way. But to date, no one had been able to figure out why he was so strange. He was full-blood Draconis and that made him strangest of all.

"Oh, stop fretting. All you do is fret."

"Sorry, Captain Horizon," Valendel said, tensing. He wasn't like the rest of them, traipsing about fancy ships or dining at the finest establishments in the stars. He was still technically a student, for stars' sake. He'd been granted special leave for the trials, because he'd been ordered to the defense team as evidence and scientific support, but he was still just a student.

"Zon," the man sighed. "You can just call me Zon, I have told you. And there's no point in calling me Captain when we're not even on my ship. Just relax, Val. I know this is all overwhelming for you, but if you'd just relax a bit, you'd see we're not all so bad."

Val nodded and tried to relax as he was told, but they were almost *there* and he was going to meet *Bikendi*, but first he had to get through another aggravating dinner and pretend he fit in with the sorts of people who saw nothing strange about travelling on the High Chancellor's private ship.

He went as agreeably as he could when Zon dragged him into the communal room, then slipped away as someone else distracted Zon and retreated to his usual corner, snagging a cup of Vrill rose wine from the table as he passed it. The wine was a silly indulgence, because after the trial, he would probably never have it again, but he couldn't resist. People had not exaggerated how good it was: sweet and light and fruity, like nothing else he'd ever drunk.

Sipping at the wine, he settled into his chair in the corner and pulled out his datapad, pulling up the article he'd been trying to read all day. It was about a ten-term study on Danubian Hellcats and the strange venom they carried. The poison had no equal, and immunization against it was neither easy nor cheap. But the poison had been crafted by the Danubians, who genetically engineered the feline warriors, later dubbed Hellcats by other planets in the IG, to help them combat the hostilities elsewhere in the IG. The Danubians themselves had always been notoriously easy prey; they were too passive and gentle in nature to defend themselves.

Val had been avidly following every scrap of the study that was published, but the article was the first of any length or detail and he'd been eagerly awaiting it. However, he was so anxious about the pending meeting, the looming trial, that every word he read slid right out of his mind again.

He gave up, put the datapad to sleep, and tucked it away again. Sipping his wine some more, he looked around the room at the other people filling it, and wondered if he would ever grow used to the idea that he would be spending so much time around them.

The most prominent person was, of course, High Chancellor Kavalerov, nephew of the Grand Chancellor and former Commander of the Authorities Special Forces. He was sitting quietly in another corner, reviewing what looked like paperwork, his in-specs flashing as he communicated with who knew how many other people. But he never failed to smile and exchange a few words when someone approached him, and his expression was always friendly when he glanced at Valendel.

In the center of the room, ensconced on a fancy red half-circle sofa, was Lady Jundel, whose son was Mendel Ekard, a Draconis convicted of murdering his father one term ago. He'd escaped from prison with a mutant human in tow, and no one had ever been able to find them. Jundel was conversing with Pyotr's bodyguard, Raoul, who was half-Fornarian to judge by his height and slenderness, with faintly dusky skin and dark hair that indicated his human half.

Zon, beads and baubles in his hair flashing in the light, leaned casually against a wall chatting with the *Shangri La's* captain. Half a dozen other personnel mingled amongst them; the only ones missing from their core group were Bikendi and the defense lawyer, who they were on their way to meet. The High Chancellor had not yet told them the lawyer's identity, and everyone else on board loved to gossip about whom it might possibly be—and it would have to be someone good, because the prosecuting lawyer was a name that even Val knew (and loathed). Lord Emil Carthage was notorious for taking on clients that everyone else agreed deserved to be put in solitary confinement at the nearest Rehab.

Val sipped more of his wine, head feeling somewhat light, and ambled over to another table to get some food before he made a complete fool of himself. Putting a plate of food together, he started to head back to his corner—only to nearly run into someone. He blinked at the steel-gray uniform just a hair from his nose, then stepped back enough to look up—and up. "Sorry."

Raoul smiled and waved the words away. "Not at all. How's our star Draconis doing? Still so quiet. I don't think you've said twenty words since boarding. Not that you need to—the rest of us can natter enough for fifty. I hear you're quite the student of the genetics of magics; you must be excited to meet Dr. Bikendi, unless of course you've met him before?"

Val laughed at the idea before he could catch himself. "Me? No way. Why would I have met Dr. Bikendi before? I'm only a student, and twenty years his junior." Eighteen actually, but it all amounted to the same. Dr. Bikendi would never give a student like him the time of day; if not for the trial, Dr. Bikendi wouldn't even know he existed.

"Well, he is very interested in meeting you, I am told," Raoul said, and like Zon had earlier, casually threw an arm across Val's shoulders and dragged him off. He led Val across the room to where Pyotr worked furiously away, one of his assistants at his side. They paused as Raoul and Val approached.

"Valendel," Kavalerov greeted with a smile. Val tried to smile back, but it was hard to act casual around the second most powerful man in the IG.

He didn't generally pay much attention to politics; he really only bothered when politics and science collided—which, really, was more often than he liked in his field, given that magics capability was always a source of contention in the IG. Val would never be fortunate enough to work alongside Bikendi, but he would not lack for jobs either.

Assuming, of course, that Val was allowed to finish school and seek proper employment, and was not terminated on order of the IG. But he was happier when he wasn't dwelling on that particular outcome. He just couldn't believe anyone would execute them; the Draconis had come too far, done too much, established themselves firmly in the stars. They were no better or worse than anyone else; why would anyone want them dead?

"I hope you are ready for a great deal of work," Kavalerov went on. "Bikendi is going to have his hands full during the trial, and you'll be his best asset since, like it or not, he will need an assistant."

Val froze with surprise. No one had told him any such thing. "Me? But I'm just a-a student. Bikendi would never take me on as an assistant."

Kavalerov smiled in a way that always made Val shiver. It wasn't a bad smile, but it wasn't a good one either; more ... that smile said *I know things and how to use them.* It was a manipulator's smile and Val had seen more of those in his life than he cared to think. He knew he was merely a sorbit piece, to be used and discarded; what else could he possibly be? He was proud to be helping his race in a way few could, but the entire thing still left him with chills. "He is going to be doing a lot of work under severe time restraints; he will need the help. You are a brilliant student, Valendel. Top marks, ahead of your studies by nearly a full term, and I am told that you will be receiving several generous grants from choice universities when you go on to your graduate studies."

"I will?" Valendel asked, startled. He hadn't bothered to really apply himself to graduate programs, yet. It was something he should be considering, but his studies were onerous enough, and his advisors had told him to focus on those and worry about the rest later. "But I'm a Draconis, hardly a safe bet."

Kavalerov's eyes flashed, and Val almost recoiled from their intensity, except he knew it was not directed at him. He didn't really know *why* Kavalerov was so intent on saving the Draconis; so far as he knew, Kavalerov had no personal stake in the matter. Everyone, even a nose-in-data scientist, knew he was a notorious loner. High Chancellor Pyotr Kavalerov, only living relative of the Grand Chancellor; he had served in the Authorities, then switched to being Lower Chancellor for a brief time, before abruptly returning to the Authorities and, shortly thereafter, assuming the mantle of Commander of Special Forces.

Rumors abounded that he had once been, or still was, part of the infamous and much whispered about Internal Affairs, the shadowy department that kept the IG itself in line. Val did not usually listen to rumors, but he tended to believe that one. "You're a very safe bet," Kavalerov replied. "After we win this trial, every university and research group in the stars will be panting to take you on. Not," he added, "that Bikendi will permit it."

Val started to ask what in the stars *that* meant, when a chime came over the ship-wide comm. "Captain," said a crisp voice. "Approaching Telve, presence required on the bridge."

The captain set down his drink and, with a polite bow to the room, departed the common area to answer his summons. A few minutes later, the captain's voice came over the comm as he announced they were landing on the moon of Telve.

Despite the wine buzzing in his system, Val's heart kicked back up to a furious pace. He was going to meet Dr. Bikendi. There were more important things to think about, he knew that, but all he could focus on was Bikendi.

He was going to be Bikendi's assistant. They thought he was good enough to *be* Bikendi's assistant. He fervently hoped Bikendi agreed, even as he told himself not to be stupid and get his hopes up. Val set his drink and plate down on a nearby table, and tried not to fuss with his clothes as they all waited to land.

Lady Jundel smiled at him and winked, making Val flush and look away. Why was everyone paying so much attention to him? They were always congenial, but largely, they had left him to his own devices during the trip—and he preferred it that way. So why were they paying him mind all of a sudden?

Before he could figure out how to ask, Kavalerov stood up and gestured for Valendel to follow him, Raoul falling into step just behind them. He rested one hand lightly on the stunner at his right hip, moving in front of Kavalerov as they reached the main doors and the captain opened them.

Raoul slipped outside and called out—then laughed and relaxed, calling out more congenial greetings. Val jumped as he heard Bikendi's voice, sharper and more curt than he'd ever heard it on the lecture vids, but recognizable all the same. He would know Bikendi's voice anywhere. His heart, already beating rapidly, kicked up another notch.

Stepping aside, Raoul motioned for them all to leave the ship.

### PLANET 2051225-3554 (MOON OF TELVE), PRIVATE ESTATE OF ITZAL BIKENDI

Val trailed out behind all the rest, fussing with his clothes and struggling to figure out what to do with his hands—what if he made a poor impression and Bikendi wanted nothing to do with him? What if he wasn't good enough, no matter what everyone said, and why hadn't anyone told him until *then* that he was going to be Bikendi's assista—

His thoughts broke off as his eyes landed on a man he had not seen in six terms: Dr. Mendel Ekard. He'd broken out of Rehab with the help of a guard there who was apparently a mutant, magics capable human ... and there he was, Val realized. He couldn't remember the man's name, but he had the look of a soldier to him and he was definitely a full-blood human, at least at a glance. Val wondered what studies had been done, to see if there was a magics capable ancestor somewhere in the blood that would explain the anomaly. If he recalled correctly, Dr. Ekard had possessed defensive magics, so his match—

"Val!"

He jumped as Kavalerov called his name, and dutifully approached as he was beckoned close, glancing shyly at Bikendi—and was only slightly disappointed that Bikendi was immersed in conversation with Lady Jundel. Val's cheeks flushed hot, as he realized that however many times he had seen Bikendi on vids and in pictures, it was nothing like seeing him in person. He was ... try as Val might to come up with something less absurd and childish, beautiful was the only word that came to mind. Bikendi was stunning, with that fascinating blend of Telve and Kemperast. His skin was a dark, dusky gold, his hair black with streaks of white and, as he finally turned to greet them, his eyes the purest violet—

Valendel cried out in pain, holding his head and falling to his knees. It *hurt*, whatever had just happened to him. It felt like someone had cracked his head open and shoved a wedge between the halves, and if his heart beat any faster, it was going to burst, he just knew it.

He trembled as someone grasped his wrists and drew his hands away from his face. He stared into the gently concerned face of Lady Jundel. "Are you all right, Val?

Matching can be pretty brutal, and of course it's always worse with stronger magics."

*Matching?* Val's eyes snapped open wide as the word sunk in. Matched—he was matched, even though he didn't have magics— He jerked his head up toward Bikendi, unable to believe it, even as he knew it must be true. He was matched to Dr. Bikendi.

Lady Jundel tugged him to his feet and squeezed his shoulder reassuringly. Val stepped forward, balling his hands into fists to still their trembling. "Dr. Bik—"

"I do not believe this," Bikendi said scathingly, completely ignoring him, blazing eyes only for Kavalerov. "Does your interference know no limits? Have you no restraint of any sort, Pyotr?"

"None," Kavalerov replied implacably. "This is perfect, admit it."

Bikendi sneered at him. "It's not perfect—it's dangerous! I am the very last person who should have ever been matched, and you are going to do more harm than good to this trial by announcing that I have a match and my magics are stronger. We don't even know in what way they are stronger!"

"Are you certain it's a bad thing?" Kavalerov asked, looking faintly amused. "I think you should calm down, Bikendi. You know this is a break for us—"

"I do not want to hear it," Bikendi snapped, then turned around sharply on one heel and stormed off.

Val looked down as he suddenly felt all eyes on him. Everyone knew, he realized bitterly. Everyone knew he was going to match with Bikendi, but no one had seen fit to tell *him.* Or Bikendi for that matter, he thought angrily.

Someone reached out—Zon, he noted absently—and Val jerked away, walking blindly off down a hallway, daring someone to chase after him. But no one did, and he wandered until he found himself in a little greenroom, the air muggy and hot, but sweet with the smell of flowers and plants.

He found a stool by the central table, then pulled out his datapad and pulled up a file that held everything Bikendi had ever published or released. Despite his efforts not to think, his mind wandered as watched one of his favorite lectures; he had watched it dozens of times, to the point he practically had it memorized. Dr. Bikendi so rarely went out in public, and as he couldn't afford to travel to those few viewings, Val had settled for watching the recordings.

Matched, Val thought dizzily. He was matched to Dr. Bikendi. It was like a dream come true, even if most other Draconis would sneer at him for being happy about being matched. His magics had always been dormant, though, and he had thought he would always be completely outcast. Matching meant he was a true Draconis, and who in the stars could be a better match than Dr. Bikendi?

But it was hard to feel truly elated when he only felt very much like the stupidest of pawns, and one so well-used that his match wanted nothing to do with him.

# Chapter Two

**PLANET 2051225-3554 (MOON OF TELVE), PRIVATE ESTATE OF ITZAL BIKENDI**

Pyotr ignored the looks everyone was giving him and strode off after Bikendi, Raoul close on his heels. He punched the button for the lift, and the doors slid smoothly open. Stepping into the lift deck, he looked out through the double layers of special glass to the endless expanse of space beyond as they were carried up.

"Bikendi is going to kill you," Raoul said with a soft chuckle. "Assuming someone else doesn't beat him to it."

"No one has killed me for being a cold-hearted bastard, yet," Pyotr replied lightly.

Raoul snickered again. "There's always a breaking point, boss. Guess it's a good thing you've got me."

Pyotr nodded in agreement, glancing over his bodyguard of many terms. Being half-Fornarian, half-human, Raoul was unusual, and therefore, drew more attention than a bodyguard strictly should, but it tended to work well for Pyotr: they noticed him and vastly underestimated him. But Raoul was nobody's fool; he was a former Black Ops soldier of the Authorities Special Forces, and would still be there if he had not volunteered to leave his position to take up full time as Pyotr's bodyguard. "We'll be leaving shortly; there's no reason for my continued presence here and I will be needed once Daie reaches Zero."

"But we can't return home until we go deal with that problem on Meltana," Raoul grimaced. "I guess I won't be able to complain of boredom once we're there."

Not bothering to reply to that, because there was *always* a fight on the notoriously problematic mining planet, Pyotr merely stepped off the lift as they reached the floor to which he knew Bikendi had retreated. The doors opened to a large, open living space, the lights dimmed to a soothing, almost intimate level. With most anyone else, Pyotr would have been suspicious of the darkened room, but Bikendi was half-Telven, and so had little need for large amounts of light.

Pyotr strode over to the small bar tucked away in one corner of the room, just behind a long, black sofa made of Telven leather. He poured a small measure of Zero brandy into a red crystal glass, then sat down on the sofa. "How long are you going to be petulant about this, Bikendi?"

"May they leave you a bloodless corpse on your mother's doorstep," Bikendi said, coming out of the shadows of the hallway, although hanging well back, purple eyes glowing faintly in the near dark. "You had no business matching me to the boy."

"No business?" Pyotr repeated, swirling his brandy idly in its glass. "I disagree. He is obviously meant for you, and I think now that he is matched, whatever untapped magics he possesses will at last come to the fore. That aside, you must admit it is quite against the odds that a Draconis would be born who matches one of the most unique specimens in the stars."

Bikendi sneered and flexed his hands, holding them in such a way that Pyotr could see them—bare, the fingers long and elegant, nary a mark or scar upon them. Hands that could kill with a simple touch, and which Bikendi usually kept gloved. "I am deadly enough, Pyotr. I did not need someone increasing my abilities. I also do not think it a fortuitous addition to our case, as you clearly do. The opposition is studying cases precisely like mine, to prove that the Draconis are more a danger than a bonus. That Draconis are being born who can match to people like me could prove that they are meant only to be weaponized, much like Cohen was trying to do a term ago. You are taunting Pixies, playing this game."

Pyotr smiled, and said only, "They are the kind of game I am best at. The Draconis will not be exterminated, not while I am alive."

"I never did understand why in the name of the blood you care so damned much."

"I have told you before that my reasons are myriad. The only one that really matters, however, is that the Draconis do not deserve to die. They're a good race and should not fall to the machinations of my greedy peers." Pyotr took a sip of brandy, and then said, "Do not take your ire out on the boy. He was kept ignorant of his potential in this matter. Until we landed, he did not even know I was assigning him as your assistant, since you cannot take Mendel with you."

Bikendi shook his head. "I don't need an assistant, and most certainly not one who is still in the nursery."

Pyotr laughed. "Still in school perhaps, but far from the nursery. Be careful with him; he's a huge admirer of yours and will take to heart everything you say and do. The Zero sharks will enjoy snacking on him. There is none better than you to keep him close, teach him what he needs to know, and ensure no one else gets to him. Try to actually get to know the boy, and you might see why he is entirely an asset to us."

"I hope you drink soured blood," Bikendi snapped. "I agreed to help you, but I told you that I was not going to be a pawn."

"Everyone is a pawn," Pyotr said, and finished his brandy. Setting the glass on a side table of black wood and smoky glass, he rose and smoothed out the stiff black fabric of his uniform. "You are expected on Zero in seventy-five hours."

Bikendi gestured impatiently. "I'm aware. When is Daie due?"

"Shortly after your arrival; I think it will make more of a show that way. It won't intimidate Cathartes, but it will give the rest of them a nasty shock." He smirked and turned away. "I will see you in three days, Bikendi. Be nice to your little assistant." Bikendi did not reply and Pyotr let it slide, rejoining Raoul at the lift and returning to the ground floor.

Raoul laughed as the doors slid closed. "If Bikendi was inclined toward illegal blood drinking, you *would* be a corpse on your mother's doorstep."

"I suppose the fact my mother is dead would not impede him," Pyotr replied dryly. "Bikendi is the least of my concerns. However much he snarls, he is a soft touch. He'll be in Valendel's palm before they reach Zero, or shortly thereafter, depending on how tetchy he insists on being." He fell silent as the lift opened, and stifled a sigh when he saw Lady Jundel waiting for him. "My lady," he greeted.

Lady Jundel ignored it, and said, "You've certainly had your dramatic moment. Was it really necessary to keep Valendel ignorant?"

Pyotr ignored the question. "I am departing. You are all expected on Zero in seventy-five hours. See to it they all get there; I would not put it past Bikendi to get wrapped up with his new assistant once he stops sulking. Be careful, all of you. I'm leaving a retinue of guards; do not be dismissive of their presence. Contact me if there are any problems."

Nodding, obviously biting back whatever she wanted to say, Jundel let him pass and followed silently in his wake. Pyotr ignored the others still clustered in the main area, and paused only to address the guard at the bottom of the gangway to arrange for a dozen men to remain. "Lieutenant Vane, have you selected men to stay behind?"

"Yes, High Chancellor," Lieutenant Vane replied, snapping a salute. "By your leave, my lord, I would like to remain behind and supervise the escort myself."

Pyotr nodded and clapped him on the shoulder. "As you like, Lieutenant." Nodding to the assembled guards in thanks, Pyotr gestured to Raoul and they boarded the ship to head off to deal with the next problem on his list.

COMBAT CLASS STARSHIP A-98147121, THE *SHANGRI LA*

Back on board, Pyotr headed straight for his office and settled at his desk. His in-lens flashed as he activated his work station, and three screens appeared in the space over his desk, arranged in a neat row. Pyotr shifted through the work, moving documents and images with commands sent via his in-lens. He held back a sigh as he shuffled through letters from the Lower Chancellors, wondering what his uncle would say if he locked them all in a room and told them they would remain in timeout until they could act like adults.

Likely, his uncle would remind him in blistering fashion of his own behavior and point out he should be in the room, as well—or in Rehab. Never mind that Pyotr's methods, while unorthodox, got the necessary results. If he obeyed every law of the IG precisely down to the minute letter, the Draconis would already be dead.

He scowled at the long list of meetings and conferences in front of him, longing for the days when he had been Commander of the Special Forces and Internal Affairs. That had had its fair share of dull meetings, but mostly it had been worthwhile work. Being forced into High Chancellor made him feel as though he were Headmaster.

"If you glare any harder at those screens, Petya," Raoul interrupted, "they will have you up on charges of aggravated assault."

"It's only vandalism with inanimate objects," Pyotr replied, dismissing the screens and sitting back in his seat. "We're going to have our hands especially full in Meltana. There are so many factions involved, Lower Chancellor Handsome cannot take care of it, and I don't think they'll settle for less than my blood. I'm about ready to find a rule that will let me disband the whole lot of them and start from scratch. At the very least, I think we need to bring in the military."

Raoul's in-lens flashed, and then various small screens appeared in the air around him as he rifled through data pulled from the IG's restricted network. "Well, if you can find a loophole for that sort of heavy reinforcement, the *Scythe*, the *Legacy,* and the *Menace* are all within three hours. I recommend the *Scythe*, myself, but you know I'm partial to that ship."

Pyotr chuckled. "Yes, but your favoritism is warranted. This is the fourth time in the past quarter that I have had to contend with Meltana. There are plenty of codes to authorize it, but I'll contact the Grand Chancellor now." His in-lens flashed and one of his screens reappeared, displaying the face of his captain. "Bridth, contact the *Scythe* and tell them to remain on standby; I may have need of them on Meltana. I do not believe they have greater standing orders, but if they do, they may proceed with those and I'll contact an alternate ship. Keep me apprised."

"Yes, your Lordship," Bridth said. "I was just about to let you know that we are ahead of schedule and should be read to jump in ten minutes."

"Excellent," Pyotr said. "Let me know when we're through." Bridth nodded, and Pyotr closed the connection, then used the same screen to contact his uncle, waiting patiently for him to answer the call. "I think Meltana will keep us busy for at least forty hours, possibly closer to fifty," he said to Raoul while he waited. "After that, we need to stop over on Vrill, before finally returning to Zero."

Raoul snorted. "Vrill. They will never let you leave, not while they are arguing over whom to make king. I'm glad I'm not part of that debate; the Vrill are furious."

"When you cling that tightly to tradition, it is bound to turn on you eventually," Pyotr said. "If Prince Teleyeveon cannot be found, then I think Kideon will do just fine—even if he is half-Krawl. I will make them accept him or put an end to their monarchy. I do not have time to linger and soothe them gently and slowly. Still, it will be luck alone that permits us to arrive on Zero in time to greet Daie before the rest of Zero sees him. I sense we'll be cutting it down to the last line."

Pulling up another screen, Pyotr activated a keyboard on his desktop and sent out various messages. When he was done with that, he scowled at his uncle's screen, still dark as he waited for the call to be answered.

"I think you're being ignored," Raoul said.

Pyotr rolled his eyes and did not bother to reply. If his uncle wanted to be pissy about breakfast, that was fine. He might loathe Pyotr's machinations, but they *worked* and that was the only thing that truly irritated everyone. *Almost everyone*, the back of his mind whispered, but Pyotr turned away from that dark path. That temptation was long gone, hidden away in the stars where no one could manage to find him. Pyotr had sent out the best scouts that Special Ops and IA could offer, and no one could find a trace anywhere.

Jade was gone and Pyotr was High Chancellor, and those were the choices they had made. He wondered bitterly if anywhere in the recriminations laid upon him, *anyone* had ever bothered to make note of that. When it mattered most, he had chosen duty over what he most wanted in all the world.

Rubbing his temples, Pyotr killed the neglected connection. "To the stars with him, then. If the mighty Grand Chancellor wants to ignore me, then I shall act as best as I am able on my own."

Raoul snorted. "Like you were going to listen to him if he said 'no'. You've already made your mind up, and you know it." He sighed, levity falling away as he said, "One of these days, someone is going to try in earnest to kill you and I won't be able to do a damn thing to stop it."

"So long as you don't die in the process," Pyotr said.

"Oh, shut up," Raoul retorted. "I don't suppose that there are plans to eat and rest anywhere on your agenda, because—" He broke off, tumbling from his seat and onto the floor as an explosion rocked the ship. Rolling to his hands and feet, Raoul stood up, slapping his hand to the wall and sticking to it as the ship was rocked again.

His in-lens flashed as he locked down Pyotr's office, protecting it from intruders and the dangers of space if the ship had been breached. Pyotr activated his own in-lens, sending out distress calls, not caring if they might be overreacting.

In front of him, the screens he'd left up abruptly flickered and went out, followed by the ship lights, leaving the two of them in absolute dark. Pyotr pulled out his in-specs, removing his in-lens and sliding the specs on in one smooth motion, transmitting two last, hasty messages just as a third explosion rocked the ship and Raoul dove for him, knocking them both to the ground.

Too little, too late, as the room filled with blinding white light. *The warp coils*. Something had gone wrong with their light jump. There was something there, in that thought, but before he could figure it out, Pyotr felt a flash of pain, and then white turned to black.

## UNKNOWN PLANET, UNKNOWN LOCATION

Cold.

Pyotr moaned as the cold registered; it was the sort of searing, bone-deep cold he had not felt since he was a child. He did not remember much of his childhood, but he remembered the pain, the blood, and the cold.

He tried to move and realized he couldn't. He lay there, slowly able to feel the snow caking his face, the bite of the wind. Shivering, he tried to collect his thoughts, make himself try to move again, but all he could feel was that terrible cold.

It was important he stay awake, get his mind functioning, but even as he thought it, Pyotr passed out again, his last thought that he *hated* the cold.

Warmth.

Pyotr opened his eyes, but all he saw was white. *Tredad?* But that was impossible, he thought hazily. He couldn't be on Tredad; it wasn't on the agenda.

Agenda. Ship. Explosion. He was dead.

Something touched his face, making him startle. Fingers, he realized. They were hot to the touch, and he groaned at the contrast to the overwhelming cold the rest of him felt. He tried to open his eyes again and wondered when he'd closed them. "Wha ... "

A husky laugh, slightly muffled, drew him, and he shuddered despite himself, though he could not say why. "Hold still," a voice said. "Even half-dead, you cannot hold still."

Pyotr shuddered again. Something ... but before he could grasp it, the thought slipped away. "Cold," he finally managed.

"I would imagine so," the muffled voice replied, sounding amused, and hot fingers once more stroked his cheek. "I should leave you out here and let the cold finish the job of killing you. One would think, 'Winter', that you would be tougher than this in your namesake."

Something ... something about those words ... Pyotr again tried to grasp the thoughts, hold on to them, but the stars forsaken *cold.* He tried again to force his eyes open, and finally succeeded, but only stared up into a mask of Tredad glass, the best possible material for working in extreme cold. It was dark, smoky, but he knew from experience that from the inside one could see clear as a perfect day on Kreska.

Framing the protective mask was white and blue fur, leaving the identity of his rescuer completely unknown. Hot fingers once again touched his cheek, and the voice said, "Do stop moving, Petya, or you really will manage to get yourself killed."

Pyotr tried to say something, but before he could, the dark took him again, the question left unspoken on his lips.

When he woke again, Pyotr groaned from pain, but his mind was working. He sat up slowly, wincing at sore muscles and an aching head. Reaching up, he gingerly felt around his head, finding the knot where he had probably endured a mild concussion. He was lucky to be alive.

He *shouldn't* be alive. Three explosions—no one survived three explosions in space. Except, he recalled with a pensive frown, they had occurred in the middle of a light jump. Tales abounded of the things that happened when things went wrong mid-light jump, and there were very good reasons the IG was so strict about passage through them. Whatever people complained about, the money made from them was merely an afterthought.

Dropping his hand, Pyotr examined his surroundings, a sick feeling in his stomach as he took in the unfortunately familiar sight of a typical Tredad home. Round, one large room with screen walls that could be pulled out when privacy was necessary. A dining area, a living area, and beds. Heat radiated up from the floor, the special walls and ceiling keeping it in, fighting back the deadly cold of Tredad's absolute winter.

Tredad. Of all the planets in the IG, he had landed on the one he most loathed. Pyotr shuddered and ran a hand over his close-cropped hair, wincing as the movement triggered a host of aches and pains.

But pain meant he was alive, and that meant he could not lie about all day. Someone had tried to assassinate him, and he suspected that everyone thought the attempt was a success. He needed to find a way to communicate with someone, preferably his uncle. Shoving back the heavy blankets covering him, he swung his feet over the edge of the bed—and did not stand halfway up before dizziness knocked him right back down. Pyotr sighed and remained still until the dizziness subsided, then stood more slowly.

He had just decided to try walking when the door in the floor swung up, then fell back and slammed against the floor. A moment later, a heavy pack landed on the floor with a muted thump, followed quickly by a figure dressed in full Tredad weather gear. Climbing up into the house, the figure closed the door and locked it, then stood up.

They stared at each other, and Pyotr tried to say something, but for some reason, the words just would not come. Something nagged at him, but he could remember little after the explosion save for a vague memory of the cold.

Slowly, the figure began to strip off the winter gear, pulling off the heavy gloves first, leaving on a much smaller, more lightweight set of gloves as he unwound a heavy scarf, then unbuttoned the cumbersome jacket. A man, Pyotr saw, and as he discarded the hood to reveal a long tumble of dark blond hair in a waist-length braid, Pyotr's gut clenched. *It couldn't be ...*

But then the man finally removed the protective face covering and the lightweight gloves, revealing scarlet-painted nails and a face too beautiful to ever be forgotten.

"Jade," Pyotr breathed.

# Chapter Three

**UNKNOWN PLANET, UNKNOWN LOCATION**

Raoul sat up with a groan, and then bit back a sob of pain. Everything *hurt*. His head hurt the most, and he slowly lifted a trembling hand to it. He stared in confusion when it came back wet and red, his first thought that he wasn't Helioran, so why was his hand red?

A moment later, he realized it was blood. His head was bleeding. That was bad. He looked around, struggling to ignore the dizziness and nausea that washed over him, and discovered he was in a forest. He stared up, wincing at the greenish light that seared his eyes. Dropping his gaze, he tried to think.

Trees. He didn't recognize them. But he could breathe, and was alive, and that had to count for something. *Where* was he, though, and how had he gotten there? He groaned again, fighting an urge to throw up, and got his hands braced on the tree he was slumped against.

Slowly, one painful movement at a time, Raoul pulled himself to his feet. Reflexively, he used his magics to stick to the tree, though the use of energy he barely possessed almost sent him falling down again, anyway. When he could mostly move without the world tilting, he let go of the tree and began walking, one agonizing, wavering step at a time.

Fear began to mingle with the pain as he realized he could be literally *anywhere* in the stars—including (and more likely than he cared to think about) a primitive planet. It was every star traveler's nightmare, to land somewhere undeveloped with no way to contact the IG.

Raoul would settle for getting out of the damn forest and finding signs of intelligent life, because at least if he could find a way to talk to someone, he had something with which to work. He held his sticky hand up to his head again, but the blood there was already drying. A rock caught beneath his feet, making him stumble and fall again. He whimpered in pain—but then noticed a road. It was only a dirt road, but that was better than nothing.

Staggering back to his feet, Raoul resumed walking, carefully making his way along the dirt road. His vision began to fray, and he was suspecting he would be spending the night in the woods, too injured to protect himself, when he abruptly stumbled out of the woods and into a clearing.

People stared at him, dressed in ragged working clothes and covered in sweat as they toiled on the fields that went on farther than he could see. Raoul almost laughed hysterically, to realize he *had* landed on a primitive planet.

But then he realized what they were farming, and that the workers included two red-skinned Heliorans, a Hellcat, a Mars human, and a *Vrill* of all things. Then the Hellcat drew a stunner and leveled it at him. Raoul laughed with hysterical relief, and then abruptly passed out.

*~*~*

Raoul groaned as he woke up, and tried to lift a hand to his throbbing head, wondering with absent annoyance just how much he was going to owe the hooker and who he needed to punch for getting him into his current mess.

But his hand got stuck and he shifted, realizing abruptly that he was covered in the kind of blanket that was not found in any whorehouse on Bangkok, but were always around in military encampments and starships.

The *Shangri La* had exploded, he remembered, everything coming back to him. Pyotr—he sat up and threw back the blanket, immediately tried to activate his in-lens, only realizing when it didn't work that it wasn't even in his damned eye. "Dragons eat it," he muttered in annoyance.

So the ship had blown, but he was alive and—where, exactly? He looked around the room, a large space divided in half by a wall that only went halfway up, the half he was in slightly raised above the other. Typical of a camp workroom, but the more he looked the less he thought the military had anything to do with it.

The guns he could see were too mismatched, though they were definitely Auth-issue weapons. To judge by the state-of-the-art military equipment, and the modifications made to it to make it work for people who didn't have the right keys and codes, he was in the middle of something seriously illegal.

He wondered if there were pain-chems anywhere in the haphazard assortment of illegal and vaguely legal equipment.

Dragons, was Pyotr alive? Raoul chose to believe he was—dragons and stars, if *he* was alive, then Pyotr just had to be. Raoul balled one hand into a fist, wishing he knew who was responsible for the damned explosion. Pyotr's ship should have been airtight; the most talented gremlin in the IG had designed the damned thing and even overseen the production. Raoul knew the ship inside and out. No one should have been able to blow the damned thing up.

He sneered at the flashy assassination; it was dramatic, messy. There were better ways to kill people if that seemed the only solution to a perceived problem. Explosions were for making sweeping statements, which meant it definitely was tied to the Draconis matter. Raoul swung his legs over the edge of the cot he was on, propped his elbows on his thighs, and rested his forehead on his fingertips.

It was damned hard to think clearly when his head felt entirely too much like it had when he'd done that undercover job on Helior. He'd sworn off alcohol for an entire *term* after that nightmare. Realizing his thoughts were straying, and that was an indication of nothing good, Raoul tried to rein himself back in.

He was tempted to try and heal himself, but he wasn't certain it wouldn't just cause him to pass out again. Better just to heal the hard way until he recovered more of his strength.

Pyotr, he needed to get to Pyotr. To do that, he needed to get in touch with someone, and the best way to do that was to help himself to the comm equipment. Nodding to himself, Raoul drew a deep breath and slowly stood up. Step by step, he made his way across the room. He was halfway to his goal when the door flew open, and surprise forced him to a halt.

Raoul almost whistled in appreciation, the Vrill was so pretty. Vrill weren't uncommon in space, but the finer vintages of that breed tended to stay at home; those who traveled the stars were considered by the rest of their race to be 'common as air'. Raoul could count on one hand the number of times he had seen a Vrill of pure noble blood anywhere but Vrill or Zero.

Vrill by nature tended toward slender, even delicate. They were still nothing next to the excessively thin build of a Fornarian, but rarely was a Vrill of real heft ever born. Pure-blood, or noble, Vrill had skin of such a pale green it was sometimes mistaken for white. Lesser Vrill had skin that was darker green or brown.

The one eyeing him warily, one hand on his stunner, had dark green hair that mostly hung loose, but with a few small braids twined with yellow ribbon scattered throughout. He was the androgynous sort of pretty that the Vrill lauded, of average height and build for a Vrill, which made him a full head shorter than Raoul and roughly the same weight. Age was hard to determine, but Raoul supposed it didn't matter.

Gold eyes met his, and the Vrill said, "What in the stars are you doing out of bed already? You do know you were concussed, right? You also lost a lot of blood."

"Well, I didn't think crash-landing headfirst on a strange planet would result in zero injuries," Raoul replied. "Where in the stars am I?""

The Vrill dropped the hand hovering over his stunner and shut the door behind him with a sharp bang. He stalked toward Raoul, grabbed him, and all but dragged him back to the bed. "Classified," he replied tersely.

Raoul glared at him and jerked free. "I don't give a dragon's ass about classified. I promise you, pretty boy, my clearances are higher than any you've got."

"You're lucky nobody knows who you are," the Vrill snapped.

The words drew Raoul up short, because in saying them, the Vrill revealed that *he* knew who Raoul was—and that was an awfully strange damned coincidence. He wasn't unknown, having been Pyotr's shadow for several terms, but no wayward Soul-dealing criminal should know him on sight. He started to ask, but the Vrill shook his head sharply and Raoul kept silent.

Not a second later, the door flew open and a Marsan strode in. He supposed the man could be from Bangkok, the only other planet that produced humans with that general look, but Raoul tended to know his own when he saw them. "Yevi," the man snapped. "Boss is waiting. What have you got on him?"

"He's been awake all of two terra-damned minutes," Yevi replied, braids snapping as he tossed his head in irritation. "I know some of you are crude enough to get what you need in two minutes, but we're not all you."

"Two minutes would do you a world of good, weed," the man replied.

Yevi sneered, lifting his nose in a way that rivaled the snootiest diplomats of the Star Assembly. "You wouldn't last two minutes with me, Truman, and I wouldn't *waste* two minutes on you. Corbin is just going to have to wait; all I've learned so far is that he's an idiot and a smartass."

Truman grunted and left again, though if the nasty look he shot over his shoulder was anything to go by, Yevi would not want to be wandering around alone in the dark later. He looked at Yevi, and said, "I see you're as friendly as any Vrill. How does that saying go? All thorn and no rose?"

"How does that other saying go?" Yevi mimicked. "All mouth and no substance?"

Raoul grinned. "I am often accused of that. So what does the esteemed Corbin want from me?"

"To know if you'll be missed if he uses you for fertilizer," Yevi replied. "You're only alive now because you were badly injured and not yet a threat to the operation."

"The operation being Soul," Raoul said, remembering the fields he had glimpsed before passing out. "Of all the planets in the stars, I managed to land on one that had a Soul-harvesting operation going on. Dragons grant me mercy."

Yevi made a face. "Your useless dragons will be the only ones granting mercy. If you ruin the operation, Corbin will kill you, and if you ruin *my* Op, Agent Haldor, I will kill you."

"You're Black Ops," Raoul replied. Black Ops was the deep undercover branch of Special Forces; they were the best of the best in the Authorities, and only the Commander of Special Forces himself knew each and every one of them. They did not even know each other. Strictly speaking, they weren't even officially in the Authorities, since most agents possessed magics and thereby weren't *allowed* to be in the Authorities. "I don't really care about you or your op," Raoul continued when Yevi said nothing. "If you know who I am, then you know what I do, and the High Chancellor could be alive somewhere. I can't stay here."

"How the fuck do you expect to get off planet?" Yevi asked. "We're locked down here. All this fancy equipment can only be accessed by Corbin. Never mind that I am *this* close to finally nailing the weeds for everything—"

Raoul shoved him into the wall, fisting his hands in Yevi's shirt and ignoring the dizziness that swept him. "If you're Black Ops, you have communication to the outside, and I repeat: I don't care about your priorities. I am personal bodyguard to the High Chancellor and someone tried to assassinate him by blowing up his ship in space. If I have to bust your entire operation to get to him, agent, you can bet your Kreskan-tight ass I will."

Yevi held fast to his wrists, eyes flashing like molten gold as he squeezed tightly, dumping out energy that made Raoul jerk away—and only belatedly realize that he felt a little better. "I have zero communication. Do you know how long I've had this cover? Going on three terms. One full year of that I've been stuck down here. I have no communication because I don't know where the stars we are. I wasn't kidding when I said it's classified. Corbin is the only one who knows. Everyone brought down planet is brought down under black out. I haven't talked to anyone else in half a term. When you showed up, I thought someone had finally found me."

Wincing in sudden sympathy, Raoul said, "I'm sorry."

"Good for you," Yevi said, but without any real heat. "I tried to salvage your in-lens but it was completely blown. How the fuck did you survive an explosion?"

"It blew while we were mid-light jump."

Yevi frowned thoughtfully. "Blew too soon?"

"Too late, I think," Raoul replied. "We jumped earlier than expected; I'm thinking we were never meant to reach that point. How the stars are we going to get off planet?"

"I have no idea. I've been trying to find a way out—or even just a way to get word out—for months. But the comm systems here are beyond my abilities to crack, and I don't know where Corbin keeps his ship. Close, I think, but that's all I've got. Without backup, I haven't been able to do much but lay low and wait for a break." He eyed Raoul critically and seemed to find something lacking.

Raoul refused to let that sting and just smirked. "Vrill: all pretty and no purpose."

"Bangkok: all display and no depth," Yevi retorted.

"How did you peg me as Bangkok?" Raoul asked, genuinely surprised. Uncouth he might be, but most people pegged him for Zero-breeding, he was that good at pretending to be what was needed.

Yevi shot him an unimpressed look. "I know my dirts."

Raoul tried to remind himself that shouldn't sting—when a Vrill mentioned dirt, it was the way most other places mentioned jewels or precious metals. Still, it was hard to ignore years of being essentially called the dirt off someone's shoe. Forcing a smile, he said, "Down and dirty, that's me."

"I wish *you* meant silent," Yevi said with a sigh. "But help is help, and if you'd be willing to help me out, I'll do everything in my power to help you find the High Chancellor once we're off planet."

"You make it sound like such a deal, I can almost forget I have no choice in the matter," Raoul said with his own sigh. "So you're Yevi, huh?"

"Yevi Lirio. You're lucky no one else recognizes you and that I've managed to convince them you're just an ordinary soldier."

Raoul nodded. "Thanks for saving me. I do owe you one."

"Then find Corbin's ship," Yevi said. He turned to the door as they heard voices beyond it. "Speaking of, you're about to meet him. He's been in the Soul business a long time, and he prefers killing to talking. He has no patience for smartass."

"Such a pity that I am one, then," Raoul said, and resigned himself to Soul farming for the foreseeable future.

# Chapter Four

CUSTOM CLASS STARSHIP Y-22932058, THE *FRANKENSTEIN*

Val walked down the hall toward where he thought he remembered the mess being, unable to tear his eyes away from the lecture he was watching. It was a guest lecture from a visiting professor of the University of Arukas on Vrill, on a study of Vrill roses and their evolution. He'd been bitterly disappointed to realize he would miss it, even as he realized it was more important that he be on Zero.

He heard someone else in the hall a moment too late, and looked up just in time to run straight into Bikendi, slamming against his chest and squashing his datapad between them. Hands grasped his shoulders, firm and warm even through gloves, and shoved him back. "Watch where you are going," Bikendi said, and brushed past him.

Face flushed, an apology stuck on his lips, Val watched him go until he turned right at the end of the hallway and went out of sight. He still couldn't believe they were matched—not that it really seemed to matter much. Bikendi had done nothing but ignore him, and when unable to do that, had merely snapped one or two words at him.

Val wished he knew how to get Bikendi to talk to him, but he was fairly certain that he was *everything* Bikendi did not want. What did he have to do to change that? Was changing it even possible? He'd always thought matching would make him fit in, not ostracize him more. Sighing, he tucked his datapad away like he should have in the beginning and resumed his hunt for the mess.

When he reached it, however, he heard voices—a lot of voices. It would seem he wasn't the only one who had gotten hungry. Cringing away, Val turned down a random hallway and wished miserably that he was back home. People left him alone there. Since matching, all anyone wanted to do was get him to *talk about it*. He was sick of hearing about how Bikendi would calm down and it would work out, and did he have any questions. Val didn't want to talk, except to Bikendi, and that was never going to happen. Matching was supposed to make everything better, so why wasn't it?

What *were* his magics? Val examined his hands and realized abruptly that he should probably be wearing gloves like Bikendi. In all the talking, no one had bothered to mention that. Were they all idiots? He shoved his hands into his pockets and hunched his shoulders. Turning around, he retraced his steps, bolting by the mess and all but running back to his room—

—only to once more crash into someone. He rubbed his nose, then saw a familiar black shirt and wished with all his heart that he would fall over dead right then. He tried to look up and meet Bikendi's eyes, but could only drop his gaze in mortification. "Sorry," he muttered.

Bikendi's hands grasped his shoulders again, but didn't immediately let go. "You seem to have difficulty watching where you're going."

Val's felt his face heat further. "I get lost in my head. I'm really sorry, Dr. Bikendi."

"Forget it, just have more care," Bikendi replied. "Why are you rushing about, anyway?"

"Uh—" Val dared to look up, but again had to drop his gaze, terrified to see in Bikendi's face that he really did completely hate Val. "It occurred to me that maybe I should be wearing gloves like—like you, now."

Bikendi said nothing, but his hands finally slid away from Val's shoulders. Val cringed inwardly, but said nothing, only took a step back and made to go around Bikendi. But then Bikendi's hand shot out and caught him by the wrist, and Bikendi said brusquely, "You'd better come with me."

Not waiting for a reply, Bikendi dragged him along down one hallway after another, and how was it possible for a custom class ship to be so *big*? They stopped abruptly, and

Val hung back as Bikendi keyed in a long string of numbers, in-lens flashing as it transmitted another portion of the complex security key keeping the room shut.

The door slid open and Bikendi pulled him inside, locking the door again behind them. A lounge of some sort, but there were also cabinets that bore the markers of various types of lab equipment. A private lab of some sort? He glanced back toward Bikendi, surprised to see that he was stripping off his white gloves—and Val got it. Whatever the room was—lab, lounge, some strange mix of both, it was a safe room for Bikendi. Was it a good or a bad thing that Bikendi had brought him there?

"Pyotr told me that you did not know you would match with me," Bikendi said, setting the gloves on a glass table and sitting down in the chair beside it. He crossed one leg over the other and draped his arms over the rests.

He was, Valendel noticed and wished he hadn't, even more beautiful up close. Was it stupid to want to stare at someone and never stop? He swore he could never get bored watching Bikendi. "I didn't," he said, trying to put his stupid mind where it should be, which was on magics and not the fact that Bikendi was beautiful. "No one told me. I just thought I was an experiment, and then they told me I was your assistant ... " He trailed off, because that thought hurt too much. Being Bikendi's assistant would have been a dream come true, and it was painfully obvious that Bikendi neither needed nor wanted his assistance. "I'm sorry," he said, unable to think of anything else to say.

Bikendi grunted. "Forget it. So your magics are entirely dormant?"

"Yes," Valendel replied, and dutifully went through the recitation of everything that had ever been done to try and figure out his dormant magics. "I've noticed no change since we matched."

Motioning dismissively, Bikendi said, "I doubt you've enough information to experiment properly. It's taken me my entire life to get a grasp of what I am and what I can do.

We can safely assume, I think, that your abilities will complement mine, but *how* is still an unknown entity. We can run some crude experiments now, but the real work will have to be done when I have the time for it."

Though he tried not to stare, Val could not quite help trying to catch a glimpse of Bikendi's palms. They didn't look that different, but Val knew that Bikendi had only to touch a person to kill him. "How—" He broke off, not wanting to be nosy and make Bikendi angry again.

"It's in the magics," Bikendi said, spreading out his fingers and displaying his palms. "This is what I brought you here to teach you. As you are no doubt aware, I have a unique form of micro-environmental magics, putting me in the same magics class as telekinetics and elementals. Contrary to popular belief, I am not in fact the only Telven-Kemperast in existence. I am merely a mutant, a rare instance of the two types of magics combining to form something new.

"The Kemperast are empathic, they absorb feelings and, in rare instances, actual thoughts, through touch. The Telven can paralyze with a touch. Somehow, those have combined into my ability to absorb energy with a touch—the way people die is merely a side effect, a shock to the system since I cannot avoid literally draining their energy away. We believe it is my body's way of feeding since I cannot process blood like a proper Telven."

Valendel stared in shock. "So—you have to-to touch people?" He'd never heard that—indeed, it was well known that Bikendi hid away on the moon of Telve to avoid any tragic accidents.

"People, no," Bikendi said tersely. "I don't need to take in raw energy often, but every now and then, I do require it. There are several animals I have found over the years that suffice; those being taken to Zero are not entirely for my experiments, though that is the only recorded reason." Bikendi cocked his head. "You do not appear to suffer from the same need, which is interesting. We will have to find time to experiment on our magics. At least you have not—" He broke off as a voice came over the comm. "Bikendi," Jundel said, and Val was startled to realize she was crying. "Report to the bridge immediately. Have you seen Valendel, we're still trying to find him—"

"Valendel is here with me," Bikendi said. "We're on our way." He stood up and retrieved his gloves. "Our discussion will have to keep, as we are apparently needed on the bridge. These gloves will be too large for you, but they are better than nothing. We'll see you receive properly fitted gloves on Zero. Come on."

Val snatched up a pair of gloves and ran after him. The gloves were too big, as Bikendi had warned, and Val already hated that he would have to wear them *always*, but he would worry about it later.

All thoughts of gloves, and even Bikendi, fled his mind once they reached the bridge and were greeted by a mass of distraught faces. "What is going on?" Bikendi demanded, looking at his captain.

Before he could speak, Jundel said, "The Grand Chancellor just contacted us. He received a distress call from Pyotr—" She broke off, covering her mouth with her hands and bowing her head to cry quietly.

"Pyotr is dead," Zon said, resting a soothing hand on Jundel's shoulder. "He managed to send out distress calls, but all we know is that his ship exploded and he did not think it was an accident."

Val stared at him in disbelief. The High Chancellor was dead? That was impossible. He wasn't the kind of person anyone managed to successfully assassinate. "Of course it wasn't an accident," Bikendi said scathingly. "We need to get to Zero before something *else* happens. Captain, contact the light gate and clear a direct jump to Zero. Someone connect me to—" He broke off as the comm station lit up with an incoming call.

"It's the *Wishing Star*, Dr. Bikendi," said the woman at the comm station.

Bikendi gestured for her to put it up on the main screen. Val stared in shock at the man who appeared—even he recognized that man. Human, fair-skinned, tall and lithe, handsome in a way Val's mother had often called 'wicked'. His hair was the color of dark, rich, Jupiter ink, and his eyes were like aquamarines. Lord Tresnor Daie, the notorious owner of Bangkok. He'd semi-retired after the death of his wife several years ago; it was his twin sons who saw to the day to day operations of Bangkok.

A lawyer, Val abruptly remembered. Lord Daie had once been one of the best lawyers in the IG. *He* was who Pyotr had convinced to represent the Draconis before the Star Assembly? Val would have smiled at the first real piece of goods news he'd heard in a long time, if they were not currently bowed down by the worst news he had ever heard. "I take it you've heard the news," he said without preamble.

"Just now," Bikendi said. "Do they know any more about it, Tresnor?"

Tresnor shook his head and took a pull from the dark blue cigar he held, looking pensive. "I'm still waiting to hear back from Zero, but I think we will learn nothing from IG channels. I'm deploying my own people now; we'll see what turns up. In the meantime, I am already getting messages that people are suggesting the proceedings be stayed until the mystery can be solved."

"Of course they are," Bikendi snapped. "They probably only just barely waited an acceptable length of time before submitting the motions to stay. I assume you are doing something about it?"

Chuckling, Tresnor leaned back in his seat, cigar smoke wafting, the jewels at his throat and in his ears gleaming, a sparkling contrast to his tailored black suit. He looked every bit the man he was: the incalculably wealthy and dangerously powerful owner of the most notorious planet in the stars. "Itzal, old friend, I had my objections written before they ever thought to make their paralegals draft the motions. What else do you pay me for?"

"To shut up and get on with it," Bikendi snapped, and killed the connection as Tresnor laughed. Silence fell in the wake of the brief conversation, and Val asked, "Are they trying to stop the trial because the High Chancellor is dead? Is that what you were discussing?"

Bikendi nodded. "Yes. It's a strategy we anticipated, though none of the three of us anticipated it would be Pyotr that they actually killed. We predicted it would be myself, Tresnor, or Lady Jundel."

"Why?" Valendel asked.

"Damage," Lady Jundel said, drawing Valendel's attention. "It's all about making the Draconis look dangerous and associating us with all the negativity they can muster."

Val frowned. "But it must be obvious they killed him, right?" Everyone shook their heads, and he wondered what he was missing.

Jundel tucked back a loose dark orange curl, and then continued, "They could just as easily accuse us of doing it, to stall for time because we fear we are going to lose—never mind that Pyotr is our staunchest supporter. Tragedy is a powerful motivator, and people will side with us now just because the High Chancellor died in defense of us. So, there is no real way to say who did it without proof."

"Oh," Val said, mind whirling, trying to process, but politics and such were beyond him. "So what do we do now?"

"Tresnor keeps them from staying the trial and we go to Zero, and we win," Bikendi said. "There are bigger games to play, and we all know this case is just the start of it. We cannot lose, even if it means we must move callously on to the trial without pausing to grieve for our friend."

He abruptly turned and left the bridge, leaving a heavy silence. Val stared at the others, but they seemed lost in their own thoughts. It was only then it really hit him—the

High Chancellor was dead and because of him, because of Jundel, because of *all* the Draconis.

Val fled, suddenly unable to bear to be around other people any longer, guilt and sadness twisting together in a knot in his chest. He fled to his room, and then fumbled his datapad out of its holster on his thigh. Sitting down on his bed, he turned the datapad on and pulled up the news feeds. Whatever else was going on in the stars, no one cared—every single headline read: HIGH CHANCELLOR ASSASINATED ON EVE OF DRACONIS TRIALS.

He had not known the High Chancellor at all, really; just enough to be in awe of him and a little scared. There was never a lack of gossip about Lord Pyotr Kavalerov: parents killed when he was a boy, taken in by his uncle, the Grand Chancellor. Former Commander of Auth Special Forces, rumors that he'd been part of Internal Affairs. Dangerous, ruthless, smart, handsome, remote—and untouchable.

Except he was dead. He'd been fighting for Val's right to live, and he was dead.

Val frowned at that, then dismissed the news feeds and flipped back to his school files, pulling up everything he had on the Telve and Kemperast races. When that proved to be only half a dozen, he logged into the university system and began to search for more, downloading those and anything cross-referenced that seemed as though it might be pertinent.

If it was his duty to be an experiment, then the least he could do in the face of the High Chancellor's sacrifice was be the best damned example he possibly could that the Draconis deserved to live, and the first step to that was to understand his magics and how they helped his match.

He jumped and cried out when a knock came at his door, dropping his datapad to the floor. Shoving it in its holster, he scrambled to the door and pushed the button to open it—then stared. "Dr. Bikendi?"

"Come along," Bikendi said tersely. "We might as well pick up where we left off—there is nothing else to do until we reach Zero, and even with emergency clearance, that will take a couple of hours."

Val nodded and followed after him, remaining silent until they reached Bikendi's safe room. Inside, he opened his mouth, and then closed it again.

"What?" Bikendi snapped.

"I-I'm sorry," Val said. "I didn't—I didn't know him, but I know he was your friend. I'm sorry he's gone."

Bikendi's tense expression eased, and he said gruffly, "I don't know that 'friend' was the word for it, but we were comrades-in-arms, and he might have deserved a thrashing, but he didn't deserve murder. Thank you. Remove your gloves; we're going to test a couple of things." Val obediently removed his gloves, then sat when Bikendi motioned he should. "I suppose we should first establish how we affect each other," Bikendi said, removing his own gloves. He frowned thoughtfully, fingers curled loosely inward.

Val glanced at his own palms, not certain if he was relieved or disappointed that they looked no different—but that was stupid; of course he should be relieved. Still, being matched was supposed to fix things, or at least change them, and so far he still felt exactly like himself. Frown deepening, he splayed his palms and looked up. "So what should I do?"

Whatever he had expected, it wasn't the hesitation and ... well, *wistfulness* was the only word that came to mind. He knew that emotion well, but he didn't know why Bikendi would feel it. Why would he need to? He was *Bikendi*. Val reached out, not thinking about his actions at all, and took Bikendi's hand—and only as Bikendi started to jerk away did he realize the risk he'd run.

But he wasn't dead. He was holding Bikendi's hand. Val stared, but Bikendi didn't notice because his gaze was locked on their hands, and he was holding Val's so tightly it hurt. Val tugged, trying to get him to ease his grip, disappointed when Bikendi abruptly dropped his hand. "Is everything—"

"Go," Bikendi said, voice as curt as ever, any hint of its softening toward Val long gone. "I think we'd do better to deal with this later."

Val opened his mouth, then closed it again, and obediently left. What had he done wrong? Wasn't it a good thing that he could touch Bikendi? He looked at his hand, opened and closed it, then shoved both hands into his pockets and head back to his room.

# Chapter Five

**PLANET 2154014 (TREDAD), UNKNOWN LOCATION**

Pyotr was not surprised to find himself alone when he woke. He still could not stay awake for very long, and Jade seemed busy with something. Though he could not say for certain, by his rough estimate he had been on Tredad for three days since waking, and he didn't know how long he'd been unconscious. In all that time, he had not seen so much as a hair of Jade. Beyond a few mocking words, Jade had said nothing to him, and Pyotr had not lasted an hour before sleep had taken him again.

He stood up slowly and stretched, gingerly feeling his head, relieved that it seemed well on the mend. The clothes he'd woken to find a day or two ago were a little too big, but warm and comfortable. There was always food, and plenty of the expensive erosa tea he knew Jade favored.

Jade ... he almost thought he was making that part up. If not for the tea, he'd probably believe he had. So Jade was hiding in Tredad, but no one had found him there. Pyotr shook his head and made the bed, then wandered over to the kitchen area to make tea.

Though he had scoured every nook and cranny of the house, he had not been able to find any means by which to communicate with the outside world. He wondered if everyone thought he was dead, or if they had been able to determine he was alive. Pyotr sighed in frustration; he needed to be on Zero, not stuck on Tredad. He needed to let his aunt and uncle know he was alive.

The same uncle, he thought bitterly, who had been ignoring his call right before the ship exploded. Pyotr grimaced and put the pettiness aside. Arkadii was a good man; he was no doubt punishing himself for ignoring that last chance to speak to him.

Sighing, Pyotr picked up the kettle as it softly chimed the water's readiness and poured it into a cup, swirling the leaves around. He sat at the little table, scowling as he thought. It had definitely been an inside job. He had hand-picked the crew of the *Shangri La*; the ship had been with him for his brief two terms as Lower Chancellor, through his several terms as Commander of the Authorities, and stayed with him as he took up the mantle of High Chancellor. The crew in all that time had changed very little; they were his crew. Betrayal was a fact of life, but it still hurt that someone amongst his crew had violated his trust.

He tried to remember everything that had happened, but the memories were no clearer than they had been three days ago. He thought he recalled three explosions, but couldn't be sure. He was almost certain he had gotten out distress calls. The last thing he remembered seeing was Raoul's face and *that* hurt. Raoul was the closest thing to a friend that Pyotr possessed, and probably the only person who had stated he would gladly die for Pyotr—not something Pyotr deserved, but given that nearly everyone else he knew wanted him dead, and the only other people he truly trusted were Tresnor, Bikendi, and Tau Ceti ...

Pyotr sighed again and sipped his tea, wishing his head would cease throbbing. He needed to get home, before whoever had tried to kill him tried something else. At least he could be confident that Tresnor and Bikendi would not let the trial come to a halt.

Stars above, he needed to be *doing* something. While he sat there, everything could be spiraling out of control, and where would his plans wind up, then? He had not come so far to fail. He hadn't, stars damn everyone who got in his way.

But hate it all he liked, he was trapped. Jade had locked him in, and without even an in-lens or a datapad, Pyotr could not crack anything. He drank his tea and wondered how long he was going to be a prisoner.

As if summoned by his thoughts, the door in the middle of the room chimed as it was unlocked from below. Then the door swung up, landing with a thud against the floor. A figure crawled up, and Pyotr could see Jade in the way the indistinct figure moved. He watched in silence as Jade locked the door, then began to slowly strip out of his cumbersome outer layers, until he at last stood wearing the same style of loose pants and long-sleeved shirt as Pyotr.

Pyotr had little need for other people, save as a means to an end. Being too close to anyone merely impeded everything—plans, goals, missions. He had an inner circle of people he trusted and relied upon as much as he must, but that same circle would be the first to say that he was 'not exactly a friend'. It was the way Pyotr preferred it, and only once in his life had he gotten a taste of what tempted a man to let someone get too close.

If he considered Tresnor and Bikendi his comrades, and Raoul as close as he would ever come to a friend ... then Jade was the only man in the stars he considered his equal. No one else met his gaze so unflinching, so lacking in hesitation—no one else made him *fight* not to be the first to look away.

"So I suppose you are done sleeping the days away," Jade finally said, and began to pick up his discarded clothes, hanging each piece up one by one on the wall nearby. His nails gleamed dark red in the warm yellow light of the room. Only Jade could be arrogant enough to retain such damning bits of himself as his nails and his tea, and still go untouched for an entire term.

Pyotr shrugged in reply, not shifting his gaze away as Jade sauntered toward him with a stride that had seduced more government officials that Pyotr had even had the stomach to count. Though Jade was beautiful—breathtaking—it was not the first adjective Pyotr would use to describe him. 'Ruthless' was the word that most suited Jade, followed very closely by 'deadly'.

Jade stopped just out of reach, and tilted his head back and to the side, an invitation to temptation if Pyotr had ever seen one. He ignored it and just met the gray eyes regarding him coolly. "How long are you going to keep me imprisoned?"

"Until I am ready to leave Tredad," Jade replied, and dropped his pose to head for the kettle and reheat the water. His braid had gotten longer, Pyotr noted, as it swayed across his ass as he walked. He'd seen Jade's hair loose only once; the memory was seared into his brain.

Pyotr sipped his own tea, watching as Jade fixed a cup, and then sat down on the opposite side of the table. "It would have been easier for you to kill me. Everyone thinks I am dead, anyway, I'm sure."

"They do," Jade replied, smile cool and amused. "Apparently there was quite an ugly fight to continue the trial, because a *shocking* number of people thought it should be stayed. Heartstone's trial dragged on for five terms, after all. Just think of all the people who could die, if they were willing to kill the *poor* High Chancellor. Your uncle is in quite the state and your aunt will not leave her home. There is to be a grand mourning ceremony tomorrow, 18:00 Zero Time, but the actual funeral is not to be held until much later, as the Star Assembly did vote to continue the trial and so it must go on." Jade smirked over the rim of his teacup. "Did you plot your own demise, Petya? It would be a clever ruse, and Tredad is an *excellent* place to hide."

"I'm not that clever," Pyotr replied, smiling despite everything. "My cleverness extends to hiring the right people and arranging their actions. Death is messy."

"Depends on who you kill and how you do it."

Pyotr did not bother to argue with that; it was true, but those days were long past for him. "What are you doing, Jade?"

Jade's expression shuttered. "Enjoying the weather."

"Your brother is excelling at Internal Affairs. I believe he'll be fit for Commander in a couple more terms." He tried not to take satisfaction in the way Jade's hand tightened around his teacup, but it was hard. Jade's only weak point was his twin brother. "I'm astonished he hasn't found you, yet."

At those words, Jade laughed. "Cyan may think he's overcome me, but he'll never look for me to prove it. Should he ever be stupid enough to try it ... " He didn't bother to finish the sentence; simply traced the rim of his teacup with one red-painted nail.

"Why did you save me?" Pyotr asked abruptly, switching back to the matter that had started the conversation.

"Leverage," Jade replied. "Leverage I doubt I will need, but I do not believe in wasting resources." He tossed his head, braid tumbling over one shoulder to land on the table, before it slowly slid off. "Anyway, why give those Zero twits their hearts' desire? I prefer to rip hearts out—as do you."

Pyotr did not reply, because it was true enough, even if he would not have phrased it that way. He smirked at the thought of all the people who would be maneuvering, believing he was dead, and just how livid they would be when he eventually reappeared. "If you kill me now, I will be most vexed with you."

"Do not tempt me," Jade replied.

"I do not believe *I* have ever been accused of tempting," Pyotr replied softly, meeting his gaze.

Jade looked away, standing up to take his teacup to the sink to rinse it out. "No, but you have been accused of everything else. That is why you were made High Chancellor."

"More or less." Pyotr finished his own tea, but held on to the cup, restlessly running his fingers over it. He'd been made High Chancellor because he was too dangerous as Commander and had allowed his objectivity with regards to Jade to falter. At least he'd been caught at it. But Jade would know that.

Pyotr watched as Jade crossed the room to the tiled area meant for washing, completely unsurprised when Jade stripped naked and turned on the water with a light touch to the master panel. Frosted glass rose up a moment later, shielding him, but not before Pyotr saw the nasty scars across his back.

Fresh, and the way the five rows of cuts were lined up ... definitely a Hellcat. Jade had gotten into a fight, and Pyotr almost felt sorry for whoever was stupid enough to sic a Hellcat on Jade. He was the only person Pyotr knew who did not need special inoculations to resist Hellcat venom—because Jade had made himself immune to it over the years and used a variation of it in some of his nail paints.

Pyotr ran a hand over his face and wondered just how long Jade intended to keep him captive. What was Jade up to, and why *Tredad?* Grimacing, Pyotr stood up and rinsed out his teacup, putting it away in the cabinet built into the wall.

Homes in Tredad did not have windows, and only the rural homes had direct access to the outdoors. Jade's home, with the door in the floor, was located in a city. To get into a fight with a Hellcat, he must have been in one of three major cities that contained IG interstellar ports. Visitors seldom bothered to visit the lesser cities or the rural areas, and a Hellcat especially would never venture that deeply into the cold.

Stars damn everything; if he had landed anywhere else, then he would probably be back on Zero already and the entire incident all but forgotten, save by those who had failed to kill him. Pyotr could not wait to figure out who amongst his crew had done the deed—it would not be hard, given the traitor was whoever remained alive.

He frowned, a belated realization striking him: if he was alive, the others could be as well. Raoul had been *with* him, so the chances were even better. Some of his tension eased, to realize that perhaps Raoul had not died for him, after all. He hoped not; Raoul deserved better.

If he had landed on Tredad, had Raoul as well? But the *Shangri La* had not been anywhere near Tredad, and light jumping was dangerous and tricky. Pyotr rubbed his forehead, tired of trying to work through it all without any way to do something about it.

He had nothing:  nothing to work with, nothing to do, nothing to distract him. He was a prisoner—Jade's prisoner, and there was nothing he could do about it. He flicked a glance toward the wash area as the water turned off, listening to the soft whir as air kicked on to dry, and the wash system began to recycle the water and prep it for the next use.

Stepping out as the glass lowered, Jade strode to the drawers under the bed and pulled on fresh clothes. His hair, Pyotr realized with equal parts amusement and disappointment, was already braided. Jade did not wear armor, but the hair and the nails might as well have been.

Dressed, Jade pulled a chest out of another drawer, and then carried it to the table. Ignoring Pyotr, he opened the case, and after a moment of deliberation, drew out a delicate crystal bottle filled with dark violet nail paint. Closing the chest, he pushed it out of his way and began to paint his nails.

Pyotr had seen Jade paint his nails before, but not for nearly three whole terms. Like his hair, Jade was more than willing to flash them, but only after they were perfect. He wondered what Jade was up to; he could sometimes read Jade's thoughts, but not as nearly as often as he would have liked.

But if Jade were easy to read, Pyotr would not be enthralled with him. "So are you going to demand a ransom for me?" he finally asked.

Jade did not reply until he finished painting another nail and examined it critically. Slowly looking up, he said, "There is nothing I need from anyone who would be willing to pay one."

"I could pay my own," Pyotr replied. "I can't stay here."

"No, I suppose you can't," Jade said, and bent to his nails again, not speaking again until he was finished. "There is always work to do, always something to fix, always something that needs the touch of the notorious Pyotr Kavalerov."

Pyotr's mouth tightened. "You were the one who chose to become a criminal, Jade. I made you an offer."

"I remember," Jade replied. "I made one as well. And here we sit, our choices made. You'll leave when and if I say. Until then, I give it another day before you are scrubbing floors or trying to use the water recycling system to build a datapad. It won't work." He put the nail paint away, and then returned the chest to its drawer below the bed.

He strode over to the wall where his weather clothes hung and began to pull them on. "Going to kill the Hellcat that scratched you?" Pyotr asked.

Jade sneered as he picked up his face covering, but did not yet put it on. "I slit his throat hours ago. His companion has been sitting in a place that keeps him just short of freezing for the past two hours. I'm going to see if he is ready to apologize for his friend's mistake. Behave while I'm gone, Petya, and perhaps I'll tell you where I keep my books."

Pyotr did not react, simply watching as Jade left. He could probably tackle him, or lie in wait and get the jump on him as he returned, but he wasn't stupid enough to think Jade had not prepared for such things—and stupid as it was, he wanted to know what he was missing. Jade knew something, was up to something, and if he was keeping Pyotr around, it wasn't because he needed the leverage—it was because Pyotr was not going to react well to whatever Jade was hiding. When all they had left between them was taunting and hurting, well ... it was better than nothing.

Stifling a sigh, Pyotr stood up to prowl the room to see if he could find the books himself. After that goad, he would be damned if he *ever* let boredom drive him to scrubbing floors.

# Chapter Six

**UNKNOWN PLANET, UNKNOWN LOCATION**

"Can't you play nicely with the other sprites?" Yevi demanded irritably, and Raoul wondered what the hell the word he'd used really was, that it translated as 'sprites' rather than 'children'. Translation programs had the weirdest damned quirks.

He winced as Yevi wiped at the cut on his face, the antiseptic rinse stinging. "I take issue with people calling my mother a whore like that's a bad thing." He jerked away as Yevi wiped his face again. "Stop trying to make it worse."

Yevi rolled his eyes and lightly slapped Raoul's good cheek. "Stop whining; it doesn't suit you. Try to remember that Corbin won't hesitate to kill you. Honestly, you're an adult. Act like one."

Raoul snorted. "First rule of Bangkok: don't be pleasant unless you're getting paid for it."

"I thought the first rule of Bangkok was 'don't leave the dragon pavilions'," Yevi replied.

"Spoken like a true visitor," Raoul said, then fell silent as Yevi treated the wound on his chest and arm as well, shirt fisted in his good hand. He watched Yevi's fingers, long and elegant, with nary a scratch upon them, the skin so pale and delicate a green, he was surprised he couldn't see right through it to the bone. His own skin, darkened by the sun, roughened and scarred by a brutal life, left him feeling like an unkempt brute, exactly the sort of reason that visitors to Bangkok were told to stay within the safe zones of the dragon towers and the pavilions in which they were situated.

Yevi didn't reply, simply bandaged the wound on his chest, and then began to clean up all his supplies. Raoul wondered what Yevi had done on Bangkok and how often he'd gone. It wasn't the kind of place anyone who worked there could actually afford; he'd only ever been into the pavilions himself when he was working, and the clients didn't take him anywhere but their beds.

Otherwise, he'd lived in a tiny little apartment in a grungy 'city' half an hour away by foot from Black Dragon Tower itself. Every day, he went to work, watching the glittering arrivals who could afford the most luxurious of the five towers, the one where the Jewels of Bangkok themselves lived, high above the world they owned. His mouth twisted and he looked down at his crumpled shirt, and then stiffly pulled it back on.

"I would think you'd be long past caring if people called your mother a whore," Yevi finally said.

"My mother was a whore," Raoul said. "So was I, for that matter. I don't take issue with the truth; I resented the tone. A whore is not a bad thing to be, and it's far better to make money from sex than to pay for sex, if you ask me." He stood up and gingerly stretched, testing his muscles. "If he does it again, I'm not going to hold back and take my licks. I'll snap his neck."

Yevi made a face and went over to a food cooler. He pulled out a glass carafe filled with the orange-colored liquid that seemed to be all anyone drank on the damned planet. Pouring two glasses, he handed one to Raoul. "Don't kill the other sprites; it'll slow down the mission. I can't see you being a very good whore; too mouthy."

Raoul shouldn't have done it—any other day, he would have curbed the impulse. Being personal bodyguard to Pyotr Kavalerov taught a man a lot about curbing *everything*. But he was still pissed off with Ree, still defensive about being the ugly half of Bangkok, and pretty boys like Yevi never gave him the time of day. Someone like Yevi had probably visited Bangkok dozens of times a term and had every luxury handed to him, and strode past Raoul without ever seeing him.

So he did it—reached out and curled one hand around Yevi's wrist, yanking him close before Yevi could react, and cupped the back of Yevi's head with his other hand, kissing him. Yevi's lips were as soft and delicate as the rest of him, sour from the orange juice, but with an underlying sweetness that seemed to be a Vrill thing.

At first, Yevi tried to jerk back—but then he relaxed and went with it, fingers curling around Raoul's sides as their mouths tangled. The kiss zinged in a way Raoul hadn't expected, made him completely forget they were in the middle of a Soul-harvesting camp where they could be shot at any moment.

It was only remembering that which finally drove him to break the kiss. He let Yevi go, and then finished his juice. "I was actually well on my way up the ranks when Pyotr found me," he said.

Yevi flicked his head, sending his hair back over his shoulder. "I guess 'mouthy' has a host of applications. Please do not tell me you met the High Chancellor in the course of your profession."

Raoul laughed at the idea of Pyotr hiring him for sexual service. "No, but that would have been hilarious. I had a regular client and Pyotr wanted him arrested. He got me to set the bastard up. Said he'd pay me in points or in a career change. I really liked the whole secret agent thing, so I opted for career change. He put me in the Authority Cadets. Once I was old enough, I joined the regular Auths. Barely a term later, they threw me at Black Ops and told them to *do something* with me. I spent a couple of terms doing that, before I became Pyotr's personal guard."

"Oddly boring job for someone who apparently likes covert work so much."

"Bodyguard to Kavalerov is just as interesting, believe me," Raoul said. "Besides, he saved my life by giving me a chance at one outside of Bangkok. I don't mind being a whore, but being an Auth is way more fun. Keeping him alive seems the least I can do."

Yevi nodded and drank his own juice, licking traces of it from his lips when he finished. Raoul wanted suddenly to kiss him again. Startled by his own vehemence, he sought for a distraction. "So how did a pretty boy like you wind up an Auth? If you're less than the Earl of Eleven Roses Castle or whatever, I will die of shock."

"You'll die from running your mouth first," Yevi retorted. "I am *not* an earl. I'm not anything, not anymore. I'm an Auth because I figured if I was going to abandon the responsibilities to which I was born, the least I could do was pick up some others. I liked the idea of responsibilities that involved shooting people."

Raoul laughed. "How oddly bloodthirsty of you, plant."

Of all things, Yevi smiled faintly. "I was never very good at proper etiquette. People always wanted to say I must be half-breed, but my lines are as pure as they can possibly be. They couldn't say poor breeding, either, because my siblings are paragons of taste and refinement, at least publically. I'm just a bad seed."

"I do wonder what your real name is," Raoul said.

Yevi shrugged. "I don't honestly know that I'd answer to it, anymore; I've been Yevi for so long, everything else sounds strange." He sighed.

Raoul grunted in sympathy.

"You'd better get back out there before Corbin sends someone to come looking," Yevi said, and did not wait for his reply; just took his arm and dragged him to the door and outside. Raoul lifted a hand, shielding his eyes from the bright, ever so slightly blue-ish yellow light. The sky was faintly green and the taste of the air reminded him of Fornar. Most planets had close living spaces with special filtered air to accommodate the host of races that travelled the stars. Raoul had chatted with an air systems engineer once; it had given him a throbbing headache (and throbbing other things, and it hadn't actually been a bad night at all).

But wherever they were, it was out in the open, the air pure and unfiltered. Where the stars were they? He looked out over the Soul fields, the camp, the sky, the distant mountains. Something niggled at the back of his mind, had ever since he'd really gotten a look around, but he had not yet been able to grasp the elusive thought or memory or whatever.

"What's wrong?" Yevi asked.

Raoul hesitated, then lowered his arm, and said, "This place bugs me, but I can't peg why. It's like ... I know I've never seen it before, but it feels like I have. Sort of like I've only ever read about it before or something. You have absolutely no idea where we are?"

"Not a one. I have tried and tried to figure it out, but to no avail. Sometimes, I think it's not even IG. Don't think it's primitive, though. From the few things Corbin *has* said, my impression is that it's a wiped planet."

"Wiped?" Raoul said. "Interesting." A wiped planet was one that had once borne conscious life, but no longer did, because that life had ceased to exist—usually a planet-wide illness was the culprit, but there were other causes. "So they're using a wiped planet for a Soul farm. Smart, very smart. But the IG will nail them eventually."

Yevi nodded. "Eventually meaning the second I get off this stars damned rock." He started to say more, but stopped as Corbin started walking toward them from where he'd been in front of his own living quarters.

Raoul braced himself; if there was one thing he had well and truly learned in the past several days it was that Corbin was a mean son of a bitch. Raoul had met starving Telvens with nicer dispositions. "Lowry!" he snarled, walking up and grabbing Raoul by the shirt, shoving him back into the wall of Yevi's building. "What the fuck are you doing, picking fights instead of working? And now I see you making eyes at my medic? I can and will—"

"Kill me, I know," Raoul replied. "Do it, then."

But Corbin wouldn't, he knew it—not when Raoul was proving very good at harvesting Soul and they were severely behind schedule, according to Yevi. Raoul might be a pain, but he was also useful.

Instead of killing him, Corbin punched him. Raoul's eyes watered and his vision went to shit as his nose broke, blood going everywhere.

"That's not going to get him back to work," Yevi snapped, striding up to them—and grunting in pain as he was shoved against the wall in turn, Corbin's hand around his throat. "Let me go, Corbin."

"Stop distracting him, weed," Corbin said, stepping in closer, splaying his free hand low on Yevi's stomach. "I always said you were too pretty to be a medic."

Yevi sneered. "I'd rather be a medic than a whore."

"How lucky for that pretty head of yours that you don't have to pick," Corbin said, and slapped his cheek with mock playfulness. "Get him patched up again, throw him back in the fields, and if I see you two slacking off again, I'll throw you in the shed." He let Yevi go and walked away.

Muttering something Raoul couldn't catch, Yevi pulled off his own shirt and balled it up, then pressed it to Raoul's face. "Staunch the blood with that. Come on, get back inside. You're nothing but trouble."

Raoul just stared at him once the door closed behind them.

Yevi made a face. "What, you think in a place like this someone who looks like me isn't going to get offers he's not really allowed to refuse?" He sighed when Raoul just continued to look at him. "It's not that bad, and occasionally letting Corbin fuck me gets the others to leave me alone."

He moved away to get fresh supplies, pointing Raoul to a seat. Sitting on his own rolling stool, Yevi laid his hands on Raoul's cheeks, his gold eyes shining faintly as he poured out healing magics. "I was surprised the first time I healed you. Being half-human, and a very public figure, I figured you must not be magics capable. But you must have some, for my healing to work." He pulled the bloody shirt away, and then cut off Raoul's ruined shirt, checking the bandages he'd only just wrapped.

Raoul gingerly tested his nose, but it was recovered from the worst of the damage. His voice was only slightly off as he finally spoke. "Officially I don't have magics, being half-human, but I do actually possess full Fornarian magics. Comes in handy."

"I have yet to meet a Fornarian who ever thought his magics were a bad thing to have, even if they like to brag they don't *need* them to climb. I personally never saw why they wanted to climb everything, but as they say: Avarri fly, Fornarians climb, Marsans shoot, Kreskans hide."

Raoul laughed, and finished, "Zeros argue, and Bangkok makes a profit off all of it." Yevi smiled faintly, and began to wash away the remaining traces of blood. They lapsed into silence and Raoul once more got lost just in looking at Yevi, in watching him move. He could not help but remember the stolen kiss ... and that immediately reminded him of what Yevi had just revealed. "I guess I'm no better than the rest, kissing you like that."

Yevi looked at him in surprise. "I seem to recall kissing you back. Trust me; Corbin doesn't waste his time on kisses. Anyway, it's not nearly as bad as you are clearly building up in your head. I'm sure you've had your fair share of flesh assignments."

"Well, obviously," Raoul said. "Who doesn't? Nothing gets results like sex. But that's different than being stuck in a place where it's possible no one will ever find you and having no back up if things go bad."

"I'm Black Ops; things 'going bad' is SOP." Raoul supposed there was no point in arguing with that; it was true. Yevi continued, "Anyway, it means Corbin cuts me a bit of slack, and I need all the slack I can get, even if I only wind up strangling myself with it."

Raoul frowned in thought. "What was that shack he mentioned?"

"The others call it a penalty box," Yevi said. "I feel I am missing something when they use that term, but I've never bothered to ask what. It's the camp rehab. Corbin has left people in there for days without food and water. He's killed a couple of people doing it, which is why we're so far behind on the harvesting. You do not want to get stuck in there."

"I think I do," Raoul said. "Any way in or out, besides the door?"

Yevi shrugged. "Technically, it's a trapdoor. He calls it a shed, but it's just a hole in the ground with steel walls and roof. It's about two hundred paces south of the camp, close to the cliffs—too far for anyone to hear the screams when they start up. I repeat: you do not want to get stuck in there."

Raoul frowned in thought, absently stroking his goatee. "No, I really think I do. Why didn't you tell me about the damned shed sooner?"

"It's too risky," Yevi said. "You think I haven't thought of it before? Get myself put in the shed, break out at night and snoop around outside the camp without real fear someone will catch me, lock myself back in by morning? One, I don't know how it locks, but I'm pretty certain Corbin is the only one who does. There is no guarantee you'd even be able to get out once he puts you in. Two, we don't know what to look for or where, so you'd literally be stumbling around in the dark. Three, you're an idiot."

"I don't think three fits with the rest," Raoul countered. "I'll take my chances, because it's better than biding our time. Corbin keeps everyone firmly northeast of the camp at all times. If he's hiding anything, it's going to be southeast somewhere."

"He always arrives from the north," Yevi said.

Raoul shrugged. "Not hard to swing around to hide the real direction of his approach. We've never heard nor seen his ship. I would imagine he flies down planet several miles from here, then travels low and quiet, tucks the ship away somewhere well out of sight and ordinary access, then makes his way to the camp on foot. It's a common trick."

"You're an idiot," Yevi repeated.

"I'm also right," Raoul said with a shrug. "It's worth trying. If it doesn't work, he'll let me out in a few days. So how do you think I should provoke him just enough that he'll put me in the shed without killing me?"

Yevi sighed and stood up, striding to the window by the door and looking out. "Well, he's on his way and looks like he swallowed a Hellcat. Please think of a better plan."

"No," Raoul said. Yevi sighed again and strode back toward him.

"What was it you said before? Nothing gets results like sex?" Before Raoul could reply, Yevi yanked him out of his chair, and then pushed him to the floor. Straddling his hips, Yevi bent and kissed him, hair falling around them like a curtain.

Raoul tried to ask a question, but Yevi's mouth was even more distracting when he was kissing with *intent*. It would take a stronger man than him to resist, so Raoul didn't even bother, just kissed back with all he had, splaying his hands across Yevi's back.

A moment later, he heard Corbin swearing, and he cried out in pain as a hard kick landed on his ribs. Yevi let out a cry of his own, but was silent when Corbin yanked him to his knees and backhanded him. "I see that sluts attract sluts and can't behave when in close proximity. I told you to knock it off or you'd get the shed."

He let Yevi go, kicked them both again for good measure, then bellowed for his goons, the three men who seemed always to shadow him. At least one of them was a former IG pilot; he had the telltale red iris of those who had spent long years tele-controlling the large freight class ships used to transport military equipment.

Raoul went obediently along as he and Yevi were hauled off, silently swearing as he realized that Yevi was going to be locked up with him. He made a face at the shed that was exactly as Yevi had described it: little more than a metal box in the ground. But the lock mechanism was one he had seen more times than he could count. It was a standard IG high security lock, and Corbin had clearly set it to respond only to his voice and touch.

It made Raoul want to cackle with glee. He eyed Corbin thoughtfully, beginning to wonder about a few things, but then he was being thrown down into the shed. Yevi came right after, landing on him in a painful collision of limbs. The door closed behind them and silence fell.

Yevi grunted and moved off him. "Good job."

"You should have just given me a blowjob," Raoul replied. "He probably would have let you off for that." He laughed as Yevi elbowed him, and reached out to tug him close. The barest threads of dusty light peaked through the top of the shed, but it was all the light his Fornarian eyes needed to see a ghost of Yevi. "Can you see at all?"

"No," Yevi said, voice thin.

Raoul tugged him close, not surprised when Yevi went without protest, and held Yevi tightly against his chest, kissing his brow. "Just wait until dark, plant. I can get us out of here."

"How?" Yevi asked, obviously going for an acerbic tone, but instead it only came out more strained than ever.

"Wait and see," Raoul replied, then laid him down on the ground and straddled him, bending to kiss him, slow and deep and thorough. Yevi all but melted into the distraction, and Raoul kept at it. If he kind of wished that they were kissing because they wanted to and not out of necessity, well, that was probably the stress talking.

He was far too smart and far too good an agent to do something stupid like get attached to another agent.

# Chapter Seven

**PLANET 0000000 (ZERO), THE PALACE OF ETERNITY**

With all the trouble and care that had gone into preparing for the trial, Val had expected ... *more.* But they were nearly two weeks into the trial that was going to determine whether he would live or die, and the only thing he really felt was boredom.

Trials, he had learned, largely consisted of passive-aggressive bickering via piles of paperwork delivered by harassed-looking clerks or the more hostile clerks who worked directly for the Grand Chancellor.

As he was a witness for the defense, Val was not allowed to roam around at his leisure. He was locked away with the rest of the team in a restricted wing of the Palace of Eternity, and even his datapad had been confiscated, leaving him with only the schoolwork he'd brought along, security-cleared books to read, and a special feed screen to watch in the main room.

He was bored to *death.* No one really needed him, except when Tresnor grilled him on his upcoming interview before the court, and that was still days and days away if he understood everything correctly—possibly weeks. If he dared to think the word *months,* he would probably do something drastic.

Val snorted. Him, drastic. He couldn't even *think* of anything drastic. That was the sort of thing people like Tresnor and Jundel and Bikendi did, while Val hid.

Bikendi ...

He had thought, after Bikendi had taken him to his safe room, that maybe something had changed. Even after Bikendi had abruptly dismissed him, he had thought eventually they would speak again. But they hadn't. Bikendi was avoiding him more than ever, and Val had no idea what he'd done and he didn't know who to ask about it.

Stifling a sigh, he stood up and went to the buffet line to get a fresh cup of tea, and maybe a snack, though he hadn't really felt hungry for a while. He dithered over the teas, fussing restlessly, scowling at his gloved hands.

However stupid it was, he had thought Bikendi would take him to get them. The way he had mentioned it, Val had been *sure* of it and he had carefully practiced what he was going to say when they went out, so he could fix whatever he'd done wrong in the safe room.

Except a clerk had shown up with half a dozen pairs of gloves in a fancy green and silver box. They'd fit perfectly, and all of Val's carefully prepared words had withered away. He glared at a box of tea, and finally made a fresh cup, then returned to his place at the enormous table where they worked, and wished there was something *he* could do.

If Tresnor made him go over what he was to say one more time, however, he would go look up 'drastic measures' somewhere. He stirred the spoon in his cup, longing for his datapad. Looking around the table, he saw that everyone else was immersed in their work. Bikendi had not been around much since their arrival, all his work confined to his labs—labs which Val had pointedly not been shown.

Did anyone need him for anything beyond a freaky purple mutant to parade in front of the Star Assembly? Apparently not. Finishing his tea in three hasty, too-hot gulps, he stood up and strode to the door. "I need to use the restroom," he told the bored-looking guards. One of them waved him on and went back to the book he was reading.

Val strode toward the bathrooms, then looked back and saw that absolutely no one had noticed he'd left. The guards paid him no mind. Turning on his heel, he strode in the opposite direction and slipped out the front doors of the restricted wing.

He waited for alarms, for someone to shout—for anything, but after standing in place for what seemed hours, he realized that nobody cared. Despite everything, nobody gave a damn. He shoved his hands into his pockets and walked off, taking in the palace in a way he had not been able to before when he had been hurried into his rooms and sequestered.

The Palace of Eternity was the kind of place that someone like him would typically stand no chance of seeing. Star travel was expensive if one wasn't part of a ship crew or had a government pass. Just a one planet hop would take saving up weeks of pay just for the ticket. Accommodations, food, passes, health checks, and with some planets, there were inoculations necessary. He shuddered to think what it had cost someone to send him first to Telve, then on to Zero. No one else had seemed to blink at it, but Val was fervently grateful that someone else was covering his costs.

If only there was something for him to do to repay it all. He sighed and turned down a random hall, examining the paintings on the wall—they seemed to represent historical moments, but he had no idea what they were. History didn't really appeal, not when the Draconis barely had a history and most of that was spent subjugated by the Coni.

He made a face and turned his thoughts elsewhere—or tried, anyway, but he didn't really have much to think about. He couldn't do his schoolwork, he didn't have his datapad to read or study other things, he was already getting sick of just sitting and reading all day, and he had no friends or plans with those friends.

Sighing again, Val turned down another hallway and slowed as he caught a sweet, familiar scent: *chopi*. Someone, somewhere, was eating chopi. His stomach growled for food he had not seen since leaving home. No one cared about what sorts of foods the Draconis might like, past making jokes about insects and other lizard food.

Val followed the sticky-sweet scent of the chopi, even though he knew there was no way he'd be able to eat it. But he couldn't resist the draw of something familiar—something he loved—and so eventually stumbled upon a small room that was filled to bursting with sunlight from the windows taking up the top half of three of the four walls. A table was laid out with a tea service, and flowers were everywhere.

A man—human—sat at the table, reading an antique book and nibbling at chopi, occasionally sipping tea. He seemed as if he'd be tall when he stood, and had dark hair just a trifle too long and the pale skin of someone who did not get much time down planet. He wore black slacks and a dark green shirt with gleaming white buttons ... and had the strangest tattoo on his left arm. Val cocked his head, trying to see all of it, and realized it wasn't really a tattoo. Well, it was, but it looked more like someone had inked a serial number into his arm, rather than anything decorative: *5133P1N634U7Y*

Suddenly the man looked up, and Val froze beneath dark green eyes that were like nothing he'd ever seen. Even Bikendi's eyes were not that intense. Then the man smiled and the intensity faded. "Well, well," he said, and his words had a strange cadence, an accent Val hadn't heard before. "I do believe the star Draconis has run away." His eyes crinkled at the corner as he smiled and Val wanted to smile back.

Then what he'd said registered and Val panicked instead. He jerked back, turned to go—and yelped as a hand wrapped around his upper arm. How had the man moved so damned fast? He whipped back around, nearly crashing into the man, and flushed as he was steadied. "I—"

"Shh," the man said soothingly, smiling in that eye-crinkling way that made Val want to smile back, even if his heart was still lodged in his throat from panic. "I promise I will not get you in trouble. Please, come and sit." He led Val to the table and pushed him into the seat catty-corner to his own. "Do you like Bangkok sweet-spice tea?"

Val stared, then gathered himself, and said, "I've never had it."

"That is a crime," the man replied, and poured a cup of tea for him. "You are Valendel, correct?" he asked, pushing the cream and sugar closer. When Val nodded, he said, "My name is Wilbur Messersmith. I'm an archivist for the IG, on call to pull records as those involved with the trial need them." He smiled again. "So far, your team has been very creative in what they require. The other team ... well, I am not permitted to take sides, of course, but I admire the way Tresnor's mind works."

"He's very smart," Val agreed quietly. "They all are."

Wilbur smiled again, and Val felt like he was sitting with one of his professors suddenly. "I believe you should have said 'we all are'," he correct gently. "You do yourself a disservice, setting yourself apart."

"I'm not here because I'm smart," Val said to his tea, bitterness slipping out. "I'm here because I'm purple."

"That is no doubt true to a point, but they would never have brought an idiot into such an important case. You are no fool, for all that you are young; that's as important to the trial as the fact that you are unique." He pushed a plate of pastries close, smiling in that gentle way. Val's anger faded away momentarily as he immediately took up one of the sticky buns he loved so much, tearing it into pieces and eating them one by one.

Wilbur chuckled. "So if I recall correctly, you study magics, correct? Rather, the genetics of magics, however that is meant to be scientifically phrased."

Val nodded. "I study the interplanetary evolution of magics."

"Dr. Bikendi's field, if I recall correctly."

"Only one of his," Val corrected. "Dr. Bikendi's primary field is actually lost magics. He believes that non-magics races should have magics, and probably did at one time, but the abilities were suppressed at the genetic level for reasons unknown. He theorizes that as people increasingly think and act with a planetary mindset, versus a national mindset, anomalies like magics capable humans will begin to increase. There are only a handful of scientists who study the field; it is not really taken seriously by the majority of the scientific community and the IG frowns heavily of course—" He broke off, realizing he was babbling.

Wilbur only smiled and poured more tea, and Val did not realize until then that he'd drunk all of his. "You seem to know a lot about it, but that does not surprise me, given that Pyotr said you were to be Bikendi's assistant in all this."

Val looked at the crumbs on his plate, and then slowly cleaned his sticky fingers. "Dr. Bikendi doesn't need an assistant, and any student would know all about his work. Lost magics is an interesting field; I would have liked to have been allowed to pursue it."

"Why can't you?"

"Funding," Val said. "I needed scholarships, and they never would have given them to me if I had listed that as my professional goal. Interplanetary evolution is interesting, too, though, so it doesn't really matter."

"Everything matters," Wilbur replied, and sat back in his seat, crossing his arms across his chest and looking pensive. "Strange that you say Bikendi does not need an assistant. The last time I saw him, he was exhausted to the point of almost passing out. But, from what I have heard of the man, that is not unusual for him. I would have thought he would jump at the chance to work with someone he can actually touch."

Val flinched. Wilbur sat up again, pushing aside the antique book next to his teacup. Val tried to read it, but the words made no sense to him. He could not even tell the planet of origin. "Why are you reading that?" he asked. "Wouldn't a normal book be easier?"

Wilbur chuckled and rapped the book gently with his knuckles. "Oh, probably. Toby laughs at me all the time; he thinks antiques are silly. But they're nostalgic for me and they keep me from forgetting my origins entirely."

Origins? Was there something strange about his origins? Before he could ask, the sudden sharp ringing of an alarm made him jump and spill his tea. "I'm sorry!" he said, trying to sit down, stand up, clean up, and hold still all at the same time.

Reaching out, Wilbur stilled him by gently grasping his hands. "Calm down, Val." His in-lens flashed, and a moment later, the alarms stopped. He looked at Val. "I believe your teammates are trying to find you."

"Oh, great," Val groaned, and slumped back down into his seat. "Now they're really going to lock me up."

Wilbur laughed. "Perhaps they've learned a lesson, hmm? Come on, I will take you back where you belong before they come running in here like anxious parents." He stood up, and Val rose with him, preceding him out into the hallway, and then falling a step behind as Wilbur led the way through the halls.

It wasn't until they passed a large fountain portraying a group of women in strange looking gowns that he'd never seen before that he realized they were not headed back to his restricted wing. "Where are going?"

Looking over his should with a faint smile, Wilbur said, "I am taking you to where you are supposed to be."

Val frowned, but didn't bother to say anything further, just following along silently as Wilbur turned down so many hallways that he no longer knew how he would ever find his way back. Finally, they stopped in front of a door that bore no markings, only a security pad. Wilbur's in-lens flashed, and the door chimed as it unlocked. Wilbur lightly touched the open/close pad, and the door slid smoothly open.

Following him inside, Val stumbled to a halt when he realized they were in a laboratory. It rivaled any he had ever seen. He didn't know where to look first, and had to curl his hands into fists to avoid bolting to the nearest piece of equipment and examining it down to the last detail. It was the sort of lab all students daydreamed about someday having—the kind of lab only a very small number of scientists ever actually got.

Movement caught his eye and he turned reflexively toward it, and then froze. Bikendi scowled at them. "What in the blood are you doing here?"

"I believe you lost something," Wilbur said, smiling in an edged away that made Val want to take a step back. "Fortunately for you, he stumbled across me and not someone else. I am returning him. You are welcome." Without another word, Wilbur turned smoothly on one heel and left, the door chiming as it locked again.

Val stared a moment longer, then looked away. "I'm sorry; I didn't know he was bringing me here. He said he was taking me back to the others."

"You should not have been out at all!" Bikendi snapped. "You have very strict orders to stay put. If someone learns you were out, that means that you are comprised and your testimony—"

"Who cares?" Val cut in bitterly, not even sure what finally made him snap. His hands shook and he felt sick to his stomach, but once the words started, they wouldn't stop. "One mutant is as good as another. All I do is sit around doing nothing except reciting my testimony, because Lord Tresnor thinks I'm too stupid to remember what I'm supposed to say unless I repeat it one hundred times a day. I'm caught up on all my schoolwork, I'm barely allowed to read, no one needs my help back in the office and you don't need me here." He turned to go and scowled when the door wouldn't open for him.

He kept trying the open pad anyway, irritably yanking off his stupid gloves to try it with direct skin contact—and jumped back with a shout as Bikendi's hand suddenly closed over his. Bikendi yanked him forward as Val stumbled back, upsetting his balance and causing him to crash into Bikendi, sending them both falling to the ground.

Val *really* wished he were dead. "I'm—"

"If you say you are sorry one more time, I really might throttle you," Bikendi said. He grabbed Val, forcing him to hold still. "Calm down, Val. You would crash about less often if you would learn to take a deep breath."

Val would settle for being able to breathe at all, but it was pretty much impossible when he was *lying on top of Bikendi and not dead yet*. "Yes, Dr. Bikendi," he finally managed, and tried to squirm free again, but he couldn't seem to sort out his limbs, and then Bikendi squeezed his arms and made him hold still again.

He yelped in surprise when Bikendi abruptly moved, rolling them over so that Val lay on the floor. Bikendi's eyes blazed purple as they stared at him, and Val wished he knew why Bikendi was staring so hard. Then Bikendi stood up, bent to pull Val to his feet, and led him over to one of the worktables. "Sit," he ordered, and then moved around the lab, turning things off and closing others, compiling notes and locking smaller bits of equipment away.

Setting the datapads with the complied notes on the table close to Val, he then went to a locked cabinet and, opening it, pulled out a small crystal bottle and two glasses. Sitting down next to Val, he poured a dark red-gold substance into the glasses. "What is it?" Val asked.

Bikendi smiled faintly and Val looked hastily away before he started gawking like an idiot. "It's generally called blood brandy, but don't let that put you off. The Telven only call it that to mess with visitors. Its traditional name translates more into 'Heart of Fire', which is even more dramatic and ridiculous, but that is Telve for you."

Val nodded and accepted the glass, taking a tentative sip. He'd drink *bleach* if that's what it took to get Bikendi to talk to him. He coughed as it went down, barely setting the glass down before he dropped it. To his astonishment, Bikendi laughed. He also, Val noted irritably, drank the stupid brandy like it was water. "Try another sip," Bikendi said. "It gets easier as you go."

Making a face, Val obeyed, grateful that the second sip didn't turn him into a sputtering idiot again. It tasted good, he realized after a third sip. Bikendi chuckled again and Val flushed, setting the glass down. "You need to learn to relax, Val," Bikendi said.

Val shrugged, but only replied, "Yes, Dr. Bikendi."

Bikendi sighed and finished his own brandy, then set the glass aside and pulled the datapads closer. "You will need to look these over if you are to help me. Read what you can tonight and we'll discuss it in the morning, and you can continue to study all of tomorrow."

It wouldn't take him *that* long to read everything, but Val did not bother to say that. "I'm allowed to help you?" he asked, astonished.

"As you so clearly pointed out, you are going to waste around here," Bikendi replied. "I also feel that being stuck in a room with those idiots for hours on end every day is considered torture, according to IG law."

Val laughed. Bikendi smiled at him; it was a small smile, but there all the same, and Val realized he was having trouble breathing again. All he could do was smile back. Bikendi finally broke their gazes, reaching up to brush back a strand of hair that had fallen into his eyes—

He wasn't wearing his gloves, Val realized abruptly. The entire time, from stopping him at the door to falling to that moment, Bikendi hadn't been wearing his gloves. "You've been touching me," he blurted. "Your gloves—you got mad before—"

Bikendi stiffened and seemed to realize himself that he wasn't wearing his gloves. Slowly lowering his hand, he flexed it, stared at it. "No," he said quietly. "It would seem I am not." He drew a breath and let it out slowly. "I shouldn't be touching you without my gloves."

Val frowned. "Why not? I thought I was safe to touch."

To his astonishment, Bikendi burst out laughing—but he didn't sound very amused. "Val, you are many things, but safe is not one of them." He stole Val's glass and tossed back the contents in one smooth, easy motion. "Read the notes. Be at breakfast by oh five hundred. There should be a guard outside by now, have him escort you back to your room. When you get back, inform Tresnor that the day after tomorrow, you will be working full time for me."

"Yes, Dr—"

"Stop calling me doctor," Bikendi snapped, and then sighed. He rested his hand lightly on Val's shoulder. "It's just Bikendi. Have a good night, Val." He strode off, vanishing through a door at the back of the lab.

Val heaved a sigh of his own and collected the datapads, all his excitement over reading them dampened by the knowledge that Bikendi didn't think he was safe. If he wasn't safe, what was he?

# Chapter Eight

**PLANET 2154014 (TREDAD), UNKNOWN LOCATION**

Pyotr had cleaned every last bit of the house twice. There was literally nothing left to clean. He gave it another ten hours before he took something apart and put it back together again. He raked a hand through his hair, grimacing. It had already needed a cut, and it was something he was going to tend to when he reached Zero again—it was beginning to drive him crazy.

He sighed and went to fix a cup of tea, longing for a good, dark, Fornarian beer or even a glass of Zero brandy or sweet Vrill wine. Anything but another day of Tredad fare and Jade's fancy tea. Leaving the water to heat, he wandered restlessly around the room, hating every last bit of it.

Whatever Jade was up to, Pyotr hoped it came to a conclusion soon, because he was going to go truly insane in only a few more days. Despite his best efforts, Jade was giving nothing away, and Pyotr knew it was only because he *thrived* on Pyotr's frustration. Pyotr would hate him for it, save that he would be no better if their situations were reversed.

The fact they were twenty years apart should have impeded that, at least a little, but it hadn't. Pyotr had been fascinated by Jade the first day they'd met: he'd only just been made Lower Chancellor, a day or two after his thirty-fifth birthday. He'd heard much of the Alexander family, but being a life-long soldier, he seldom was on Zero long enough to meet anyone not in the Authorities.

Lord and Lady Alexander had been fascinating—ambitious in a way he recognized all too well, though he also recognized they were not willing to be quite as ruthless as he. Their children, however ... Cyan Alexander had the look and feel of a soldier, a fighter, and the fading bruises on his arms to prove it. Pyotr had looked at him and known the boy would go very far in life if given the correct opportunities.

But it was Jade who had taken his breath away, with that cool calculation in his eyes that belonged in men with twice his years, not a boy of fifteen. He was beautiful, more so than his brother because he knew it, enhanced it—used it, where Cyan seemed interested in diminishing his looks as much as possible. They looked so dissimilar that he would not have known they were fraternal twins if his uncle had not told him ahead of time.

Jade had smiled at him, young and beautiful and too smart, and Pyotr had been hooked. He hadn't wanted to fuck Jade, then, but he'd been aware enough to know someday that would change. He had wished them all the best and gone on his way.

But after that day, confined to the life of a Lower Chancellor, he had seen them more and more over the course of the year. Most of it was because of the fight over the Temperast and the notoriety the Alexander family gained by wanting them exterminated. Jade had been right there in the heart of it all, learning far more than anyone realized, manipulating people who should have been smarter than that and thriving on it.

No one else had seen it, but Pyotr had. Jade loved being a predator in the political ocean of Zero, and if he continued to go unchecked ...

But barely a year had passed when the Alexanders were killed. *That* was the night when the strange watch-and wait-tension between them changed. He remembered Jade screaming, the look in his eyes, holding him as he shook, continuing to hold him after Jade was finally sedated. Whatever else Jade might be, he was still a child—and one who had just been thrown into adulthood in the worst possible way.

It was the only time he'd seen Jade lose his Zero polish, the only time Jade had let someone else in. By morning, he had locked himself away again, his exterior harder and sharper and colder. Whatever Jade's plans had been the day before, Pyotr could see they were long gone, replaced by revenge.

Pyotr turned away from those thoughts, not willing to follow them to where they wanted to go.

Instead, he went to turn off the kettle and pour his tea, deliberating between disassembling the kitchen or the wash area. It had been a long time since his mechanical days—stars, he'd been so young and stupid then, was it really thirty-five years ago?—but he still knew his way around a toolbox.

Of course, he realized, that assumed there was a toolbox, and he had not thus far noticed one, which meant Jade probably had not left tools anywhere about for him to find. Pyotr balled his hands into fists and pressed them to his temples, elbows braced on the table.

He needed something to do. Pyotr slowly relaxed his hands, picking up his steaming teacup to take a sip. Beer, he thought mournfully; the very least Jade could give him was a stars damned beer. But it simply was not in Jade's nature to do something so ... simple and kind.

Pyotr sighed and wondered how the trial was proceeding. He hoped Bikendi was over his snit and taking care of Val. He hoped his team was proving as successful as he had anticipated they would. He fervently hoped that should he never make it home, his uncle told them about Haven after the trial was won.

He was bitterly disappointed that he would not get to announce it himself; he had worked for terms on Haven—on the entire Draconis problem. He would have liked to see his plans come to fruition, before he moved on to the next step in his overarching goal.

No doubt his uncle would say he was getting exactly what he deserved, for going about everything in the manner he did—but if Pyotr had done things the 'proper' way, then nothing would have been done. The IG suffered from outdated laws and stigmas; he'd seen it all his life. Everything needed to change, and the Draconis were the first step to doing that.

Pyotr looked up from his tea as he heard the door unlock, and frowned when it started to open, then crashed shut again. When it happened a second time, he stood up and went to it, grabbing the handle and pulling the door up, letting it fall to the floor with a muffled thump.

Jade lay at the bottom of the stairs, a trail of blood in his wake, more pooling beneath him. Pyotr swore and leapt down the stairs, gingerly examining Jade as best he could, before rolling his onto his back. He tore open Jade's jacket, then stripped off his own shirt and folded it into a compress, holding it over the wound low on Jade's chest.

The sound of movement—of people running—made him look up just in time to avoid stunner fire. Rolling away, Pyotr gained his feet, dodged another shot, and then threw himself at the man holding the stunner.

Snapping his neck was easy. Pyotr took the stunner as the body fell to the ground and shot two of the other three men. They couldn't be more than low level goons, with such poor reaction times. The last man ran and Pyotr fired, hitting him square in the back. He glanced at his commandeered stunner and saw that it had been illegally tampered with to make it fire fatal rounds. So they were all dead. A pity; he could have used some answers. Well, another opportunity would probably present itself in due course.

He dropped the stunner and returned to Jade, carefully lifting him and climbing the stairs back into the house. Setting Jade on the floor, he turned to close and lock the door, and then put the kettle on. Returning to Jade, he rifled through Jade's clothes until he found a dagger, and began to cut the clothes away.

Pyotr grimaced when he saw the wound—Jade was lucky to be alive. The kettle chimed and he returned to the kitchen, pulling out a medkit and pouring hot water into a large bowl. Grabbing some clean rags, he returned to Jade again, and began meticulously to clean and bandage his wound.

By the time he'd finished, Jade was stirring. Though he must have been in extreme pain, his eyes were clear and sharp as they met Pyotr's. "Are they all dead?" he asked.

"Yes," Pyotr said. "I wasn't able to capture one."

Jade made a face, and then tried to sit up. Pyotr pushed him back down and kept a hand firmly on his chest. "Don't move; you know better. Stay there." He carried all of the med supplies to the table, then returned to Jade and finished getting rid of his clothes. When Jade was naked, he gingerly lifted him up and carried him to bed.

Throughout, Jade just stared coldly. Pyotr settled him in the bed and pulled the blankets up, then reached out to touch a smudge of drying blood on Jade's cheek. "Since when do amateurs lay so much as a finger on you?"

"There were six of them to start," Jade said with a cold smile. "Every now and then, I am taken by surprise by how stupid people can be. No matter how much stupidity I credit them, I always underestimate."

Pyotr shook his head. "Rest. I'll go take care of the bodies."

"I would have thought, Petya, that you would already be long gone."

"You know that isn't true," Pyotr said quietly, and called it a victory when Jade looked away first, his hand almost clenching the blankets, before he caught himself and made it relax. Standing up, Pyotr crossed to the door and opened it again, going quickly down the stairs to the dark passageway below.

There was only just enough light to see by, affixed to the stone-faced walls at regular intervals. It was cold, though not as cold as it would be if he were to travel to the end of the tunnel where it joined with several others to form a larger tunnel. That, in turn, would lead to a hub, and so on and so forth, until at last they reached the city.

Pyotr sighed as he looked over the bodies, retrieving the stunner he had dropped earlier and shooting them all again to be certain they were dead. He tucked the stunner into the waistband of his pants, then went to the body furthest away and dragged it closer to the others, lining all four up at the base of the stairs.

Next, he wandered a short distance down the passageway, until he found a narrow door set deep into the wall. A cursory examination confirmed that very little had changed about Tredad since he had first left it: no one bothered to repair the service door locks. The door opened easily when he gave it a shove, sliding smoothly into its recess in the wall.

A blast of cold air hit him in the face, with enough force that he suspected the access door at the end of the tunnel was gaping open. Turning around, Pyotr returned to the bodies and grabbed the first one, hefting it up over his shoulder. He carried it down the service tunnel, until he reached the door to the outside that gaped exactly as he had anticipated.

So it was possible that someone else was already outside, but he suspected it just meant people were that apathetic. Shoving the door all the way open, he climbed the special heated stairs up into the snow, wincing as he left the shelter of the tunnels entirely and was assaulted by the crippling cold. Gritting his teeth, he walked as far as he dared, then threw the body into the snow.

He doubted it would ever be found. He knew it wasn't the only body disposed of in such fashion. Retracing his steps, Pyotr repeated the process with the remaining three bodies. By the time he was finished, it took all his remaining strength to stumble his way back into Jade's house and close the door.

Jade, he saw with surprise, was passed out on the bed—but not, Pyotr realized in the next moment, as he'd left him. Jade was dressed again and lying more awkwardly, as though he had passed out before he could properly settle himself. The idiot; he shouldn't have been moving around after so much blood loss.

Pyotr sighed and made himself keep moving, shivering as he stripped off his clothes and activated the wash area. He turned the water up as hot as he could stand it and shuddered beneath the spray, until the heat began to penetrate. Stars, he *hated* Tredad.

He was days away from turning fifty, he thought tiredly. It was the life he had signed up for, but sometimes, he wouldn't have minded living the way someone his age normally did. But most men his age—or any age—didn't long for unattainable, unstable beauties bent on destruction.

Discarding the useless thoughts, Pyotr finished washing and waited impatiently while the air dried him. As the glass walls around the unit lowered, he stepped over them and strode to the dressing cabinets, pulling out clean clothes. He retrieved his stunner from where it lay amongst his discarded clothes, sliding it into place in the holster he had also found in the wardrobe.

Pyotr stared at the closed door, painfully aware it wasn't locked. He should go. The unlocked door was his chance. It would take mere minutes to reach a contact point, and mere hours for someone to retrieve him. He would be back on Zero before the day was out.

His gaze slid away from the door and landed on Jade, still lying on his side on the bed. Pyotr walked over to him and gingerly moved Jade until he was lying on his back, brushing back a loose strand of dark gold hair.

*"You don't want to go down this path," Pyotr said softly.*

*Jade regarded him coldly, the gray of his eyes delicate against the elaborate black and silver robe he wore. He had not always dressed so flamboyantly, and Pyotr knew the look of a man who hunted by drawing the unsuspecting into his trap. "What path?"*

*"Don't insult us both," Pyotr replied. "I know the look of a man willing to sacrifice everything for revenge."*

*"I suppose you would, if even half of what they say about you is true."*

*Pyotr shrugged, dismissing the rumors that people loved to whisper. "It's not a reason to live."*

*Jade tossed his head, braid snapping in the air. "What would you do, in my place?"*

*"I don't live for revenge."*

*"That's not what I asked."*

*Pyotr shook his head. "Revenge is a waste of energy. It won't fix anything."*

*"Good. I don't want to fix anything."*

*"Find a different path, walk away from this one," Pyotr said. "You deserve more than the kind of life I've led."*

*Jade moved in closer, stopping just short of being within reach. Pyotr tried not to notice that he was beautiful, tempting, and reminded himself that Jade was too young for him to look at, and so lost in rage and grief, that it was out of the question, anyway.*

*But he smelled like sandalwood and musk, and stood as though inviting every stolen glance. He had been dangerously beautiful three months ago when his parents had been alive—in so brief a span of time, he had become far more than dangerous. Pyotr had been ordered to kill people like Jade, back when he was still an assassin in the Authorities.*

*"What would make you walk away from such a path?" Jade challenged.*

*"Nothing," Pyotr admitted, even as his mind whispered* you. *"It's too late for me."*

*Jade finally looked away, granting Pyotr relief from the intensity of his eyes. "Then I suppose our paths are set, Lower Chancellor." He walked away, braid swaying against his back, and Pyotr watched him until he vanished from sight.*

*Drawing a breath, Pyotr let it out softly and continued on his way, headed in the opposite direction.*

# Chapter Nine

**UNKNOWN PLANET, UNKNOWN LOCATION**

Raoul punched Yevi, catching him on the jaw, and then nailed him in the gut before he could recover. He backed up a step, tensed to strike again. "You're nothing but a lying slut."

"You're a gullible fool, especially for someone who's equal parts Bangkok whore and rock spider," Yevi retorted, wiping blood from his mouth. "Blame yourself for your own stupidity; it's not my fault."

"Fucking weed!" Raoul snarled, and lunged at him—then reeled back when Yevi caught him square in the face, damn near breaking his nose. "You know what? Dragons take you for the fool you are and leave you bare, weed. I hope you choke on the dicks you suck. I'm out. I don't need you or the rest of this stars-forsaken camp." He turned sharply and stormed off, vanishing into the forest at the south end of camp.

When he was just out of sight, he leaned against a large tree and wiped away the blood dripping from his nose as best he could. After a good fifteen minutes had passed, and it was clear that no one had followed after him, Raoul resumed walking. He hoped Yevi would be all right left to his own devices—but that was stupid. He rolled his eyes at himself. Yevi had been stranded alone for the past year; he was better equipped than Raoul to deal with fuck everything.

Raoul slipped through the trees as quickly as he was able, fervently hoping he was remembering the way correctly. It had been a long time since he'd had to trek across anything more arduous than a government building.

He'd needed three bouts in the shed to do it, between days of working hard enough to make himself useful and not worth killing, but he *had* finally found a very likely hiding place for the ship they sought. All he had to do was get down to it.

The sky was just beginning to darken by the time he reached the cliffs, and the ocean was so dark it looked black, crashing against the base of the blue-gray cliffs. A familiar thrill shot through Raoul; there was *nothing* like climbing. His mother had laughed at him growing up and told him that he was very much his father's son. Raoul had spent countless hours scaling buildings as a boy, and more than a few of his Black Ops assignments had made full use of his unique skill set.

But the tallest building was nothing like scaling a cliff face, with only his skills and his magics to keep him from a fatal fall. Raoul stripped out of his jacket and tucked it out of sight in a copse of bushes. Moving back to the edge of the cliff, he knelt and braced himself, then swung over the edge. Once his footing was secure, he moved his hands, magics activating to stick him to the rock face whenever he touched it.

When he was sure of his balance, he began the slow climb down, moving parallel to the marks that had first drawn his attention—scorch marks where a ship had gotten too close, and clearly on several occasions. A little over halfway down, Raoul found exactly what he had hoped to find: a hole in the cliff face that had probably started out natural, but been expanded and shaped by man, just large enough to fit a scout ship. Moving sideways along the cliff, he swung neatly into the opening and looked around for any obvious security. Seeing none, he ventured on, making his way slowly down the long tunnel. It abruptly widened into a large cavern, a ship dock, and what looked like unloading and work stations, a small office area that seemed to hold nothing useful at a cursory glance.

There was no doubt at all that he had found where they hid the ship. A pity that the ship itself wasn't around, but if he waited long enough, he'd get his wish. Corbin had already been gone three days, two days longer than normal. It was the only reason he had been able to walk out of camp without issue, after he and Yevi had argued.

Raoul looked around the cavern again, going to the office area and the work station, unsurprised when he came up empty. It was obviously a temporary thing, to be used while the ship was there and completely abandoned when it was not. His curiosity about who was really behind the operation expanded; he was going to have *fun* helping Yevi catch the bastard.

His eyes lit on a ledge three quarters of the way up the rounded cavern, where they had obviously not bothered to carve any farther. Nodding to himself, he climbed up the wall to the ledge and settled in, pleased that he had found such a handy place to see without being seen.

Once he was settled, however, he had nothing left to do but think until the ship showed. Soon, he would have communications access. He and Yevi would be safe and on their way back to Zero, the bust of the decade on their records. They would be back to their normal lives, something he was certain that Yevi, especially, desperately wanted.

He didn't like that the elation he should have felt, thinking of going home, wasn't quite as strong as it should have been—that it was tempered by a strange disappointment. He hadn't known Yevi long enough to be disappointed by anything. He'd known people a hell of a lot longer and felt a lot less when their paths diverted. His Fornarian heritage meant he wasn't inclined to get close very often, even if the other half was human. It was one of the main reasons he was good at his job. He also knew that whatever he thought he felt right then was more than likely going to change once normalcy returned. It was something he had seen any number of times: people who worked well under duress, who were a perfect team in the field, falling completely apart once they were safely home again.

There was nothing between them that needed to work, anyway. The sex was great, but sex usually was, and there was no telling who Yevi had waiting for him. If all of that managed not to matter, somehow, Yevi was clearly Vrill nobility and that would *always* matter. Raoul frowned at himself and tried to put his mind on work, where it should be.

In the end, though, it was sleep that took him. He'd gotten very little of it in the past several days while he worked to find the ship, and there was nothing for him to do until it finally showed up again. Thanks to his fight with Yevi, the others in the camp hopefully believed they'd seen the last of him (and all the better).

He woke to the sound of roaring, training keeping him still, even as his eyes opened, body tense and completely alert. A ship—Corbin had finally returned. He wondered what time it was, but had no way of knowing. Light flared, but thankfully, did not reach enough to cast any problematic shadows. He watched as best he could, unable to see much from his vantage point, but more than enough to recognize Corbin and two other men as they disembarked.

One of the men, he noted, wore an Auth uniform. That gray color, the shape of it, was unmistakable. So there were Auths involved in the ring—and Auths who were able to steal a battle-class scout ship. That spoke of higher rank than Raoul liked. It turned his stomach to think some high-ranking officer was dealing Soul. He waited and watched, tried to catch what they were saying, but the voices were just too low.

An hour or so later, by his best estimate, Corbin finally departed with the man in civilian clothes, a grunt Raoul recognized from the Soul fields. The Auth vanished back into the ship; that particular class of scout ship could only hold a maximum of five, a standard scouting party.

So at most, he had three with which to deal. Raoul waited until roughly half an hour had passed, when it seemed relatively certain that no one else would be coming or going. He wondered absently how Corbin and the other guy had gotten topside, but that was a question to answer later.

He slipped off the ledge and climbed down the wall, tensed for motion alarms, but not really surprised when nothing tripped—it was rare anyone bothered to equip simple scout ships with anything more than basic security. Anyone needing more tended to use better ships.

Raoul crept up to the ship and strode up the gangway that had been left down, punching a long string of numbers into the control pad. When it chimed and opened, he let out the breath he'd been holding. He might have been presumed dead, but no one had yet deactivated his master codes. They had worked on the shed, but he knew he was working on borrowed time. Eventually, some overworked clerk in the Grand Chancellor's office would notice a dead man's master codes were still live, and deactivate them. Hopefully, Raoul would be home before that happened—getting all knew codes would be a pain in the ass.

Inside, he encountered only an empty hallway. The bridge must have been notified someone had boarded—

The sound of footsteps made him draw back, ducking out of immediate view. He waited until the man reached the door and saw him, before striking, hitting the throat first so he couldn't cry out, and then knocking him out and catching the body before it could hit the floor.

Raoul glanced around and saw a storage room, rapidly typing in his access code. He hefted the body inside and stole the two stunners the man carried. Last, he gagged and bound the man, then locked the door and changed the passcode.

Tucking one stunner away, he checked the other and turned up the setting, noting with interest that it had been illegally modified to kill. Hopefully, it wouldn't come to that. He made his way to the bridge, and was able to see from the hallway that there was definitely one more man inside.

Whether or not the total was two ... well, only one way to find out. Raoul took aim and fired. The man at the captain's station dropped, hitting his head on the master control panel, before falling all the way to the floor.

No shout came from the possible second man, so either he was elsewhere on the ship, or there had only been two. Given the small confines of the scout ship, Raoul was reasonably confident there were only two men aboard.

He dragged the second to join the first, deciding to figure out what to do with them long term later. His first priority was figuring out the ship. All the designating numbers had been removed from the hull, which meant he needed to access the data.

Thankfully, his codes had that covered. Returning to the bridge, Raoul said, "Ship, switch to vocal commands."

*"Acknowledged."*

"Security Code 3-2147151-IGSA1B-7012118004."

*"Password."*

"Bangkok Spider."

*"Acknowledged. Full access granted."*

Raoul sat down in the captain's seat, and asked, "What is your mother ship?"

*"Combat Class starship B-65891154, the* Forsaken.*"*

The realization struck him like a blow to the gut, and Raoul only asked his next question as a formality. "Ship, what is our current location?"

*"Unregistered Planet, temporary PSN 4181774, codename Haven."*

"Dragons' *dicks*," Raoul swore. They were on Haven. No fucking wonder it had all seemed familiar, but not. He stayed out of Pyotr's work as much as possible, because if *he* ever fell into the wrong hands, the less he knew, the better for everyone, but Pyotr had been working on Haven for terms. It was coded at the highest possible level of security. Other than Pyotr, his ship, and the hand-picked scouts he'd assigned to study the planet, only the Grand Chancellor and the Archivist would know anything about it.

Of all the planets in the stars, he'd landed on *Haven.*

But, he wondered, was it really such a coincidence? The coordinates for it must have been in the ship log, for though he'd never been down planet, he knew they'd visited it before. It was one of their more recent stops, in fact. The way they'd blown mid-light jump ... well, it made sense to him, and there was probably an expert on the subject who could explain it properly.

And he was getting completely off track. So he was on a lost or stolen scout ship being used by drug runners ... but no, some of them had still been in Auth uniforms. Raoul frowned at that, and said aloud, "Ship, what is your itinerary?"

*"Fourteen hundred to twenty-two hundred, private mission for General Vane. Twenty-two oh one, return to the* Forsaken."

"Dragons!" he cursed, slamming his fist down on the armrest. Lieutenant Vane was scout leader for the *Shangri La*. He'd stayed behind to lead the forces left with Bikendi and the others. "Wait until I get my hands on you, spineless son of a Kreskan," he muttered, fingers itching to grab a stunner, set it to kill, and find the bastard right then.

So the ship wasn't stolen, and General Vane knew about Haven because his brother had told him, which meant the drug running was likely a family business. He wondered what other Auths they had dragged into the mess. Dragons' dicks!

The entire matter had just moved from 'debacle' to 'monumental nightmare', and he did not relish telling Yevi just how far and deep the rot had spread. He wondered just how much worse it was, because he doubted they'd be lucky enough that it stopped at a general and a handful of other Auths. The sorts of resources involved with commandeering an entire planet to grow Soul ...

Especially when they must know that Pyotr had staked the planet to be populated by the Draconis once the trial cleared them.

Raoul's head was spinning, trying to keep up with it all. Shaking his head to sort out the fine points later, he tried to figure out what to do for the present. Stick with the plan, he decided. Yevi was set to meet him in two days—probably a day and a half at that point. He'd promised he'd be able to get out, though he'd cautioned that there would be no turning back once he made his escape.

So he would wait and Yevi would meet him. Then, as the saying went in Bangkok, it would be the kind of night that nobody wanted to remember the next morning.

# Chapter Ten

**PLANET 0000000 (ZERO), THE PALACE OF ETERNITY**

Val wasn't sure where to put his attention—well, where to put it when he made himself stop paying avid attention to Bikendi. If he was permitted, he would be more than happy to watch and listen to no one but Bikendi all day. They would probably be on Zero for weeks, or even months, still, but all he could think about was when he would say goodbye and probably never see Bikendi again.

He sipped his tea and tried to pay attention, but the conversation had gone over his head a long time ago. He wasn't entirely certain why he was there at all; Tresnor, Wilbur, and Bikendi were in a different galaxy entirely. Val started to ask any number of questions, but dreaded sounding like an idiot, and so just kept quiet and tried not to stare at Bikendi.

It was more difficult than he really liked admitting, but there it was. Still, he'd only ever thought of Bikendi ... scientifically, he supposed. He knew Bikendi through his reports, lectures, studies, books, and articles. He knew him through lab experiments. It was strange to see Bikendi socializing, to walk into a room and see him reading or watching something—acting like a normal person, if on the reclusive and acerbic side. That was almost easier to deal with than someone like Tresnor or Lady Jundel, who lived and breathed socializing.

Val flicked his gaze to Tresnor, who was waving his blue cigar animatedly as he related a tale of something his sons had done recently, talking about some room in Black Dragon Tower. That was, Val thought, the central of the five dragon towers at the heart of Bangkok, but he wasn't really sure.

Shifting his glance to Wilbur, who laughed quietly and spoke quietly, but still somehow seemed a very loud presence, he studied the serial number—or whatever kind of number it was—on his arm. He had written it down and run it through every search he knew, but nothing ever came up and he'd felt guilty about prying, so had stopped. He really wished he knew what it meant, but it seemed the kind of thing he definitely wasn't supposed to ask.

Nibbling at another little cake, liking how spicy they were, he looked again at Bikendi. He remembered thinking before that he could stare at Bikendi forever and never grow bored. After so many days together, he knew it for certain. Bikendi wasn't loud and animated the way Tresnor was, or quiet and calm like Wilbur. He was rigid, sharp, closed off—but he never missed anything that happened and always listened, even when people thought he wasn't, and the more time Val spent with him, the more he realized that much of Bikendi's manner had to do with the fact that for nearly all his life, he had not been able to touch anyone, not the way people touched one another every day. Even Val could walk up to anyone he wanted and touch their hand, their shoulder.

Well, not anymore, but he never really did that sort of thing, anyway, so he had yet to acutely notice the loss. The only person he wanted to touch was Bikendi. His face flushed and he dropped his gaze to his tea. Stupid, he reminded himself. He was Bikendi's lab assistant for the foreseeable future and they were matched—that was more than he could ever have dreamed. It would be stupid to get carried away and think about things that would *definitely* never happen.

Thoughts collided suddenly in his head. He had always assumed that after the trial concluded, they would go their separate ways. But they *were* matched, which meant ... what, exactly? Perhaps Bikendi would prefer he left, since with matches, the further apart they were, the more their magics weakened. It was a quirk no one had been able to explain, yet, something that had not been in the original schematics (like so many other things in regards to the Draconis). So if he returned to Coni, Bikendi would be free to live as though he had no magics whatsoever.

It was, Val realized with a sudden despondence, perfect. He was stupid not to have thought of it sooner. Bikendi had probably realized it almost immediately. At least he hadn't been stupid enough to think Bikendi might take him on permanently. Val picked up his cake to eat another bite, then just set it down again, no longer really hungry.

"My, my, what a long face," Tresnor said, drawing his attention. "Why so suddenly glum, Val? The story was meant to be amusing, not depressing." He winked.

Val flushed. "Oh, no—my thoughts wandered, I'm sorry."

Tresnor chuckled. "Well, trust me; thoughts should not wander into such gloomy places. My wife never tolerated it when I fell into such a mood. She and my assistant, Mythril, were very good at bringing me out of them. Perhaps—"

"Perhaps you should shut your mouth before something comes out of it that should not," Bikendi snapped.

"Never fear, my dear doctor," Tresnor drawled, pulling idly at his cigar and blowing the smoke at Bikendi. "I've neither reason nor desire to poach. I was going to say that perhaps you should cheer him up."

Bikendi shot him a withering look and poured more tea for himself, before directing his sharp look at Val. "So what is wrong with you? I know Tresnor does tend to go on and on, but he's not—well, yes, he is that awful, but you've endured much worse, I would imagine. I cannot remember a single school lecture that was remotely stimulating."

Wilbur chuckled. "No, school lectures never are, and I think for two such brilliant pupils, they must be all the more dreadful. What was it you were studying? Something about magic between planets."

"The interplanetary evolution of magics, or how the fact we think and act with planetary identities, rather than, say, national identities, is affecting our magics and altering how we use them and how they will evolve."

Bikendi frowned, setting down the teacup he had just picked up. "An interesting field, but it can't be your primary. You are far too familiar with lost magics for your field of specialty to be anything as mundane as interplanetary evolution."

Val flushed at the unexpected phrase, but only shrugged, and explained, "Funding."

"Bah," Bikendi said. "The Coni are a pile of idiots and deserve what is coming to them." He picked his tea up again and took a sip.

Wilbur cast Bikendi an amused glance, then turned back to Val, and said, "So how do your experiments proceed? I have seen the reports, of course, but as I mentioned once before, it largely goes over my head. The closest I ever got to such scientific experiments was *being* the experiment." He gestured at the serial number on his arm. "It did not go well. I know you are studying the Draconis genetics, especially how they are in present day versus the original genetic map laid out by the Coni, and something to do with the matching ... ?"

Val looked at Bikendi, who only rolled his eyes and did not reply. It made Val smile, briefly, because when Bikendi did that, it was his own way of avoiding the fact he would not mind speaking at length about it, but refused to do anything as silly as *babble*. On anyone else, Val might have described it as cute. "The matching is the important thing—it proves beyond a shadow of a doubt that the Draconis have a place in society, that we serve a purpose. We have actually switched to studying our own magics lately, as it could be a stronger argument than we first realized."

"Oh?" Wilbur asked, casting reproving looks at Bikendi and Daie. "No one told me of this."

"It's still in the early stages," Bikendi growled. "All the studies in the world will not endear people to the fact that I can kill with a touch. That has not changed, though we had hoped it would make it controllable."

Val flinched, feeling bad even though he knew it wasn't his fault. Still, if he was going to match, wouldn't it have made sense that he at least add an ability to control whether or not a touch could kill?

"So what can you do now that you couldn't before?" Wilbur asked.

"Give the energies to someone else," Bikendi replied. "Before, I could only use what I absorbed on myself, or not use it at all. Now, I can pass it along to someone else, either as magics energy or life energy. It's strange that Val had the ability to transmute and share energy all along, but no ability to actually draw it in order to change it and pass it along."

Wilbur nodded. "Magics don't usually complement quite that ... intentionally, I suppose, do they?"

"No," Bikendi said, frowning. "It's true they always complement, since that is part of the matching element, but I do not have any other matches on file that seemed so customized. If that element has been there all along, it opens up a whole new way to look at everything I've done." He rubbed his forehead, looking suddenly tired.

Val had often been lectured by his professors for working too hard, too long, but he thought compared to Bikendi, he must seem like a slouch. All he could do was keep up and work just as hard, and hope it was good enough. He didn't know what he would do if he ever let Bikendi down.

"How are you taking to it, Val?"

"Uh—fine," Val said quietly, balling his gloved hands in his lap, not willing to discuss how shaken he'd been the first time he'd killed a lab lizard just by touching it. He'd stared at the lizard and really appreciated why Bikendi acted the way he did, why he had been so angry. "I'm fine," he repeated, when he realized the silence had stretched on too long.

He looked up and caught Bikendi staring at him, a pensive frown on his face. Val flushed and looked down at his plate, wishing he were anywhere else.

"Well, I think you will get the hang of it," Tresnor said. "You will probably get further than the cranky demi-vampire here, I would bet good money on that." When Val looked up, startled, he winked. "You're as brilliant as your match, but possessed of manners and a pleasant demeanor."

"Oh, shut up," Bikendi said. "I cannot wait until you return to your damnable moon, Tresnor. You are a fine one to speak of *demeanors*, you old letch."

"Hardly old, yet," Tresnor smirked, leaning back in his seat, the picture of indolence (or perhaps indulgence). "Fifty odd years is not so remarkable. You're not even forty, what do you know?"

"I know an old letch when I see one," Bikendi drawled, and Val laughed, unable to help it—and just laughed harder when Bikendi stared at him in surprise. He looked down at his plate again, trying to get control of himself, but even after the laughter faded, he could not stop smiling. Watching Bikendi and Tresnor was like watching a lizard and a kip: they fought just so no one would figure out they were playing.

He only wished Bikendi was that easy around him. Val looked up and flushed when he saw Bikendi still eying him, even as Tresnor looked around the table in a particularly smug fashion and opened his mouth to say something that would not doubt provoke Bikendi—but a discrete cough from the doorway stopped him.

They all turned and looked, and Mythril said in his soft, even voice, "My lord, the call you have been waiting on has come through, if you would like to take it?"

"Of course," Tresnor said, and rose, depositing his cigar in the tray at his elbow. He sketched them an elegant half-bow. "Gentlemen, it's been a pleasure. I will see you at supper tonight." He left the room, Mythril at his side.

Wilbur sighed softly. "I suppose that is my cue to get back to work, and I did promise Toby I would call him around about now. Enjoy the rest of your day, my friends." He rose and left, leaving Val and Bikendi alone in the tearoom. Val stood and moved to the windows, gazing down at the courtyard below, where an elaborate maze had been made from a combination of stone and shrubbery. It looked like something out of the books he had read as a child.

He heard Bikendi move, and turned—and jumped back when he proved to be closer than Val realized. "Uh—should we go back to the lab?" He stared up at Bikendi, confused that he didn't reply, just stared—then abruptly drew back.

"Yes," Bikendi said, shaking his head, black and white hair sliding across his face. Val wanted to reach out and brush it back, ask him what was making him so ... restless. But the only times Bikendi touched him were in the lab when they were experimenting. Beyond that, it had only been the two times by accident, and Bikendi had not been thrilled either of those times, even if the second incident had persuaded him to make Val his assistant. "We have lingered long enough and should resume our own work. Come on."

Val obediently followed, disappointed for a reason he could not name. What had he expected, for Bikendi to suggest they do something else? Bikendi did not spend time with him unless it was in the lab or with a group of people. It all reminded him of his earlier realization, further cementing his idea that Bikendi would vastly prefer that they occupy different quadrants when everything was over and done.

When they reached the lab, he automatically headed for his work station, stripping off his gloves as he went—and yelped when Bikendi grabbed his arm and tugged him back. He dropped his gloves in surprise, heart kicking up a notch the way it always did when Bikendi touched him, because stars take it, no matter how hard he tried to deny it, that was what he wanted: Bikendi touching him. But they were nearly twenty years apart and Bikendi didn't want to be matched, so Val would only ever be able to take what he could get, and that thought did *nothing* for his mood.

"You are looking wretched again," Bikendi said, and if he had been a kip the words would have been a long, deep growl. "What is the matter?"

Val shook his head. "N-nothing, Dr—I mean, Bikendi. There's nothing wrong, I'm fine. Just meandering thoughts. I'm sorry, I'll focus on my work, I really will."

Bikendi let go of his wrist and pinched the bridge of his nose, sighing. "Do leave off the apologies, how many times must I tell you?" Val opened his mouth to apologize, then shut it as he realized what he was about to say.

"It's nothing, really," he said, and when Bikendi only glared at him, relented slightly. "I just wondered what I would be doing after all of this was over. I didn't know I was going to be matched, and I still have school to finish, and ... " He shrugged, not willing to say that he wanted to remain with Bikendi, because he didn't want to hear Bikendi say that would definitely not be happening. "Like I said, it's nothing."

"Finishing your formal education is not 'nothing', for all that it may as well be," Bikendi replied. "Of course it should be a concern, though I don't think it requires such a long face. Who is funding you, that you are pursuing a course of study beneath you? What sort of imbeciles would block you from where you should be spending your time?"

Val flushed with humiliation, but he wasn't Bikendi or Tresnor or—or anyone, really. He didn't have their funds and resources. His parents were just hoping that he would someday. Until then, they largely ignored him. "Uh, it's from the IG scholastic fund."

Bikendi made a face. "That would explain it. Well, I cannot see why we can't get you better funding than that. You should be studying—"

"It's not your job to see to that," Val interrupted, discomfited and annoyed, mostly because it got his hopes up and that was a stupid thing to let happen.

Scowling, Bikendi replied, "Yes, it is. We're matched—"

"That's the whole point of all of this!" Val snapped, wishing he could just go home and back to normal, where he didn't lose his temper over the stupidest things—where he didn't lose his temper at all. He didn't even know he *had* a temper, until everyone had tricked him into matching with Bikendi. "To free the Draconis, to prove they're more than reserves and supplements to the rest of the stars. You don't want to be matched. You don't want to be stuck with me. It's not your job to—"

He froze as Bikendi's fingers covered his mouth, acutely aware of how soft and warm they felt. Val stared at Bikendi, equal parts startled and still angry. To his astonishment, Bikendi laughed softly, a husky note to it that Val really wished he *hadn't* noticed. "You are not nearly as quiet or complacent as you seem; it makes me wonder how you will behave when you're more comfortable with yourself and your surroundings."

Something flashed in Bikendi's eyes, something Val didn't recognize, but suddenly, he felt that hand on his lips more than ever and the room had gotten entirely too warm. He pulled back, feeling stupid. "Sor—" The word turned into a yelp as Bikendi yanked him closer, and Val barely avoided crashing into him.

"I will find a way to punish you every time you say that word, if you do not cease using it," Bikendi said, and if Val didn't know better, he'd vow Bikendi was *teasing* him. He was used to Bikendi's occasional flashes of humor; they appeared more often when it was just the two of them working together in the lab. Teasing was something new. "I don't need you helping me," he muttered to Bikendi's chest. "You don't really want me, anyway."

Bikendi made a rough noise, and then his hands curled around Val's shoulders and urged him back a bit. "I do not like being manipulated and I was not looking for a match, it's true. But I am not entirely an idiot. Being matched changes everything for both of us, that is a foregone conclusion. How exactly it will change everything is not, but it is something we cannot sort out until the trial is concluded. Whatever we do, finishing your schooling is a priority, far more important than me simply returning to my moon to resume ignoring the majority of the stars."

Val stared at him, wondering suddenly if it hadn't occurred to Bikendi, after all, how much better off he would be with Val far away from him. He wanted it to stay that way—but he just couldn't withhold it. Doing so seemed like cheating, or lying. Besides, it was better to ruin everything sooner rather than later, wasn't it? He didn't want to get used to the idea of being with Bikendi, only for Bikendi to suddenly change his mind and walk away. "But if you're on Telve and I'm on Coni, our magics won't work. You can go anywhere but Coni and not have to worry about your gloves or anything."

The hands on his shoulders tightened nearly to the point of pain, and the unguarded look on Bikendi's face was one of shock. It really hadn't occurred to him. Val waited for him to say something dismissive, to declare that was stupid, or reckless, or of course he wouldn't just discard Val like that.

But the seconds passed and Bikendi said nothing; just let him go and shook his head. Val wished he'd kept his mouth shut, ignored all the reasons for speaking up. Whatever Bikendi said about working together, he didn't mean. Val had just handed him exactly what he'd always wanted: to be able to touch people freely. All he had to do was stay far away from Val.

Obviously a trivial price to pay. Val fled the laboratory and walked as quickly as he could back to his assigned wing of the palace, ignoring everyone as he passed through the main room and headed straight for his bedroom.

He sat down on his bed and stared glumly at the hands fisted in his lap. It wasn't fair. All he wanted was Bikendi, and all Bikendi wanted was never to see him again. Why did no one ever want to keep him?

# Chapter Eleven

**PLANET 2154014 (TREDAD), UNKNOWN LOCATION**

Jade, true to form, was a terrible patient. Pyotr was sorely tempted to sit on him, and didn't only because he was neither stupid nor a masochist. "The medication will speed the healing, but not if you insist on behaving as though you are not injured," he said, raking a hand through his hair. "Sit down or I swear I will tie you to the bed."

"You would hardly be the first to offer to do so," Jade drawled in a tone that would have made a veteran Bangkok whore blush.

"It wasn't an offer." Jade just smirked and resumed making tea. Pyotr sighed and strode over to him, but was not quite stupid enough to try and grab him. "Jade, you're going to tear those stitches open."

"Do stop being my caretaker, Petya; the role doesn't suit you. I have dealt with worse before and shall again."

Pyotr fisted his hand to avoid the ever-increasing temptation to grab Jade and carry him back to bed. "You would be dead if I had not been here."

"If you had not been here, I would not have been meeting with them," Jade replied, voice entirely too smooth.

Refusing to take the bait, even though he badly wanted to know what Jade had been up to, Pyotr only said, "If you do not lay or sit down and give yourself proper time to recover, I will not return your nail paints."

Jade slammed down the cup he'd just pulled from a cupboard and spun around sharply, gray eyes narrowing at Pyotr. "What?" he asked in a soft tone that people learned quickly meant they should run.

Pyotr held his ground. "You heard me."

"I am not interested in playing childish games, Petya," Jade said coolly, and resumed fixing his tea. "Keep the nail paints, then; I will not be coerced. Honestly, the idea of you as a caretaker is laughable. You excel at taking lives, as I recall, not saving them." When Pyotr said nothing, Jade continued, "Rumor has it your first kill was when you were still a cadet."

"That story has not faded from popularity, I see," Pyotr said, and sat down at the table. "It was not a 'kill' in that sense, only self-defense." He didn't bother to add that he had done it so well that certain people had made note.

Jade finished fixing his drink, then sat down opposite him, sipping the tea delicately, before saying, "Nevertheless, you were made a regular soldier at only eighteen, when normally the age to join the Authorities is twenty. When you were twenty, you were inducted into Black Ops, or so the rumors say." His smile said he knew very well they weren't rumors.

Pyotr replied in flat tones, "At twenty-two, I was recruited for assassin work, is that what is coming next? I did two and a half terms of that before I was moved to Internal Affairs, where I continued assassin work in addition to more mundane covert ops. They pulled me when I was thirty-two and forced me to rest for a term. My uncle saw to it I was given a political position, and a term later, I was made Lower Chancellor. I am a very talented murderer, it's true, but that doesn't mean I'll just let you die."

Jade laughed coldly and abandoned his tea to slink closer to Pyotr, not quite looming over him as he said, "That is not what they say about the notorious Winter."

He might be days from fifty, but Pyotr could still *move* when he wanted. Even Jade stood no chance, eyes wide and furious as he stared up at Pyotr while pinned to the wall by a hand to his throat. Pyotr squeezed tightly, but not quite hard enough to leave bruises. "Is that what you want, Jade? For me not to care? To walk away from you while you're injured and still at risk of dying from your wounds if you're careless with them? Do you want me to be as worthless as everyone else is? Abandon you like Cyan?"

There was no reply, but Pyotr hardly needed one with the way those gray eyes met his, the color of a stormy sky and as hard as gremlin steel. "You excel at getting underneath the skin of every person you cross, one way or another, Jade. Why does it bother you so much that you did the same to me?"

"Let me go," Jade finally hissed, right before taking a swing. Pyotr let him go, but only to grab his hands instead, pinning them to the wall, using his body to keep Jade in place. So close, he smelled of medicine and tea, traces of the fragrant soap he favored. Pyotr hated using the stuff; such frivolous scents seemed too young on him. He liked smelling it on Jade, however, the way it tangled with the warm, male scent of Jade himself.

Pyotr chuckled softly, meeting the eyes so dangerously close to his own. "You're deadly, Jade, but don't think for a moment that you can best me in all ways. I've been a soldier all my life, and most of that as a professional assassin. And my first kill wasn't at fifteen."

Jade smirked at him, a purr in his voice as he replied, "I don't think I've ever seen you display the skills everyone whispers about. So icy and calm, is that how you came to be Winter?"

"One of them," Pyotr replied. "Isn't this what you want? To see me snap, to prove to you that you *should* have left me in the snow? It's not going to happen, Jade. We took separate paths, but—"

"Don't," Jade snapped, something flashing in his eyes that Pyotr would have missed had they not been so close he could feel Jade's heart speed up.

Pyotr ignored him. "But that doesn't mean I ever lost sight of you."

Jade made a noise like a choked off snarl, breaking their locked gazes to stare angrily at a point beyond Pyotr's shoulder.

"And I don't think you ever lost sight of me, either," Pyotr finished softly.

"It doesn't matter," Jade said coolly, but Pyotr heard the trace of bitterness. After so many terms, was Jade having second thoughts? "My plans are set in motion; there's no going back."

"You can always turn off to another path."

Jade finally looked at him again, smirk returning. "Why ever would I do that, when this path is dead on course to take me to Haven?"

Pyotr's eyes narrowed. "How do you know about Haven?"

"You would do better to ask how General Vane knows about it, and with whom he decided to share the secret," Jade replied, relaxing in Pyotr's hold on him, confident he had regained the upper hand.

Vane—Pyotr knew that name. A general that was more bluster than backbone, though he muddled through his job well enough and was useful for unwittingly transporting IA and Black Ops agents whenever Pyotr needed them to slip through military channels. His younger brother was scout leader on Pyotr's ship. Until that moment, Pyotr had always thought him a good man.

Jade smiled in that cold, sharp way of his. "I see you've put some of the pieces together. Let me guess, your lieutenant wasn't on the ship when it blew?"

"He stayed behind on Telve; he should be on Zero by now," Pyotr replied. "Who else is in on this?"

"Carthage."

Pyotr narrowed his eyes to hear the name of the lead lawyer for the team fighting to have the Draconis annihilated. The pieces were laid out neatly before him, but he could not quite bring them together and Jade knew it. "I do not get the correlation," he said. "What in the stars do an Auth general and an IG lawyer have to do with Haven?"

"They're spreading religion across the stars," Jade said.

"Stars damn them all!" Pyotr snarled, letting go of Jade in his fury. Soul dealers. He had been played and used, and missed they were stars-damned *Soul dealers.* Soul was the bane of the IG; the harder they fought it, the more of it was illegally grown and sold. He knew Auths must be involved, but he had never noticed Vane, and the damned man was right under his nose the entire fucking time!

He slammed his fist on the table, and then balled both hands at his side. The moment he got back to Zero, he would have both Vanes arrested and Carthage alongside them. He couldn't believe it. "What does all this have to do with Haven?" But even as he asked the question, he knew the answer. "That's where they're growing it. They have an entire damned planet to themselves, and I handed it to them by way of Lieutenant Vane." Pyotr half-turned to look at Jade, still leaning against the wall, saffron-painted nails gleaming. "How do you know all this?"

"The good general has long been slated for comeuppance," Jade said, and in any other person, that tone would have been described as cheerful. "Who do you think really pulled the trigger of the weapon that killed my parents? That pathetic soldier the IG found already dead in his cheap hotel room?"

Pyotr grunted in acknowledgement, not surprised by that revelation in the slightest. "What do you have against Carthage?"

"Nothing. He's simple crossfire," Jade said dismissively. "He is remarkably easy to get information out of, but then, most men are fairly pliant after you've made them think you've never sucked a finer cock."

Pyotr chuffed briefly in amusement. "Most men, Jade. Not all."

"No," Jade agreed, gray eyes steady upon him. "Not all."

Permission had never been so prettily granted, but Pyotr was too, well, jaded, to believe it was that easy. "You're still injured," he replied. And no matter how much he wanted to be a fool and indulge in the only thing he'd ever wanted, he just wasn't that stupid. Jade never did anything just to do it, and Pyotr wasn't doing anything until he had all the pieces and they formed a picture.

Jade didn't reply, simply pushing off the wall, and Pyotr saw that he had squeezed Jade's throat harder than he realized; already faint bruises were forming. He tensed as Jade crowded into his space, dragging his nails lightly along Pyotr's cheek, along his throat, then down his back. Pyotr couldn't feel the scrape of them through the thick fabric of his shirt, but he felt the pressure almost as acutely. He didn't move; just stared into Jade's eyes and waited for the moment when the teasing caress turned into painful scratches. Jade's hands slipped beneath his shirt and Pyotr drew breath to tell him to stop it—but was cut off by Jade's mouth, moving over his as though they had kissed a thousand times.

He tasted of bitter tea and the medicine Pyotr had thought he hadn't actually been taking, but beneath all that was something shockingly sweet. In all his imaginings, he hadn't thought Jade would taste sweet. Pyotr let Jade have his way for a moment, enjoying the soft, teasing, too gentle to be believed kiss—then he grabbed both of Jade's wrists, jerked them behind Jade's back, and shoved him into the wall again. He pinned his arms so he couldn't pull them from behind his back, and kissed Jade hard enough to bruise his lips.

Pyotr grunted when Jade bit down on his lip, drawing blood, but didn't break the brutal kiss, only pressed it deeper. Blood mingled with the flavors of medicine and tea in Jade's mouth, but still did not hide that underlying sweetness.

If Jade was troubled by Pyotr's behavior, he gave no signs of it—and that was the first clue Pyotr had that he really had been played for the fool. He drew back, and the wave of dizziness that struck him was the second. "What did you do to me?" he said, letting go of Jade and stepping back—only to stumble and fall to his knees, avoiding falling to the floor entirely only by bracing himself on one hand.

Jade knelt beside him and gave a hard push, sending Pyotr toppling over to lie on his back. He stared up at the kitchen ceiling, everything going fuzzy and faded, his head beginning to pound. He should have remembered Jade's love affair with poisons; that explained the sweetness. Jade draped himself over Pyotr, lips brushing his jaw, tongue dragging across his lips. "I have a drug deal to finish arranging, Petya, and I can't do it with you trying to play nursemaid. Sleep." He kissed Pyotr one last time, then stood up and walked away.

Pyotr passed out.

When he woke some indeterminate time later, he was in bed and all the lights were out. Pyotr swore softly, then pushed away the bitterness and disappointment. He had known better, just like everyone Jade fooled knew better. It never stopped them and it hadn't stopped him. Pyotr slowly sat up, wincing at his throbbing head. He had no idea what Jade had slipped him and would probably never know.

He sat up slowly and threw back the blankets, bemused that Jade had put him in bed before leaving. What had he said? He had a drug deal to finish, that was it. "Half-lights," Pyotr ordered, and the lights came up slowly and remained dim. Standing up, Pyotr went to get the medkit out of the kitchen cabinet where it was kept, and fumbled out the small bottle of anti-pain powder. He dumped a double measure in a glass, then filled it with water and stirred it just long enough for the powder to dissolve. He drank it down in one long swallow and set the glass down hard on the counter.

Flipping the kettle on, he pulled out the makings for tea, then pulled out a container of soup and set it to warm up. He glanced at the clock on the far wall and saw that he'd been out for nearly six hours. Just what in the stars had Jade doped him with? Pyotr sighed and wondered if he *was* getting too old for such games. Suddenly, settling down in the role of High Chancellor didn't seem as awful as it had before.

He looked around the room, looking for—stars, he did not even know what. Pyotr froze as his gaze landed on something new. A book. He strode across the room to the small, flat black book sitting on the bedside table. How had he missed it before? He sat down on the edge of the bed, headache already fading away, and turned the book on. There were hundreds of files; as long as he did not get tired of holding still, he would not grow bored. Fiction, non-fiction, poetry, and scores of articles from every academic branch imaginable.

There was also absolutely no way to use it to do anything but read. Pyotr would have smiled in amusement, if he hadn't still felt like finishing the job he'd started when he'd put bruises on Jade's delectable throat.

The kettle chimed, and he returned to the kitchen to fix his soup and tea. Sitting down, he browsed through the files on the book and settled on one to read while he ate.

He'd only just finished cleaning up the dishes when the door opened and Jade climbed in—and promptly dropped to the floor. Pyotr heaved an aggravated sigh and strode toward him. He knelt and checked Jade over, ensuring he would be all right for a few minutes. When he was sure of that, he went outside to see if there was anyone to be dealt with, but found only an empty passageway. Frowning, he went back inside and closed the door.

Kneeling again, Pyotr stripped Jade out of his clothes, then carried him to the bed and went to fetch the medkit to re-bandage the wounds that Jade had opened up again. As he sat down on the edge of the bed, Jade's eyes flickered open, dull with pain and exhaustion. "You're a fool," Pyotr said quietly.

"You've no room to talk," Jade whispered, then passed out again.

Pyotr sighed and brushed a loose bit of hair from Jade's face, caressing his cheek lightly, then drew back and focused on the wounds.

# Chapter Twelve

**UNREGISTERED PLANET (T-PSN 4181774, CODENAME HAVEN), SECTOR FOUR**

Raoul reached the top of the cliff and pulled himself up onto level ground, wiping his hands off on his pants before slowly standing up. He looked around the moonlit clearing, but saw nothing. The temptation to call out was strong, but he dared not give himself away on the chance he already hadn't. Where was Yevi?

Just as he began to worry he would have to go raid the shed or the camp and pull Yevi out, a figure appeared from the trees, the orange light of the moon making his green skin look decidedly strange. "Raoul."

"There you are," Raoul said in relief. "All clear?"

Yevi nodded. "Yeah. They won't be waking up anytime soon. It was always a risk, making that shit and keeping it around, but I knew it would come in handy should I ever get a real chance to escape. So is the ship where you thought?"

"Yeah, about halfway down. Ready to go?"

"As if I have a choice," Yevi groused, and stepped closer. He moved in a way Raoul recognized, as though he were afraid he would promptly fall off if he got too close to the cliff.

Raoul snickered. "You're afraid of heights."

"I believe that if I was meant to be high up, I'd be a bird. Roots don't flourish in the sky," Yevi said sourly. "You needn't sound so amused, rock spider." He jerked away when Raoul reached for him, but the movement was half-hearted at best. Raoul stepped in closer and wrapped his arms around Yevi, and that time, Yevi let him, even tilting his head in an invitation Raoul gladly accepted.

Whatever happened between them when they returned to civilization, he would always remember Yevi's kisses fondly. Reluctantly pulling away, he said, "Come on down to my place; I'll show you everything I got."

It was too dark for him to see it, but Raoul could practically feel the way Yevi rolled his eyes. He didn't deign to reply; simply strode to the cliff and knelt—then froze. Raoul joined him, kissing his cheek softly, and saying, "I won't let you fall."

"You won't have anything to do with it," Yevi said, then swung down over the edge before Raoul could reply. "Hurry up," he said in a thin voice, "I don't know where I'm going."

Raoul obediently swung back down onto the cliff face himself, leading the way down, going slowly and braced to go after Yevi the moment he showed any sign of slipping. To his relief, they reached the entrance to the ship hold without incident, though when he pulled Yevi close to check on him, he could feel him trembling badly. "You're one of a kind."

"Technically, I'm the youngest of four," Yevi replied, most of his usual sharpness in his tone. "Come on, let's get this over with. I want to go home."

Letting him go, Raoul focused on work, leading the way to the cavern where the ship was being kept. "I was worried Corbin would return and we'd be back at square one."

"He's been too busy with a bunch of sick plants," Yevi said, his smirk in his voice. "He tried to pin it on me, but Vrill can't make plants sick anyway that other people can't, and I did manage to heal several. He's busy babysitting the afflicted field right now, and he has all hands watching the others to be certain the disease hasn't spread. He won't notice I'm not in my position until he makes rounds again, which gives us an hour to get out of here."

Raoul nodded and quickly keyed in his access code as they reached the ship. "It won't take us ten minutes; she's prepped and ready. Welcome aboard the scout ship of the *Forsaken.*"

Yevi's brows shot up. "That's General Vane's flagship. General *Vane* is part of this?"

"Yeah," Raoul said. "His brother was on the *Shangri La*, which explains how they know about this planet and how they were able to assassinate Pyotr. Once we're off planet, I'll contact Zero and get someone out here to take us all the way in. This poor scout ship can't make that kind of journey."

"We also don't want the general getting back our prize piece of evidence against him," Yevi said grimly, as he settled into the comm seat on the bridge while Raoul took the captain's seat. Ten minutes later, they were out of the cave and flying low, well away from any chance of the drug camp seeing them when they headed into space.

The minute they were well out of range of Haven, Raoul fired up the main comm screen, and ordered, "Contact Zero Command, emergency code HC-181152112." Raoul waited, but the code had barely transmitted when the screen flared to life with a face he had not expected to see. "Grand Chancellor!"

"Raoul?" Grand Chancellor Arkadii asked. "How the stars are you alive? Is Pyotr with you?"

"No, Grand Chancellor," Raoul said, bowing his head in apology. "I've been trapped on Haven and have vital information regarding it. I'm currently on a scout ship assigned to the *Forsaken*, accompanied by Special Agent—" He stopped, realizing he didn't Yevi's real name.

"Teleyeveon Kao," Yevi said, stepping forward.

Arkadii's brow shot up. "Of all the people to finally reappear after being presumed dead. I'm glad you're alive, Highness."

Raoul could not believe it. How in the stars had he not recognized Yevi?

"Your family will be happy to hear that you are not dead, after all," Arkadii said. "Obviously, there is a lot going on here. Are you returning to the *Forsaken?* I believe it's near your loca—"

"No," Raoul said. "It's vital the *Forsaken* know nothing about our possessing the scout ship, and someone should be assigned to watch General Vane carefully. I also suggest locating Lieutenant Vane, his brother and a former member of the *Shangri La* crew, and sequestering him. Send a ship to rendezvous with us and take us back to Zero, where we can make a full report."

Nodding, Arkadii said, "I am sending coordinates of the ship nearest you and will relay all pertinent information to them. Expect to rendezvous with the *Penitentiary*, helmed by Captain Karmikel Aurum, a Draconis. He and his three team members are all Internal Affairs—"

"I remember them," Raoul said, surprised. "A gold Draconis, matched to a Fornarian. I haven't seen that group since Pyotr made them IA."

Arkadii grunted. "I forgot you knew them. Yes, they will return you to Zero. Keep me notified, and I'm glad you're alive, Raoul."

"Thank you, sir," Raoul replied, and the screen went dark. He looked at Yevi, who was staring far too intently at the comm screen. "*You're* Teleyeveon Kao?"

Yevi scowled at the screen. "You needn't say it that way; it's not that big a deal."

Raoul laughed. "Not a big deal that Vrill's runaway prince was left for dead on Haven—"

"I'm not a prince!" Yevi snarled, slamming his hands down on the console, whipping around to glare at Raoul, braids smacking him in the face. "I surrendered all claims to the throne, not that I was ever going to get it with three siblings in front of me. Not that I wanted it. I told you—I walked away from the responsibilities to which I was born."

"When did you last catch up on family gossip, Yevi?" Raoul asked quietly.

Yevi looked up sharply, eying him. "I heard something, right before I went undercover for this assignment, about Cevoli being shot. But I ascertained he was all right ... "

"You've been out of touch with your family for three terms?"

"It's none of your business," Yevi snapped. "My family and I never got along. They're a bunch of elitist thorns and I wanted no part of it, and that is only the bud at the end of a very tangled and thorny vine. You have no right judging me, Raoul."

Raoul held his hands up, placating. "Wasn't judging. I was surprised. Yevi ... "

"What?" Yevi asked, worry filling his face at Raoul's quiet tone. "They're not—"

"Cevoli and your sister are dead," Raoul said, saying it as gently as he could manage. "I'm sorry."

Yevi went pale. "What about Bevel?"

"Sick," Raoul said. "He's not expected to survive to the end of the term. You were presumed dead, as well; your eldest cousin is expected to take the throne."

"My cousin? Not *Kideon*," Yevi said, and he sounded so affronted that Raoul almost smiled. "He's half-Krawl! You can't put him on the Vrill throne; people will riot. As much as I wish Vrill was more progressive than that, there is no way they would ever tolerate someone with Krawl blood on the throne of Vrill."

He turned away and stared bleakly at the dark comm screen again. Looking at him twisted Raoul's gut. How in the dragons had he never put two and two together? But it had never occurred to him that a Black Ops agent of such high caliber would ever be Vrill royalty. That was like expecting a Fornarian to excel at swimming. Raoul stood up and walked over to him, tugging Yevi out of his seat and just holding him close. "I'm sorry. I should have known. You shouldn't have found out this way."

"I prefer people don't figure out who I am. Usually I go by Yevi and nobody connects the dots. I only announced myself to the Grand Chancellor so he's braced for my arrival; I had a feeling everyone would think I was dead after going so long with no communication. The Vrill delegates will burst spores, especially in light of all these problems I did not know of ... "

Raoul let him go to cup his face, and drew Yevi into a kiss, refusing to stop until Yevi made a soft noise of concession and kissed him back, fingers holding fast to the fabric of Raoul's shirt. Raoul kissed him until merely kissing was no longer enough, then drew back only to put his mouth to Yevi's jaw, nudging his braids out of the way to nibble at his ear, working slowly down to his throat. He sucked up a mark on the pale green skin and tugged at the laces of his shirt, opening it.

The fingers in his shirt had becomes nails just biting into his skin through the fabric, and raked through his hair when Raoul knelt. He wasn't good for much, but he was good at distracting. Raoul opened Yevi's pants and proceeded to distract him with all the skill a seasoned Bangkok whore could provide.

He made it last as long as he could, drawing back and slowing down whenever Yevi was right on the edge of coming, pulling off his cock to put mouth and hands to his sac, returning to his cock to resume the slow torment—and chuckling when Yevi finally yanked on his hair and ordered him in imperious tones to stop being a weed.

Raoul sucked him down, worked throat and tongue, and finally let Yevi come, spilling hot and sticky in his mouth, hands still fisted almost too-tight in Raoul's overlong hair. Raoul stood up again and kissed Yevi hard, committing the smell and feel and taste of him to memory, because when they reached Zero ...

Distracting other people was easy; it was himself Raoul had never been very good at distracting. He softened the kiss, made it last as long as he could, then drew back and pulled away to head back to his seat. Yevi gave him a startled look and reached out to drag him back, but Raoul moved out of the way before he could—

And yelped in surprise when Yevi tackled him to the floor and pinned him there. "You don't get to turn all mopey," Yevi said. "If I'm not allowed to be upset, you aren't, either."

Raoul said nothing, tugging at Yevi's hold to test it, and then relaxing. "I'm not moping."

"You're acting like a sprite again," Yevi snapped. "Don't make me—" He broke off as the comm station lit up with an incoming call and the warnings flared of an approaching ship. "Thorns and roses," Yevi snarled, and let go of Raoul to climb to his feet and stomp over to the comm station. "Who approaches?" he snapped.

A sharp, precise voice replied, "This is the *Penitentiary.* You needed a ride?"

"Affirmative," Raoul said, before Yevi could voice the scathing reply on his lips. "Thank you for the assistance, *Penitentiary.*"

"Sending out cables; we'll reel you in and secure you in the dock. Brace for transport." The comm clicked off and Raoul sat down just as the ship jerked. Several minutes later, they were safely inside the *Penitentiary*. He put the ship in stasis and led the way out. In the dock area, six familiar men were assembled, and Raoul was pretty certain he recalled all their names: Karmikel, Lark, Einn, Mendel, Sean, and Cyan. "Long time no see, gentlemen," he drawled. "What brings you to this side of the stars?"

"We just finished up an assignment," Cyan said, dropping his folded arms. "How the stars did you end up out here after being blown up mid-light jump?"

Raoul snorted in amusement. "Do I look like a scientist to you? That's his department." He pointed at Mendel.

"I'm a geneticist; I barely know more than you with regards to light jumps. They most certainly are *not* 'my department'," Mendel replied, rolling his eyes. "Let's go to the bridge." He did not wait for anyone to reply; simply strode out, clearly expecting them to follow.

Yevi obediently went—but not before grabbing Raoul's hand and holding fast, shooting him a warning look as they followed the others out. "We're not done talking."

"Yes, Highness," Raoul said, and immediately regretted the words, the way Yevi looked as though he'd just been slapped. "I'm sorry."

"Good for you," Yevi snapped, and dropped his hand.

Raoul shoved his hands into his pockets and slumped in a corner when they reached the bridge.

"So what in the stars is going on?" Karmikel demanded, as he resumed his place at the captain's station, shoving irritably at the loose strands of his gold hair.

Yevi replied in flat tones, "General Vane is consorting with criminals to operate a Soul-dealing ring. The planet from which you just rescued us is where his ground team grows it, and I assume he must have other contacts within the Auths who help him transport it."

"Vane?" Karmikel demanded, the word snapping out.

Raoul stood up straight, and replied, "Afraid so." He quickly explained all that had transpired since he'd woken up on Haven right up until the moment they'd left, with Yevi filling in all the pieces. When he finished, he wasn't certain which of them looked the angriest.

Cyan cracked his knuckles and smirked in that cocky way that belonged exclusively to Auths and Rehabbers. "Let's get to Zero and start cracking some heads. The Grand Chancellor is going to have kittens, and then he's going to drink someone's blood."

"I wonder who else is involved," Yevi said, and they all turned to look at him. "Even the general would not be able to get the kinds of codes and protocols he would need to transport Soul around the IG. That would take a government official, or a civilian with comparable power. The very last thing we want to do when we get to Zero is make a fuss about the Soul; what we need is to distract them until we can figure out who else is in on it."

"I have my theories," Cyan said. "What did you have in mind for a distraction? I can see you've thought of something."

Yevi sighed, looking more exhausted than Raoul had ever seen him. "What could possibly be more exciting than the return of a long-lost Vrill prince, when apparently the rest of my family—" He broke off, and abruptly turned and walked out.

Raoul went after him, reaching Yevi in the hall and jerking him close, holding him tight when Yevi tried to break loose. "I'm sorry, Yevi," he said. "I really am. If you don't want to return—"

"Just shut up," Yevi replied, burying his face in the crook of Raoul's shoulder. They both reeked from days of hiding in caves or working in the fields, from exhausting themselves looking for the ship and getting very little rest. He was so tired, the world was starting to go blurry at the edges. He could only imagine how much worse *everything* was for Yevi, returned so brutally to the real world after a year on an unregistered planet with only criminals for company, at the end of three terms of undercover work.

Not certain there was anything he could see to make any of it even just a little bit better, Raoul obediently shut up and just held him tight.

# Chapter Thirteen

**PLANET 0000000 (ZERO), THE PALACE OF ETERNITY**

Val had never been so miserable in his life. He was supposed to be at the lab, but he just couldn't bring himself to leave his room. He'd tried—gotten up, showered, dressed, and headed to the door. Then he'd broken down and crawled back to his bed.

He didn't want to face it, the way Bikendi didn't want him around. When Bikendi had finally taken him on, when they'd started experimenting ... he had thought Bikendi really had changed his mind. Then the insistence that Val finish his schooling, as angry as it made him ...

People had knocked on his door, but Val refused to budge until absolutely necessary. He had snacks and his own bathroom; if he wanted to hide in his room like a loser, then he could—for a couple of days, anyway.

He sighed at himself, knowing full well he was being stupid. A child. He just couldn't make himself actually care. Val pulled out his datapad and activated a full keyboard, typing up reports from all the notes he'd taken in the lab over the past several days. He didn't know who had left the datapad outside his door, but he was grateful he'd found it.

Maybe he couldn't bear to face Bikendi, but he could still do *some* of the work he was supposed to be doing. He wondered what it would take, what he would have to do, to make keeping him more important than getting rid of him.

Val thought of his parents, eager to ship him off to school. The people who thought him too strange or too smart to call 'friend'. The team eager to use him as an exhibit, but not much else. Didn't anyone want to *keep* him? Just because he was Val, not a mutant or a genius or anything else? Wasn't there something else about him that someone might want?

He tried to shake the thoughts away, hating how whiney he sounded, even in his own head.

Why hadn't Bikendi come to see him? Wasn't he at least angry that Val wasn't showing up to work? Val sighed and cast his datapad aside, scrubbing at his face. He *should* be working; the trial was more important than his hurt feelings. The entire Draconis race should not be put at risk because he was a child with a crush who had gotten a reminder of how adults behaved.

Bikendi didn't want him. Okay. He would get over it. Eventually. Maybe. He'd learn to deal with it, or ignore it, or something. Scooping up his datapad again, Val slipped it into its holster at his side and strode to the door. He faltered there, his hand hovering over the control pad, but then he forced himself to open the door and walk out.

The main room, he was surprised to see, was completely deserted. Where was everyone? Val shrugged it off, too relieved that he would be left alone for a few more minutes to question it. Maybe they were at the trial; he could never keep track of when exactly it was in session.

He was surprised no guards lingered, but he had been locked in his room for a couple of days, so probably he had missed an important development that explained everything. Maybe there were still guards stationed outside. Striding to the door, Val opened it and saw the guards outside were missing, as well.

What in the stars was going on? He hovered in the hallway, not certain what he should do. Since the first time he'd run off and the trouble it had caused, he'd been careful not to go anywhere unless he was with Bikendi, Wilbur, or escorted by a guard. He wanted to head for the lab, but didn't dare if no one was around to take him.

Val sighed and had turned to go back inside when someone came around the corner—a guard, he realized. One he recognized, from the High Chancellor's ship. He'd stayed behind to escort them all to Zero. Val smiled hesitantly when the man spotted him. "Uh—Lieutenant, wasn't it? Where is everyone?"

"Emergency meeting was called," the lieutenant said, nodding in answer to Val's first question. "Didn't you hear?" He narrowed his eyes in silent inquiry about how Val could have *not* heard.

"I was—not feeling well," Val said. "I was in my room sleeping."

The lieutenant's face cleared, and he smiled. "Ah, I see. Well, it's nothing much. They found a survivor of a recent disaster in space. Everyone has gone to hail his return." Val fought a sudden urge to take a step back, not certain why he'd want to get further away from a stupid smile. "Where are you headed?"

"The—the lab."

"Well, I'll be happy to escort you there," the lieutenant said. "This way."

Val fell into step beside him, telling himself it was stupid to be nervous. "Thank you," he said quietly. "So who was the survivor you mentioned?"

That sickly smile he didn't like appeared again. "Someone from the High Chancellor's ship, actually."

"What?" Val asked. "But how is that possible? Who? One of your comrades?" It was only as he asked the question that he realized the man's indifference made absolutely no sense. He should be ecstatic that someone had lived, not wandering the halls looking displeased.

He seemed to know the moment Val realized something was wrong, and grabbed his arm, squeezing it painfully tight. Val drew breath to say something, but only cried out in pain when the lieutenant shoved him into a wall and covered his mouth. "You say a word and I'll snap your neck. Walk with me, say nothing, cause no trouble. All I have to do is give an order, and your friends won't know what hit them, understand me, mutant?"

Val nodded, feeling sick.

"Good. Don't try anything funny, either. I see you try to remove your gloves and I'll give that kill order." He pushed off the wall and dragged Val with him, walking more briskly through the halls. Val felt like he was going to throw up, and only the thought that he might get the others hurt kept him from succumbing to panic.

He should have stayed in his room. No—he should have faced Bikendi like an adult, instead of hiding like a coward. Suddenly, he really didn't care *what* Bikendi thought of him, or if he never wanted to see Val again. All he wanted right then was to know he would see him one last time.

But he knew the statistics on kidnapping. He'd read about kidnappings nigh on religiously when he heard that Bikendi had been kidnapped a term ago. No one had been more relieved than him when Bikendi came out of it alive and well.

Val had the sinking feeling that he would not be so lucky. He held back another wave of panic, eyes stinging as he realized he was probably going to die somewhere in space the moment he was no longer needed. What did the lieutenant need him for, anyway?

He shivered as they left the Palace of Eternity and walked down a long, chilly passageway. Where were they? It didn't look like a public area—of course it wasn't, he realized. The lieutenant didn't want to be seen for some reason, that's why he'd been walking halls he knew would be empty for at least a little while.

Why, though? Val cried out in surprise and pain as the man threw him down on a teleport pad. He stood up just as they vanished, reappearing in the docks—but again, it was a deserted area. Worker area, maybe? Val knew nothing about the ports and wished suddenly that he did.

The lieutenant dragged him along, until they reached a massive ship that Val recognized as a freight class ship. Why in the stars would he need such a massive ship? Freight ships were slow, made to carry extremely heavy loads over great distances. They took weeks or months, where other classes took days or weeks. "What—"

"Shut up," the lieutenant snapped, and cuffed him so hard Val felt momentarily dizzy. He shut up and went unresisting, as he was dragged up the gangway and into the belly of the ship.

FREIGHT CLASS STARSHIP 20589325, THE *TERRIMAY*

"It's about time you got here, Vane!"

Vane gestured crudely at the man who had reprimanded him, then all but threw Val at another group of men, who roughly grabbed him close and looked to Vane for orders. "Lock him up, make certain he can't communicate with anyone. Then let's get out of here. Where's my brother?"

"He left you a coded message with his coordinates," one of the men replied in a thick Helior accent, his skin such a dark red that it was nearly black. "Come on, then, little one." He turned and jerked Val to go with him, causing Val to trip and stumble into him, upsetting their balance enough that they both went crashing to the floor.

He winced as his elbow took the brunt of his weight and looked up to apologize—and cried out as the man backhanded him so hard Val's lip split. His eyes watered to the point he couldn't see anything but a blurry impression of the Helioran. He tried to wipe the blood from his lips as he was yanked to his feet and dragged along.

They stopped at a door and the man quickly punched in a code. The door slid open and he threw Val inside, then followed him in and made quick, rough work of searching Val thoroughly for anything he might be carrying. Val said nothing as the man destroyed his datapad and shoved the pieces into one of the pockets of his own pants.

When he was satisfied there was nothing problematic on Val's person, the man struck him upside the head and pushed him back against the wall. He backhanded Val again, causing him to fall to the ground, and Val bit back another cry as the man knelt and, pulling what proved to be cuffs out of another pocket, locked them around Val's wrists. "Be quiet and obedient, and you might get to live," the man said, and then he was gone, leaving Val alone in the dimly lit room.

Val wiped his face on his sleeve as best he was able, grimacing at the mix of tears and snot and blood. His face throbbed with agony, and he wondered morosely why his magics had to be so useless—he could take and give energy, and in taking, could kill, except they'd never figured out how he was supposed to kill.

Not that he thought he would be able to, and it didn't seem as though killing anyone was going to solve anything. Val slumped, wondering what he was going to do. He wished he'd just faced Bikendi; then he never would have gotten kidnapped. He wondered what Bikendi had done when he was kidnapped. He probably hadn't just gone along with it—he'd probably fought his kidnappers as hard as he could until they simply overwhelmed him.

But that wasn't true; Bikendi wasn't a fighter, not that Val had ever seen, and he'd followed Bikendi for as long as he could remember. Bikendi wouldn't fight, just because he ran the risk of killing, and he didn't even like to kill the lab lizards unless it was absolutely necessary.

No ... Bikendi would have ... he would have bided his time, Val decided. He looked up, studying his surroundings. An empty storage room, by the looks of it, and by the smell, it usually held machine parts or something like that. It had the smell of oil and metal that seemed unique to starships.

A freight ship, he recalled, and wondered again at the oddness of that. He didn't know much—really, anything—about star travel, but he knew that a freight ship was not the vessel of choice for a quick getaway.

Val slowly climbed to his feet, unused to the weight of the cuffs or the way his arms were forced to remain in front of him. He walked to the door and peered out the small window at about eye level. Beyond, he could see where they came in—and a small starship he had not noticed before.

To judge from the way they were loading it, they had plans to be using it very soon. Val took in whatever else he could from his limited vantage point, but saw nothing else helpful, past the fact the freight was filled with cargo.

Were they ... using the freight to sneak out of Zero, and then going to fly away on the smaller starship? That made more sense. But how would they get clearance? Surely the ships were inspected and—

He knew nothing about it, Val conceded. He could talk forever about genetics and magics and evolution, but he was at a complete loss presently. Abandoning the door, he slumped in a corner and tried to distract himself with other thoughts, such as: when would the others notice he was missing? He thought he was safe in assuming they would eventually notice.

Eventually being the primary problem, he thought morosely. Given the way he'd been so locked in his room no one had even tried to get him when the survivor had arrived ... how long would it be? A few more hours? A couple more days? Val drew his legs up against his chest, arranging his cuffed hands as best he could over them.

They would definitely notice when Bikendi's magics stopped working. His stomach twisted as he looped right back to the problem that had started the entire debacle. Being kidnapped like a gullible idiot certainly would not help him build a case for all the reasons Bikendi should want to keep him. Val drew a deep breath and let it out slowly.

How long he was in the corner like that, he didn't know. Long enough to get hungry and tired, and long for a place to piss. He jumped when the door opened and the dark-skinned man from before reappeared. He stalked across the room and yanked Val to his feet, dragging him from the room.

Val kept pace as well as he could, but his legs were stiff from being still, which didn't help on top of the fact he was already worn out from fear. The man led him up the gangway of the smaller ship, but instead of shoving him into another closet, Val was taken to the bridge.

"Gag him," Vane ordered from the captain's seat. "I don't want him given a chance to say something."

The man grunted and pulled a long strip of fabric from another of the many pockets on his pants. What sort of man just happened to carry around handcuffs and gags? Val tried to glare at him, but he flinched when the man raised his hand as though to backhand him again.

Laughing in a mean-sounding way, the man wrapped the gag around Val's mouth and knotted it tightly behind his head, catching some of his hair in the process and making it pull painfully. Taking Val by the arm, the man dragged him up the captain's area and threw him down in front of Vane's seat.

Val jerked away as Vane tried to touch him, turning—and froze as he saw the faces of Tresnor, Bikendi, the Grand Chancellor, and a man Val recognized as the High Chancellor's bodyguard on the main comm screen. They'd clearly been angrily discussing something before he'd been brought in. But what? Him? How had they noticed so fast?

"Vane," Raoul said flatly. "This is a mistake. Return to Zero, give Val back to us, and this matter can end peacefully. It doesn't have to go this way."

"Shut up," Vane snarled. "You have my terms. If they're not met, then your little pet here and the good doctor there will both die. I'm not debating the matter." He kicked Val hard, and then kicked him again when he fell to the floor. Val whimpered into the gag and tried to curl up in on himself. "This discussion is over, gentlemen."

Val opened his eyes, turned his head just enough to see Bikendi in the lower right portion of the screen. He looked—frightened. Angry. "Val, it'll be okay," Bikendi said, and started to say more, but the screen went dark.

Tears stung Val's eyes, and he went along numbly as the dark-skinned man once more dragged him away and left him alone in a small room with two beds. Food was set out, and there was a place to clean up and go to the bathroom. Val worked for several minutes to get the gag off and threw it under the nearest bunk when he finally managed to work it free.

He pissed and cleaned up as well as he could still cuffed, then sat down on the left-hand bunk, wishing there was *something* he could do. Wondering what was going to happen to him. Hoping fervently that he would somehow manage to live through it all, and not be responsible for both killing Bikendi and ruining the trial to save his people.

# Chapter Fourteen

**PLANET 2154014 (TREDAD), UNKNOWN LOCATION**

Pyotr looked up from his book when the door opened, and set it aside as Jade threw a heavy sack inside before following it. The door closed with a thud and chimed softly as Jade locked it. Pyotr turned the kettle on, and then went to help him unpack the supplies he'd brought back.

There was very little to put away, making him frown. The bag was still full, but Jade dragged it away and stowed it before Pyotr was able to see what was inside. He let the matter go for the time being. "How are your wounds?"

Jade did not reply; simply stripped off his clothes and went to get cleaned up. The wounds in question, however, looked to be doing remarkably well, considering how bad they'd been. Jade must have found someone able to give him a heal-accelerant. Illegal for a host of reasons, but it had never stopped anyone from using them. "Here you are, locked away, wholly of your own free will by now, and *still* you managed to muck up my plans, Petya."

"Even I am not talented enough to ruin your plans with nothing but a book and erosa tea," Pyotr replied, preparing said tea and placing two cups of it on the table. When—*if*—he was freed, he was never drinking tea again. "What did I do?"

Jade ignored him as the water came on, and Pyotr gave in to the urge to roll his eyes. He picked his book back up and resumed reading an article debating the real reasons the gremlins were nearly annihilated. The generally accepted reason was a plague, but there were some who argued the plague was merely what happened to finish a job already begun by the gremlins themselves.

Pyotr's mouth quirked to think of what his gremlin, Tau Ceti, would have to say on the matter. He was distracted from the thought by the sudden silence as Jade turned off the water. Jade left the washing area and Pyotr's mouth went dry when he saw that the long hair was loose. He'd seen men and women spend fortunes in an effort to get their hair to look exactly like that long fall of dark gold. The color only made the soft gray of his eyes all the more delicate.

Jade dressed slowly in pants and shirt, pulling on thick socks before he began the arduous task of brushing his hair. To Pyotr's astonishment, he did not braid it when he was done; simply bound it loosely back in a ribbon.

He strode to the table and Pyotr pushed his cup of tea toward him, and then settled back. "I guess your venture out was not successful?"

"No," Jade said, and sipped his tea. His nails, Pyotr saw, were painted a soft, silvery blue. "I've worked a term for this deal to go down. I've worked years to bring Vane and the rest to this point. Do you *know* the work that has gone into this plan? I would have had him sooner, if I hadn't been concerned that bringing down Vane would spook Cohen. Now it's ruined because *you* did not have the decency to be assassinated."

Pyotr cocked his head thoughtfully. "Did you know they were going to assassinate me?"

Jade sipped his tea, ignoring the question.

"Did you know?" Pyotr asked more sharply.

When he had finished his tea and set the empty cup on the table, Jade finally replied, "No. I made the mistake of thinking they realized it would be to their detriment to do something so desperate. Assassinating you has put more notice on the trial, on Zero—on everything. If I had caught wind of the assassination, I would have altered courses more to my liking. As it is, the entire matter has ruined everything. Your bodyguard's ignominious return has certainly closed the door on the matter."

"What?" Pyotr said, setting his own teacup down so hard it nearly broke. "Raoul is alive?"

"It's being broadcast everywhere," Jade said, a hint of irritation slipping into his carefully modulated tone. "The scientific community is embarrassing themselves in their excitement to figure out how he survived. But he landed on Haven after the explosion, so now they are aware of General Vane's involvement and it will only be a matter of time before they figure out Carthage is involved, as well. It's possible they already know, by this point."

Pyotr was still annoyed about that. "Carthage."

Jade's mouth quirked. "Come now, Petya, are you still put out by their deceiving you?"

He barely heard the words, he was so lost in a haze of anger. Carthage. "I am angry that their entire reason for wanting the Draconis dead was so that there would be no need for Haven as a planet for the Draconis to call their own. They wanted to destroy an entire race of people so they could continue drug trafficking."

"It's a rather admirable level of ruthlessness, if remarkably stupid," Jade said. "I think they realized pretty quickly that it was probably never going to work, however, and settled for stalling it until they could think of something better. But the Kavalerov family is the very definition of ruthless, hm? Your uncle would never call off the trial over something as trivial as his nephew's death."

Pyotr shrugged. "What would be the point? Quitting would not bring me back to life. Better to keep moving forward. I don't see why you're upset, however; you get chaos whether the deal went down or not."

Irritation flickered briefly across Jade's face and he traced the rim of his teacup with the tip of one finger. "It will be contained; that was not my plan."

Standing up, too restless to sit still any longer, Pyotr deposited his cup in the sink, and then prowled the room. He wanted to punch somebody—Vane, Carthage, all of them. Even he had never been so twisted that he would annihilate an entire race to get what he wanted. He was not above casualties, much to his uncle's despair, but he drew a line. "Would you have let them destroy the Draconis?"

"The Draconis are in no danger of going the path of Heartstone," Jade said. "They probably *should* be destroyed, for all the reasons you want to keep them alive. They are upsetting the balance; one day, they will be a force to be reckoned with, all the more powerful for the people they are matched to and so bring together. Their existence will, exactly as you have always wanted, reshape the IG."

Pyotr smiled faintly and stopped prowling to look at Jade. "It was a stupid question. Of course you want them to live. You want to see their existence destroy everything else."

Jade tossed his head. "You want to see that destruction, too, Petya. Maybe your end goal is rebuilding, but seeing it all come crashing down first will not upset you."

"If I wanted destruction, we would have trod the same path," Pyotr replied quietly. "I don't want to destroy anything; I just want to change it."

"Bah," Jade said, and stood up, prowling close to him. "If you really believe that, Petya, then you're a fool, after all. The IG is rotting and we both know it. To build a new house, you must first tear down the old one. Anything else is just dressing up the rot, and you are not that lazy, Petya." Jade dragged out the diminutive of his name, sing-song and intimate all at once. He stood so close that Pyotr could smell him, could reach out and touch, but he wouldn't fall for that trick a second time. That he'd fallen for it once still bruised.

He stared into Jade's pale eyes. "Why are you so bent on destruction?"

"They destroyed my world, why shouldn't I destroy theirs?"

Pyotr lifted a hand and lightly touched his fingertips to Jade's cheek. "Poisonous in every respect." Jade's eyes slipped shut for a moment, and though he did not move into the caress, he did not pull away, either.

When he finally opened his eyes again, they were the color of ashes. "You said your first kill wasn't when you were fifteen."

Pyotr wondered why it had taken Jade so long to ask about that. "I was five," he said. "I killed my father, after he beat my mother to death. I used his hunting knife."

Jade regarded him pensively for a moment, and then asked, "Which one of them was the mutant?"

Laughing softly and trailing his fingers down to Jade's throat, Pyotr lingered there a moment, before finally his hand fell away. "How did you guess?"

"Humans don't just choose to live on Tredad for the fun of it. If your family lived there, they were hiding something. You care too much about the rights of the magics capable and allowing them to take up positions within the IG for it to be anything but personal."

Pyotr's mouth quirked. "My grandfather, and he passed it on to my father. He couldn't stand being left behind, being nothing, because he was a mutant. He took it out on my mother, until he finally went too far. If he had been allowed ... "

Jade's too-pretty mouth twisted in another sneer. "If he had been allowed. If my parents had not been killed. There is no point in 'if'."

"Only in changing the laws so people in the future don't have to worry about it," Pyotr added.

"So lofty, you and your change. I don't care what people build upon the ashes. I only want the ashes."

Pyotr nodded, and said quietly, "I know. But it wasn't what you always wanted."

"Petya, Petya, still trying to talk me off my path," Jade said, tossing his head in such a way that the ribbon loosely binding his hair slipped free and fell to the floor. Jade hair tumbled loose, so long it nearly reached his knees, a spill of dark gold that Pyotr wanted to fist his hands in, use to pull Jade close and make him forget about things like revenge and destruction.

"There is no reason you have to stay on it. You could take another path."

Anger flashed in Jade's eyes and he shoved Pyotr away, causing him to stumble into the wall behind, head cracking against it. "Again you try to tell me what I should do, Petya, but I do not see you leaving your path. Justice for daddy, a miserable mutant who murdered his wife and was slain by his son. You're no better than me."

"I have never denied that," Pyotr said quietly, standing up straight again. "What if I said I would walk away? Give it all up."

"You're a liar," Jade hissed, but Pyotr didn't miss the slight pause before he spit the words out. "When you return to Zero, you'll have all you need to begin remaking Zero according to your grand design. You'll be able to bring all your precious little IA pets forward."

Pyotr didn't deny it. He would return a miracle, and winning the case for the Draconis would be easy. Another decade would see him crack the impenetrable rule against magics capable and he would die seeing his plans come to fruition. All the magics capable persons who helped from the shadows and far too often died in the dark, all those whose efforts went unknown, would be able to step forward and at last be seen.

He wondered when he had stopped caring. "Walk away, Jade. Walk away and I'll be right beside you." He never thought he'd say the words, be *able* to say the words—but they were said, and a weight lifted off his chest.

"I don't believe you," Jade said, but didn't resist when Pyotr reached out and pulled him close, tilting his face up for a kiss.

He still tasted sweet, which surprised Pyotr, because he had thought that sweetness must have been the drug Jade had used to knock him out. He pulled back slightly to ask, "You're not poisoning me again, are you?"

Jade laughed and Pyotr was surprised how genuine it sounded. "Not this time." He stared to pull away, but Pyotr tugged him close and kissed him again, sliding his hand around to cup the back of Jade's head, sinking his hands into that long, soft hair he had admired for what seemed most of his life. Jade let him, tilting his head to improve the angle, tongue sliding along Pyotr's as the kiss deepened.

His hands splayed across Pyotr's chest and he could feel just a hint of the long nails. How long before Jade ceased to tolerate the intimacy and left him bleeding? Pyotr slid his other arm around Jade's waist, pulling him even closer, unable to easily slip away. To his astonishment, Jade's hands slid up to wrap around his neck, and then Pyotr was no longer in control of the kiss. He let Jade have it, groaning at the feel and flavor of the man so long denied him.

All the reasons he should not be succumbing flitted through his mind—Jade was *Jade,* first and foremost, a man who manipulated people for fun, had tortured his brother (and more than once), and whose only goal in life was to destroy the Infinitum Government. He was a wanted criminal and Pyotr was High Chancellor, nephew to the Grand Chancellor.

Pyotr just didn't give a damn. He let go of Jade's waist to fist both his hands in that magnificent hair and take control back, kissing Jade hard enough someone's lip split. When he finally was forced to break the kiss, he drew back panting, and finally realized it was his own lip that was bleeding. He licked the blood away and stared into Jade's eyes.

Jade stared back, unflinching as always. Even his uncle could not look him in the eyes the way Jade always had, unafraid of what made everyone else run or jump to do Pyotr's bidding. Pyotr wasn't sure who moved first the third time, only that they were once again kissing, Jade's teeth digging painfully into the split in his lip; but it was the sort of pain that shivered down Pyotr's spine and pooled hot low in his gut. He slid his hands down Jade's back, tugged him flush again, and delved into his mouth as though it would be his one and only chance to do so.

He refused to think about the fact that it probably was.

When Jade pushed, he obediently let go and stepped back, if reluctantly—but Jade only led him to the bed and pushed him down upon it. Pyotr pulled Jade down to join him, and then shifted so that Jade was spread out beneath him on the bed. He didn't wait for the comment poised on Jade's smirking mouth; just kissed him again.

But kissing wasn't enough, anymore. He'd had a taste, and he wanted the rest. He pulled back and pushed hands beneath Jade's shirt, running one over the smooth, warm skin that had tempted more than a few men to a course of action that had ultimately ruined their lives. He glanced at Jade's closed face, but his eyes were so pale they almost looked silver, the pupils blown, and Pyotr took it as permission to divest Jade of his clothes.

Naked, Jade was even more beautiful than before, his skin pale, flawless, smooth and warm to the touch. Pyotr bent and nuzzled at Jade's throat, shivering as nails dragged along his side, nothing but a teasing pressure through the fabric of his shirt. He worked his way down Jade's chest, licking over one pale nipple, and then nipping with his teeth. He treated the other to the same, until Jade's grip tightened to the point he could feel the bite of those nails, regardless of fabric.

He fisted Jade's cock, hard and leaking, crowned by hair even darker than that on his head, the only other hair on his body. Jade made a soft, rough noise that he quickly cut off, and then abruptly sat up, forcing Pyotr back. He looked Pyotr up and down slowly, and Pyotr had never felt so undressed with all his clothes still on. Jade just looked at him, never saying a word, but the order was clear enough. Pyotr stood up and discarded his own clothes, then climbed back into bed. He crawled over Jade, grabbing his wrists and pinning them to the mattress, before taking his mouth in another hard, hungry kiss.

Jade bit his lip, hard, making it bleed again, but as he drew back, Jade licked the blood away himself. He pulled at his wrists, casting Pyotr a warning look, and Pyotr obediently released him. Jade drew him down into another kiss, hands curving around Pyotr's sides to his back, and that time, when he raked his nails, there was no buffer. It stung, all the more because Jade's polishes always contained some sort of toxic addition.

The pain only made Pyotr groan and rub against him, attacking Jade's body with hands and mouth, determined to leave marks in a way no one else had likely ever been permitted. Jade's tacit permission to do so, that Jade *wanted* him to do so, was the headiest drug in the stars. Pyotr worked his way slowly down Jade's body until he finally reached his cock, licking the length of it, sucking on the head, before he finally swallowed Jade all the way down. The noise Jade made then was exquisite, made Pyotr desperate for more of them, and he might be fifty, but having Jade writhe and moan because of *him* made him feel immortal.

He pulled off Jade's cock, mouthed at his soft sac, fingers pushing behind to tease—and he hissed in surprise that Jade was more than ready to be fucked. He looked up and could only chuckle at the smirk that flitted across Jade's mouth. Pyotr laughed and bit down hard on the soft skin of Jade's inner thigh, then levered himself up and spread Jade's legs wide, dragging them around his waist and lining up his cock. He leaned over Jade as he pushed in, bracing himself on his hands, kissing Jade as he shoved all the way in. Jade's nails dug into Pyotr's back, right at the shoulders, adding new marks to the ones already there.

Pyotr felt a bit dizzy as he began to move, but ignored it, attention only for Jade as he drove into him over and over again, fucking Jade harder than he'd ever bothered to fuck anyone else. Blood and sweat exacerbated the scratches on his back, his sides, driving him on, faster and harder, Jade meeting him full measure. Jade's long hair stuck to his sweat-soaked skin, his lips swollen from Pyotr's kisses, and his eyes blazed in a way Pyotr had never seen before. He doubted anyone had ever seen Jade so genuine, so vulnerable.

The thought drove him over the edge, and with a last brutal thrust and a cry muffled in Jade's mouth, he came, fisting Jade's cock so he spilled hot and wet and sticky between them.

Dizziness swamped him again as he collapsed alongside Jade and buried his face in Jade's hair. He splayed one hand across Jade's mostly healed wound, breathing in the mingled scent of them, and wished with a pang that Jade would still be there when he woke.

The last thing he remembered was a light scrape of nails down his cheek. When he woke a short time later, Pyotr was unsurprised to find he was alone.

All signs of Jade were gone; nothing remained of him but a single tea cup on the table … that sat beside a pile of clothes and a small box that could contain only one thing. Pyotr threw back the blankets and stood, wincing at sore muscles, his stinging back and sides, and a throbbing head. He strode across the room to examine the items on the table.

Black slacks, boots, a gray shirt, and a black jacket, and they would probably fit him perfectly. They were high quality, of Mars cotton and Parthon silk. He picked up the box and flipped it open, staring at the in-lens inside. He didn't have to activate it and put it in place to know it would do everything he needed; he didn't bother to wonder how Jade had managed it, either. Another box, one he'd missed before, contained a datapad, and no doubt it was just as equipped as the in-lens.

Knowing Jade, every last bit of it had been in the house the entire time. Pyotr set the box down again and went to get a shower. Hopefully, by the time he had managed to scrub away every last trace of Jade, he would be ready to resume the role of High Chancellor.

# Chapter Fifteen

**CUSTOM CLASS STARSHIP 22932058, THE *FRANKENSTEIN***

"I'm going to kill whoever let them get off Zero," Raoul snarled as the screen went dark, barely resisting an urge to put his fist through the console in front of him. He turned to the captain of Bikendi's ship. "Can we track them at all?"

"No, the—"

Raoul cut him off with a motion, not interested in the reasons why at present. "Where is General Vane? Have we found that out, yet?"

"His ship was seized in port on Trax; when they boarded, however, he wasn't there. The agents on board now are still working on how he managed to escape, when they had confirmation he was still aboard."

"So he got away and is no doubt going to shortly rendezvous with his brother and Carthage. Was anyone doing their job today?"

The captain glared at him and nearly everyone else on the bridge recoiled, but Raoul just scowled back. He wasn't afraid of a fucking Telven, and even if he was, he had more important things to worry about than the very unlikely possibility that someone was going to drink his blood. "Everyone on this ship is, I can assure, performing at peak. As to the rest of Zero, I daresay they were distracted by your miraculous survival."

Raoul didn't think it was possible for the man to pour another drop of sneer into the word *miraculous*. He almost laughed, liking the captain despite himself. He had the distinctive black skin of Telve, and dark purple eyes with just a touch too much red in them. Raoul thought that red-heavy purple was unique to a particular region or something, but couldn't remember for certain. "I don't suppose the *Penitentiary* is doing any better?"

"No, sir," said the Telven manning the comm station. "They report no success."

"Dragons' dicks," Raoul said sourly. It seemed they had well and truly lost their prey. He turned and left the bridge without another word, prowling the ship in search of its owner. Any other day, he would have been all but drooling over the ship. The *Frankenstein* was a beautiful ship, even better than some of the military ships on which Raoul had been aboard.

Right then, however, he could not have cared less if they were on a junker. The bastards were getting away and they had taken a hostage, and Raoul would not let them kill Val and have the trial, everything, end with a tragedy.

He stopped short as he caught something out of the corner of his eye and saw Bikendi staring morosely out a window in what looked like a small meeting room. He was impressed by the window; not only did it exist at all, it was of a large, non-standard size and looked to be made of extremely high-quality glass. Raoul hadn't gotten much look at the *Frankenstein* the last time he'd been on it, too busy with security. He was probably missing plenty of details he would kill to examine, but there was no time for admiration.

Slipping into the room, he called out, "Bikendi."

Bikendi turned at the sound of his name, and Raoul was startled by how haggard he looked. For all he easily displayed his notorious temper, Bikendi was oftentimes described as cold; he had always been a remarkably contained person, though most said that was the Telven in him. "No sign, then?" Bikendi asked, huffing out an irritated breath and swiping at the hair that had fallen in his face. Not like him to be so restless, either—and, Raoul noted with a start and a chill, Bikendi had removed his gloves.

He stayed a few steps back so as not to add to Bikendi's tension, but Bikendi shoved his hands in his pockets and beckoned him close with a sharp jerk of his head. "Not yet,"

Raoul said quietly in reply. "I was hoping you might be able to tell us something, given you've been dealing with that group in some fashion for the past few weeks."

"No," Bikendi said with another sigh. "I've met Carthage on any number of occasions; it's impossible to avoid one another in our circles. I avoided him as much as possible, though; he makes me think of a *Tella*."

Raoul almost laughed to hear Carthage described as one of the 'hunters' who had once killed thousands of Telvens because of religious fervor. The entire race had been wiped out by the Telvens and each other shortly before Telve had joined the IG.

"You would know the Vane brothers better than I," Bikendi continued. "Especially Lieutenant Vane, I should think."

Making a face, Raoul leaned against the wall and folded his arms across his chest. "I'm not really close to any of the crew. Friendly, in a passive way, maybe. I'd never turn my back on helping them, but there's always a line between me and the regular crew. Their job is to fly the ship and keep Pyotr as safe as possible. My job is to protect Pyotr and, if necessary, die for him—even if that means I have to choose to let them die to save him. But Vane always seemed like a good guy. Nothing about him ever struck me as off. Until a couple of days ago, I would have told you he *was* good guy and completely incapable of things like Soul-trafficking and kidnapping. Clearly, I don't know anything. What I *want* to know is how he ever managed to get to Val. Why wasn't Val with the rest of you?"

"He was upset," Bikendi said, and the set of his shoulders made it clear that he was the reason for the upset. Raoul looked at him in silent query, and Bikendi continued, "I told the others to leave him be or else. I wanted to talk to him myself, without the others interfering. He wouldn't leave his room, however, so I thought to give him a couple of days before forcing the matter ... " He trailed off and rubbed irritably at his forehead with one hand.

Dropping his hand a moment later, Bikendi stared out the window again, then continued, "I was about to say forget about waiting so long and was on my way to speak to him when you arrived, and everything went crazy. I knew he wouldn't be comfortable in the crowd, so I ordered him left alone. I didn't think he'd leave his room, but he must have, because otherwise going to grab him would have been dangerously out of Vane's way." He started to say more, but only fell silent.

Raoul wasn't certain what to say; he wouldn't insult Bikendi by promising him they'd get Val back safe and sound. Bikendi knew the stats on kidnapping better than anyone. "Why was he upset?"

Bikendi's mouth tightened, and for a moment, Raoul thought maybe he'd been wrong in thinking Bikendi wanted to talk—but then Bikendi broke with a sigh, and said, "I'm an idiot, that's why. It completely escaped me that as I am matched, the further I am from Val, the weaker my magics grow. Given enough distance, my magics will stop working. I was startled by the revelation and stunned it had not occurred to me. I was also angry with Pyotr, who probably had that in mind the entire time. I didn't know what to say, and I think Val took my silence the wrong way. Though what, exactly, is going through his head, I have not the slightest. I can imagine, however."

"I see," Raoul said, chuckling. "I wouldn't worry about it, doc. That kid thinks you built the stars."

"Well, I didn't," Bikendi said unnecessarily. "I am sure by now he is quite aware of that."

The words gave Raoul pause, making him forget the next joke he was about to make. He stared harder at Bikendi, and laughed as comprehension dawned. "You want him. You actually like the kid. The cold Bikendi wants to fuck his pretty little match, and maybe not kick him out of bed immediately afterward."

"Shut up, blood bag," Bikendi snapped, and Raoul just grinned. It was rare Bikendi's Telven roots displayed in anything but his purple eyes and the black strands of his hair; Raoul always found it amusing when his Telven turns of phrase or snootiness slipped through.

He just laughed again, unable to believe it—Bikendi had been snared by the little Draconis. "That's just cute."

"Shut up," Bikendi repeated sourly.

Raoul ignored him. "So what's the problem? It's not like he'd be against it. Everyone can see—"

"I don't care what everyone can see," Bikendi snapped, eyes flashing. "You have said it twice yourself—he is a kid. He is barely nineteen and I am going to be thirty-eight soon. Never mind that, as he is the only one I can safely touch, I am more than a little biased. I know an advantage when I taking one."

"I think—"

"What you think doesn't matter, and it will matter even *less* if we cannot find him before he is killed," Bikendi cut in, not quite bellowing the words.

"You're right." Raoul pushed off the wall and rested a hand lightly on Bikendi's shoulder, in what little comfort and reassurance he could offer. Leaving Bikendi to his brooding, he made his way back to the bridge.

He stopped halfway there when he came across two figures in the hallway:  Yevi and one of the other two Vrill who had insisted on coming along when Yevi declared he was going to help. Raoul's mouth tightened at the way the other man stood with his head bowed deferentially as he spoke, as was custom for Vrill when addressing royalty. They were speaking too low for him to catch the words, and when they saw him, they stopped entirely.

Yevi dismissed the other Vrill by tilting his head in the direction of the hallway just behind him, a smooth, easy motion done so reflexively that it made Raoul's heart plummet to his stomach. That imperious way of silently giving orders was another mark of Vrill royalty. It seemed so stupidly obvious that Yevi was a prince.

He still could not believe he'd missed it. When they'd arrived and everyone had seen Yevi, the room had exploded with shock. He swore the Vrill coalition on Zero had nearly burst into roses, and he had not even gotten to tell Yevi goodbye, before they had grabbed him and started to drag him away.

When only a few minutes later they had learned of Val's kidnapping, the Vrill had been furious that Yevi had insisted on going along, not relenting until two of them had gone along, as well. Raoul would definitely be happier if Val had not been kidnapped, but he wondered if it was the only reason he would get to spend a few more minutes with Yevi without having to lower his head and call him 'Majesty'. "So what are you doing here, anyway? You should be on Zero."

"My job," Yevi snapped, that dangerous glint in his eyes.

"This—" Raoul swallowed and forced the words out. "I figured the moment we landed on Zero, you were retired."

Yevi scowled and looked away, some of his braids falling into his face. Raoul fought an urge to brush them away and tilt Yevi's face up for a kiss. "I will be resigned when we return and this fiasco is wrapped up. There's just no one else to do it, though stars know I don't want the throne. But I can't let it go to those of unworthy blood, or collapse entirely, because of my selfish behavior."

Raoul said nothing—what could he say? It was all true, and whatever Yevi said about being selfish, he wasn't.

"So after all this is wrapped up ... " Yevi trailed off and looked up at him, and he looked so suddenly sad that Raoul stupidly felt a little better about his own misery.

"I'm no longer a bodyguard," he said slowly. "I could probably wrangle a posting to Vrill. Do you think a lowly Bangkok spider could finagle an audience with the king now and again?"

Yevi's shoulders dropped from relief. "Yes, you weed. Of course."

Raoul smiled and figured that was good enough for a start; there were only a thousand other problems in front of them, but that was a start. He stepped in closer and kissed Yevi briefly—then could not resist taking a second, longer and deeper kiss. "We need to work," Yevi said. "As delightful as this is, Val and catching those bastards is more important."

"I know," Raoul said, and reluctantly stepped back. "Everything I try brings me nothing."

Yevi grunted and irritably flicked his braids from his face. "Vane could be anywhere at this point. I'm not having any luck narrowing down the options. No one arrested on Haven is willing or able to provide useful information."

"They must have a bolt hole somewhere," Raoul said. "At least we know they can't run forever. The Grand Chancellor was forced to let them escape, but the moment they were gone, he put their identities on high alert. We may not know what ship they're on, but eventually we'll figure it out. They can't even think about a light gate without tripping an alarm."

Though Yevi nodded in agreement, he looked about as confident as Raoul felt.

Raoul was still trying to think of what else to say when the sound of feet ringing on metal startled them both, and they turned to see one of the Telven soldiers running toward them. "The bridge!" he said. "You're needed—"

"Did they find the ship?" Raoul demanded, heart thudding in his chest.

"They've found the *High Chancellor.*"

Raoul's mouth dropped open, and he bolted past the man and raced straight to the bridge. He nearly tripped flying through the door—and could not think of a single thing to say as he saw the face of Pyotr Kavalerov filling the main comm screen, looking as calm as could be, as though he had not been presumed dead for the past few weeks. "Raoul, it's good to see you survived, as well."

"And you, High Chancellor," Raoul said, only barely remembering to address him properly instead of using his given name.

Pyotr smiled faintly, looking for all the world like his usual tired, stubborn, but always firmly in control self. "Raoul. I am informed you are aware of the culprits behind this and that they have taken Valendel hostage to ensure their escape."

"Yes. But they can't hide forever."

"No, but Valendel will not live forever," Pyotr said. "I am luring them here to Tredad, though a separate part of it. Use the omni-codes and get to Tredad as quickly as you can. Seeing as you are on the *Frankenstein*, I doubt you will have any trouble on that point. After you have saved Valendel and secured the criminals, retrieve me from Whisper City. I've forwarded the tracking codes in my in-lens."

"Copy that."

Pyotr nodded in parting, and said, "I'll be waiting." He killed the connection.

"Bastard," Raoul said with a laugh. "Nearly blown to pieces, lands on *Tredad* of all places, and reappears completely in control of the entire situation. If I didn't know how much he hates Tredad, I would think he did all of this on purpose. Thank the stars he works for the IG and not against it."

"I'm glad he's alive," Yevi said quietly, but his tight smile reminded Raoul abruptly that their stupid little start was effectively shattered. He was a bodyguard again—there would be no stationing on Vrill. But, he forced himself to remember, his personal woes didn't matter.

That didn't mean, however, that he had to neglect them entirely. He hadn't gotten as far as personal bodyguard to the High Chancellor by giving up. Ignoring everyone around them, he leapt neatly down from the platform he'd climbed to be closer to the comm screen and grabbed Yevi by the shoulders. Jerking him close, he kissed Yevi hard enough to leave their lips bruised and throbbing, chuckling at the outraged noises made by the other Vrill.

Finally letting him go, smirking at Yevi's half-hearted scowl, Raoul went off to find Bikendi, satisfied he had made it clear that Yevi was his until further notice.

# Chapter Sixteen

**CUSTOM CLASS STARSHIP Z- 21212605, THE *BLAZE***

"I still don't like it."

"We don't have a choice, in case you didn't notice. Kidnapping him only gets us so far, and we've gone that far. Escape is going to take dealing with *him.*"

"There should always be a better option than him," Lieutenant Vane muttered. "I told you not to deal with him at all; he's a dead man's coin if ever I've encountered one. He poisons everything he touches—worse, he *enjoys* it. I've seen him—"

"I've seen him more than you," snapped General Vane. At least, that's who Val assumed he was; the two men were nearly identical, save for the fact they were several years apart. A couple of hours ago, he'd been dragged out of his room and back to the bridge, but since then, he'd largely been ignored. The ship had stopped briefly and General Vane had boarded.

Val still wondered why he'd been brought to the bridge, but wasn't in a hurry to remind anyone of his presence. He was scared to death it meant that death was exactly what should be scaring him. The fact they'd removed his gag did not reassure him in the slightest.

General Vane cut his brother off when he tried to speak again. "I killed his parents; I can kill him, too, if it comes to that. But it won't. He's even more of a fugitive than us. He won't do anything that jeopardizes his freedom. Alexander is only dangerous if you drop your guard. I'm not that stupid."

"You—" Vane the younger gaped at his brother.

Ignoring him, General Vane finally turned his attention to Val. His eyes were a sickly sort of green and made Val recoil, wishing he had more space to put between them. "So you are the mutant Draconis." His gaze dropped to Val's hands, still gloved and cuffed. "So can you kill with a touch, too?"

Val nodded. "Y-yes."

Grunting, General Vane said, "I still don't see what makes all of you deserve an entire fucking planet. If you and Kavalerov had just done what you *should*, none of this would have had to happen."

"Planet?" Val's heart kicked up yet another notch at those words. The High Chancellor had gotten the Draconis their own planet? Is that what General Vane meant? What did that have to do with anything? Were they really going to get their own *planet* if they won the trial? Val wanted to cry at the thought of it—a place where most Coni wouldn't hate them for becoming such a high-profile, controversial, and ultimately failed creation. Where they could be their own race, make up their own laws and culture and everything. They could be the Draconis and nothing else.

Val was so startled by the news, he didn't hold back his reply to General Vane. "You're the one breaking the law. If *you* had done as you should have, nothing—" He bit back a cry of pain as Genera Vane punched him, eyes watering, jaw throbbing. He lay still on the floor, curled up as much as he possibly could on the chance someone decided to kick him again.

"Scientists," General Vane spat. "Keep your mouth shut or we'll gag you again."

Obediently, Val subsided. He missed Bikendi, who had never hurt him for being stupid or saying the wrong thing—who might not have liked that they had been forced to match, but had relented and been nice ever sense. Well, as nice as Bikendi got, but it was far more sincere than some of the niceness Val had encountered before.

They'd worked so well together in the lab ... Val closed his eyes and wished fervently that Bikendi would show up and save him. That Bikendi would come at all. If Bikendi would just—just pretend to *really* care for only a few minutes, Val would be okay. He'd leave and never bother Bikendi again, after that. He just wanted to be okay and to know Bikendi was okay. "What are you going to do with me?" he blurted out, and then remembered he wasn't supposed to be speaking. He braced himself to be hurt again.

General Vane only glanced at him impatiently. "I guess you'll find out, won't you? How much longer until we reach Tredad?" he asked, turning to his brother.

"Fifteen minutes until planet approach, but it'll take us nearly an hour to get down planet."

"Can't we go faster than that?"

Lieutenant Vane shot him a disgusted look. "No, we can't, not unless you want to get noticed by patrol. I'm sure they would *love* to chat with us."

"Shut up and get us there."

"Yeah, yeah," Lieutenant Vane muttered, pointedly ignoring it when General Vane glared at him again. He jerked his head at Val a moment later. "What are we doing about him once we're done with Alexander?"

"What do you think?"

Val started crying, but didn't bother to say anything. He *had* to get away, he just had to—but how?

They went back to ignoring him after that, discussing things that Val didn't really understand. How much longer did he have to live? Minutes? Probably until they were down planet, which gave him an hour and fifteen minutes, give or take.

What could he possibly hope to do? He couldn't get out of the cuffs, or even his gloves. Pretending for two seconds he somehow managed to escape, anyway—it was Tredad. He wouldn't last five seconds aboveground on Tredad. He wouldn't survive five seconds belowground, either.

Val had never felt so useless in his life. It was no wonder everyone treated him like a child! Self-loathing washed over him. He wasn't good at anything but assisting with lab work and making a fool of himself. He couldn't even stop his kidnappers from beating him; it was stupid to think he could stop them from killing him.

He huddled in his corner and tried to sit still, but his entire body ached and throbbed with pain, and being exhausted and hungry and scared did not help anything. Val drew a breath and let it out slowly. If he somehow managed to survive, he would make certain he was never able to be easily kidnapped again. He refused to continue being useless.

Letting out another deep breath, Val tried to find the calm that came so easily to him when he was working. He loved being in the laboratory, because everything else went away, and it was just him, the machines, the experiments—and the addition of working for Bikendi just made it perfect. It was easy to keep calm, keep his hands steady, to pay attention to everything.

If only he could figure out how to do it right then, it would help him, he thought. He froze as he felt the ship slow, felt that drop in his stomach that said they were headed down. Despite himself, Val started crying anew. He didn't want to die.

As Lieutenant Vane had warned, an hour passed before the ship finally came to a halt and the engines slowly died down. "Bring him," General Vane snapped.

"No!" Val shouted, as the dark-skinned man reached for him, stumbling to his feet and moving away—only to be grabbed from behind and held so tightly he cried out in pain. He recognized the well-manicured nails and dark red skin of Carthage, and went still.

"I've got him," Carthage said. "You stay on the ship." He didn't wait for the man to reply, just strode off, dragging Val with him. Val stumbled along as best he could, heart in his throat, tears blurring his vision anew. Blood and snot smeared his face, made it hard to breathe. Would they leave his body in the snow? Would anyone ever find it?

Val hissed as the door opened and the cold struck him, and went half-sliding, half-stumbling down the gangway alongside Carthage, who finally hit him when he tripped one time too many. His soft slippers, so perfect for the halls of the Palace of Eternity, were soaked and frozen in seconds. Val was shaking by the time they left the snow behind.

They slipped into a dimly lit room that smelled of dust and disuse. Val wondered why they had brought him—wouldn't it have been easier to leave him on the ship or in the snow? He wished desperately that he had some way to clean his face; if he ever got a chance to save himself he wouldn't be able to see it.

"He isn't here," Carthage snapped, fingers biting into Val's skin again. "We should go." He had barely finished the sentence when the lights went out.

"You're not going anywhere," a voice rang out—Raoul, Val realized, and suddenly found it hard to breathe.

Carthage jerked him close and pressed a stunner to his throat. "I leave, unless you want to see your mutant die right in front of you."

"No one is dying except you," said a soft, cold voice. Carthage made a faint noise, like a choked off gasp, and then dropped to the floor, pulling Val down with him. The stunner clattered to the floor nearby, the sound startling in the sudden silence.

Val scrambled to get away, tried to stand, only to fall over again, struggling to *breathe,* but so choked with fear and relief—

Someone grabbed him, pulled him into an embrace, and as suddenly as that, Val recognized Bikendi's warm scent. It was Bikendi who had spoken, he realized, and in the next moment, comprehension dawned. Bikendi had killed Carthage.

Bikendi rested a hand against his cheek and Val felt a flood of energy pour through him, steady and strengthening him slightly. Val shivered as it washed through him, and finally faded off; he should be upset that Carthage was dead, that it was Carthage's stolen energy he was using, but it just wouldn't register.

"Come on," Bikendi said softly, and held him as close as possible without impeding his ability to walk. Val tried to stop crying, but his attempts only seemed to make it worse. He clung tightly as Bikendi led him up what was clearly the gangway of a ship.

CUSTOM CLASS STARSHIP 22932058, THE *FRANKENSTEIN*

When they finally stopped moving, Bikendi urged him to sit down on what Val realized was a bed. He listened, tense, as Bikendi moved away; heard the sound of water running and Bikendi fussing at the cabinets. He lifted his hands to wipe at his face, and immediately felt stupid for somehow managing to forget that his hands were still cuffed.

Val startled as a warm, damp cloth covered his face, and Bikendi began gently to clean it off. He blinked when the cloth was finally removed for good, wincing at the light for a moment. When he could finally see clearly, Val stared at Bikendi.

Bikendi strode to the door and opened it, then spoke in low tones to someone outside. A moment later, he returned with a key. Val slumped in relief when Bikendi inserted the key into the slot on his cuffs and triggered the lock. Removing the cuffs, Bikendi threw them aside and gently took Val's wrists, rubbing a soothing ointment into them.

Val just wanted to start crying again. "S-s-so everything is okay, now? No one was h-hurt?"

Bikendi's head jerked up and he stared at Val in surprise. "No, Val. You were the only one in danger, and I'm sorry for that. Everything—everyone—is fine now. Again, I'm sorry we let this happen to you."

"It's not your fault I was stupid and got taken. I was afraid—afraid I'd get u-us killed." And there he went crying again, so upset he was shaking. He jumped slightly as Bikendi's hands cupped his face, unable to do anything but stare into Bikendi's eyes.

"Val, it is not *your* fault. If it's anyone's fault at all, it's mine." He gently squeezed Val's shoulder. "It's okay, Val. You're safe now and I won't let anyone touch you ever again. I promise."

"But you—you want me far away," Val said, and it seemed like such a *stupid* thing to dwell on, but it still preyed on him. Plus, he'd promised. He was okay, Bikendi was okay, so he would leave without fuss.

Bikendi moved to sit next to him, and Val tried not to be so painfully aware of how close they were, but trying not to be acutely aware of Bikendi was like trying not to breathe. He just couldn't do it. "I don't want you going anywhere, Val," Bikendi said softly. "I'm sorry I gave you that impression."

Val stared at him. "But—but you didn't *say* anything and you looked so surprised! Of *course* you want me far away. Everyone does, and if I'm gone, you can touch people whenever you want, why wouldn't you want—" His eyes popped wide open as he realized Bikendi was kissing him.

Bikendi. Was kissing him. Val tried to process that thought, but it just couldn't complete the circuit. He opened his mouth to say something, but Bikendi just kissed him deeper. Better. Val didn't know what to do, except try to kiss Bikendi back.

When they finally drew apart, he wondered how and when his hands had wound up on Bikendi's shoulders. "What—" He jerked his hands away, flushing. "Why did you do that?"

Looking amused, Bikendi said, "It might surprise you, Val, how many people would not mind taking you to bed. Not that they're ever going to."

Val shook his head, dismissing that. "But—I'm—I should go. So you won't have magics."

"I have gone my entire life with gloves; I don't really care if I must continue doing so. I never wanted to touch everybody in the stars, Val. I just wanted *one* person; someone I got along with, who actually could put up with me—keep up with me, instead of resenting me when they fell behind." He rubbed his thumb over Val's lips, making him flush anew, and smiled faintly in a way that made Val struggle to remember how to breathe. "Though it might have been better if you were not so damnably distracting."

"Distracting?" Val asked, confused.

Bikendi gave a rough-sounding laugh and shifted to bury his fingers in Val's hair. Val barely braced himself with his hands splayed on Bikendi's chest before they were kissing again. Oh, the second time was even better than the first. He moved and tried to get closer. He *must* be dead, if Bikendi was actually kissing him. He'd never been crazy enough to dream of Bikendi actually kissing him, so it had to be he was dead.

Val tried to ignore the way he whimpered when Bikendi finally pulled away. "You need to rest," Bikendi said in his growly way. "I shouldn't be mauling you."

"I—I don't think that was mauling," Val replied.

Bikendi's mouth twitched. "You still need to rest."

Val shrugged. "I'm just glad I'm alive, that you're alive, and that I can stay?"

"Of course you're staying," Bikendi replied. "You had damned well better. Nothing that happened is your fault. If anything, you should want nothing to do with me."

"That's stupid," Val said, shaking his head. "Of course I want—" He flushed, but finished what he'd started to say. "You."

"Are you sure, Val?" Bikendi asked quietly. "You've been through a lot, and just because we're matched—and you're nearly two decades younger—"

"I don't care," Val said, interrupting him. "I don't know much, but I always knew what I wanted to study, and I always knew I would do anything to meet you. I *don't* want to leave."

Bikendi smiled and kissed him again, brief, but sweet, then drew back with clear reluctance. "Then stay. We have to return to Zero for the formal halting of the trial until further notice, but then it's only us and the *Frankenstein*. We'll figure out the rest later. For now, rest."

"Stay?" Val asked, before he could stop himself.

Though Bikendi looked surprised by the request, he nodded and stood up. Moving to the door, he spoke with the guard outside, then closed the door again and locked it. He shrugged out of the coat he still wore, stripped down to his slacks and a black t-shirt, toeing off his shoes before he returned to the bed and got Val settled in it. He sat down on the other side and took Val's hand. From the table by the bed, he pulled out a book and turned it on.

Val watched him for as long as he could, and even managed a couple of question to which Bikendi replied with a smile, but finally fell asleep while Bikendi was still explaining something about the Traxen genetic history.

# Chapter Seventeen

**PLANET 2154014 (TREDAD), WHISPER CITY**

Pyotr disconnected the call and set the datapad on the table, then picked up his cup of dark, hot, Tredad tea and drained it. A woman came by, pale and gray as most Tredad natives were, and refilled it without comment, leaving a fresh bowl of sweetberries. Pyotr dropped five of them in the fresh cup of tea and stirred until they dissolved.

Sipping it, he flicked his datapad back on and read the latest communications on the transport of prisoners from Haven. It was a pity the trial had been put on hold indefinitely; he had hoped to see that wrapped up by the end of the term to begin the process of giving the Draconis their own planet. Well, it would just take an extra term or so. He would see it done.

Weariness washed over him, so abrupt it left him reeling, struggling for breath. Pyotr shoved it aside, ignored it, but the feeling persisted. He didn't want to do it anymore—any of it. Perhaps seeing Jade was just what it took to admit that, no matter what, he just didn't want to be Pyotr Kavalerov anymore.

The datapad slipped from his fingers and clattered to the table. Pyotr scowled at it, but did not reach to pick it up again. Try as he might, all he could think about was Jade's hair sliding through his fingers, the smooth warmth of his skin. He could still feel the wounds on his back and sides, throbbing, almost burning from the poison in the polish Jade had been wearing.

Once he was back on the *Frankenstein*, it would be easy to get a heal spray or cream and be rid of the pain. He just didn't *want* to be rid of it.

Of course Jade hadn't accepted his offer. Jade manipulated and murdered; the only thing he liked more than using people was hurting them. When he completed his plans to destroy the IG, he would reclaim his brother and finish the job there that he had never been able to finish. Why give up all of that to run away and do only the stars knew what with a washed up High Chancellor?

They were not the sorts of thoughts Pyotr was accustomed to having and he did not care for them. People did what he wanted, one way or another. He had not become head of Special Forces, head of Internal Affairs, just because he was good at it. Everyone did what he wanted.

Except Jade.

Pyotr made himself pick up his datapad, in-lens flashing as he directed the datapad to contact the *Frankenstein*. Captain Cyk filled his screen and nodded politely. "High Chancellor. We are securing the prisoners now and locking down their ship. I apologize for keeping you waiting—"

"Not at all," Pyotr interrupted. "The prisoners are more important; I want everything done by the book, Captain. There will be no getting off on a technicality for that lot. How did the capture proceed? How is Valendel?"

"There was one casualty—Lord Carthage. Dr. Bikendi was forced to kill him as he had Valendel hostage and would have likely killed him had we dealt with the matter any other way. Did you wish to speak to Dr. Bikendi?"

Pyotr shook his head. "No, that won't be necessary. Bikendi knows what he's doing. If he killed Carthage, I believe it was necessary. How is Valendel?"

Captain Cyk's mouth quirked in a half-smile. "From what little I saw of him, he is shaken, but will recover. Can't say for certain, though, because Bikendi took Valendel straight to his own room and they have not reemerged. I doubt we will see much of them until we return to Zero."

"I see. How is my bodyguard?"

"Currently inciting the wrath of the Vrill delegation," Cyk drawled. "He and Prince Teleyeveon are securing the prisoners, much to the distress of the other plants aboard ship. Expect a formal complaint from the Vrill delegation upon your return."

Pyotr chuckled. "I saw on the feeds that the trial has been put on hold. I assume my uncle is managing to keep the knowledge that I am alive a secret?"

"To the best of my knowledge, my lord."

A soft chime alerted Pyotr to a new message and he pulled it up with his in-lens, redirecting it to the tabletop. He read it a moment, and then dismissed it. "I have just received word that Haven has been secured. The *Penitentiary* is en route to Zero with the prisoners. Notify me when you are done and on your way to me."

"Yes, my lord," Captain Cyk replied, and Pyotr closed the connection. He'd only just set the datapad down and picked up his tea when it began to chime an incoming call. He knew it was only a matter of time before he was forced to talk something other than business. Sighing, Pyotr set down his tea and accepted the call.

"Hello, Uncle."

"Petya," Arkadii said in his gruff way, one of only two people who ever used the diminutive of Pyotr's name with real affection. If Pyotr *still* preferred to hear it in mocking, seductive tones, well, he would be the first to say he was a fool. "Only you would manage to survive that explosion—well, you and that crazy bodyguard of yours. Where have you been all this time?"

"Tredad," Pyotr replied. "I was badly injured for several days, and then I simply had no means of communication."

Arkadii grunted. "Your aunt is beside herself. The news of your death almost killed her."

"I'm sorry," Pyotr said quietly, thinking of his poor aunt. She had always treated him like her own, and never did anything but love him. He could count on one hand the people who had always been that kind to him, and it meant all the more because he knew he didn't deserve it. "The betrayal slipped by me and it should not have."

"No one is perfect. I'm glad you're alive and well." Silence fell, and then Arkadii tilted his head, the blue eyes that were exactly like Pyotr's regarding him far too knowingly. "Something is different about you."

Pyotr opened his mouth to dismiss the notion, and startled them both when he said, "I'm tired."

Arkadii stared at him silently for a moment, and then said, "You should be. If you're tired, rest. I know you want to save everyone in the stars, even those too long dead to save. You're fifty years old, Petya. It's long past time you looked after you, instead of everyone else."

Pyotr said nothing, only sipped his tea.

"You're a good man, Petya. Whatever faults, no matter how many times I wanted to throttle you for your actions, you always had the best of intentions."

Pyotr scoffed at that. Good men did not want to destroy things, for any reason. Good men did not become professional killers. Good men did not let a psychotic criminals get away—or fall in love with that same criminal. "You're going senile, Uncle."

Arkadii ignored the old joke. "Good has nuances. You deserve to rest as much as anyone."

He tried to shrug the words aside, retain the notorious cool that had earned him the codename 'Winter' when he had first turned to black ops. "There's too much to do."

"It can be done by other people," Arkadii said. "It is not the duty of any one man to carry the weight of the stars forever. What is meant to be, will be. You've done your part, Petya."

Pyotr shook his head. He had to do it; he'd chosen his path and he would walk it until he reached his destination. But just as he finally began to regain control of himself, Arkadii said, "We will always love you, Petya. You're the only good thing that ever came from my brother's side of the family. I think he would have been the first to agree—no matter how he died. Whatever you choose to do, your aunt and I will always love you."

Pyotr's throat suddenly felt tight. "You know—how do you know?"

"I know you," Arkadii said gruffly. "Severely injured or not, the very first thing you would have done was find a way to contact me. If you contacted no one else, you would have sent a message to me—unless there was someone worth remaining silent. I know of only one person in all creation, Petya, who can keep you silent and in one place for more than a day. God knows your aunt and I have tried. I will never understand what you see in *him*, but he was the only one who ever made you *stop.* You were the only weakness, the only threat, he never removed. I will never understand it, but there's a lot I don't understand."

Suddenly feeling more fifteen than fifty, Pyotr replied, "It doesn't matter. He's gone."

"Mmm," Arkadii said, not looking entirely convinced. "If there is one thing I have learned about his sort, they are never *gone*. But no matter if he is, you should rest. I would like to know you have finally found some sort of happiness before I die, so do it."

He meant to refuse, to say he would be returning—but he just could not bring himself to do it. Swallowing, Pyotr nodded, and said, "Yes, Uncle. Give my love to Aunt Veronika."

Arkadii returned the nod, and then closed the connection without another word. Pyotr could not remember the last time his heart had beat so fast; it felt like it was going to pound out of his chest. Was he really going to do it? Just ... walk away?

The datapad chimed again and he looked down to see a message from the *Frankenstein.* Damn, he would have to be quick. Picking up the datapad, he acknowledged the communication so they would not think anything was amiss. Then he typed out a quick resignation, approving his uncle to make all decisions on his behalf. Finally, he typed out a letter to the Vrill delegation, recommending Raoul as personal bodyguard to Prince Teleyeveon. His uncle would see they obeyed. Setting the datapad down, he removed his in-lens and set it on top of the datapad. Standing up, he set the datapad on his chair and tucked it under the table so that it was not immediately noticeable, but could be easily found by Raoul.

When all was set, he gave it one last look over, then nodded and turned away. He left the café and walked down the street at a brisk pace, pulling down the tight-fitting cap covering his pale hair, pulling up the collar of his coat. So far, no one had recognized him, but he couldn't afford to have that luck finally turn.

He made his way quickly through Whisper City to the port, where he bypassed the public and military ships for the private sector. At the main station, he looked over the list of ships willing to take on extra passengers, looking for one headed to Bangkok, or at least somewhere that he could then get easily to Bangkok.

From Bangkok, he could get in contact with Wilbur, who would be able to get him to the *Sweet Dream*. There was no better place to build a new life, and completely bury his old one, than on the ship about which only a small handful of people knew. And no one would understand better than Wilbur.

Hopefully, he would be long gone from Tredad before the others began to look for him. But he would not be going anywhere if he could not find a suitable ship. Pyotr skimmed the list of ships impatiently, though not quite yet frantically, annoyed that no one seemed to be going anywhere near Bangkok—then froze as he saw a ship near the bottom. Destination: Bangkok. Ship: The *Fool*. Captain: Ilia Winter

It couldn't be. Could it?

Pyotr noted the location of the ship and all but ran to the designated dock, staring in disbelief when he saw the ship. It was a G-line leisure class ship and must have cost a fortune to build. A fortune, Pyotr did not doubt, that Jade had acquired by means of playing with a recently-arrested gang of drug traffickers. It made him smile faintly.

The ship was a beauty, and from the look of it, was still very new. He must have been getting it ready at least as long as Pyotr had been on Tredad. The gangway was down, the main door wide open, as if in invitation—though Pyotr was not certain to what he was being invited. If the invitation was for him at all. But it must be, if Jade was using the name Ilia Winter.

Pyotr strode up the gangway and into the ship, pausing to punch the close command into the control panel. He waited until the ship was sealed, then slowly made his way through it until he at last found Jade curled up in a chair in the captain's quarters, a book in his lap. He did not look up as Pyotr stepped into the room.

His hair was loose, Pyotr noted, not even bound back with a ribbon—just left to cascade around him in a wild tumble of dark gold. He had also resumed wearing his ornate clothing; his robe was only a couple of shades darker than his hair, embroidered with ivy and flowers in lighter gold. By contrast, his nails were the same delicate gray of his eyes. "It's a bit stupid to leave your ship open like that, for just anyone to wander aboard."

Jade slowly looked up, a smirk curving his too-pretty mouth, and didn't bother to voice a reply.

"I thought you'd be well off planet by now."

Jade remained silent and shifted in his seat slightly, before bowing his head back to his book. Pyotr left him there, and went to prepare the ship for departure. It did not take long—the clearance codes needed only to be punched in, and Jade had also already obtained protocols and clearances for the light gate they would need to get to quad three.

Two hours later, they were far enough away from Tredad that Pyotr felt he could relax. He ran diagnostics of the ship, and then ran a check of their surroundings. Finally satisfied that all was well, he set the ship to autopilot.

Leaving the bridge, he returned to the captain's quarters, where Jade was still curled up with the book in his lap. "You didn't leave."

"I was leaving shortly," Jade replied. "Right after the High Chancellor and his faithful pets departed."

Jade had been waiting to see what he would really choose, Pyotr realized. He'd set Pyotr up to go back to his life as High Chancellor, given him everything he needed to do precisely that. But then he'd waited. "I thought you were long gone."

Setting the book aside on the table by his chair, Jade shoved his hair back from his face and looked up. "I was waiting for clearance to take off. What are you doing here, High Chancellor?"

"I retired," Pyotr said, moving closer, but still keeping back a few steps. "I walked away."

Jade said nothing, but did not protest when Pyotr closed the last few remaining steps of space between them. Neither did he protest when Pyotr took hold of his wrists and tugged him to his feet. Jade always felt so slender, so close to frail, but Pyotr would never voice the thought. "Say it, Jade."

"Say what?" Jade asked, irritation slipping into his voice. "I would say it is patently clear that we are both fools. I give it a week before we cannot stand it any longer."

Pyotr smiled and bent to kiss him, chuckling when Jade jerked his wrists free to wrap his arms around Pyotr's neck. His hair slid through Pyotr's fingers like threads of Parthon silk, and he tasted sweet and bitter. Pyotr drew back just enough to speak, Jade's breath warm against his skin. "Say it."

"There is nothing to say," Jade said, digging his nails into Pyotr's skin. When Pyotr did not reply, he dug them in deeper, but added, "I walked away, Petya. Do not ever give me a reason to kill you for doing it."

"I won't," Pyotr said, and kissed him again, finally content to let the rest of the stars take care of themselves and narrow his own world to just one, however deadly and unstable it might be.

# Fin

# About the Author

Megan grew up a military brat and traveled extensively with her family. She is now firmly settled in Ohio, with two roommates and their four cats. She has always been book obsessed, and writing obsessed since she first gave it a whirl in college. Romance and fantasy are her primary obsessions, but she's game to write just about anything and enjoys a challenge. She is a sucker for stories of enemies becoming lovers. When not writing, Megan is drinking too much coffee, reading still more books, and harassing family and friends, or otherwise doing whatever possible to avoid editing.

She loves to hear from her readers, and can be found all over the place:

@amasour
maderr.livejournal.com
meganderr.blogspot.com
maderr.tumblr.com
maderr.com

CPSIA information can be obtained at www.ICGtesting.com
Printed in the USA
LVOW062352251012

304456LV00001B/218/P

9 781936 202935